"KIRK HERE. WHAT'S GOING ON?"

"Bridge, sir—hull breach on deck eight."

"Alert security and damage-control teams. Get visual confirmation. Clear those areas and seal those breaches."

"Aye, sir!"

"I'm heading to deck eight." Kirk bolted toward the turbolift at the far end of the shuttlebay.

Spock didn't wait. He crossed to the shipboard terminals and cued up the graphics of ship's integrity. Even he couldn't contain a reaction as the graphics showed him what was happening. Across the bay he called, "Rupture now on deck nine, Captain!"

Boots skidding under him, Kirk spun around. "Are you sure?"

"Another one . . . deck ten," Spock called. "And deck eleven . . ."

STAR TREK

NEW EARTH

BOOK SIX OF SIX
CHALLENGER

DIANE CAREY

NEW EARTH CONCEPT BY DIANE CAREY AND JOHN ORDOVER

POCKET BOOKS

New York   London   Toronto   Sydney   Singapore   Belle Terre

This book is a work of fiction. Names, characters, places and incidents are products of the author's imagination or are used fictitiously. Any resemblance to actual events or locales or persons, living or dead, is entirely coincidental.

An *Original* Publication of POCKET BOOKS

POCKET BOOKS, a division of Simon & Schuster Inc.
1230 Avenue of the Americas, New York, NY 10020

A VIACOM COMPANY

STAR TREK is a Registered Trademark of Paramount Pictures.

This book is published by Pocket Books, a division of Simon & Schuster Inc., under exclusive license from Paramount Pictures.

ISBN: 0-671-04298-X

First Pocket Books printing August 2000

10 9 8 7 6 5 4 3 2 1

POCKET and colophon are registered trademarks of Simon & Schuster Inc.

Printed in the U.S.A.

This novel, our 41st, is dedicated to

Barc Lavengood and Dan Thorsby
of "Tullamore Dew"

to Mary, Cathy, Keith and all our friends
at the Rathskeller,
where much of this book was written.

What else can we say, but . . .

"McINTYRE!"

Chapter One

"How COULD threat vessels get so close without tripping our sensors?"

"What do you expect from me? Look at the monitors. Completely gamma-seized."

"Then we better saddle up and learn to ride blind."

The sci-deck of Starfleet Cruiser *Peleliu* stank and smoldered. Part of the carpet was on fire, but nobody was bothering with it. Hot damage crawled like parasites through the mechanics under the sensor boards' tripolymer skin. Burst connections caused tiny volcanoes of acid in ripped-open sheeting. A third of the pressure pads and readouts had quit working or were crying for damage control.

Nick Keller swiped his uniform's dirty sleeve across his forehead, bent over the sensor boards, and tried to focus his stinging eyes. A fleck of insulation hung from a wing of his briar-patch-brown hair and blocked part of his view. For an hour they'd fielded attacks from enemies they couldn't see, couldn't target, and hadn't expected. How had any hostiles known they were on their way out to Belle Terre? Or was this some new enemy that nobody in Starfleet or out at the colony even knew about yet?

The question went unanswered. Sensors couldn't see through the bath of gamma radiation spewed by a pulsing neutron star so far away that even working long-range sensors wouldn't have picked it up.

Beside him, Tim McAddis dribbled sweat from his pale forehead onto the sensor dials. His blond hair glistened with a frost of perspiration. "I'm used to seeing things a solar system away, not a lousy five hundred yards. Now that our deflectors are on full, we can't even pick up phantom data like before."

It was a hard thing for a science officer to admit.

Keller pressed a hand to McAddis's hunched shoulder. "Look at the bright side. You'll get the blame instead of me."

McAddis grinned nervously. "The mighty second mate stands defiant."

A knock on the cold-molded lattice grid near his knee got Keller's attention. He found the first officer's reassuring face peering up from the command deck seven feet below, through the lattice fence that prevented crewmen or tools from falling under the sci-deck rail. "What've you two got up there? How'd they come up on us?"

Without a good explanation, Keller knelt to meet him under the rail and handed over the unhelpful truth. "Derek, they must've cruised in cold. No engines. Coasting, like the old days of rocketry. We were looking for exhaust signatures, not solid objects. All I can figure is the bad guys are accustomed to blackout action and know how to maneuver on inertia. Without engines, they're really invisible."

"Mr. Hahn," the communications officer interrupted, "sickbay reports thirty casualties."

"How many dead?" Derek Hahn asked.

"They just said casualties. I don't think they want to tell us."

Kneeling up here in only a pretense of seclusion, Keller gripped the rail at the tremor in Tracy Chan's voice. Everybody was shaken badly. They weren't even sure yet how many of their shipmates were dead. Suj Sanjai at tactical had been killed in the first hit less than an hour ago. That grim hello had brought in critical seconds of attack before the *Peleliu* got its shields up. Since then, the minutes had been long and bitter, landing percussion after percussion on them from unseen foes who understood better than Starfleet how to fight during Gamma Night.

"Phasers direct aft," the captain ordered. "Fire!"

Both Keller and Hahn looked at the command deck.

Staccato phaser fire spewed from the aft array, at targets no one could see, jolting the ship much more than normal. That was the damage speaking. The cruiser convulsed under Keller's knee.

Keeping his voice low, he murmured, "What's he targeting? He can't possibly know where they are."

Hahn shook his head, but said nothing. He watched Captain Roger Lake, stalking the center deck.

From up here on the half-circle balcony, Keller clearly saw the command arena below except for the turbolift. The science and engineering balcony where he knelt rested on top of the lift's tube structure, a design meant to maximize use of the cruiser's support skeleton. Two narrow sets of ladder steps, one to his left and the other to his right, curved down to the command deck on either side of the lift doors. Below, Crewman Makarios at the helm and Ensign Hurley at nav both hunched over their controls, staring at the main viewscreen, which stubbornly showed them only a static field interrupted every twenty seconds or so by a grainy flash of open space, fed by McAddis's tedious attempts to clear the sensors. The largest screen on the bridge—on any Starfleet bridge—was their window to eternity. The two fellows at the helm were hoping for a lucky glimpse of the attackers, maybe get off a clean shot with full phasers.

To port of the helm the half-demolished tactical station was still unmanned, with Captain Lake's stocky form haunting it as he tried to keep one eye on the main screen. Why hadn't he called for somebody to replace Sanjai? Why was he so moody?

To starboard, Chan's communications console was the only board on the bridge that had so far evaded damage, either direct or repercussive. Everybody else was struggling just to make things work at half capacity. Those first hits had done some nasty work.

Up here the engineering console on the balcony's starboard side beeped madly, reporting dozens of damaged sites all over the ship, but there was no one to answer. The engineers had split for their own section as soon as the attack came, and behind him the environmental and life-support board went wanting too. Keller and McAddis were up here alone.

Almost alone.

The sci-deck offered a certain amount of privacy. Sound insulation and clever design of the ceiling shell prevented travel of much conversation from up here to the lower deck, where command conversations were also taking place. The two sections, then, could be functionally close, but not interrupt each other. Usually, Keller liked it up here. This was second-officer territory if ever there had been any. During this voyage, though, an added presence haunted the upper deck.

4

He glanced to his right.

There she was. That Rassua woman, Zoa, along for the haul. A cross between an ambassador and an inspector, she wasn't in Starfleet, but she was here most of the time anyway, fulfilling her mission of "determining whether the Federation is up the standards of the Rassua."

She stood on the upper deck as if someone had leaned an ancient Egyptian sarcophagus against the console, both legs braced, her gold face and thick hair in a waterfall of severe skinny plaits, her lined lips giving nothing away. In the months of travel, Keller had only heard her voice a couple of times. If she was any indication, the Rassua weren't talkative.

Dressed in woven strips of leather that left her heavily tattooed shoulders bare, Zoa was markedly disparate from the Starfleet crew in their black trousers and brick-red jackets. If only she had boots on. Instead, she wore only some kind of crisscross thong sandals with thick soles, allowing her two-inch toenails to curve down like a hawk's talons hooked over a branch.

And she never moved her face. Her blue-dot eyes followed the crew action here and below. It was like having a sphinx watch every move they made. Keller wished he could order her off the bridge. Roger Lake wanted her here. He liked showing off to an alien who was being courted by the Federation. The UFP wanted the Rassua alliance to guard their zenith borders.

So here she was, observing. If they got out of this, she'd have a real story for somebody back home.

Keller had hoped she'd get the hint and go below when the battle started, but apparently this was what she'd been waiting for all along and she wasn't about to leave. He tried to ignore her. His skull throbbed.

Derek Hahn reached up and caught Keller's wrist. "You okay? Your left eye's dilating."

His swollen temple ached under Keller's probing fingers. "Feel like I got mule-kicked."

"You got ship-kicked. For a minute there I didn't think we'd come out of that spin. Harrison's hands are full in sickbay, but I'll have Ring come up here."

"No, don't. Savannah's a passenger this trip. She shouldn't have to be on the bridge."

"Won't hurt a Starfleet medic to work her passage. She wants to start a Special Services Rescue Unit at Belle Terre, she can start right here."

"Were you a drill sergeant in a previous life?"

"Everybody needs a hobby." Hahn looked under the sci-deck balcony toward the communications post. "Tracy, call Savannah Ring to the bridge with her bag of tricks."

"Aye, sir. Medic Ring, report to the bridge with a field kit. Medic Ring to the bridge, please."

"Nick!" McAddis erupted from the science board. "I'm getting a shadow! I think they're coming in again!"

Without even attempting to confirm the readings, Keller glanced at the stocky form of their captain, pacing the lower deck between the helm and the command chair. "Tell him, Derek."

Accepting Keller's instincts, Hahn spun around. "Captain, brace for another pass!"

On the command deck, Captain Roger Lake didn't order the crew to brace or any other preventive action. Instead he made a completely unexplained order. "Thrusters on! One-eighth impulse power!"

Hahn stepped away from the rail and croaked, "Sir, we shouldn't be moving during Gamma Night!"

Lake shot him a glare. "We've got to outrun them while we can. I know how these people think."

Keller pushed to his feet and spoke up, "Sir, I agree with Derek. One full-power hit from *Peleliu* would demolish any ship in this sector. They don't have anything that can match—"

"They've got everything we've got. Fire!"

Lake's eyes were fixed on the forward screen, as if he saw something there. But there was nothing. Only a clicking blue cloud of static. Yet he was shooting, over and over, depleting their weapons, sending unthinkable destructive power racing through space behind them without effect.

Hahn came back to the rail and peered up at McAddis's scanners. "If only we could go to warp speed . . ."

Gamma Night laughed in his face.

Hahn turned to watch Lake from behind, analyzing the set of the captain's shoulders, the quick breathing, the cranky movements, the petulant glances. "We're dead if we keep moving." He jumped to the nearest ladder, climbed it, and joined Keller at the suffering sensors. His voice was very low. "He's snapping, Nick."

Cold dread washed down Keller's spine. He glanced to his side, afraid the science officer had overheard, but McAddis had moved down the sensor bank and was preoccupied.

Keller's hands turned icy. "Now, let's not pick our peaches before they're fuzzy."

"We gambled," Hahn said. "We lost."

"We don't know that yet, Dee," Keller downplayed.

"His judgments are sluggish, he's irrational—this stuff about how they've got everything we've got—who does he think is out there?"

Desperate to hold together whatever they had, Keller resisted the urge to face him and obviously be having a conversation that might get the captain's attention. Quietly he said, "Harrison did a psych scan two weeks ago for chemical abnormalities. The results were indeterminate. This is just stress. He hasn't been in battle for years."

"Neither have I, but I'm not—"

"Hey, I've got blips on the short-range," McAddis interrupted. "I think they might be moving away!"

Keller spoke past Hahn. "Captain, they might be moving off."

"If we hold off on weapons fire," Hahn added, "they might lose us. Sir!"

"Don't believe the equipment!" Lake whirled around, meeting everyone's eyes one by one. "They've done something to our sensors! Sabotage. We have to rely on instinct. We know they always attack in a wedge formation. Like bees."

At that, Hahn stepped forward. "Captain, how can you recognize something we've never encountered before?"

"Don't joke around, Dee," Lake said. "It's typical Klingon formation. Hurley, did I tell you to stop shooting?"

Beside Keller, McAddis bent forward as if he'd gotten a cramp. *"Klingons."*

"Shh. Anybody can misspeak. He means Kauld."

But he peered past Hahn, down to the command area. A few steps to their right, the Rassua woman now had her inkdot eyes fixed not on Lake, but on Keller and Hahn. Gold face, a zillion little braids, and eyes with no pupils, just solid blue, grilling them with an angry message.

This could get out of hand. Turning away from her, Keller pressed a couple of fingers gingerly to his aching head and used the other hand to play the suffering sensors, but he overturned the dial and lost the image.

McAddis nudged him. "All right, Nick?"

Beside them, Hahn complained, "What's taking Ring so long?"

Keller waved them off. "Swamped in sickbay. I'll just put a patch over the dilated one. You can call me the Santa Fe Bandito."

McAddis smiled, then murmured, "I'd feel better if *she* just wasn't here all the time."

"Captain likes having her here, watching," Hahn reminded, almost casting a glance back at Zoa, then changing his mind at the last second. "Her people have a taste for frontier living. They weren't interested in the UFP before Belle Terre broke wide open."

"Funny," Keller commented. "Nobody wanted to go out there when it was peaceful and pretty. Now hell's broke loose, they discovered stable olivium, and all bets are off."

Uneasy, McAddis sighed. "Those colonists are in for a shock with people like the Rassua prowling around."

Keller peered at the reflection of Zoa's stiff face in the polished rim of the number-two scanner. "Naw, she's just going out there to open a young ladies' academy. Zoa's Charm School and Small Engine Repair."

Though he managed to get chuckles out of the two other men, that was all the relief they would get. On the engineering console, across the sci-deck from where the three men huddled, the severe-malfunction lights came on with a corresponding alarm. An instant later, half the board exploded in what was obviously not another hit, but internal damage finally blowing.

While Hahn pulled the leather-strapped presence of Zoa out of the way, Keller stumbled to the unmanned engineering console and tried to make sense of the flashing and smoldering. "Tetragrid overload! We need an engineer on the bridge to lock down the static pulses!"

"I'll do it," Hahn volunteered. He skimmed down the ladder, dropped to the lower deck, and crossed to the tactical boards.

Keller fought to tie his controls in to the tactical, racing the damage before it caused a calamity. "Starboard PTCs read amber!"

"Leave 'em alone!" Hahn turned briefly toward aft to make sure he was heard over the mechanical whine. "Cool those plasma injectors right now! Try the—"

The ship slammed sideways, driving Keller first backward, and then elbow-first into the environmental grids. The enemy had found them again and struck them in the main section's port side, hitting the skin of the cruiser mere feet from the bridge. A tumor of smoke and shrapnel burst out of the tactical displays.

The blast swallowed Derek Hahn completely. The last thing Keller saw of him was the wedge of his chin as the explosion struck him in the back.

"Oh, cripe—!" Keller was down the steps before he realized he was on his feet.

"Out of the way!" Roger Lake shoved Helmsman Makarios right out of his seat and plowed to Hahn.

He and Keller met at the first officer's writhing form. Lake pulled from one side, and Keller caught Hahn as they rolled him over.

Hahn's uniform was actually sizzling in Keller's hands, but the exo was conscious, talking, and trying to stand.

"I'm all right," Hahn gasped. "The injectors—"

"Pick him up." Lake pushed off the deck and veered back to the helm. "Blanket the phasers! Set up a grid and open fire!"

"Our weapons are depleting," Keller reminded, but it was like talking to a tree. "Blanketing shots without a target just wastes power!"

Derek Hahn reached out. "Roger!"

The captain didn't honor them with a response, turning instead to the frightened helm crew. "Ahead, quarter impulse!"

"Oh, no—" Hahn pressed a hand to Keller's knee and forced himself to his feet.

When Hahn stood up, Keller was choked by a heart-clutching sight of Hahn's uniform and the three inches of metal sticking out of the first officer's back on the right side, an unidentified piece of the blown board material.

Three inches out—how far in?

And how could he avoid a panic? He grasped Hahn from behind. "Captain, permission to drag Mr. Hahn kicking and screaming to sickbay?"

"What?" Hahn belched. "Get your hands off me!"

"Granted!"

"Come on, Derek." Looping an arm around the first officer, Keller hoisted him to the turbolift vestibule. Overhead, one leg pressed against the balcony rail, Tim McAddis stared down at them in a momentary lapse from the science boards.

He and Keller locked gazes for a moment. "Be right back, Tim," Keller undergirded.

The turbolift doors parted and he pulled Hahn inside. Hahn tried to help, but only one leg was working. Instead the exo clasped Keller's arms and shrieked, "It's the methane! Roger!"

"Hush," Keller warned, "don't make me rope you," and pulled him all the way in. The lift doors gushed closed, but before Keller could grasp the destination controller, Hahn collapsed against him and Keller devoted both hands to holding him.

Valiantly Hahn braced his legs and tried to stay upright, but slipped a centimeter with every agonized gasp. "He's snapping! Did you see—his—eyes?"

"It's just Gamma Night," Keller said. "He's never fought like this before."

"We shouldn't be moving—not a foot, not an inch, they—could lay mines in front of us—If we move, we're easier to find even on blinded sensors. It's the methane, Nick, I know it is—I know it is!"

Still holding him, Keller cranked halfway around. Where was the control arm? There! He gave it a twist. The mechanism felt sluggish in his hand. "Sickbay," he said.

Though the confirm light went on, the lift did nothing. Outside the closed doors, he could hear the action on the bridge and wanted to go back. The wound in Hahn's back was now bleeding into the fabric of Keller's sleeve, almost the same color.

"Sickbay!" he shouted at the sound-sensitive panel. "Dang box of rocks—"

Responding this time, the lift started to move downward, then chunked under his feet to a sudden dead stop and threw him and Hahn against the wall. Hahn gasped out his pain, and the lift began to descend again.

Less than ten feet down, the whole cab shifted a good two inches, tilted at a noticeable angle, and jammed to another grating stop.

"The guides!" Hahn choked out.

Keller looked up at the flashing warning lights. "Must be bent."

"If he'd sit still, the sensors might be able to pull in something. Open the doors—I've got to get back in there."

But Keller pressed him down, feeling desperation and his own fears rushing through his arms. "You sit still."

He craned around to look at the lift's control panel. How could he get it moving? The doors were jammed. There'd been a power surge.

"Did you see him?" Hahn coiled his arms around his own body. "He's not acting right. We don't need to be moving. We survived the surprise attack. We can stand

toe to toe with anybody—there's nobody—read the reports—who can stand up to a destroyer point-blank in
this sector. But if we're moving we can collide, we can
hit anything else that's out there, our own thrusters and
shields muck up our sensors . . ."

Maybe he was babbling, except that people who bab-
ble don't usually make perfect sense. Keller nodded in
frustration and unhappy agreement, then broke the
panel off the wall and got to the direct-feed cables. A
puff of gray acid smoke piled out at him, souring the
air in the lift. When it cleared, he looked into the panel
opening. What he saw in there—he didn't even want to
touch it, never mind stick his arm all the way in.

"Fused," he reported, more to himself than Hahn.
"We're stuck."

"They'll break us—out in a minute." On the deck,
Hahn's breathing grew more labored and his voice
weaker. "I was hoping we could make it to Belle
Terre. . . . Captain Kirk could take over . . . situation . . ." He pressed a bloody hand to his side again,
but couldn't reach the wound in his back. As his head
dropped against the lift wall, his waxy eyes beseeched
Keller's. "We're overpaying our debt, Nick."

More concerned about Hahn than the lift, Keller divided his mind and knelt beside the injured officer, seeing their four years together dancing in front of his eyes.

Hahn grimaced and arched against the lift wall. "I—
feel it now—I feel it—!" Pain twisted through him. He
clutched toward the wound he couldn't possibly reach.
"Is there something in me? I feel something solid. Pull
it out!"

"There's nothing in there," Keller lied. "You're just
ship-kicked."

Drunk with blood loss, Hahn couldn't raise his head.
His eyes began to glaze. "He'll be poisoned. . . . Tavola

13

exposure—you know what that means . . . but he saved our asses. Don't tell them, Nick . . . he'll cover for you. I will too . . ."

Stunned, Keller held his breath a few seconds before he realized what was happening. He dug his fingers into the chest placket of Hahn's uniform and shook him. "Derek, that was three years ago! Come out of it!"

"What?" Hahn murmured. His eyes cleared with a surge of adrenaline. "Oh, sorry . . . took a trip, didn't I?"

Angry now, Keller snapped, "Tavola exposure shows itself in the first ninety days—you know that!"

"Usually," Hahn gagged. "And usually the person's watched like a hawk by every doctor within a light-year. Nick, he's snapping and it's our—"

"No, no," Keller insisted, feeling himself sweat under his jacket. This couldn't be rearing its ugly skull, could it? Not now! "He hasn't been in battle in over six years. It's just stress."

Forcing a shake of his head, Hahn argued, "The pressure's bringing the reaction out. We can't protect him anymore . . . We made a hell of a mistake. Today we . . . we pay."

From above, a faint voice filtered through the sound-muffling insulation. "Nick?"

Keller bolted to his feet. "Savannah! The lift's jammed! Break us out! We need help!"

A response thrummed through the shaft, but he couldn't make it out. For a moment he wondered how Savannah Ring had made it onto the bridge, but then his head cleared some and he remembered the companionway ladder leading down to the next deck. Then they must know the lift wasn't working.

"Open up the hatch," Hahn said. "Let's get back to the bridge."

"You're going to sickbay," Keller said. At least he could do that much.

"Till I get back," Hahn gasped, "keep our shields up, no matter what."

"If we run with full shields, the sensors won't work at all." Keller tried pushing at the ceiling hatch. The twisted lift must have jammed the hatch too. It wouldn't budge. "Not even the little bit of data we get trickling in—dang crippled thing, open up!"

Hahn flinched at the protest and grasped Keller's leg. "We shouldn't be running at all! Roger's cracking . . . you watch him. I—I—can't breathe . . ." His eyes cramped shut and he slipped sideways, his face a twisted knot.

Abandoning the hatch as he heard noises thunking from above, Keller quickly knelt again and pulled Hahn up, then yanked open the placket to loose the exo's jacket. "Let's get your belt off."

"You always—wanted an excuse—to get out of uniform. . . ."

Keller tried a grin. "At least the new ones have pockets in the britches. The other ones were just fancy PJs. What's a cowboy to do with his thumbs?"

"Still got those wranglers on . . ."

"Don't give me grief about m'boots. You don't outrank me that much."

"Nick—" Hahn fought his way back from the edge of consciousness again, battled down the pain that obviously had him by the body, and hooked his bloody hand on Keller's neck. "Nick, listen. It's time, it's time."

"Now, Dee," Keller moaned. "He's got thirteen years' command experience. That's better than what you and I got between us, even if he's a little shook."

"We let it go too long," Hahn wheezed. His gaze was now shockingly lucid. "As soon as I get back from sickbay," he vowed, "I'm relieving him."

More roughly than he meant, Keller tightened his grip. "Sit still. Let me get us out of here. Everything'll be better in a few minutes. Just sit."

On thready legs he stood again, reached up, and tried pulling on the hatch instead of pushing. The hatch squawked and moved this time, but it was meant to push out, not pull in, and the rim wouldn't give. "Come on, bust open," he grumbled. "What've I ever done to you?"

If only he had something to stand on, he could apply his weight onto the hatch with a well-arranged elbow. Muffled thunks and rasping of tools and metal told him they were breaking through from the bridge. He wanted to call out for them to hurry, but the lift tube was clustered with electrical outlets and access points that might be hot, dangerous. They couldn't hurry. He braced his legs and tried to push straight upward, but his boot heel skidded on the deck. His leg slipped out from under him. He staggered.

He looked down.

Hahn's blood painted the deck, a red smear across the lift floor, with a slashing imprint of the heel of Keller's left ranch boot.

Maybe if he'd wear regulation footwear, none of this would be happening. If one decision had been different somewhere way back—

Derek had tried to tell him. Why hadn't they made a different decision three years ago? Why couldn't they go back and fix it?

Below him, Derek Hahn sucked a lump of air and wheezed it back out. "The crew . . ."

"What about 'em?" Aggravated and taking it out on the hatch, Keller pushed harder on the stubborn panel.

There was no response this time. After a few seconds, the silence made sense.

"Derek?" Keller knelt again.

Hahn's eyes had lost their focus. Though sweat trailed down his face, his lips were relaxed now, his arms resting on his thighs. A breath gurgled in . . . out.

"Derek! They're almost through!"

Though the first officer was still breathing, he no longer blinked or responded. His eyelids began to sag, his tight facial muscles to go limp. His face turned pasty. Another choked breath clawed its way in.

Terror seized Keller by the heart. This was supposed to be a milk run. An easy mission. A six-month flight out to Belle Terre, the same heading all the way, boring, quiet, peaceful, simple, then take over picket duty at Belle Terre and relieve the *Enterprise* to return to Federation space.

Suddenly everything shattered around him like a glass bulb he held too tight in his hand. His fingers crushed the bulb into ever smaller shards.

Something thumped on the lift roof. The access hatch cranked open with a ghastly shriek. Bent metal, crying, weeping.

There it was. The way back to the bridge. A hand came down.

Whose?

Chapter Two

Starship Enterprise, in orbit, planet Belle Terre

"THIS WAS INEVITABLE. Quantum olivium is so valuable, somebody was bound to try stealing it in larger quantties."

The most precious commodity, Captain James Kirk thought, discovered in the settled galaxy for over a hundred years, was disappearing in large quantities from their holding facilities.

When had a simple escort mission turned into a safari to hell? Right around the third light-year out, as he recalled. Seemed far back.

At his side in the hangar deck of their only oasis, the United Federation of Planets flagship *Enterprise,* Captain Spock, currently the ship's acting first officer, drew and released a long uncharacteristic sigh. "I'd hoped for a grace period," he commented, "before losing quite such a large grip."

No "sir," no "Jim," no nothing.

Spock's angular features were drawn and etched with fatigue. He hadn't slept in days, and not well in weeks. Not since the storagemasters discovered the slow leaks of thievery from the olivium vaults. Spock had no comforts of delusion for his commanding officer, or even the simple reassurances of logic to offer. His statement left a grinding emptiness. Why wasn't he saying something to make Kirk feel better?

Couldn't have everything all at once, apparently. Today, they couldn't have anything at all but questions.

He'd noticed a difference in Spock over the past few months, since the trickle of olivium thefts had begun to plague the colony. Spock overworked himself now, hardly slept, delegated his other responsibilities to lieutenants all over the colony.

Did he think he was working alone? That he was the only one who could solve the problem?

A familiar discomfort. Kirk had shouldered this kind of burden himself many times, but something about this was different for Spock. Spock was the one everyone went to for answers. He didn't have any yet.

"I feel like a fractured bone," Kirk said, hoping there might be comfort in collaboration. "We've hardly seen any of our command staff for weeks. We're supposed to be a ship's crew, leaders of an expedition, not tutors in a survival clinic. Scotty's been running engineering projects and ship refits all over the planet, Chekov's off exploring on the *Reliant*. Sulu's been checking up on the flight teams he trained after that mess in the Big Muddy, Uhura setting up communications and emergency networks, McCoy's off who knows where, working on making sure the crops are getting the right amino acid balance from the changed soil. I wish he'd get back here to complain and grouse. After all, that's his number-one job, isn't it?"

When Spock, strangely, had no tidy retort about the absent doctor who was ordinarily a fixture in their lives, Jim Kirk started answering himself in private. Quips, comments, satiricals and snidisms flitted back and forth like a badminton birdie between the imaginary Spock and McCoy in his head.

He and Spock were isolated. Not physically, but in their souls. They were in their ship, but they weren't in a crew. Instead, they were advisors, field guides, mentors, assistants, tutors—duties usually left to other Federation emissaries. But there weren't any Federation emissaries this far out who could take over those jobs, no one to step in and fill the gaps, allowing the starship to go on its way and to do the job it had been built for, the job the crew had imagined and trained to do. The ship's complement, largely, had been dispersed all over that planet down there, the new colony, the dream of thousands. Suddenly they were parents to a confused and ragged colony of people amiably determined to stay and slog through the wake of disaster.

That alone had kept Kirk and his people on target.

"I hope the *Peleliu* arrives soon," he commented in a less than commanding way. "I'll be glad to cede this mess to somebody else. Escorting the colonial expedition out to Belle Terre was one thing. Staying here and helping them carve a living out of a half-wrecked planet speckled with the most valuable ore ever discovered and solving a planet-threatening crisis every other hour . . . that's not what I suspended my admiralty for. Now I find myself in charge of a new Gold Rush. It'll be my pleasure to hand this over to Captain Lake and the specialists he's bringing out with him."

The only answer was the click and twinkle of Spock's tricorder and the tie-in to the ship's mainframe. He had, for days now, been coordinating quantity broadcasts from olivium repositories all over the planet and in orbit. Ordinarily this would be a grunt job, except for the fabulous value of the stuff they were storing.

Here in the wide white hangar deck of *Enterprise*, several sealed drums holding olivium in flux stasis stood in sentinel form, a little taller than Kirk and twice as thick. Quantum olivium that lent itself to stability. He could hardly believe it was here. Until the discovery of the Quake Moon at Belle Terre, this remarkable stuff had been only a scientific fantasy, created in minuscule amounts in laboratory conditions. The advancements it would bring were a feast for the imagination. Spock himself, Spock the understated, Spock the subdued, had referred to the discovery's value in his most extreme of terms ... "inestimable."

The people who now lived on Belle Terre had come for a whole other reason—a dream to establish a Mecca, a cultural hub, to live with their own laws and polish up the tenets of basic individual freedom. They hadn't come for the olivium. They hadn't known it was here.

The unstable Quake Moon had spewed its wondrous shimmering prize all over the planet, to be mined at the will of the human occupants, but it had also made Belle Terre a target for those who would use and abuse the olivium. That meant this was still Jim Kirk's problem.

Even if there were no Federation citizens here, he

Diane Carey

couldn't leave the olivium until the area was secure. This was one resource which couldn't be allowed to fall into the hands of hostile cultures unless it was also in the hands of everybody else. The colonists had bitten off a pretty volatile mouthful.

"Still," he went on, aloud, "for people who signed up for paradise and got stuck with a woolly frontier shagtown, the colonists digested the turn of events and plowed ahead. I hadn't really expected that of them. Sometimes we intrepid starship types get the idea that everyone else is a pampered citizen used to secure homes and a threatless existence. These folks, I have to admit, tightened the ranks, explained the tragedy to their children, locked their knees and faced all the problems. They gave up their chance to turn around and go home, even with all the attacks on the planet. They're not really colonists anymore, supported by the Federation. They're as much on their own as anyone in history ever has been. They're citizens of an independent planet, in their own right. They refused to let that go, even though things turned sour. You've got to give them credit. Of course, they now hold the claim to the richest diamond mine in the universe. If this planet doesn't kill them in the next couple of years, they'll all live very good lives eventually."

"Yes, sir." Spock barely muttered his response.

Kirk paused and looked at him. Spock wasn't listening. Hunched over a computer terminal with twelve interconnected screens feeding information from over a thousand recovery points and storage sites on Belle Terre, the Vulcan remained consumed by his quest to solve their newest problem.

A big problem. A collision of moons had been the citizens' only chance to save their far-flung planet, but that collision had left Belle Terre storm-swept and inclement. Though disappointment showed on every face for the shining spaceport that for now had to be back-pocketed, plain human resilience had risen and sustained them.

Theirs was a noble enough mission, as packed with activity as any he had led. Yet somehow he felt like half a person, missing critical limbs that he needed to walk, talk, live. Somehow he imagined that if McCoy, Scotty, Sulu, Uhura, and the others could be here on the ship and still do their jobs, he would feel better. With all the family members dispersed around the perimeter, the house had a sad echo.

Of course, the other portion of this feeling in his stomach had do with the fact that he didn't know which action to take, or how even to begin solving the problem of the missing olivium. He knew what the problem was—he just didn't know what to do about it.

He pivoted on a boot heel and crossed the deck to Spock, deliberately coming around into Spock's periphery so the Vulcan would see him clearly.

"Any luck?" he prodded.

Beneath the straight eave of black hair, Spock's brow was creased and his complexion pallid. His eyes were wedges of worry, squinted and dull. Even his deep-red Starfleet jacket seemed to sag.

He leaned back in his chair. "I've no idea how these disappearances are happening," he said, listless and ragged. He was completely discouraged, and as baffled as Kirk had ever seen him. "If I had any information . . . knew *how* these shortages were being perpetrated, I could form a hypothesis. With even one clue, I could begin to—"

"Don't apologize," Kirk interrupted. "Even Vulcans can't form theories with information they don't possess."

Frustrated, Spock tilted his head. "Yes, but, Captain,

you must understand. The shortfall cannot simply happen within a closed storage system. It must be *caused* by outside forces. The containers are unbreachable by conventional means, yet none shows any sign of rupture. In spite of this, we have a steadily decreasing amount of olivium. The loss does seem to occur in transit . . ."

Kirk straightened. "Well, that's something, isn't it? We'll start looking between the mining operations and the storage facilities. Who's handling that?"

"Commander Uhura is the coordinator. She's traveling around the planet, overseeing all the preparations for shipment and processing. We get regular reports, and she has mentioned no security breach or other troubles, despite being notified about the steady decreases."

Prowling around Spock's computer table, Kirk shrugged. "Mmm, we know *she's* probably not stealing it." He'd experienced palpable tension before, but this business of stalking around while waiting for a computer to cough up answers that he sensed just weren't in there was irritating.

He ran his finger along the back of Spock's console. "When this is over, we both need a vacation. How about if after we get back into Federation space, we lay off in some quiet solar system for about a month, and not tell anybody where we are?"

Spock just sat there, ignoring or not even registering Kirk's grumbles.

As Kirk parted his lips to make a comment of his own, what came out was the honking emergency klaxon so familiar and so dreaded aboard a ship. Red alert!

Spock came to his feet. Around them, the scarlet light panels began flashing, determined not to be missed.

Danger, destruction, and disaster. At last! Kirk plunged for the nearest comm unit and hammered it.

"Kirk here. What's going on?"

"Bridge, sir—hull breach on deck eight."

"Nature of the breach?"

"Unknown—the automatic alerts just popped on and the sensors reported a rupture! Sir, there's minimal atmospheric loss—I don't understand these readings!"

"Alert security and damage control teams. Get visual confirmation. Clear those areas and seal those breaches."

"Aye, sir!"

"I'm heading to deck eight." Kirk bolted toward the turbolift at the far end of the shuttle bay, stopping along the way to grab two phasers from the weapons locker.

Spock didn't wait. He crossed to the shipboard terminals and cued up the graphics of ship's integrity. Even he couldn't contain a reaction as the graphics showed him what was happening. Across the bay he called, "Rupture now on deck nine, Captain!"

Boots skidding under him, Kirk scratched around. "Are you sure?"

"Another one, on deck ten," Spock called. "Deck eleven!"

"Phasers, Spock!" Kirk drew his sidearm and looked up at the hood of the hangar bay.

"I hear it!" Clapping a hand to one of his elegantly upswept ears, Spock used the other hand.

"Hear what?" Kirk squinted and strained to listen. Yes—there it was! A thrumming sound, pulsing through the body of the ship. He couldn't exactly hear it. Instead he felt it in his bones, his nerve endings, every sinew, every brain cell, so tightly attuned to the fiber of the *Enterprise* that the two were nearly one. Something indeed was coming, punching through his second body, layer by layer.

A moment later, he heard the whining sound that had shaken Spock's more sensitive hearing. Spock—he was still picking at his controls, zeroing in with sensor analysis.

"Spock," Kirk called, "arm yourself!"

He no longer had to run to meet the crisis. Whatever it was, the force was smashing its way through the ship and was on its way to them.

Above his head, the ceiling structure began to dissolve. Ringed with phosphorescence that cast a glow on Kirk's face and Spock's, a hole appeared and spread its edges, burning away the deck layer by layer. Jagged rims of structural material peeled back as if the ceiling were exacting a maniacal grin, showing its teeth of superhard reinforcements that were the last to burn back.

James Kirk had seen in his time many strange things, innocent things that turned out to be deadly, horror that turned out placid, and he fought to hold back his drive to open fire on the unknown force drilling its way through his ship. How many were dead up there, in the decks where this thing had come in? Were his crewmen being sucked out the gaps punched into the ship's skin? How many of these young people wouldn't settle into their bunks tonight? To how many parents, wives, husbands, children would he as their captain be writing personal notes of consolation?

These thoughts rocketed through his mind as quick as that, within the three or four seconds it took for that hole to burn itself a wide presence in his hangar bay.

Down through the hole floated a glowing, whining, metallic mechanism, completely unfamiliar in form, and not very big. Only a couple of meters long by the time it got its legs through the hole, the thing had a cylindrical structure that fanned at its opening, and behind it were three legs that arched out and back in undeniably artistic curves. Its metallic surface kept changing colors, and Kirk wasted a few seconds figuring out that the effect wasn't just reflection.

"Robotic!" Spock called, glancing at the sensors on the screen, now out of reach. "No life readings!"

"Stay back!"

Unfortunately, though Spock did obey the order by backing away, he backed in the direction of the olivium casks. Kirk realized a millisecond too late what was happening.

The 'bot swung its maw around to the casks without paying the slightest attention to Kirk and his obviously pointed phaser. Over the singing shriek, Kirk shouted, "Spock, get out of the line of fire!"

But the noise was too loud. He could barely hear his own voice. The electrical thrumming—was a maddening sound! It almost had a human quality, as if some *Rigoletto* tenor were being strangled.

Leaving Kirk behind, the 'bot swerved past Spock's makeshift computer setup and for some reason bothered to steer around a parked shuttle. Why would it drill right through the ship's body, then politely avoid wrecking a shuttle?

Raising his phaser to eye level, Kirk opened fire. Set to kill, the phaser should easily destroy the flying object.

The whining sound increased slightly. That was the only effect. He might as well have been spraying it with water. The 'bot didn't even slow down, but made its way with determination toward the casks. Just before it would've run them over, it paused and spewed out a vertical search beam with a scream of its own. The beam washed back and forth across the casks of olivium, then over Spock. The storm of energy knocked him flat on his back and somehow held him down while the vertical beam panned back and forth along the entire hangar bay in an obvious search pattern.

"Fire on it!" Kirk shouted.

He squeezed his own phaser again.

Again the searing beam struck the 'bot's legs, its crotch, its cylindrical body, and had no effect at all except to cause an increased whine. Did it have shields? He saw no shield reaction, but that might mean nothing.

Spock rolled over and crawled to his knees, then was drummed down by the glowing blue energy beam. He managed to twist around, aimed his phaser into the thing's maw, and opened fire.

The blue beam stopped, but the thing swallowed Spock's phaser beam without a belch. It moved in on the olivium casks. Using a second kind of beam, this one with sizable floating particles that sprayed onto the casks and began to sizzle the containment systems, the thing cracked every cask like an egg.

As Kirk and Spock watched, unable to act, chunks of gleaming raw olivium swam out of the cracked casks and twisted into a long thin tornado and flew inside the 'bot's maw. Hundreds of pounds of ore was sucked into a structure the size of a shuttle nacelle. How?

Spock shielded his face against sprinkles of ore and bits of the stuff that had cracked the casks. He flinched as the spray burned his raised hand.

Dropping to his knees, Kirk shuffled ferociously under the thrumming 'bot, ignoring the crackle of energy on his head and back, and reached for Spock's ankle.

Just as he grasped it, as he was about to pull Spock out of the funnel of energy, the last of the olivium spun into the maw. Everything shut down. The beam, the sound, the whine, the particles—cut off sharply.

Now silent, the 'bot hovered over them passively, as if deciding what to do next. Kirk blinked up at it.

A little hatch opened up in the more or less front of the shiny cylinder, on the bottom. A nozzle popped out. Kirk ducked back.

A lather of greenish-white foam splattered Spock where he lay. Only a last-ditch reflex allowed him to hide his face. The green stuff bubbled a bit, then quickly began drying.

Over them, the 'bot upended, shined its vertical beam on the nearest bulkheads until it found something it wanted, then impudently burned itself an escape hatch in the bay door.

Lying on the deck, Kirk braced himself to be sucked into space, a sudden death he hadn't anticipated.

Instead, the gaping hole grew big enough to accommodate the 'bot, which pleasantly flew through the gash into open space. The last Kirk saw of it was a plume of webbing spat from the three arching legs. The webbing formed itself into a crude sheet and sealed the gash in the bay door with a clouded bandage.

As he gathered his legs and stood up, Kirk realized his limbs were tingling. Felt like an electrical charge. Some kind of converted power had been at work here, despite the fact that he hadn't seen anything big enough to do that kind of work. Just their curious visitation, a device about as long as Kirk was tall. Of course, the power of a phaser wasn't obvious in its size either.

Most phasers. He looked down at his hand weapon and glowered at it.

His knees shuddered. He stepped to Spock and knelt beside him.

"Spock, you hurt?"

"No . . . I am . . . quite . . ." The once-tidy Vulcan looked down at the foam dripping in moist cakes from his clothing to the deck.

Kirk pulled him to his feet, then wiped his hand on his jacket. "What is this mess?"

Thoroughly annoyed, Spock picked up a tricorder from his desk area and turned it on. "Reads as inert . . . blend of petroleum gel, chloromas cellular bond, and semi-fibrous particles . . . some trace readings . . . some kind of decontaminant."

Glancing up at the ceiling, then at the shimmering web that sealed the hole in the bay door, Kirk scowled and sighed. "That thing took our rocks."

Sadness and disappointment weighted Spock's expression. He said nothing.

Kirk stepped to the comm button. "Kirk to damage control. What's the condition of those hull breaches?"

"Captain, Ensign Baker, sir. My damage-control teams report that the hull breaches have been sealed. Whatever that thing was, it plugged up the holes as it came through. The patches are some kind of filament, rough to the touch. Seem to be holding though."

"Don't believe what you see. Reinforce them. Kirk out." He turned again to Spock, sympathized briefly with the indignity suffered by his unprovincial companion, and forced the subject forward. "Ever seen anything like that before?"

Dripping, Spock shook his head. Far-flung implications showed in his troubled eyes. "I will investigate further."

"I'm not waiting," Kirk declared. "We'll decentralize the ore storage. Find some bosuns to organize the changes. Let's see if we can hide the olivium from . . . whatever that was and whoever's running it."

"Very well, sir," Spock murmured. He sounded doubtful. His eyes fixed sorrowfully upon the remains of the cracked-open storage casks.

With the toe of his boot, Kirk flipped over a piece of plating from one of the destroyed casks. It buzzed with residual energy, then went silent. He peered into the empty receptacle.

"Well," he offered, "you have what you wanted. Back home in Iowa, this is what we refer to as 'a clue.' "

CHAPTER

Chapter Three

Peleliu

IT WAS Tim McAddis's hand that pulled Nick Keller out
of the lift, but the first face he saw was Savannah
Ring's. She was running a diagnostic scanner over him
even before he got both legs through the hatch, which
Ring had opened with a cutting torch.

"Hold still, sheriff," she said, trying to read the
scanner.

"Stop that!" He knocked her hand away. "Derek's
down there. Go, go!"

"Climb up to Tim," she told him. "Don't come down
again. I work alone."

The cavity was clogged halfway across by a safety
rig of cables to keep the lift from continuing its drop if
the twisted guides decided to crack. Savannah Ring's
stocky figure and straight redwood hair disappeared
without assistance. McAddis climbed up to the bridge,
then pulled Keller up after him.

Keller grasped the science officer by the arm. "What's the story?"

"Phasers seized up," McAddis said, keeping his voice low. "We're at all-stop. He's got the engineers working on the phaser banks. He wants to keep shooting. Savannah came up through the companionway, but now the automatic hatches are sealed, so we're stuck here."

"Why? Did we have a pressure drop?"

"Big one, deck four. We're trapped on the bridge with the Mask of Tut." McAddis cast a punitive glare up at Zoa, where she still hovered near the sci-deck rail.

Just a few steps away, Captain Roger Lake fixed his eyes on the forward screen even though there was still nothing to see. The bridge was hot, sticky. Life-support was still on, but the comfort index had been tapped and rerouted to the suffering sensors on the outer skin of the ship, scooping the beach of space for invisible grains.

"What did Savannah say about below deck?"

McAddis lowered his voice even more. "Thirteen dead, thirty-four wounded."

As if he'd been gut-shot, Keller clamped his eyes shut and groaned. *Thirteen. Thirty-four.*

Why were they being attacked? Who was doing this? Why? He forced himself to think, dismiss the ugly numbers, think, think.

Somebody was trying to discourage the cruiser from going out to Belle Terre, or kill them before they got there, before they could join the *Enterprise* in its defense of the new colony and the precious substance discovered there.

Must mean the *Enterprise* was already encountering trouble out there. Whoever was attacking *Peleliu* understood something about Starfleet configuration and knew where to aim. Now *Peleliu* was stumbling in its own wreckage.

Still, a cruiser was a tough breed, built for exploration, yes, but also equipped to defend itself against anyone who objected to being surveyed. With a man like Roger Lake in command there wouldn't be any turning back.

But their captain wasn't himself, just as Derek Hahn suspected. Against his own will Keller read the change clearly in the set of Lake's shoulders and the fact that he hadn't even looked down the hole to see about the condition of his two mates. Down in the lift, with Derek there to make the decisions, it had been easier to resist.

Here, with Hahn out of commission, Keller was abruptly, and for the first time, unprotected against whatever the captain might choose to do.

Thirteen . . . thirty-four . . . out of a crew of only eighty.

The past rushed up to claw at him. His midsection tightened as if he'd strapped on a corset. An expedition, an abandoned outpost. A captain and two young officers stumbling through a half-contaminated site. Unsecured chemical tanks . . . ruptured, and a lieutenant who forgot to secure the site before clearing the captain through to investigate. Simple procedure, if only the ranch hand from New Mexico had followed it.

All those years, and here the error came rushing forward to have an effect on today. Keller was trapped between his loyalty to his captain and what might be the right thing to do.

Around him, the crew stepped over wreckage. Open trunks, strands of insulation, burned carpet, and datacrystal membranes peeled back like banana skins. He squeezed his eyes shut and let the sounds of the bridge ring and jingle through his skull. *Peleliu* was singing to him. Not as pretty or sleek as a starship, the Chesapeake-class cruiser was an advanced defensive picket ship. A no-frills vessel meant for multiple duties from exploration to medium-range rescue and relay, she had limited lab space and the most utilitarian of quarters. There was hardly any room on board to get away from each other. Their job was to go out to the Sagittarius star cluster, replace the *Enterprise,* and work toward stabilization of anterior space and opening up the cluster under Federation jurisdictional law. Simple.

With a captain who might be unstable? Keller found himself his own judge and jury, with no one else to answer to.

Tim McAddis was watching him. "What is it you're not telling me?"

Self-consciousness squeezed a little cough out of Keller. He winced at the knots in his stomach, put up an officer front, and gave McAddis a hopeful nudge. "Pretty perceptive for a late paleolithic hunter-gatherer."

Both relief and dread washed over him as he saw Savannah Ring's chestnut head appear in the lift cavity. She was climbing out, slowly.

He was glad she was here. A fair number of people in his life circle had earned his trust, but he trusted Savannah Ring most. Stocky and quick, a mix of Polynesian bloods and some Eskimo, with brown eyes and a slick of dark red hair whose color she couldn't quite decide upon, Ring was smart and maverick. She neither coddled nor balked, and made up methods as she went along. She was heading to Belle Terre on a last-ditch deal with Starfleet—take a discharge or take frontier duty. Follow the rules, or go where there aren't any.

Here she was, climbing out of the lift hatch and up the safety cables without anyone's help. When she stood again on the bridge, her uniform was smudged with blood and grease.

35

Keller's silent eyes probed. He felt them burning in his head like separate beings.

With a towelette Savannah wiped blood from her hands, then repacked the field kit at her hip, using slow and deliberate movements. Finally she met his eyes. "We'll take him below later," she said. "He's pretty compliant now."

At Keller's side, Tim McAddis covered his face with trembling hands and mumbled unintelligible grieving.

And Keller stood there, and just stood.

Hours passed. The enemy had stopped shooting. Maybe they ran away, lost the cruiser in the sensor darkness, ran out of power themselves, or were overwhelmed by the phaser blanket. Nobody knew. Maybe they were still out there.

Nick Keller sat on one of the crew chairs on the scideck. His arms stuck out before him, resting on the balcony rail. His head was lowered almost between them. He stared at the carpet and his two feet, with a hole in his heart the size of his own fist.

Below, the mutter of reports threaded up from the lower decks, everything from damage assessments to the captain's relentless efforts to get the phasers on line so he could keep shooting, even though nothing had shot at them for hours now.

Over the dangerous final hours of Gamma Night, Savannah had floated around the bridge, giving first aid where it was needed, but that was finished now. She'd done all she could, and had retreated up here to the scideck, where she had finally done what she'd been called to the bridge about in the first place. She'd checked Keller's head wound, looked into his eyes and declared them green. Then she, McAddis, and Keller had fallen into a squirming brand of silence that stretched out until nobody dared break it. Long enough for old memories to crawl in.

Tavola methane. Two shipmates determined not to wreck their captain's career on a maybe. Swearing to keep silent about the lieutenant's slip.

Not reporting Tavola exposure was a Starfleet court-martial offense, because there was no other way to know, no other way to detect it. Exposure only resulted in pathological change in one of about eighty victims. The symptoms never came up, doctors never said a thing at Lake's regular physicals. Milk runs in interior space, easy missions, mostly handled by the crew. Until this mission.

Symptoms never came out. *It's the methane, I know it is. We gambled—we lost. Today we pay.*

Now what? Relieve Lake of command based on an incident that happened three years ago and they couldn't even prove happened at all? People change with age. Could be just stress.

Now that he was out of the lift, without Derek Hahn helping him think, making the decisions, suddenly stress could only explain so much.

A young officer breaks regs to protect his captain. Not the first time.

Seldom also did such an error result in rolling thunder. This might be the time.

Somebody was rubbing his back. Savannah or Tim. Might be that Rassua woman, but he had the feeling his skin would be in shreds by now if she were doing it. She didn't seem like the back-rub type.

Probably not Savannah. Her bedside manner was more of a slap in the rear than a rub on the back.

Must be Tim.

Far as Keller could tell, Roger Lake had buried any feelings about Derek Hahn, had done nothing more than take a silent look down into the lift cavity. Then he put aside any mention of the cloying loss, personal or otherwise. Maybe a good captain did that kind of thing.

So much for me.

The hand on his back went away. A squeak on the deck told him McAddis was moving back to the sensors. Keller didn't raise his head. The science console twittered sluggishly.

McAddis's voice startled him a little. "Captain, I'm picking up shadows again on the mid-range."

Below, Roger Lake came toward the balcony. "Describe them."

"They read generally the same as the ionized clouds we went through a couple of nights ago, except for some flickers of solidity."

"Clouds? I don't believe it."

"I could run a comparison, sir," McAddis offered. "But these readings are . . . real muddy. I don't think they'll clear any."

Lake turned to the helm. "Thrusters on."

Keller's head snapped up. "What'd he say?"

"One-sixth impulse," Lake finished. "Steady as she goes. What's the story on those phasers?"

As the crew yanked themselves out of all-stop and back into the ugly pattern of before, tension shot out to engulf the bridge again. At the helm, Makarios looked over his shoulder to Keller. The desperation in his face communicated what he dared not say. Beside him, Hurley worked the navigation controls, but there was no way to know where the ship was heading or what might be in their way.

Moving again—without an order to raise deflector shields.

"Cripes," Keller mumbled. "Tim?"

"I got flickers, Nick," McAddis quietly said. "Could

be the people who attacked us, or just sensor shadows, or it could be nothing. I'm bettin' on nothing."

"But he's responding to them. It's enough to keep us moving forward . . . but forward toward what?"

"He won't let me scan forward."

Dangerous words.

Usually sublight speed was slow for a deep-space vessel. But under the conditions of Gamma Night, they might as well have been shot out of a supernova. Everybody was nervous, bruised. Savannah had made the rounds, patching injuries and doling out medication, unable to transfer anyone to sickbay.

The bridge was locked up. The pressure drop on deck four had cut them off. Damage had to be repaired before the hatches would allow themselves to be opened. With the crew severely depleted, there were only so many hands to go around. The broken lift still hung ten feet down the useless tube, with Derek Hahn beginning his eternal walk inside it. Getting people on and off the bridge had become a low priority.

"He's got it in his mind there's a big force tracking us," Savannah breathed through her lips.

"He could be right," Keller reminded. "We don't know."

"In my medical opinion—"

"You're not a doctor."

Her dark-island eyes stung him. "And you need one?"

In a fume, Keller snapped, "What if he's right and there's somebody behind us?"

McAddis thrust his opinion in. "If we keep moving during Gamma Night, what's *behind* us won't make any difference."

The thought explored its way through Keller's mind. If they kept moving—what?

"You better get ready to hold this hot potato." Wide-eyed, McAddis pressed a warning hand to Keller's shoulder. "Because, guess what, wrangler . . . you're the first officer now."

Keller's whole body turned cold, as if there were holes in the bottom of his feet and his blood suddenly drained right out.

"Great snakes," he moaned. "We'd be better off flippin' a coin. . . ."

"I'll give you one." McAddis dug in his trouser pocket and thumbed a shiny coin onto the console's microfoamed face. "Have a half-dollar."

The coin was soft burnished silver or some other white metal, with a gold edge around the outside, struck with a picture of some kind of ship. Keller leaned over it, then finally picked it up and held it so the overhead lighting didn't obscure the impression.

"Oh—the early moon shuttle program! Well, isn't this mighty pretty."

"Not moon shuttle," McAddis corrected. "An 'orbiter.' "

"They were called 'shuttles' though, weren't they?"

"I guess, but they never went to the moon. It's a commemorative coin, struck for the NASA sesquicentennial or something-centennial back when they had a grand opening for the first lunar mall."

"Is it silver?"

"Platinum. Rim's gold. If you can believe Bonifay."

"Zane Bonifay?" Keller held the coin higher and looked at the cluster of rocket-powered contraptions neatly standing on a launch pad. "Orbiter *Challenger.* These names around the rim . . . who're they, the crew?"

"Must be."

"Where'd you get a thing like this?"

"From Bonifay, just before he left for Belle Terre. I won a bet. I had a choice of that one or a Roman emperor. Should've picked the Roman one. It would've gone with your nose."

"Bonifay—you mean that rascal is out at Belle Terre waiting to spring on us?"

Savannah came up closer and commented, "That brat put a curse on me!"

"He said it's for luck," McAddis said, pointing at the coin. "You need it more than I do. Maybe you can hypnotize the captain and get him to heave to during Gamma Night before we get netted by a nebula."

A nostalgic smile tugged at Keller's sweat-stiffened cheeks. "Those were the days, y'know? Countdowns, blastoffs, whiplash trajectory . . . Mission Control always right there with you on the radio vox . . . must've been some time to live, eh? Everything just out of reach enough to keep you scratching forward . . . wish I'd been there."

The coin turned in his fingers. The faces of seven people, in three-quarter profile, were etched into the flip side. He didn't recognize them, or their names.

What a wondrous time that must have been, those days of early exploration so close to Mother Earth. Just those few miles projected wondrous adventure. Even the planets of the Sol system were sirens in the night. Those stalwart first few men and women were held to Earth only by the thinnest threads, by mere whispers in the darkness.

He sank against the rolled foam edge of the science console, his imagination clicking, held the coin in his fist, and peered down at the forward screen's fractured vision.

"I've seen dogs," he began, "bite at the flanks of sheep in order to herd them in a direction. And dogs are smarter than sheep." His brow tightened. "What d'you figure the dogs know that the sheep don't?"

Though aware of Tim and Savannah gazing at him,

both disinclined to comment, he paid them no attention at all. For a few seconds there was only Nick Keller and the blind forward screen in the whole universe. Even Roger Lake faded away for a moment and he forgot all the other forces pressing on him. In his fist, the commemorative coin was warmer than his flesh.

"Gives me an idea." Leaning forward again, past McAddis, he touched the comm panel on the science board. "Tracy, Nick."

Below, Tracy Chan turned to look up at him, wondering why he didn't just talk to her over the rail.

With a motion for her to remain silent, Keller quietly said, "Patch me through to Hurley, very low vox."

For a moment, she didn't understand. Then she did. She touched her controls with subtle gestures, and nodded to him.

"Joe," Keller uttered, "it's Nick. Pretend you're talking to Makarios."

He saw Hurley's posture change, but no more. The navigator turned slightly toward Makarios at the helm. *"Copy that."*

"Can you read our heading?"

"Direction, but not clutter. Our best sensors are trained aft."

"Deflector reactions? Heat? Fragments? Dust? Radiation on the hull—anything?"

"You're asking me to read a book through cheesecloth. Talk him into slowing down. We're dead if we keep mov—"

"Hurley! What're you whispering about!" Roger Lake's round face, with its flush of anger and locoweed eyes and a glaze of sweat under the five-o'clock shadow, leveled a glare on the navigator. "If you think you two can conspire on my bridge, you've got something coming!"

"We were just double-checking our readouts, sir," Hurley covered. His guilty expression didn't help him. "We have to be careful during Gam—"

"Don't believe the instruments! Keep all the sensors trained aft, you understand? This one, and this one! And this one!"

Lake punched buttons on the helm, forcing the pilots to turn their sensors away from the direction the ship was traveling. What little information they managed to draw in would be useless. Unhappy, he speared his glare up at the sci-deck. "McAddis!"

"Sir?"

"You a science officer or a janitor? Keep scanning behind us! You expect Hurley to do your job for you?"

"Aye aye, sir. . . ." With a suffering glance to Keller, McAddis shrank to his console.

"Nick, keep an eye on them up there."

"Aye, sir."

Everything settled to a surreal quiet.

Hiding her curiosity behind a padd she'd picked up at the environmental station, Savannah moved forward and pretended to be interested in the little screen. She even went to the trouble of pulling out the onboard stylus and pretending to write things. "You're sweating, Sheriff," she commented.

"So are you, tumbleweed." Keller's words rumbled in his throat.

"I like to sweat. Makes me feel alive. At least I don't look like *her*."

Keller glanced to his right, at Zoa, not really caring anymore whether she saw or heard them talking about her. She either wanted in on the shipboard community or she didn't, and she apparently didn't.

"Don't pay her any mind," he said. "We can't do anything about her."

Savannah nailed the Rassua guest with a bitter glower. "She found out about my snakes yesterday. I thought she was just interested. Know what she did? She stole them and beamed them into space."

Though he knew she was manipulating him by changing the subject, Keller tried to make his stomach muscles relax. "I know. Derek said there's some kind of taboo on her planet against reptilians. I don't think she understands your species."

"But what kind of a savage does that?"

"What kind of a pet is a snake? I mean, a tail with fangs?"

"They're silky, they coil around your neck, and you don't have to worry about any preschool children hanging around for long."

"You don't have a reflection, do you?"

Nope, changing the subject wasn't helping.

"Tim," he began.

At the console, McAddis flinched. "Huh?"

Keller slipped closer to him. "Be real sly about this. Turn your sensors forward. If we're going to slam into anything, that's where it'll be."

"But his orders—"

"Hush." His finger touched his lips. He pointed at the science boards.

If they could hold out till Gamma Night ended, survive without being cut in half by a ten-mile-wide asteroid or an icy meteor or a tendril flare, they'd have twenty full hours before the next sensor blackout and he would have time to work on his problem.

Problems, plural.

The science board bleeped and twittered. McAddis had to be careful, switch over only certain screens, or the other bridge crew would start making reports that they were no longer scanning aft with their best sensors. Or Lake himself would notice.

As each screen shifted, Keller felt his innards turn over. Even from down here, Keller could look up at the top row of McAddis's dynoscanners. He pointed at the mass/density screen and murmured to Savannah.

"What's that look like to you?"

"Looks like . . . gravity."

McAddis frowned. "Could be just another magnetic cloud. We've gone through ten of them already."

"Pretend it's gravity," Keller said. "There's only one thing that causes gravity, right?"

"Mass." McAddis stiffened. "God—you don't think there's something solid in front of us and we can't see it. . . ."

"If he's right and we're being pursued, why wouldn't they just attack us like they did before?"

"Uh . . ."

"How long till Gamma Night's over?"

"Only seven or eight minutes," McAddis said. "Long enough to get killed."

Keller looked at the scatter on the forward screen, and at Roger Lake, who was now hovering over Makarios at the helm. "Why would they start showing up behind us again now?"

Savannah's eyes narrowed as she inferred information from his tone. "Because . . . we're . . . being herded?"

Keller rewarded her with a squeeze around the shoulders. He touched the comm again. "Tracy, patch me through to Hurley again, ultra-low."

Without acknowledging, Tracy Chan winked at him from communications and worked her controls.

A light came on next to Hurley's right hand. He pressed the button.

"Don't talk, Joe," Keller whispered before Hurley

said anything. "Plot emergency vector courses, four different directions . . . just be ready."

Toiling at inconspicuousness, Joe Hurley lowered his chin, his fingers poised on the multicolored control chips. His arms moved slowly, cautiously. His fingers tapped one directional sensor. A second. Then he had to adjust.

Keller barely breathed. This was a court-martial offense if they were wrong, to countermand orders in a battle situation. If the captain's suspicions were right, they'd be giving the enemy an opening to attack.

He stiffened. Hurley had stopped what he was doing.

Roger Lake was pacing around the helm, scanning Hurley's and Makarios's boards, and their hands, prowling like a dog in a junkyard. At the helm, Anton Makarios looked perfectly terrified and wasn't able to hide it. Keller wanted to sell him a poker face.

Slowly, Lake passed by the helm and circled around to the communications station, where he bent to look at Chan's frequency data.

Hurley began to work again. His left hand on the astrogator. Click, click . . . click. Three.

Now the last one.

Four lifelines, just in case, *if* they could know early enough to use them.

Now the courses had to be logged into the nav computer. Hurley moved with deliberation, while beside him Makarios mopped his drenched face and breathed in little sucks.

Heading . . . mark . . . adjust . . . auto-helm response . . . connect to thruster . . . guidance system . . . cued . . .

Lake snapped alert at the bleeps of the guidance computer. "What? What is that!"

Keller and McAddis spun to the rail.

Below them, Lake knocked Chan right out of the

comm chair to get down to Hurley, then drove his arm into Hurley's neck. He twisted his fists into Hurley's collar and hauled him halfway out of his chair. "What're you doing! What're you changing!"

Hurley's face flushed. "Plotting—alternate—courses, sir, in case you need them."

"You're trying to escape, aren't you?" Lake drove him backward, punishing the navigator's spine against the tilted chair. "You're going to abandon me and Nick out here in the middle of nothing! Nick, get a security team up here! This man's under arrest!"

Stunned by the order, Keller grasped the rail with both hands and begged, "Captain!"

"Sir!" McAddis called. "Sensors clearing!"

Like desert venturers recklessly stumbling into an oasis, the screens all around them began to flash and suck information previously denied. Free-flowing data raced around the horseshoe of optical displays. Graphics went suddenly from blank to optimal, and instantly shot to red-line. Alarms began to clang.

On the forward screen, the static blinked, then cleared. It showed not the black starry velvet of space, but instead a perfect view of wall-to-wall sulfur storms and blinding fume.

At the pilot's bench, Makarios quacked out a shout.

"Gas giant dead ahead!"

Chapter Four

Planet Belle Terre

WIND MOANED across the ice desert. Bits of broken
branches twisted into tumbleweed and ran like billiard
balls after the break. Under the wind's grief there was
another sound, a deep pulse that came into James Kirk's
skull as if someone were knocking on a distant door.

He sensed it first, then actually heard it. Regular, mechanical, but somehow also a natural hum with the
asymphony of bees on the swarm. A throbbing sound,
with a saw-blade irritation inside. As his teeth grated at
the sound, he opened his eyes and looked through the
hoversled's windshield. There really was something
coming. It hadn't been just a mirage on the local sensors.

And he'd made a bet with himself when the Starfleet
attendant at this silo had notified the starship about the
surge in impulses on their security screens. Now he
was here, leading a contingent of hoversleds, trying to
chase down a demon.

But darkness had crashed in on the afflicted prairie. The pinkish-yellow sun had chickened out. Kirk squinted, saw only a breath of tumbleweeds rush past the tormented terraces, a sad echo of the beauty this planet had been. There used to be meadow flowers sweeping from bank to bank across this valley. Now there was ice dust. Beautiful Earth.

As the cold sunset closed up, there was no more distance. Invisible mountains were shrouded in advancing night. The buzz-saw noise took on a second chorus, a sound like a human voice, high-pitched, crying a single unending note—a sound that if heard from a castle tower or an opera stage would strike the ear as enticing, haunting.

Throaty gusts hammered his face, drove his hair into a wicked weapon that slapped his scalp, and he was forced to pilot his hoversled backward out of the storm. When he opened his eyes they watered and hurt. He strained to look out again onto the featureless prairie.

Within the arms of blowing ice-sand, a vortex began to take some shape against the mud-brown night. The knotted mass was visible only because some kind of shale bits or glass particles were caught in it and were reflecting Belle Terre's angry formation of moons just now coming up over the western horizon.

Kirk spoke into his hoversled's high-gain comm, which connected him to the other six sleds and their pilots. "Target the center and fire!"

Just before the flash of phaser fire lit up the night, he realized he should've made sure none of the hoversleds were in each other's line of fire. Some things did have to be left up to the guy behind the trigger. That's what training was for.

Since no streak of energy came to cut off his head, he figured they had the sense to look out for each other.

Flanking the vortex, the horseshoe of hoversleds were engaged in a race with a force that was traveling in a clear lateral course from the direction of the wind, thus nothing natural, not a storm, not a twister. Though the readings hadn't been clear, there was something unnatural inside that storm.

Before them, growing swiftly nearer, the hopper silo reached three hundred feet into the unhappy skies over Belle Terre. The structure began horridly to sway and shudder. Despite a certain amount of movement built in to tolerate winds, the silo cried and screeched. This was no prairie wind.

As the churning mass drew closer and the hoversleds became more than just slashes of white and blue plasticore against the night, Kirk made out the other forms in the open-canopied cockpits, Starfleet personnel wearing desert goggles with their standard-issue, holding their phaser rifles and shooting them freely. The hoversleds surfed wildly on waves of white sand, throwing the pilots back and forth even as they fired their weapons again and again.

Kirk closed one eye from the bruising wind and forced himself to focus on the sled at his far right—Spock's—and to move aside himself, thus giving the sharpshooting Vulcan a clear shot at the nose of the vortex.

His stocky form braced with his knees against the edge of the cockpit, Kirk led the running battle against the unidentified force at the epicenter of that storm. Like an electric shock, the storm surged right up to the open door of the bunker at the foot of the silo—just as quick as that, as if summoned, as if pushed, swept by a titan's hand along the ice desert's skirt.

There, in the open sliding door of the bunker, Kirk saw three young Starfleet persons of unidentifiable rank, except that the woman among them was with the security division. He could see her molded torso shield even through the storm.

Beside the woman were two young men, one built like a moose, the other like Robin Hood, and they were both raising their hand phasers. The leaner of the two was an ensign, Kirk could see now.

Phaser rifles had no effect—what did those kids think they could do against the invader with a couple of handhelds? Besides get themselves mowed down—

"All stop!" Kirk shouted, and held his left arm high in the air for the other pilots to see. "Hold your fire! Ensign, hold your fire!"

Shots rang from the ensign's phaser.

"Zane!" the young woman barked. As the wind pulled at her dirty-blond hair, she grabbed the brave kid's arm and pushed his phaser high. The last two shots broke into the clouded night sky.

As the whole bizarre entourage came to a sudden halt outside the silo, the ice-dust spun and began quickly to settle, weighted by its many complex heavy particles. Within a couple of breaths, most of the shroud dropped.

The hoversleds buzzed in place. The dust in the middle settled too, sheeting off a metallic form. At last, the monster in the mist was revealed and Kirk stood staring at his nemesis.

The contraption showed no signs of life at all, nor any place even to put life if it wanted a ride. In fact, the thing was no more than the now recognizable three arched table legs without a table, attached at one end by a buffed green trunklike drum with some indistinguishable carvings. Each table leg had an extension that looked like a foot coming off a leg, but it didn't set itself down onto these feet. Instead it hovered, then pivoted until the legs were pointed out the back and the top of the trunk now pointed at the bunker. The whole mechanism couldn't have been more than five feet on its longest side.

And it was still singing.

"What the hell is that little thing?" the security woman blurted. She stepped out of the bunker with her phaser raised.

"Hold fire, crewman!" Kirk jumped down from his hoversled and stopped every movement with his presence alone. Behind him, around him, the other sleds hovered as if frozen in the air.

Of all the armed men and women stocking the sleds, only Spock moved. The Vulcan stepped down to the ground, frosted sand pelting his legs, his phaser rifle braced and ready against his narrow torso.

At the mouth of the bunker, the wiry ensign shoved his two companions to the sides of the bunker doors. He clearly ranked them both, and was making a decision, the kind Kirk recognized even without words. Then the young man prepared to stand his ground.

He made a bizarre sight, Kirk noted—over his shoulders, right over his uniform jacket, the ensign wore a brightly striped shawl or scarf with a mane of gold fringe that whipped mercilessly, slapping the kid about the head and body. Why would anybody wear such a thing over a Starfleet uniform while he was on duty?

The table-leg thing hung in the air about four feet over the ground. The maw of its drum faced the ensign. Its three flying buttresses splayed out behind, with one aimed directly at the ground, a gathering of drum and sticks that had no apparent purpose. It was still humming, buzzing, with the almost human voice singing under the sound. Inside the maw he could see a spinning light show of crystal bits, a miniature of the thing's travel across the ice desert. Was it about to eat him?

Skin prickled at the back of Kirk's neck. Only the ensign stood between the 'bot and the silo.

Inside the maw, the crystal centrifuge spun faster, faster, then even faster. The suction pulled at the ensign's black hair, the skin of his face and the fabric of his uniform jacket, and finally his entire body.

The 'bot shuddered, began moving forward. Kirk waved his phaser rifle and shouted, "Clear out, you three!"

The security woman and the huge muscular crewman shifted out of the way. The ensign in the middle seemed not to hear him.

"Bonifay!" the big one called. As Kirk's sled drew nearer he saw that this young man wasn't just big—he was *thick*.

The woman also shouted. "Zane, move!"

But the black-haired ensign was caught in the suction and the other two were being pushed back by a secondary force blown sideways by the 'bot.

The ensign couldn't move his head or his arms. His knees bent, but froze in place. The force of suction distorted his face and sent a percussive shudder across his whole body. The 'bot bared its spinning gullet inches from his face. It sang to him, cruel and tempting. He tried to close his eyes, to shut out the promise of being rendered into pieces like a chicken caught in a saw blade. His eyelids were blown open again by the sheer impact of suction and pressure.

All the young man could do, in the end, was part his aching jaws and bellow a warning. At the last moment Kirk saw the face of the Starfleet ensign distorted into a gargoyle of sheer will.

Determined not to lose the ensign, Kirk jumped out of his hoversled and charged the 'bot, aimed his phaser rifle and fired, even though he knew the force would be rejected or absorbed, or whatever that robot did with the energy. He sucked for air and got ice crystals instead.

Despite his bravado, the 'bot ignored him. Of all the insolence.

Thrum thrum thrum . . . the 'bot flew into the bunker. When it got inside, only inches over the ensign's outstretched arms, the thing rolled like a doorknob turning, then upended again to put its flying buttresses downward as if it meant to stand upon them.

Under it, the ensign winced and writhed, his face driven sideways into the deck by some force blowing downward. He lashed out with both legs, only to flail at empty air.

If only the singing would stop! If only it would roar or hiss or make some kind of ugly sound instead of doing its opera imitation—there was something unheroic about being killed by something that was trilling a melody.

The drumstick started moving away, moving up, toward the bottom loading hatch of the hopper silo. If it opened that hatch without activating the antigrav loaders, four hundred gross tons of raw olivium pellets would pour down on them! The container strata would automatically fill from each successive level until the hopper was drained.

"We'll—be—buried alive!" the ensign squawked.

His voice was sucked away, leaving him dry-throated and gagging. The hatch whined as it was yanked open with sheer force of suction. A swishing sound descended. Ore pellets shifting!

"Captain!" Spock called.

"Stand back and hold your fire!" Kirk left Spock with the distasteful order and charged the 'bot. What could he do if a phaser had no effect?

54

Yes, he was being irrational in a way. But something inside him demanded that he get in there, show those young people that even the admirals and captains and famous icons were willing to die with them, even in the age of light-year communication.

He skidded onto his side under the 'bot, and landed beside the ensign twisting underneath.

Unlike the ensign, Kirk didn't try to fight the forces pinning them down. He wanted something different from escape—he wanted information.

Overhead, as he lay here on his back, he saw a tornado of polished olivium pellets whirl in gorgeous and deadly form. But they weren't falling. Jangling furiously, the pellets were sucked into the maw of the drumstick as it hovered, shuddering merrily, a few inches from his dust-caked face. Ton after ton of olivium pellets drained into the maw, flushing into an opening far too small to accommodate the sheer volume of stored ore going in. The drumstick was sucking up a thousand times its own volume of the valuable ore. Where was it going? It was being stolen, but how? How could a two-ounce rat eat a hundred-pound pig?

A few stray pellets fell next to his head and boinked around in the spinning force from overhead. The jangle sound faded down to nothing, leaving only the drumstick's singing voice. Just like that, it ate its fill of the stored olivium, sheer tons of it, until over their heads the silo was empty.

Without a bit of ceremony, threat, or apology, the drumstick stopped its sucking noises, folded its flying buttresses into a kind of point, turned on its side again, and floated out of the bunker like a cannon being hauled over a rampart.

Just as simple as that.

Outside, in front of the confused detail of uniformed personnel who were now out of their sleds, the thing turned with a little twinkle of delight, and vaulted straight upward into the dark sky. Gone. Just like that.

How humiliating!

His ego thoroughly scratched, Kirk coughed some air into his compressed lungs and rolled over. He managed to roll onto his knees, and something hard bit into his right kneecap. He was kneeling on a candle. Next to it was something that looked like a wooden clothespin he'd seen once on another colony planet. What would anybody want with a candle and a clothespin out here?

He plucked the offending candle out from under his leg, picked up the clothespin also, shifted his weight and stood up.

"Who're you?" he asked, aware that he probably presented a monolith of reputation to the ensign.

The black-haired kid blinked up with sore eyes. "Ens . . . Zzz . . . Bah-hanonifay . . ."

"What's your duty here?"

"Secure the processed ore for shipment . . . I inspect, seal, catalogue, and authorize . . ."

"Very well, on your feet. Pull yourself together. You lived." With a first grasp on the wrist, Kirk hoisted him up.

The ensign coughed and spat dust. "How could it—eat that much!"

"We're not sure. Spock, is everyone out there all right?"

Spock came to Kirk's side, still scanning the scene of the crime, and nodded away the question. "Obviously some sort of transcendental portal," he postulated, voicing his thought process still in action.

Kirk huffed a frustrated sigh, then looked down and lifted one boot. "Why's there melted wax on the floor?"

"Where'd that thing come from?" Bonifay belched. "How'd it—how could it—where—"

"We don't know yet."

Inside the deathly darkened bunker, a weak rose-colored haze was thrown by tiny worklights along the far edge of the floor. Emergency lights on the black-painted planks illuminated scratches from loading pallets. The junior officers were little more than wraiths hovering about.

There were the big crewman and the security officer, outside the bunker door, brace-legged and caked with ice-dust, looking like a couple of abominable snowsicles with just their eyes blinking on and off in shock. Alive, anyway, not sucked into that thing.

Accepting the reality quickly and already thinking about alternatives, Kirk indulged his curiosity. He fingered the gold fringe on the kid's shoulders, a shawl or scarf of some exotic fabric, tied into a sailor's knot in front. "Ensign, are you out of uniform?"

The young man's expressive eyes worked. "Oh . . . It's ceremonial, sir."

"You look like a yenta. And these?" He held up the candle and the wooden peg.

"Time-tested charms, sir."

"Is something on fire in here? Or are you cooking?"

"Oh, that's just some incense, sir. And bay leaves."

"You had open flame inside a containment bunker?"

The ensign steeled himself, but already didn't seem to like his own answer. "Candle . . . the shadow had to fall across . . . there had to be a forty-degree . . . em . . . it's hard to explain."

Not that he didn't believe whatever he was talking about. He just didn't like telling it to Kirk.

All right. Change the subject. Let him off the hook.

"Why weren't those processed pellets inside a forcefield?" he charged, even though he knew no forcefield would've stopped the 'bot from stealing the lode.

The ensign didn't seem to feel quite as guilty as Kirk was fishing for. In fact, he displayed the confidence of someone who knows his job and knows he did it. "We were waiting for the last shipment. It's been slow going in this precinct. The processing stations are having trouble separating the olivium from a lot of gold and platinum and other trash."

"Bonifay!" The muscle mass charged in, flushed and overwhelmed. "Did you conjure up that thing?"

The ensign waved him down. "Not on purpose."

"If my pecs deflate because of your voodoo, I'm coming after you."

Now embarrassed in front of Kirk and Spock, the ensign gritted his teeth at his companion. "Shut up, Gyler, or I'll kill you and make some vain attempt to hide the body."

"Who are you two?" Kirk asked, pointing at the muscular one and the security woman as she hesitantly joined them.

"Phaser Gunner Ted Gyler, sir," the big kid said.

"Security Specialist Lucy Quinones, sir. It's an honor, Captain Kirk."

"Thank you. What's your duty on Belle Terre, Specialist?"

"I'm finishing a two-year hitch, sir." The hard-shelled Quinones deposited her phaser into the pressure-molded Security Division chest shield that dominated her upper body. "I'm planning to go into Commander Giotto's Planetary Law Enforcement Agency. With my service record, I'll go in as a precinct deputy."

"There isn't any Planetary Law Enforcement Agency," Bonifay countered.

"There will be," Quinones reacted.

Gyler held up a little vial in his gorilla fingers. "Here's your little momento, jerk."

Bonifay rolled his eyes. "It's *mem*ento. From *mem*ory. 'Momento' goes with 'mo-ron.' I'll take charge of that."

"What's that?" Kirk asked. "Water?"

"Glycerin, sir," Bonifay answered. What choice did he have? "Symbolizes tears of yearning. Canonizes the long-lost homeland."

"Whose?"

"His people," Quinones said unrevealingly.

"What people?"

Quinones faced Bonifay. "Spanish, right?"

"Some."

"Greek? Italian? Jewish? Come on, give!"

Kirk snapped his fingers and pointed at Bonifay. "I remember you now! Two weeks ago, cargo dock sixteen. You told one of my delivery yeomen you were a quarter Klingon."

"I sensed Klingon blood in him, sir. I assimilated."

"That was no Klingon!" Quinones snarled.

Bonifay's charcoal-mark brows and bedroom eyes crawled into an expression. "He had Klingon in his heart. I flowed with it."

Pulling out his flameproof cosmopolitanism, Spock commented, "Humanity prides itself upon being a melting pot, Ensign."

Despite his embarrassment, Bonifay raised his chin. "We're in the pot, sir, but we refuse to melt."

Kirk eyed him. "You'd better explain that one."

Gyler pointed at Bonifay. "He wanted to get on your good side. He was casting a spell."

"Why do you want to be on my good side?"

"He wants a transfer off Belle Terre."

Bonifay's tan flushed pink. "Have I got a voice? Can I speak for myself?"

Kirk pressed down a smile. "Yes, you may."

"I have the right to remain silent."

"Mmm. Well said."

Did everybody want to get off Belle Terre?

Maybe. Somehow these young people, with their bits of contention and odd desperate measures, were a microcosm of the strange effect this planet seemed to be having on people. Something about the frontier of Belle Terre, the pressure of olivium possession and the prospect of losing it all, was driving both citizens and uniformed personnel to bizarre actions. Industrious, desperate, confused, trying to find ballast in an inclement storm. Amazed by the wide variety of methods people had of solving their problems, Kirk shook his head and turned to gaze out onto the open prairie, half expecting the drumstick to come back.

"Spock," he began, "that probe . . . it only measured about two meters at its longest, correct?"

"One meter, nineteen centimeters, at an estimate," Spock offered.

"Yet we hit it with phaser rifles at full charge and it didn't even heat up."

Fluidly Spock moved closer. His clear enunciation and something about the deep timbre of his voice commanded absolute attention. "Not only that, Captain, but my tricorder registered a density flux. The probe registered a few hundred kilograms to a few hundred *million* kilograms."

The ink-slash brows went up to make his point.

"Impossible," Kirk gruffed.

Spock held out the tricorder before him.

Kirk's aching hazel eyes crimped. "Then where's the energy transferring to? And where'd the olivium go?"

"No idea. Physical laws cannot change, yet for some reason, they are not applying. However," Spock said, shifting his weight and tipping his head, "I also note a purely mechanical behavior. There were no life signs. Its actions were clinically simple, suggesting computer-based steps of progress. With that level of complex energy absorption and transmutational power, we don't know how much more aggressive it's capable of becoming if we stand in the way of its programming."

"You're saying, if it shows up again, we shouldn't make it mad."

"Phasers obviously have no effect." Spock looked down at his rifle. "Thus we should refrain from provoking the probe until we discover something that does have an effect."

Troubled, Kirk finally allowed himself to accept that they'd failed again despite a masterful effort and a good thought forward. It was annoying to admit. "We've got to keep this from happening again, Spock. Belle Terre's future depends on the olivium now. The whole Federation too. If we let it fall into someone else's hands in these kinds of quantities . . ." He paused, sought an end to his sentence, then dismissed the complex possibilities and simply finished, "I just don't trust anyone else."

"On the *Enterprise*," Spock offered, "I will be able to analyze the tricorder's readings more thoroughly. Perhaps find a theory."

He seemed dissatisfied that he couldn't provide all the answers. Bonifay was watching him, catching subtle communication that Kirk usually kept private between the two. This kid wasn't missing anything.

"I'm counting on that," Kirk said, both kindly and sternly, and turned to the ensign. "What's your name again?"

The kid opened his mouth, but the sound stuck in the bottom of his throat.

"Bosun Zane Bonifay, sir," Spock smoothly provided. "Lately of the CST *Beowulf,* reassigned to planetary cataloging and loading of the olivium consignments to *Enterprise* after the wreckage of *Beowulf.*"

"Oh, yes." Kirk let the harsh edge pass from his voice in lieu of sympathy. "Sorry, Ensign. A spacefarer should be in space. Unfortunately," he continued as he handed his phaser rifle to Quinones, "we all have to serve triple duty here now."

Zane Bonifay shook his head clear of the cobwebs and tried to deal with one thought at a time. "That thing sure was happy. . . ."

"Happy?" Instantly Kirk picked up on the odd comment. "How do you know it was happy?"

Bonifay frowned. "You heard it singing, sir . . . didn't you?"

Kirk looked at Spock. "I thought that was just engine noise. Did you pick up feelings?"

"I failed to register any subjective emotion," Spock said, "but Mr. Bonifay's observation should be noted."

"All right, it's noted. We still have to do something about this. There has to be some way to isolate the olivium from whoever's got the nerve to confiscate it in these kinds of quanities. That was enough to fill a quarter of *Enterprise*'s hold capacity. We can't have this, Spock, we just can't have it."

A few steps away now, Bonifay halfheartedly offered, "I could try to transfer a shipment directly from one of the processing operations. I know you want the *Enterprise* filled to capacity before you leave . . . there's another silo on this island—"

"*Enterprise* isn't leaving as planned, bosun." Sparing him any illusions, Kirk explained, "We're staying to work this out. Small doses of olivium have been disappearing from installations all over the planet. We thought it was being raided by people here, but obviously, since we just witnessed the impossible, there's something much bigger going on. This is the first time a major quantity's been hijacked."

That figured, didn't it?

A few steps away, Lucy Quinones grimaced in empathy for Bonifay, but what could anyone say?

"We need a plan of action," Kirk went on, but now he was speaking to Spock, who stood in elegant repose very near him. "The colonists are up in arms."

"Pointless," Spock mentioned, "since weapons are apparently ineffective against these raiders."

"And they may get hurt trying to defend the mines and storage facilities. We'll have to take over planetary security." Kirk's brows came down on his plans.

Spock, toneless, said, "Governor Pardonnet will resist."

"I know. I would too, if I were in his shoes, but I'm not. Have Starfleet guards take over every installation and recovery operation. Advise them to abstain from confronting these things and keep the colonists from confronting them. Have them log all contacts for activity and duration, then report all findings back to you for analysis. And Spock . . ."

"Yes, sir?"

"These things seem to be happening at sources of large quantities of olivium that have already been mined. We'll split up what we've got into smaller increments and stop mining the rest. We'll decentralize the ore and store it in much smaller quantities, spread out farther from each other, until we clear this up."

Spock digested that, then reminded, "The governor

Diane Carey

will be unhappy about shutting down the first major planetary operation to recover from the Kauld's nano-machine attack."

"Well," Kirk grumbled, "Evan Pardonnet's always unhappy about something and happy about something else. If I were clairvoyant, I could tell you which way he'll go. When McCoy gets back from globetrotting all over this planet, I'll have him nail Pardonnet with a calm-down shot."

"The governor's concern is justified, Captain, as the advocate of the private sector. These people have waited more than five years to establish——"

"They'll wait longer," Kirk snapped.

Spock had hit the wrong cord with that one.

"Sir?" Bonifay surprised himself by squawking through his dust-coated throat. *That's it, stick your head into the grinder.*

"Yes?"

"We should . . . why don't you try—well, I'm a bosun . . ."

"You're a bosun, yes?"

Forcing the idea lingering in his head to actually form into words, the impetuous Bonifay coughed up a dustball and continued. "We should store small quantities of olivium in different kinds of containers and see if the things can find them. Maybe there's something inert that could hide it. Polymer or paraffin . . ." He threw in a last shrug. "Maybe they can't see though lead."

Spock skewered him with a glare. "Most logical," the Vulcan congratulated, his voice actually lilting.

His own eyes twinkling, Kirk pointed at Bonifay, but looked at Spock. "Do that. And put Mr. Bonifay here in charge."

That done, he suddenly just wanted to get out of here. He moved out until the doorway of the bunker

64

framed his form. The cold wind plucked at his sandy hair and swirled around his boots. He peered upward, threatening and thoughtful, into the darkened sky of this alien world that had seemed so beckoning yet had provided nothing but trial since Humanity arrived here. When he spoke, the level of conviction was as compact and clear as his skyward glare.

"Somebody's stealing a priceless cache of the Federation's future. I mean to reclaim it."

Though he started to walk out, Kirk now paused. He turned to Bonifay one more time.

"You stood your ground," he sanctioned.

Bonifay straightened up some, and met the captain's gaze. "Maybe I froze, sir."

There was a touch of insubordination in there somehow. Bonifay felt it pop out, on a little skid of resentment. He expected Kirk to snap him down, but Kirk liked the sliver of defiance. He shifted from one foot to the other.

"Sometimes they're the same, ensign. Carry on."

He turned away, toward Spock's calm gaze. Shoulder to shoulder they stepped out of the bunker.

As Kirk and Spock headed back to their hoversleds, Quinones and Gyler wandered in a daze to Zane Bonifay's side. They seemed not to know what to say to him. He saw that in their eyes, sensed it in the way they were breathing. All his hopes had been pinned on this last few minutes, and been dashed to bits.

"Stuck here," Bonifay muttered.

Quinones ran a raw hand over her ice-flecked face. "Maybe a red candle next time?"

Chapter Five

ROGER LAKE dropped Hurley back into his chair, which fell over and dumped the navigator onto the command deck. Lake stared at the forward screen as it fritzed and fought to clear. He couldn't change his thoughts from the danger aft to the danger forward fast enough.

"Roger!" Nick Keller shouted to break the shock in his captain's face.

Lake's jowls shuddered. A droplet of sweat freed itself from the pucker of his chin. The screen-wide glare of the gas giant flung itself back and forth in his eyes and turned his face a pasty blue. "But they're aft of us. . . ."

At Keller's side, the rock of Zoa impulsively came to life with a series of short calculated movements. She plucked the stylus out of Savannah Ring's hand, and placed it on her forearm, which she raised quickly to chest level. One of the straps on her wrist brace turned out not to be leather at all, but some kind of elastic. She fixed the stylus into the strap, pulled back, and *pwinggg*—the stylus speared Captain Lake in the back of his right shoulder.

"Ah!" Lake howled and spun around, clutching at his shoulder, then spun full about again, his face monstrous.

Keller met Zoa's eyes for a fleeting instant, then he seized the distraction for what it was.

"Vector port!" he called. "Hard over!"

Hurley and Makarios fumbled briefly, but hammered the helm.

With one hand on the rail and the other holding Savannah by the arm, Keller braced his legs. Under him the *Peleliu* tilted up on a nacelle and wheeled hard. Ring slipped out of his grip and disappeared behind Zoa. A tangle of arms, legs, and wrecked hardware slammed into Keller's left side as McAddis lost his balance and brought pieces of the smashed science trunk with him. Together they skidded across the sci-deck and hit the environmental station. Keller's shoulder and the side of his face smeared across the starboard consoles. McAddis's bulk pinned them both there, breathless and squashed. Centrifugal force drove them efficiently to helplessness while the ship screamed in their ears, all systems hitting tolerance in only seconds.

The shields fended off radiation and heat, engines fighting gravitational pull, thrusters ruddering off the deadly course. On the main screen, visible in Keller's one good eye, the gas giant's swirling poisonous atmosphere dominated second after second. Ten—fifteen—the ship whined and whined. They'd almost been on top of it, almost incinerated in its thick atmosphere.

Would Lake take over? Get them out of this? Keller wanted to shout orders, but the idea of two officers giving directions made a horrid vision of good practice simply shredding. This couldn't go on. The crew would start dividing. Efficiency would shatter. The ship would crack or the crew would.

Still pinned to the deck, Keller forced his hand into the air and grasped the edge of the engineering console next to where he'd fallen. He raised one boot and thumped the lattice blockade under the sci-deck rail, enough to make a muffled clank.

"Braking thrusters, boys!"

Even from up here he caught a flash of Hurley's face and could see Makarios struggle to stay at the controls and work them.

Suddenly the whine tapered down. Pressure fell abruptly off and Keller could move again. He was sprawled in his side behind Zoa and Savannah, in the crease between the carpet and the trunks. Beside him lay the lower trunk lid with torn wires and a nozzle dripping the last of its lubricant. Above, over there on the port side, the science opticals showed a blue monster's swiftly growing distance. He pressed his hands to the carpet and pushed himself halfway up under McAddis's weight and looked forward.

"All stop!" Roger Lake called. He was slumped in his command chair like Santa Claus after a long day.

"All stop," Hurley rasped. He reached over to tend the helm controls. Makarios was nowhere to be seen.

"That was close," Lake huffed, wincing at the stylus that had saved them, still impaled in his shoulder. "We missed the damn thing! That was a hell of a thing . . ." He rubbed his hands and glanced about at the monitors, which did their regular jobs now that sensor blackout had lifted.

What now? Would he explode that his command had been snatched away?

Let him.

Blue eyes crinkled with fear and a million other

things, Tim McAddis rolled to his knees and pulled Keller to a sitting position.

"Nick!" he gasped. "You hurt?"

Keller touched his reddened jaw. "Carpet burn. Now I'll get a tan. How about you?"

"You saved our skins!"

"Hush."

Glancing up at Zoa, who had somehow stayed on her feet, McAddis steadied himself with effort. "I think our lady guest has a crush on you."

"Tim, the woman *wears* a crossbow." Keller got to his feet and pulled Savannah out from Zoa's shadow.

As he straightened, he met Zoa's blue dots for a moment of bizarre communication. She was proud of herself. How she felt about him and their rash cooperation remained a mystery, but clearly she thought she'd done the rightest thing around by assaulting the captain.

Assaulting the captain.

Keller backed away a couple of steps. He hated himself. He thought it was right too.

On the lower deck, Lake was turning his shoulder to Hurley. "Can you see what pinned me? Pull it out."

Tentatively, Hurley glanced at Keller, fumbled briefly, then yanked the offending sticker out of the captain's flesh.

Lake peered at the stylus. "How'n hell did that get in me?"

Hurley mopped his face with a dirty hand. "Must've been the ship turning so fast, sir. I don't know."

At Keller's side McAddis wobbled, but caught himself on the science board. "If the course hadn't already been locked in—"

A gesture from Keller cut him off. "I told you to hush."

"Look!" Makarios reappeared in front of the helm and shot a finger at the main screen.

In the deep distance, a small cluster of blips were just now winking out.

"Who were they!" Lake thundered. "Get a trace on those bandits! Read their emission trail!"

Pestering an answer out of his banks, McAddis croaked, "Emissions read similar to the bandits who attacked us before, sir."

Somehow irritated and also relieved by that, Keller moved to the sci-deck rail. "You were right, Captain. They were behind us."

Lake clapped his hands so sharply that sweat sprayed from them. "Hell, you don't spend twenty-eight years in space without learning a thing or two. Nick!"

"Yes?"

"Great job watching our blind side. I can always count on you!"

"Oh . . . yes you can, sir."

Rubbing his receded hairline, Lake clumped to the communications station, where Tracy Chan was readjusting herself after the tumble. "Sure could use a rest. I'm bushed. Can we get somebody up here to clear the tube and companionways? Let me talk to the damage-control chief."

His conversation with the lower decks faded as he bent over Chan's connections.

Savannah Ring heaved a shuddering sigh. "Be sure to close the coffin lid," she said, "you saturated headcase."

"Secure that," Keller admonished.

"Oh, right." Her eyes flared. "Bad me."

As the ice-cube mood on the bridge began to dissolve, Keller turned toward the science station and took a step. His left leg folded under him and he stumbled into McAddis. Pain shot up his thigh and sent him gasping. The deck swam under him.

McAddis caught him on one side, and Savannah on the other.

"What is it?" Savannah asked. "Your leg?"

"I tripped on the ship . . . 'scuse me while I writhe in agony. Done in a minute . . ."

"Sit here." McAddis pulled him to the science chair.

Keller folded into it and gritted his teeth, letting the pain in his knee overtake him. Savannah wrapped her analytical hands around his knee, feeling for whatever medics felt for at a time like this. "Don't make a fuss," he warned.

"You're just worried Lake'll make you wear regulation boots if he sees you limping."

"What's wrong with my Durangos? They just prevented a sprained ankle."

"Too bad they're not thigh-high," McAddis contributed. "Would've saved your knee too. I gotta git me some a them someday, Nevada."

"And show me up?"

"Think they were Kauld?" Savannah asked. "Those ships running away?"

Throat tight, Keller managed, "Like it or not, he was right. Wasn't just shadows following us. His command instincts are still bankable."

"Denial," Savannah stated. "Seems to me your job description just changed in more ways than one."

Irritated, he pushed her hand away. "I'm not leading a mutiny just to please you."

He stood up and turned, then stumbled back a step— there was somebody in his way. He found himself beak to beak with the Rassua woman who had haunted the entire voyage like a gargoyle.

Here she was. Right here. Did she expect a warm thanks or what?

"Ah—hello," Keller stammered. "Can we help you?"

71

Now that she was standing ten inches in front of him, Zoa didn't look as monolithic as she had in her perch over there by the end of the rail. In fact, she was noticeably shorter than Keller, though still taller than Savannah and muscular as a bodybuilder. While her body was not a man's, her torso was thick with mass, her bare shoulders and arms made of glazed knots. Her braided coif fanned around her face. Those heavily lined eyes never blinked.

Up close now, Keller saw that the bird-wing decorations on her eyes weren't makeup. They were tattooed on. Her eyelashes were long and severely curled and stuck that way somehow. He got the idea that was permanent too.

"You are an commander crew officer," she said, in thickly accented English that forced her to speak slowly. "You will take possession of thy battling-ship."

She turned the last phrase into a drumbeat of syllables, and Keller's problem into a mountain. Nobody else was saying it right out like that.

Fielding a glance down to the lower deck, hoping the captain hadn't heard, Keller swallowed a lump. "Ma'am, I can't do that."

Her expression never changed. There wasn't a flicker of warning, except her left shoulder tilting back like a spring. When it came forward, the rest of her arm launched like a cannon shot.

All Keller saw was the brown tips of his boots splaying out in midair. His head hit the rail, and he fell butt-first to the deck with his spine against the rattling lattice.

Before him—above him—McAddis charged the woman, but was knocked back when she simply raised her hand and knuckled him in the forehead as if flicking a bug. Savannah, standing back by the enviro controls, had the sense not to move against the Rassua.

McAddis recovered, his face an angry grimace. He

snatched up a spot-welder from the deck clutter and swung around to Zoa's golden face. She turned her head and looked casually at the welder muzzle as if she were about to take a bite out of it.

"No, Tim!" Keller thrust out a hand. "Stand down!"

McAddis drew back. He didn't lower the welder.

"What's going on up there?"

On the lower deck, Lake and the helmsmen and Tracy Chan were all peering up here.

Keller ignored the pain in his left hip, where he'd collided with the rail, and scrambled to his feet. "Slipped, sir."

"Well, be more careful."

"Yes, sir."

Zoa's blinkless eyes swung back to Keller with iced-over passion broiling under the surface.

"You will," she proclaimed.

Having had her say, and still completely unintimidated by McAddis or anyone else, she turned to the steps and descended from the sci-deck. Apparently the command deck wasn't terrorized enough yet.

Keller sank back to rest against the rail. "And your little dog, too. . . ."

If only they weren't locked together on the bridge. What was taking damage control so long?

Tim McAddis still had the spot-welder tight in one hand. With the other hand he got a grip on Keller. "Good grief, Nick, I'm sorry! I didn't even see her move!"

"What'd she hit me with?"

"That was her hand. Anything broken?"

"Just my hopes for galactic peace. . . ."

Savanah shook her head in disgust. "Ambassador Nick Jacob Keller speaketh."

He rubbed his hip and added it to the roster of sore

spots. "Heshup . . . I just got a switchin' from a croco-
dile in a leather jumpsuit. Gimme a minute."

"Let him alone, Ring," McAddis scolded. "It's none
of your business. You're not in the crew."

She was unthreatened. "We *all* almost ended up real
small and toasty, so shut up. You should've hit her
back, Nick."

"Can't. UFP wants the Rassua to join up, and the
Rassua are interested in the excitement out at Belle
Terre. They sent her to have a look at us and the planet.
See if we're good enough for them."

"You mean *she's* the diplomatic corps?"

"Yep."

McAddis gazed down to the lower deck, where Zoa
had taken up position near the forward screen, her
back to them as she watched space unfold before
the eager sensors. "Wonder what the soldiers are
like. . . ."

Savannah drifted back farther under the ceiling shell
that cloaked their words. "If we can stay alive out to
Belle Terre, we can put Captain Lake on medical leave
and get him some help."

"What if he snaps before we get there?" McAddis
pointed out.

"Hush," Keller groaned. "Both of you . . . hush."

He moved away from them, to the back of the sci-
deck, as far from them, from the captain, as he could go
on a sealed bridge. There, he turned away, faced the
chittering environmental opticals, and closed his eyes.

Lake's judgments were sluggish, he was making
some irrational accusations, motivations were a little
twisted . . . but was it enough to declare him unfit for
duty? Would the admiralty regard these changes as
quirks of command style? Keller would be expected to
produce a log of the captain's erratic behavior. Neither

he nor Hahn had kept documentation. The behavior hadn't shown up until the attack came.

Or had it? He began to sift back over the past few weeks, over the orders to check the supples, then check them again. The ship's stores, the manifests, weapons-locker inspections . . . running diagnostics twice, three times per watch, on the same systems, security analyses of crew quarters, assigning crewmen to different departments arbitrarily—

But there were sensible shipboard reasons to do all those things, especially on a long-range mission. Keller had never been on a long-range with Lake. Maybe this was his long-range command style.

Had Derek Hahn been suspicious of the curious custodial orders? Keller combed back over the conversations, even momentary exchanges, between himself and the other watch officer over the past months. He found sentences both suspicious and not, in and out of context.

His head throbbed. The argument kept going inside his head. He shoved his hands into his pockets and tried to flex his shoulders. The carpet blurred as he gazed downward.

How many more Gamma Nights could they survive if Lake insisted they keep moving? How could he justify taking Roger's command? Never mind Starfleet— what would the crew think? Dr. Harrison would have to certify a medical report of debility. But there was no trace of Tavola methane. There never would be. Keller and Hahn hadn't reported it immediately, instantly. Physical evidence went the way of the winds.

Below, he heard a loud scraping noise, then a clank deep in the bones of the bridge. The damage-control crew must be breaking through to the companionway. Getting the hatches open. Freeing the trapped bridge crew. Next would be the jammed lift. And Derek.

He could confess on the record. To whom? Himself? Starfleet was months behind them, Captain Kirk weeks ahead. Like it or not, the ranking authority out here in the snowy Yukon was standing right here in a scuffed pair of Durangos.

Throw the captain in restraints and himself in the brig? Who would that help?

There were so few situations when mutiny was the right choice . . . in all of history he couldn't even count ten. What were the odds against *Peleliu*'s being number eleven?

Could a man actually blow up and strangle at the same time?

One pile of manure at a time.

Inside his pocket, his knuckle bumped the commemorative coin. In his mind, he flipped it.

"Roger, we need to parlay."

"Sure, Nick, come on in. Sit down right there. You did a great job out there, just great. When we lost Dee, I thought we'd have ourselves a mess without an experienced exec, but you stepped right up and showed me I can depend on you. A captain without a good first officer, he's got the whole galaxy on his neck. I know it's a big bite for you to swallow. Field promotion from lieutenant commander to commander—that doesn't happen to everybody."

"It won't stick," Keller reminded as he came into the dimly lit captain's quarters. "HQ'll rescind it and replace me with a qualified exec once we reach Belle Terre. Captain Kirk'll handle it. He's got a starship full of people with ten times my experience. The sooner, the better, for me."

Lake looked at him. "But you're headed for command, Nick, someday. And you can depend on me for support when that day comes. Sit down. I want you to review this tape."

"Sir?"

"They did a hell of a thing out at Belle Terre. This is Captain Spock's Quake Moon report on telemetry. It's the damndest thing."

His computer terminal, keyed to command encryption, displayed several security protocols before clearing the portrait of one of Starfleet's most valuable assets—Spock of the *Enterprise*. The Vulcan's archetypal features possessed an unexpected ease of being, not like a lot of Vulcans Keller had met. He wasn't stiff or arrogant at all. Everyone Keller's age had grown up with the stirring tales of Captain Kirk and Mr. Spock, two men who had opened up the reaches of the galaxy, and who were now doing it again. Surprise made Keller miss the first few words spoken by Mr. Spock's historic baritone voice, one of the few voices of household familiarity Federation-wide.

". . . initial readings indicated that the moon was hollow. It was not. The material inside was simply not read by conventional instrumentation. Since we often do not see what we're not looking for, instruments and probes saw only the volcanic moon, but not the slight shifts in mass. The body read as volcanic with a hollow core, which of course made no sense."

"Captain," Keller interrupted quietly, "we really need to talk. Can we listen to this later?"

"Shh! This is the good part."

"Only later analysis at close range," Spock went on, "revealed a cascading effect. The more the moon heated up, the more the olivium went in and out of flux, creating more friction and thus more heat."

"I know the feeling," Keller blistered.

"By the time the colonial expedition arrived at Belle

Terre, the moon's flux was actually visible from the planet's surface."

Keller fell suddenly silent as a blue planet rolled by on the screen. Belle Terre. So that's what it looked like. It really was a second Earth. Dawning over an ocean was a surging black and red moon, its surface scored from beneath by fissures pulsing a strange neon white.

Keller shivered at the raw natural force that would soon be in his life. "Look at that thing boil. . . ."

Mr. Spock's voice continued to explain while a free-floating satellite toured the surface of the hostile moon.

"The moon's history involved an asymptotic curve, bumping along for uncounted centuries at the bottom of the curve. For thousands of years, the flux was only a small vibration. Our early probes and scouts missed it completely. Then it reached its vector and suddenly spiked upward, paralleling the vertical line but never quite reaching it. Friction reached the moon's point of tolerance. The olivium was in constant quantum flux, causing exceptional heat. The more it flowed in and out of existence, the less accurate our predictions became. After millennia of housing the olivium successfully, the moon was about to destroy itself. Only a safety-valve release would keep the moon from destroying Belle Terre as a livable planet."

Vulcan or not, Spock's delivery was anything but stoic. Keller heard the tenor of concern, fascination, and worry. This plainly meant a lot to him. Spock paused as the camera continued its tour of the angry moon.

"It's incredible what they did," Roger Lake said, squinting in respect at the screen. "They use all their ships, or most of them, to alter the moon's orbit just a little by adding energy. The moon collided with a smaller moon, and ruptured in a controlled manner. The pressure went *pssssshhhhh*—right out into space!"

"Played hell and high water with the planet's weather, I'll bet," Keller commented, fidgeting. "I guess it's not a very nice place anymore."

"It'll settle down in a few years. Shh. Here comes the rest of it."

"When the moon collided," Spock's voice went on, narrating a stunning vision of what he was talking about, "there was a momentary burst of gamma radiation bombarding the planet. We could only protect our livestock and civilians, and hope that when we stepped outside, the planet would allow us to continue living."

The screen went to several more protocols, flashed the UFP standard with its leaf-brackets and star chart, then a shimmering delta shield, and finally the receiver frame of *Peleliu*'s call letters and a confirmation of delivery.

"That was a hell of a thing, by golly, Nick," Lake evulsed. "In the lunar blast furnace, the olivium was even more unstable. The more unstable, the less they could anticipate orbital status. They had to coordinate like a damned dance teacher! Effect the maneuver to make the moons collide a glancing blow, but not be knocked out of orbit, or slow the orbits so much that they crashed into the planet. I can't imagine it! What a day that must've been! Damn, I wish we'd been there!"

"I don't," Keller told him. "I hear there were glacial repercussions, tectonic shifts, blizzards—"

"Hell, the air remained breathable and the oceans stayed pretty much in place, give or take the odd tidal wave."

"Well, I'm from Santa Fe. I don't do blizzards." Trying to steady himself and keep anchored to the reason he'd come here, Keller found himself instead recalling Mr. Spock's intelligent face and animated eyes from the beginning of the tape. What was going on at Belle Terre that could shake a tempered obelisk like Spock?

The phenomenon of stable quantum olivium had made interstellar news all over the Federation. Every scientist in thirty star systems was salivating. And Spock was right there.

"They should've turned back," Lake proclaimed. "That's what I'd have done. They sacrificed almost every one of their ships to that moon move, and then they got attacked by the Kauld twice. If the planet had been unlivable, what the devil would they have done with sixty-four thousand civilians?"

"How could they turn back?" Keller asked. "Kirk found himself holding a bag full of the most valuable scientific discovery since I don't know when. He couldn't just fly off and leave it unguarded. Besides, he's not the type to back off. I hear he's got an ego that bends light."

Lake shrugged. "A captain can do anything he wants. His only responsibility is his ship."

"How can you say that?" Keller quarreled. "The whole Federation's future is tied to that hunk of hot stone. If a hostile power gets to develop the olivium, we could be on the edge of a whole new age of tyranny."

Lake wiped his face with his bare hand. "Well, we got our own problems anyway." Stretching his arms, he pulled down the chest placquet of his jacket, then decided to shrug the jacket completely off. "That was something, what happened today. It's been a long time since I was in a battle. I forgot how tough it is. Getting old, I guess."

The humility, the doubt, peppered with a sense of sidewise victory, somehow soured on the vine.

"You're only sixty-two," Keller said. "Not exactly Moses. There might be something else at work—"

"I just need to remember how to stop doing everything myself and depend more on you, like I depended on Dee. Guess I was just shook when we lost him. Still am. Look how good you did your job, catching that gas giant thing."

Getting nowhere, warp six.

Carefully, Keller asked, "What about the . . . Klingons?"

Lake looked up and scowled. "Klingons? There's not a Klingon within eight months of here. You mean the Kauld. Get it right, Nick. You'll have to deal with those people once we get to the cluster."

He shifted from the lounge chair over to his desk and called up the crew manifest and started scanning the names, pausing over certain personnel files and reading them as if he hadn't read them before.

"Roger," Keller attempted, "you need rest . . ."

"You do too," Lake said. "Go ahead and put McAddis in charge of the next watch and get some shut-eye. It's not like he's got a job to do out here in Emptyville. We'll get to Belle Terre, take over planetary security for a few months, let the *Enterprise* get back to starship business, and then rotate out of there and stick somebody else with the Sagittarian trash heap."

Who turned down the temperature? The sweat in Keller's shirt turned cold against his skin. His shoulders sank. "That's the spirit," he stewed.

Lake sputtered an unintelligible agreement, then kicked off his boots and toed them under the bunk. "But what are we going to do about the rest of the crew?"

Keller's blood turned to paste. "What . . . about them?"

The captain's gray eyes flared. "You saw. They purposely followed my orders slowly, moving us in the wrong directions, heading us toward the gas giant to make me look bad. You think one of 'em's a spy?"

Without looking at Keller, Lake pivoted the monitor more to face him and tapped his computer's controls, not using the voicelink for some reason which Keller didn't want to know.

On the screen, though Keller could see it only at an angle now, scan sheets of the personnel came up. Why?

"They're plotting against us," Lake went on. "I think a mutiny's brewing. You're the only one I can trust. You should see this manifest. I've been going over it. I keep seeing new things in their backgrounds that I didn't notice before."

Was the chair shrinking? Keller's hands turned clammy. His ears buzzed.

"I've been watching Savannah Ring," Lake said. "The way she looks at me. I checked her record. She's had nothing but trouble in her past. We better arrest her before she takes actions we'll regret. Put her in the brig, will you?"

"Roger, Savannah's not a member of the crew. She's a passenger. She's got an assignment waiting at Belle Terre."

"Wouldn't stop her from sabotaging us. I want her locked up."

"On what charge?"

"Her whole personnel file is faked. None of this is true. Haz-mat specialist, emergency rescue field training, experience in toxins, fungae, spores, plague manifestations—nobody does that kind of thing in real life. This is all fake. She can't do this stuff. She faked the record so she could escape to Belle Terre."

"Escape from *who?*"

"From me. Who else?" Lake pressed forward and put his hand on Keller's wrist. "Nick," he said sincerely, "you're the only person who's not trying to betray me."

There it was, in a nutshell. In his mind, Lake wasn't linking Keller to the crew's actions. The only person

Lake didn't see as a threat was the one who would take over if dismissal became unavoidable.

For now, Keller's job was to find a way to avoid it, to find a way to make the situation work, use what was left of Lake's good qualities and talents to their advantage, and play down the bad things that were surfacing. Lake had been around the block more than once. That couldn't be tossed out the airlock. His behavior, though, would not remain secret for long.

How could the crew's resolve be kept from shattering?

"And one more thing," Lake added. "Dr. Harrison."

Keller stiffened. "What about him?"

"You know when I had the flu last week?"

"You had a flare-up of that viral infection you caught on Berengaria."

"He tried to poison me."

"Harrison? He cured it in a day!"

Lake's eyes, now red-ringed with exhaustion and glazed over, met Keller's. "He *said* it was an infection. I know it was poison. I quit taking his medicine, and that's why I got better."

"Great snakes . . ."

"I was hoping we could make the end of this voyage, then put these people on trial and let Kirk and Spock adjudicate the courts-martial. I was hoping we could get there before these people get us."

"Get *us* . . ." Keller's stomach cramped at the nice tidy paranoid delusion blooming before him. "Captain, the only real problem we have here is this business of forward progress during Gamma Night. We've got to do something about it."

"Oh, we will," Lake said. "We're going to keep changing the orders and surprising the crew, so nobody can get a pattern out of our behavior. That's the first

Diane Carey

thing you do when you have an enemy. Become unpredictable. Don't let anybody anticipate—"

"Bridge to Captain Lake! Emergency!"

Keller sat bolt upright, barely restraining himself from answering the call before Lake did.

Lake tapped the comm. "Yeah, what?"

"Incoming vessel, unfamiliar design, approaching from vector nine-one-seven, speed warp factor three!"

"Yeah, all right. Red alert. Battle stations, Nick."

With every fiber in his body on edge, Keller shot to his feet and hit the shipwide. "Red alert. All hands to general quarters. Everybody saddle up—here we go again!"

Chapter Six

Converted Olivium Chaser
Pandora's Box

ENTER BILLY MAIDENSHORE, Belle Terre's answer to the mug books.

Lieutenant Commander Uhura swiveled around in the only chair provided to her as the big man with the chinchilla hair, rosy complexion, and swaggering eyes, the universal snake-oil salesman, the user-ultimate, strode into her converted stateroom dragging Dr. McCoy in one of his paws.

Dr. McCoy had borne the suffering Uhura had been spared. His narrow body had been denied rest and proper food, his skills forced into use on behalf of the lowlifes, stooges, criminals, and thugs keeping company here on this converted olivium chaser. His frosted brown hair was dulled, his blue eyes bagged, shoulders stooped, while somehow his spirit remained vibrant and his cynical mind quick as ever. The fascination of the problem around them kept him going, and the drive to get out alive hadn't flagged in Leonard McCoy over the weeks they'd been trapped here. Whenever Uhura saw him, though her heart shriveled at his discomfort, she got an injection of hope and determination fostered in those years of adventure with James Kirk and Mr. Spock, flashing back on the many times when the situation seemed so wicked, hopeless, yet somehow could still be forged into unexpected wins. She clung to that, because she saw McCoy clinging to it.

Their autocratic captor didn't look as good as he thought he did. Not anymore. Looks were important to Billy Maidenshore. The past several weeks of upheaval had taken a toll on him which he didn't seem to perceive. He had overrun the prison facility so hastily constructed on Belle Terre. Nobody even knew yet that the prison had been taken over by the prisoners. But Billy hadn't escaped—he'd simply confiscated an asset. He'd stayed right there at the prison, pretending everything was fine, while he killed or bribed every guard. When the olivium chaser *Pandora's Box* had appeared to pick up a work force of released prisoners for its mining operations at the asteroids, Billy had simply taken over that asset too, with great joy at the irony of confiscating a ship he had once owned under an assumed name. Now he had a ship, one of very few available to the Belle Terre community, and a ship that could mine the splatter of olivium thrown around the solar system by the moon explosion.

He'd cleverly kept up the illusion of order, established his system, and gotten it working. Everything was a machine to Maidenshore, from far-ranging human desires to getting daily things done. He'd been incarcerated here, in a ship he previously owned under an assumed name, a private olivium chaser that had been converted with some gleeful irony into a mining ship. Maidenshore and his crime connections were the colony's only hard criminals, give or take a few stragglers, those who had used the colonial movement to escape trial back in Federation space. There were always those, in every wagon train, caravan, or outpost, as far back as time remembered. Those types of people quickly gave themselves away.

And now they had their own ship.

Unfortunately, Uhura and McCoy had stumbled into a mess when they'd come out to rendezvous with the mining vessel on its supposed mining run. All they'd wanted was to check for radiation and set up communications boosters.

Now Uhura was locked in these quarters, once the captain's quarters, fairly luxurious but now generally stripped. Other than a blanket and sheets on the bunk, there were none of the decorations the ship had previously enjoyed. Almost all electrical connections had been stripped out, the hatches converted to manual controls with coded magnetic locks. The hold and other cabins had been converted to racks for miners, the galley and lounges also stripped for minimal comfort and rigged for almost constant use. The ship now housed escaped convicts, a working force of criminals who should be somewhere else.

Here, nothing was elastic. Billy Maidenshore had taken over. In fact, the former prisoners here were still incarcerated. They thought they were working for themselves, with Billy as their benefactor, but stupid people often thought those things. With a savvy for politics, charismatic bottom feeders like Billy Maidenshore often remained in power despite flagrant acts of betrayal.

"Howdy, ma'am," Maidenshore crowed. "The doctor and I need to talk to you again."

He tossed McCoy onto the bunk, where the doctor managed weakly to push himself to a sitting position, probably just to retain a thread of dignity.

Uhura immediately went to McCoy, not bothering to pretend she didn't care. "What did you do to him this time?"

Maidenshore puffed up as she looked at him. "Me? Nothing. I never do the messy work myself. Other people do things for me. Half the time I don't even have to ask. Just brought him in so you'd know he's still alive. I'll leave him here for a while. You two can get reacquainted and talk about me behind my back." He stepped closer and tucked his chin to gaze at her. "Brought you a pillow, see? Velvet. Got little leaves on it. Ivy or something."

In a bizarre boyish gesture, he held out a plush bolster that didn't seem as if it had gone with anything here. He'd probably pulled it out of a bribery shipment.

"Thanks," she said, and took it. No point making trouble. "What I really want is a makeup kit. How else can a girl keep up her maidenly airs?"

"I'll get one for you." He smiled and wobbled his silver brows. "You shorted out my listening devices again."

"That's right," Uhura told him firmly. "I gave them a triple feedback on a charged frequency this time. Just one of a thousand tricks. Learn from this, Mr. Maidenshore. Nobody listens to me when I don't want them to. You can hold me here, you can threaten me, you can torment my friends . . . but you may *not* eavesdrop on me."

His eyes crinkled as he indulged in his effective and disarming smile. "I like that. That's good."

He continued gazing at her in some kind of appreciation, but somehow this was more as if he were looking in a mirror than at another human being. He was a swaggering, self-involved man who joyed in the confusion of others, to whom lies were legal tender, yet who somehow had the formidable gift of charm and deception that made people trust him when there was no reason to, usually by convincing them that he could get them everything they wanted if only they would hand him all they had. The wizardry of convincing people that making them poorer could make them richer had carried Billy Maidenshore and men like him to places of influence, but always with a trail of trodden victims crawling behind. Somehow people fell for the charm of Billy Maidenshore. This insecure planet was the perfect playground for a smart man with no conscience.

"Hey, Doc, how about a cigar?" Maidenshore attempted. "We can hate each other, but no reason we can't be friends."

McCoy cleared his throat. "Ah . . . no thanks. I think I'll just live longer."

"Your loss. I need Milady here to go to work again."

Waiting until Uhura met his eyes, he slipped a computer cartridge into the intake. It was his personal encryption, which allowed the outgoing signals to come back on line. A whole bank of lights and screens flashed to life.

"I put another APB out on myself this morning," he said, "including charges of felony flight and, oh, about six others. So I need you to send a message from Commander Giotto's northern continental unit on the planet, notifying him that they found an abandoned camp and it had my prints all over it. That ought to keep them busy looking for another couple of weeks, sled dogs and all. If they think I'm on the planet, and where else would I be, they'll part every blade of grass like the good little beagles they are."

"Pretty clever, Billy," McCoy rasped. "Stage an escape that never happened and engineer the illusion of a fugitive without taking a step outside this ship. I have to give you credit for this one."

"Why run around when you don't have to waste the energy?" Maidenshore said. "Let them waste theirs. And this—it's a perfect place to hide. A ship that's still doing its job is the one place they'll never look for an escaped convict."

"I admit," McCoy went on, "I wouldn't have thought of it."

"Think of this." Maidenshore raised his hand. In it was a simple but quite deadly laser knife, which he knuckled up to McCoy's gullet as the doctor stiffened. The laser blade buzzed and fritzed its very real threat, causing a visible burn on McCoy's skin even without contact. How could a man hold a blade at another man's throat and never even change his expression? Maidenshore looked at Uhura. "Send the message, Cleopatra. Or I'll guillotine Hippocrates right here and now."

Uhura tried to keep her regurgitating horror from showing in her eyes. "If you kill him, he can't treat your neuropathy," she told him. The pretense of fearlessness wasn't working. She knew her terror showed clearly, no matter how she controlled her voice.

"There are other doctors to kidnap," Maidenshore bluntly claimed. "Don't make me go get somebody younger and dumber for you to protect. The stand-in's first duty will be to jettison Dr. McCoy's scrawny carcass into space, just to make sure I'm completely understood. So broadcast."

But he lowered the knife. She didn't know why he did that.

The threat remained, though, because she knew he had her with that one. Maidenshore knew how much James Kirk's core crew cared about each other, and he was willing to use that as a weapon. As the color began to return to McCoy's squarish features, Uhura moved to her tattered chair and passed her large hands over the controls.

She pulled herself up to the comm station.

This station had been rigged before she came here, put into place by whatever agents Maidenshore had on this ship who knew anything about electronics and computers. They'd set it up, but hadn't been able to use it effectively to do what he wanted. They could fool the planet into thinking their mine ship was merrily loping around the solar system, collecting stray chunks of olivium—which it was—and they could skim olivium without arousing suspicion. But without a skilled communications officer, they hadn't been able to redirect olivium from other sources, which was what Billy wanted.

He'd captured Uhura and gotten McCoy as a bonus as their shuttle passed by. Over the past weeks, he'd used her to send false messages that kept up appearances and allowed him to skim far more olivium from the planetary sources than this one ship could collect in space. What a racket.

Maidenshore had been using Uhura to keep up the mask, but also to redirect and redistribute other caches of olivium.

Fleeting ideas of sabotage teased her for the tenth time today, but she resisted them. The buttons and pressure pads were warm under her fingers. Lights changed. She felt them play across her face. The channels opened. Redirectionals cued up and waited for her to send her message.

"Don't use your voice," Maidenshore warned at the last second.

Too bad he'd thought of that.

She scowled briefly and went about tapping out the message that Billy Maidenshore, consequently escaped and now on Belle Terre's first Most Wanted list, had been tracked to the North Forest Peninsula. The site is being investigated. Further information will be forth-coming.

"All right, it's gone," she sighed.

"Good. Now send the one I wrote up this morning. I'm listening. Identify yourself nice and clear this time."

"Yes, fine." She touched her console again, aware of McCoy's unhappy glare. "Lieutenant Commander Uhura here. All subcontinental precinct stations, pack and trans-port no less than four thousand grams to the nearest col-lection point. Authorization ZXY-90, Code 24. Confirm on Channel Zebra-Echo and contact with three-second quickflash when you're ready. This is Central Processing standing by."

"I like that one," Billy Maidenshore congratulated. "That was good, how you did that. Now send a mes-sage from Dr. McCoy to yourself. Make it a cheery one. He's off in the tundra, things are cold, little boring, but he's getting a lot done. He'll take another four weeks before he can be sure there's no residual effects from the olivium exposure and the moon collision, say hi to Spock, yak, yak, yak, bumble, bumble, and he can't possibly get back before, oh, maybe spring. Make it eleven weeks. Nice uneven number. Then you send the relay to Mr. Spock and tell him how much you're enjoying yourself in your duty station waaaaaayyy out here and you got a new boyfriend, so you don't want no company. Got it, queen bee? Send, send."

She did it, without a single word. When she was fin-ished, Maidenshore was ready with the next one.

"Third," he continued, "send out a message that *Pandora's Box* is finished mining the sector seven and we're moving on to the next two. Crew is working very diligently, using all safety precautions, and will be shipping thirty more tons of contained raw olivium that got sprayed all over the belt, very rich deposits, good cache, men working well, guards having great time, et cetera et cetera and thus'n'such. You know the drill. We'll hold back ten tons and the idiots'll never know the difference."

"Yes, I know."

Once again she tapped her board with his report, geared to fool the people back on Belle Terre into thinking their little floating rehabilitation effort was actually doing some good. Didn't take long, actually. At first, she had bothered to make the messages long and sluggish, wasting as much time as possible, but soon she'd found this added up to no more than minutes here and there and had no effect. She had also tried to send wrong messages, coded messages, and even exaggerations, but he had read every one over her shoulder and made McCoy suffer. She didn't do that anymore. She sent what he said, just as he meant it. No codes, no clues, no tricks.

She leaned back when she was finished. "That's it, Mr. Maidenshore. Every communiqué's been accepted and confirmed. You can extort, skim, and shave quantum olivium off those shipments as they pass through the outlets you've set up. For all the good it'll do you."

His smile fell away to a sort of wounded look. "Why would you say that? It'll do me plenty of good. Belle Terre's going to be the diamond belt of the Federation. And I'm going to own the buckle."

McCoy knuckled his bruised lip. "How long do you think this can go on before Captain Kirk figures out what you're doing, Billy?"

"He's not going to figure it out. He thinks he won. As long as I let him keep thinking it, he won't come looking for any of us. Jimmy's got his hands full. You'd think I dreamed this month up and stamped MAIDEN-SHORE on it and got the blessing of Olympus." He moved to the door and coded the magnetic locking sys-

tem, which had been reintegrated to his personal speci-
fications. "Don't entertain any ideas about escaping.
This ship has been fully converted for maximum-secu-
rity incarceration."

As Maidenshore pulled the cartridge out, once again
darkening the bank of outgoing signal readouts, McCoy
droned, "How'd you manage to escape?"

Maidenshore put his unlit cigar in his teeth and held it
there. "That's the beauty of the rumor. I never did escape.
I just hijacked the ship and sent out an APB on myself.
Every guard's been bribed or replaced, the warden
knows I can scorch his family to cinders any time if he
doesn't behave. Off the little Starfleet soldiers go, searching the reaches for the escaped racketeer Billy Maidenshore, while I keep living right here, in the last place
they'll ever look. Okay, so it's not exactly splendor, but I
eat good. The last report you picked up was priceless—
how they suspect I've taken up residence with the Kauld,
maybe! Can you imagine me living with those blueber-
ries? How perfect is this? Your pals don't even monitor
the signals coming from here. After all, what's a mining
ship got to say? Goddissimo, I love a simple plan."

"What can you do with the ore you're skimming?"
McCoy asked. "No one's going to deal with you for
olivium when we've got a whole hemisphere shot with
the stuff—"

Maidenshore waved his unlit cigar. "You think all
wrong, Doc. If you can steal one percent of a diamond
mine, you're going to be pretty damn powerful."

"You won't be able to hold on, Billy. You can't do
this alone."

"Who's alone? All these men incarcerated around
you who couldn't make it any other way, they'll be
royalty at Chez Maidenshore after they help me take
over this little piece of heaven. So don't forget, Doc.

If I die, these men'll carry out their orders on your girlfriend here." Leaving the door once again, Maidenshore came back to loom over Uhura, finally to stare down at her. "And you, queen bee," he warned, "if the codes are wrong and the signals get shady, the doctor here's going to be in a whole new experiment. Both of you understand, I can see it in your beady eyes. Keep on understanding and you might see another Christmas."

She shook her head in cold disgust. "You're a whole other kind of artwork, Billy," she said. "Humanity doesn't deserve you."

"Got that right," he approved. "Redistributing of wealth is a time-tried method of stealing. I'm only doing what politicians have done since Man discovered slavery. This is just the modern form—the approval of the slaves. I love suckers. 'Take my life's earnings and do anything you want with it, just keep blowing in my ear.' The priceless part is that they beg you do to it. Priceless! I made a joke. Get it? Priceless."

He paused, still looking at her, and now kicked over an empty supply cannister that had been sitting here the whole time she'd lived in this room. Lowering to sit on it, he clasped his hands around the cigar and leaned his elbows on his knees.

"You know, gingerbread," he began, "I won't be in this filthy business forever . . . the last thing I want is to stay out here and hobnob with the common. I'm building up a nest egg. Enough wealth and power to set up my own planet, then be left alone without society gumming up the scenery. I'm only doing all this so I can blast free, and there's no legitimate way to do it fast. I want to go away and be able to protect myself. Captain Kirk put the squash on my motherlode. Now I need a new one, to build an organization big enough that everybody'll have to leave me alone. Is that so wrong? Who've I really hurt?"

His pathological innocence was amazing. He really didn't think he'd done anything wrong. Of course, that was because anything done for Billy Maidenshore couldn't possibly be wrong. As Uhura sat here returning his gaze, she found herself wondering what kind of a mother he must've had.

"What do you care, really, about these people for?" he went on. "Humanity's just a pack of technological apes. It's not just Humanity, either. I tried other races. You just get technological lizards or technological seed pods or some other brand of plop. Sure, they develop warp speed, but they just use it to go get more bananas."

A scent of cologne wafted from him as he shifted on the cannister. Despite the wear and tear of his operation, he was still trying day after day to appear in control and to maintain his physical appeal. That was the only manifestation of caring what anyone else thought. His pewter hair was always immaculate, despite the worry lines on his face or the lingering aroma of cigar tobacco that eternally clung to him. Other than seeming a little nauseated, he was trying to keep up a front as he spoke to her.

"Me, I'm not interested in the petty," he continued. His eyes never wavered from hers. Few people could look someone in the eyes this long and never flinch. "I don't want to spend my life out on a rock running a piddly syndicate. You know what I love? Classical art. It's the only true sign of civilization. Not population, not factories, not commerce, not sanitation, not cities or sports or any of the things people think of. Only art is a sign that once every million or so apes, a virtuoso is born. Just enough to keep civilization pretending it's worth something."

Uhura shifted back an inch or two, away from him,

angling away from McCoy to keep Maidenshore from noticing the doctor, whom he seemed to have dismissed during this private conversation.

"Well," she said, "even a snake likes sunshine."

He grinned, but she didn't think he understood her meaning. "I had a private collection before Jimmy Kirk busted my motherlode and confiscated everything. Now my da Vincis and Laviolettes and Michelangelos are marking time in museums. Can you think of a stupider place for a work of art?"

He lowered his head a little more, his brows drawn in a kind of beckoning question.

"I've known a whole parade of women," he said. "But you, you're different from all of 'em. You don't give in. I like that. You don't want me to hurt people? Okay, I won't hurt 'em. You want me to leave them alone? The sooner I get my motherlode and bug out of here, the sooner they'll be left alone. You can help me do that. And when it's over, I'll surround you with masterpieces." He leaned a little closer, and his voice grew softer. "I can put the stars back in your eyes."

Pressing his lower lip inward against his teeth, he nodded in agreement with himself, as if listening to music he liked.

In the background, Uhura noticed McCoy's expression screw up. She prayed he wouldn't say anything.

Maidenshore slapped his knees. "Gotta go. Need a shower. I'm expecting company. Bye."

As if suddenly uneasy, he simply tapped the door controls and ducked out. The door slid shut behind him, and the magnetic lock whistled its security confirmation.

"He *is* a work of art," Uhura grumbled. She turned to McCoy and touched a bruise on the side of his face. "Have you been volunteering for tackle dummy again?"

"Why don't you ask your boyfriend?" he suggested.

She glowered. "He's just putting on an act."

McCoy clasped his arms tightly and rubbed the circulation back into them. "I don't think so."

"Are you kidding?" she blurted.

"I've been paying attention. He talks an awful lot around you."

"He talks a lot anyway."

"No, no. I mean he talks excessively when you're around. Compulsively. You have an effect on him."

"You mean when he looks like he's about to give birth through his face? I certainly don't like the angle of this conversation. Pardon while I get back to doing absolutely nothing of any consequence."

"Uhura," McCoy said with a sigh, "if it comes down to it and you have a chance to warn the planet of what he's doing . . . let him kill me. You think I want to live to be a hundred and thirty?"

She settled back at her chair before the console of equipment that once again locked her out. "I'm not letting him kill you, Leonard. It's just stones. I don't care how precious they are, they're just stones. I'm not letting him kill you over stones. The olivium's not being destroyed, it's just being moved around. Eventually we'll move it back. So be quiet and live."

McCoy shook his aching head. "Another chronic optimist. You people are a plague."

"Optimist?" She gave him a saucy expression. "Don't mistake my anger for something else. He's using my personal authority to skim ore from the planet's repositories. Mine, not yours."

"Mine wouldn't work. It's a medical priority."

"And he knows that. That's why he's keeping me alive, to use as leverage against you, so you'll keep treating him."

"Oh, he'll keep you alive," McCoy guaranteed, "because I won't treat him if he harms you, and killing me means he dies of the Klepstow's neuropathy he contracted when he really did try to escape. If I hadn't been the one to come here to treat him, none of this would've happened."

"He would've tried it with someone else," she said. "You heard what he said about another doctor."

"He knows I'm the only one outside of Federation central with Klepstow experience. That's why he intercepted the shuttle with both of us on it. He wanted you for communications and me for treatment. We were sitting ducks."

"Doesn't mean he won't do something worse to you than just kill you," she pointed out. "Men like him have twisted imaginations. He didn't look very good," she added. "Are you sure you're treating his neuropathy right?"

McCoy's blue eyes mustered up a twinkle. "Oh, yes. In fact, he's been cured for two weeks. He just doesn't know it. All he's had lately is morning sickness. Next week he gets a maddening itch."

Uhura swiveled toward him and looked into McCoy's tired eyes, worried about his pallor, his slumped shoulders, his papery skin. Did she look the same to him? Had her usually lustrous dark complexion gone tawny with fatigue and almost constant dimness in this chilly compartment? Was his cell any warmer? Could he hold on under these conditions, day after day?

"We have to keep this up," she encouraged. "It's our duty to stay alive. We're the best hope of stopping Maidenshore's long-range plans."

He sagged down to sit on the edge of her cot. "Suppose you're right about that. Nobody realizes that *Pandora's Box* has been hijacked. Maidenshore's skimming olivium and shipping it—what's he doing with it? Do we know?"

"I'm not sure. We're collecting it and skimming off a certain percentage, but since he's in charge of how much gets collected, he could be skimming fifty percent and no one would know. I'd guess he's walking the line of sending just enough to keep suspicion from rising. Since *Pandora's Box* is supposed to be moving around, earning its keep, no one notices our travels."

McCoy frowned at the truth in her words. This actually could go on for months. "We've got to get a message out somehow."

Sweeping her hand across the communication units, Uhura shook her head. "You saw. He took the enabler with him. He only lets me send when he's here. All this system can do now is receive. I can listen, but I can't broadcast. I've tried to override his systems, but he's anticipated every move. The system's so simplified now that I can't undercut the efficiency. He's smart, Doctor, along with all his other magnificence."

"He's certainly happy with himself—" McCoy grasped the carved bunk support as a loud chunking noise rumbled through the ship from deep below decks. "What was that?"

"Sounds like docking clamps," Uhura told him. "But there's no other ship this far out, is there?"

"There shouldn't be."

"Let's have a look around."

"How?" McCoy asked.

"Just a few tricks I've been inventing when our friend Billy wasn't looking. Watch that little screen. I tied into the interior sensors. He doesn't figure I'd want to look around inside the ship."

McCoy pulled up the cannister Maidenshore had

been sitting on and positioned himself beside Uhura, to watch the small screen she indicated.

"First, the passenger lounge." She tapped the controls. On the screen appeared a view of the lounge area, converted from a comfortable sitting and viewing area to an exercise run for the miners. A few of Maidenshore's lackeys were enjoying a wrestling match. There was no sign of Maidenshore.

One by one, they scanned other areas of the ship. The hold, the galley, main salon, midships salon, racks—

"Empty," McCoy noted. "How could he be nowhere?"

"It's a big ship, Doctor. Let's check the docking collar itself."

"Why would anybody be in there except to load or unload?"

"Let's look anyway."

Pictures flashed of other parts of the *Pandora's Box,* now a seamy hole in space, littered and untended.

"Can't you just sabotage this console beyond repair?" McCoy asked. "He can't have you send signals if everything's smashed."

"He'll just find another way," Uhura said as she continued scanning the ship through the security line. "This way, at least I know where everything's being moved to. You don't think I'm staying here much longer, do you?"

"Does that mean you have a plan for escape?"

"No. I'm just psychically willing Maidenshore to have an infarction or something. Meanwhile, all we can do is manipulate him into keeping us alive and letting us see each other every few days."

"He lets us see each other," the doctor muttered, "to keep us pliant and willing to protect each other. He's holding us hostage with each other's lives. I could compromise his health, but he knows that and he's on watch for it." He sighed. "I suppose . . . I could incapacitate him . . . medically."

Uhura turned to him, reached out and clasped his hand tightly. "No one's asking you to do that, Leonard. Besides, I believe him when he tells us he has backups if he ends up out of the picture. Eventually, Captain Kirk and Mr. Spock will figure out the messages aren't really giving them any information and they'll start asking questions. Until then, we have to hang on and stay alive."

McCoy rubbed his arms and paused, then said. "I think I may have the ticket to that."

She looked at him. "How so?"

"You've managed to impress him. He wants to impress you. We can use that."

She shied back. "Are you out of your little ol' mind? What do you mean, exactly?"

"I haven't figured that out yet. Give me a—look! It's him. There he is."

Uhura's hands drew fluidly over the console as she focused in on the form of Billy Maidenshore, standing with—

"Of all the gall!" Uhura blurted.

"Vellyngaith!" McCoy leered with contempt. "Dealing with the Kauld! Why didn't we figure that out? Now that I see it, it makes perfect sense. Can you move in? Can you get sound?"

"Yes. I just have to keep from initiating any feedback." Uhura turned the dials carefully, very carefully, each hand moving independently from the other. Tap this switch with the ring finger without disturbing the dials . . . nudge that one, disconnect this one . . . Element by element she summoned years of experience with touchy and delicate modulation equipment. A less experienced technician wouldn't have been able to do this at all, with equipment so heavily filtered and inhibited. The slightest crackle would incur Maidenshore's suspicion.

She hungered to get sound out of the inhibited system. Maidenshore was talking to Battlelord Vellyngaith of the Kauld. Vellyngaith was a stunning man, strongly built, with his long white hair decorated with feathers and beads, his gull-wing complexion starting to look normal as Uhura got used to the residents of this cluster, the blue-pigmented Blood and Kauld. As outrageous as this was, it suddenly made sense. So that was where the skimmed olivium was going!

But what could Vellyngaith be giving Maidenshore in return? Nothing else was of more value out here.

Voices. She could hear the beginnings of a sound pickup.

"There we go," she murmured, victorious.

McCoy leaned close. "Very good."

"And the doctor had doubts."

They fell to silence as the voices of Maidenshore and the senior Kauld veteran crackled through the system. She filtered out the residual noises, and they began to listen.

"You people, you don't even know what you want," Maidenshore was saying, dripping with disrespect for a man who, though an enemy, deserved respect. "You got two choices. Fold to the Federation, or get your asses kicked *then* fold to the Federation. Either you're going to be their friend, or they smash you and make you be their friend. That's what they do. Except they don't have me. You have me. I'm giving you a third choice. The Blood have already folded. You still have a chance."

Battlelord Vellyngaith glared at Maidenshore in something that sure wasn't affection. "These things are new to us. We have never dealt with other cultures come to live in our place. No one else has ever come.

We know only Blood and Kauld. Every day we must learn new lessons."

"Here's one," Maidenshore said snottily. "Ask yourself, why is the Federation so hot to come here? Why are they staying on this decimated planet? Why are the Blood here? Why are you in trouble? It's because of this stuff that moon spat all over the solar system. You've tried to knock them off the planet twice, and it didn't work. So let 'em have it. Just own the stuff."

"I understand," Vellyngaith said, "but why are you taking the olivium in so loud and thundering a manner? Now everyone knows it's being taken!"

"Oh, damn!" Uhura blurted. "He's about to tell him! Quiet, quiet, quiet! Oh—"

"What?" McCoy flinched. "Tell him what?"

On the little screen, Maidenshore paused. "What're you talking about? Nobody knows anything yet."

"Everyone knows!" Vellyngaith raised his hands in fists. "Your mechanical devices are blasting their way into containment facilities all over the planet, taking huge amounts!"

"I don't have any mechanical . . ." Maidenshore stepped back a few paces, stopped to think, then looked up at Vellyngaith. "Wait a minute . . . you mean somebody's stealing more than me?"

"It's not you?" Vellyngaith asked. "I was certain it would be you."

"Quiet. Let me think about this a minute."

At Uhura's side, McCoy lowered his voice instinctively, even though they couldn't be heard. "Somebody's been stealing the olivium? More than him?"

Uhura also spoke quietly, silly as that was. "I've been hearing reports from the captain and others. I didn't tell him. I hoped an investigation would lead them to us."

"What's going on?"

"No one knows for sure. Some kind of mechanical units have been raiding olivium stores down on the planet, taking huge amounts and streaking off into space at high warp. Whatever they are, they can swallow a full phaser hit, so their tech is way beyond our power to stop them. I hoped that if we could keep the information from Billy, somebody would pick up on the fact that our broadcasts never mention any trouble—" Frustrated, she interrupted herself. "It doesn't matter now. Vellyngaith's spilled the beans."

"Tell you something else," McCoy told her, "look at Vellyngaith."

"What about him?"

"Look closer. Maidenshore's so full of himself, he doesn't even notice that man is ill."

Uhura squinted, only now noticing Vellyngaith's dry lips, his sallow gray complexion, his sunken eyes. "He doesn't look good, does he?"

"Something's wrong with him. His complexion's sallow, his eyes are glazed . . . listen to his respiration. He's got fluid in his lungs. And both legs are braced. He's having trouble standing. He doesn't want Maidenshore to know."

"What do you think is wrong with him?"

As Uhura waited, McCoy studied the visiting enemy battlelord as closely as the small screen allowed. "Almost everything."

On the screen, Maidenshore was just now pacing back toward Vellyngaith, waving his still-unlit cigar. "This could be perfect," he decided. "It could cover my tracks. I'll have to find out more about this. Mechanicals, you say? Robots?"

Vellyngaith just stood there, completely annoyed, as if he'd rather be anywhere else.

Unaffected by the presence of the formidable general, Maidenshore treated Vellyngaith like another of his thugs. "What about the *Peleliu?* Did you kick that ship in the tail?"

Vellyngaith's features further hardened. "We could not stand against that ship even during the Blind."

Shaking his head and rolling his eyes, Maidenshore put on a show of disappointment. "Can't you jerks do one simple thing?"

"We fought them!" Vellyngaith thundered. "They were stronger. They deserved to prevail."

"Did you do some damage, at least?"

"Yes, much—"

"But not enough. They're still coming." Maidenshore pointed rudely at Vellyngaith's face. "Look, I don't care what it takes. You have to beat them right now, hit 'em again while they're weak. When'll they get here?"

"Perhaps a day. Two."

"When they get here, Kirk'll set Montgomery Scott on it and fix that ship. If you don't wreck the *Peleliu* while she's down, then there's two fully operational Starfleet ships out here and I can't handle two. If *Peleliu* has time to be repaired and joins forces with *Enterprise,* you'll have a fight to make your little spat with the Bloods look like a footnote. You've seen what the Federation can do—do you want two of them here?"

Vellyngaith paused, his tense muscles obvious even over the small screen. "No."

"See? I knew you had a brain cell still working. Let that second ship get back to strength, and you're dead. Stop it right now, and we'll have olivium and the power to use it. This is your last chance to hit them behind the knees. It's time to finish off that ship."

"I have no magic to bring me close to that planet, close to that ship while it remains damaged—"

"I have the magic," Maidenshore claimed. "Leave it to me."

The Kauld battlelord clearly didn't trust Maidenshore, but seemed to be making some kind of bet whose boundaries he didn't understand. "How do you know, Maidenshore, that I won't betray you?"

Maidenshore chuckled. "What difference does that make?"

"I want to know why a man trusts me who has no reason to. I give trust to you because I must have an ally among my enemies. What is your reason?"

"My reason is you don't have any choice but to trust me. Second, you don't know how to use the olivium. I've got access to technology that's magic to you backward buzzards. I can make you more powerful than the Federation, because you'll be right here with the motherlode and they're still way the heck over there. Proximity to the lode is an advantage we can use. Third, you can blow me out of space, but I have it set up that if I disappear, messages beam directly to Captain Kirk about who's got their olivium and he's gonna be knocking at your door with photon torpedoes."

At Uhura's side, McCoy mumbled, "Sweet Uncle Billy, always thinking of others."

On the screen, Vellyngaith wavered, irritated, but mightily kept his temper in check. "I only asked for one reason. I won't be cheating you, will I?"

"Nope," Maidenshore declared. "People don't cheat me."

"You are a disgusting creature," the Kauld leader said. "I have no joy in dealing with someone so despicable."

"Thanks. Give us a kiss."

"How do I know you won't cheat me instead?"

Maidenshore waved his unlit cigar. "Oh, you don't.

If it was in my advantage I probably would, but it's not right now. At least you know where you stand."

"Yes," Vellyngaith tightly observed, his voice hardly more than a chafe. "I know where I stand."

"Then you better get going, gather up some firepower to hit *Peleliu* when she comes limping in," Maidenshore instructed. "I'll figure out a way to distract *Enterprise* so you can hit *Peleliu*. Don't look at me like that, chump. How long do you think you have? Every month they'll be sending in new ships and new supplies. I know the situation between you and the Blood. You were about to win. Then the Federation shows up, the Blood toss in with them, and Kirk hands you your purple head—twice. Now you're about to lose. Do what I say and things might change. Take the olivium I give you, fly it back to your solar system, stick it on the second planet on the left, and get a good night's sleep on your way to beat the *Peleliu* to cream."

With an artistic pause, Maidenshore pulled out a pocket lighter and flipped the red-hot diode merrily in Vellyngaith's face, toying with the idea of lighting his cigar without actually lighting it. "Get together every ship you can find. Get ready to attack *Peleliu*. This time, make it count. Get ready, but let me tell you when to attack. Got it? Don't do anything till I signal you. This is how you can win. So cheer up."

The discussion ended. Maidenshore had gotten all he wanted out of the encounter, and more than he expected, and now it was over.

Without farewell Vellyngaith turned, moving cautiously, and simply stalked away, apparently to return to whatever vessel had docked with *Pandora's Box*, to go off and prepare to hit *Peleliu* again, thus encouraged.

Uhura shivered as her skin prickled. "Something tells me our survival just became a lot less important."

Aching for a way to warn the incoming Starfleet crew that they were in trouble again. Uhura took a chill all over her body, and McCoy's beside her, as Billy Maidenshore gazed upward in the general direction of the sensor camera. Slowly he lit his cigar and indulged in a long draw, then exhaled the bluish smoke in a single unbroken trail.

"Uh-oh," McCoy murmured.

Looking up at "them," Maidenshore now spoke clearly, and with certainty that someone was listening.

"Isn't that right, milady?"

Vellyngaith's Kauld Battlebarge

" 'Gather up firepower.' 'Strike while they are weak.' And what are we? We are the weakest fighting force ever to exist."

"Battlelord." Fremigoth greeted Vellyngaith glumly, holding a breathing-treatment mask in case their general needed another one today.

Vellyngaith knocked the mask away. "Stop keeping me alive, physician. The sooner I die, the better for my memory."

"With so many already dead in our army," Fremigoth assured, "we need you more. Stop whining."

"Before I die, I think I'll kill you first."

"What did the ghastly man say?"

"He spoke a ghastly truth." Vellyngaith slumped onto the bench outside the spacelock as the vault slid closed, blessedly cutting him off from Maidenshore. A sound worth worship.

No one else was here, and he was glad of the solitude. The barge was tomblike, so few men remained standing to man it.

So many dead, suffering, ill—

"Half our fleet is dead. Our army, crawling to their beds," he murmured. "The rest, doomed . . . how can I man a dozen vessels to face the two of Starfleet? Nine, ten men to a ship that requires fifty? Hardly enough to keep moving forward. . . ."

Beside him, Fremigoth slumped against a computer housing. "He wants us to attack again? When? How soon?"

"He will tell us when to attack."

Fremigoth, unsatisfied with that answer, slumped more and began wiping his own face with a moistened cloth so vigorously that Vellyngaith found bizarre fascination in waiting for the physician to wipe off his deep blue skin completely. In their condition, this was not so much a fantasy.

"That insufferable man," Fremigoth uttered.

"We must suffer him," Vellyngaith said. "We're helpless to win in a fair fight. We must use trickery and guile and have help. All those are Maidenshore—"

The bile he had managed to hold down now belched into his mouth and out his lips. Blood and bits of flesh splattered his knee. He hadn't turned his head quickly enough. Another cough brought up even more solid matter, speckled with the white pustules from his poisoned lungs. He stared at the mess, seeing the fate of all Kauld military men who had been living in their base, their only fortress, as the contamination spread in that one horrible day.

They hadn't even known they were being poisoned. There had been no panic, no warnings, no chance to escape. Experiments with the systems of dynadrive had done this to them, and there was no undoing it. Nearly all the Kauld fighting forces were contaminated. A great secret. How could he fight two Starfleet ships, and keep the awful truth hidden?

"We're weak, Fremigoth. Poisoned, weak, dying, dead . . . our soldiers, young and old . . . I have watched both my own students and my own teachers die twisted deaths in the past months. The rest of us will be gone before the next eclipse . . . punishment for housing all our fighting men in one place. We must somehow preserve our civilization until a new army can be trained, to carry on our work, protect our people from Blood and Federation. For this, we need . . . the ghastly Maidenshore."

Fremigoth said nothing. He seemed smaller than ever before, as if he had actually shrunken by a percentage.

Vellyngaith wiped his bloody lips on his sleeve, catching a decorative bead briefly on the corner of his mouth. For a moment he gazed hatefully at the bead. "This is a universal payment to us. We were willing to fight Blood to extinction. Now they have Federation, and we face extinction ourselves. We waited too long. We should have erased Blood Many when we had the chance."

"They would do the same to us," Fremigoth wheezed. "They would admit it. Even Shucorion, who flirts with Federation in person and calls them friends."

"Shucorion is not the only Blood avedon. He's only the most dangerous one at this time. He uses them as we must use Maidenshore. When he is done with them, we will be done with him. I will use his skin for my fire shroud."

To provide a kind of example, if only to himself, Vellyngaith forced himself to his feet, battling his own clouded mind to think clearly for one more moment, one more day.

"Gather all the men who can still stand," he ordered. "Give them treatments and put them in ships. Make ready to assault *Peleliu* and this time rend it to ruins."

Chapter Seven

THE BRIDGE was in efficient chaos as Keller followed Lake back to the command deck. They had to use the ladder companionways because the lift tube was still out of order. Only the deepest of personal restraint kept Keller from plowing upward in front of his captain, maybe tripping him on the way in, hoping he'd hit his head.

Around them, everything was in a knot. Even the two security men Lake had ordered to man the bridge were sweat-glazed and pasty-faced, worried about what might happen. Apparently rumors were wicking to the lower decks already.

"Speed is one half sublight, sir," McAddis reported, taking refuge in convention, "heading nine-four mark three. Incoming vessel's at six-nine-nine mark one and closing. They dropped to sublight as soon as they made contact."

"Phaser banks on full," Lake ordered immediately. "Open fire as soon as we bear. Hit the bastards where it counts. Hurley, prepare for attack maneuvers. Keep

112

your bow shields to 'em. I'm not letting 'em get the best of me again."

Keenly feeling the absence of Derek Hahn's steadying influence, Keller knotted his hands at his sides and stepped into the big shoes. "Warning shots only, I assume, sir."

"No, we're shooting to kill."

A terrible claw closed itself around the throat of the entire bridge crew as if they shared a single body. The captain couldn't possibly have assessed the situation before giving that order, hadn't even had time to look at the forward screen, note the small dot of a ship on approach vector that would in moments be forced to bear off.

Instantly the ship's phasers whined, breaking the peaceful fabric of open space. A clean miss.

Keller glanced at Hurley. A miss, on purpose? That would be an egregious breach. Still, could he blame Hurley for it?

Up on the sci-deck, Tim McAddis's face was a thumbprint of ghostly white framed by the colorful upper graphic monitors, his blue eyes fixed on Keller.

The dot on the main screen began to take some hint of shape, and a deeper purple color. Keller couldn't make out more than maybe a wing formation and a yellow propulsion stream. "Have we got ID?"

Typical of a professional comm officer, Tracy Chan banished the tension from her voice. "They're broadcasting a signal. I'm trying to bring it in."

"Hurry," Keller encouraged.

"They're on a standard approach vector, sir," Makarios reported. "No suspicious maneuvers of any kind."

There was anguish in the helmsman's voice, panic in his eyes as he scoped out Keller for some kind of help, answers. This couldn't be happening. Taking potshots at shadows during Gamma Night was nothing like this.

They were targeting for clean full-power shots at an enemy that couldn't possibly match their might or speed.

Lake hunched his shoulders and gripped the arm of his command chair. "Come around to z-minus two-seven and fire as you bear."

Time to face the music. Turn and look him right in the eye. Wait till he looks back. Now—talk!

"Captain, are you ordering us to open fire on a vessel that hasn't been declared an enemy presence?"

As if he had a psychic tie to the whole sector, Lake calmly proclaimed, "There's nothing out here but enemy presences, Nick."

"It could be an innocent passage, sir. Those people could be just moving through."

"In all these weeks, how many 'innocent passages' have we stumbled upon?"

"Captain!" Tracy Chan came to life with a flinch. "They're broadcasting Federation frequency, encoded to Starfleet encryption! Authorization code reads as James T. Kirk, Commander *Enterprise*."

What a relief! Keller turned to find that Chan might have been addressing Lake, but she was looking at him. "Confirm that, Tracy," he requested, because he wanted Lake to hear it twice.

The captain, though, peered at the forward screen with eyes like slits. "Does that look like the *Enterprise* to you? What do you take me for?"

"Sir," Keller pointed out quickly, "they could've been given the authorization code by Captain Kirk, to carry a message to us. That's standard proced—"

"Or they could've hijacked the code and they're using it to lull us into a passive state. Look at it. Nobody's ever seen that design before. They're trying to trick us into dropping our shields. I'm not falling for it.

Helm, come to zero-zero-four. Increase speed to point seven-zero sublight. Come in under them, then increase speed to point seven-five and come to nine-five true."

"Zero-zero-four, sir." Hurley was panting.

Beside him, Makarios shivered and worked his board. "Coming about, sir."

The ship clawed her way around. Paranoid or not, Lake was good at this. Within two short maneuvers, he had boxed the blue ship between *Peleliu*'s tough phasers and the scorching presence of the nearest star. The little ship, without engines as powerful as the cruiser's, was forced to veer hard over, right back into the trap, in order to avoid the gas giant's hungry gravity.

"Captain," Chan insisted, "they're sending a properly encoded recognition signal with James Kirk's personal encryption! I believe this constitutes confirmation!"

"Sure. I would too, if I were them."

Torn up by the desperation in Tracy's face, Keller bent forward and grasped the bridge rail, "Let's find out what they want, sir. Let me hail—"

"We know what they want. Fire!"

His legs thready, Keller moved up the deck ramp until he was standing right over his captain. He leaned into Lake's face, almost blocking his view of the screen.

"Captain, this is a whole new territory out here. You saw that briefing. We have enemies *and* we have friends, in ships we might not have catalogued yet. Please break off while we ascertain the condition over there."

Offering him a passive and parental gaze, Lake waved the idea away. "You're a fine man, Nick, you'll be a fine shipmaster someday, but for today we've got nothing but my instincts to call on. I've seen this kind of thing before. Don't be so quick to believe what you think you're seeing. That's how people get killed."

"Sir," McAddis protested from overhead, "they're

not returning our shots! They haven't fired on us once yet!"

"Because I didn't give them the chance to. Helm, fire!" As the phasers barked, Lake glanced around for a moment of rationality and noticed the crew's distress. Unfortunately, it had little effect on him. "This is the oldest trick in the book. These are the same people who attacked us earlier. This is just round two."

McAddis came to the sci-deck rail. "Sir, respectfully submit you don't know that! Those people fled. This ship came in on a completely diff—"

"Stand down, McAddis," Lake snarled. "I don't trust you anymore. Fire! Nick, get to the sci-deck and keep your eye on McAddis."

Right this way, folks, for a little tap-dance in hell.

Keller glared at Lake with acrimony the captain would've seen even through his mental fog if he'd been looking, then simply turned and skimmed up the ladder to McAddis's side. Was Lake really getting him out of the way?

Just climbing the steps caused the muscles of his back to seize and ache. He waited to field more of the captain's wrath off McAddis.

Lake, though, was involved with his pursuit, staring without a blink at the ship on the screen as he relentlessly dogged it.

"Direct hit on the other ship," Makarios said miserably. "Their shields are faltering."

"He fights like a badger," Keller grumbled, "you gotta give him that."

"Listens like one too," McAddis uttered with contempt.

Simple reason wasn't working. The faces of the crew around him, of McAddis and Hurley, Makarios and

116

Lewiston were palettes of desperation. One by one they looked at Keller. *Try something else!*

Thinking quickly through the crash of his own brain cells arguing with each other, he shook his hands to get the blood back in them, then tried to appear much calmer than his roiling innards suggested. "Captain, I've got a new report up here."

Lake blinked up at him. "Let's have it."

"Sir, we now have reason to believe they might have Federation hostages on board. I strongly recommend cease-fire until we can confirm status. They may be attempting to negotiate."

His chest was tight with the weight of his deception. What if Lake asked for details of that report? How could they possibly have such information? Lake might be paranoid, but he'd never been stupid. He knew this bridge and all its signals and every button, bleep, glint, and graphic as if he'd designed them himself. He'd worked every station on a dozen ships' bridges in his long career. They wouldn't be able to fool him for long.

But for a moment—just a moment—

The *Peleliu* closed in on the blue ship, which now spewed a trail of serious damage. It simply couldn't stand up to the might of a Starfleet cruiser that wasn't pulling punches. That alone proved the other ship wasn't here to attack them. Nobody in his right mind would think a patrol vessel like that could take on a flying gut punch like *Peleliu*.

Sweating in empathy for the crew of the other ship, Keller turned to McAddis's science monitors and scanned the horrible report from the infrared and ultraviolets.

"Nick, Nick—look." McAddis pointed at the optical between them. "Are you seeing this? This is a transporter signal. A *transporter*. And it's on a Federation-compatible standard. They're trying to beam somebody over here, but they can't get through our shields."

"Tim, are you sure about this?"

The frightened science officer pointed at the screen's view of the small purple ship twisting out a desperate pattern, failing utterly to shake the pit bull from its tail. "I'm telling you, that ship's been fitted with a Fleet-standard transporter. We could be killing Federation emissaries!"

"Sounds like a desperation move," Keller mourned. He could see himself doing such a thing if he had to, try a crazy last-ditch beam-over in an attempt to communicate.

Tortured, McAddis met Keller's eyes. "If those people aren't dead already, they're going to be soon. You better pull out that old coin and get him to pay attention, because we're about nine seconds from open murder."

Chapter Eight

NICK KELLER sank his meathooks into Tim McAddis's arm, and at the same moment seized a course of action he never imagined himself prosecuting.

"Put the shields down, Tim. Use the override."

Bent over his controls, McAddis choked on his own whisper. "You—we can't do that!"

"I can't let him do *that*."

"Are you thinking straight?"

"Beats me. What's a stroke feel like?"

"What if they're trying to bomb in a beam? Beam in a bomb?"

"Take the chance."

McAddis's face twisted. "Dropping shields in the middle of a battle—"

"Authorization code Keller Four-Zero-Five Delta India Tango. Do it, quick."

"What's if he's right?"

"Don't make me flip the coin."

"Oh, mother . . ." Clamping his lips, McAddis

hunched his shoulders over his controls for a jump into gross insubordination. The ship's phaser banks sang and sang. Assisting some, Keller knew that if he touched the boards too much, his actions would attract Lake's attention and the captain's wrath would come down not upon him, but upon McAddis.

At the helm, Makarios dutifully blurted, "Captain, our shields are falling!"

"Why?" Enraged, Lake swung in every direction. "Who's doing that! Who's dropping the shields! Hurley, if it's you I'll kill you with my bare hands!"

"No!" Keller croaked, spinning so hard he almost went all the way around. "It's a malfunction—up here. We're working on it."

He held his breath, hoping Lake accepted that ridiculous claim.

Before Lake had a chance to digest what he'd heard, Chan called, "Transporter beam incoming, direct to the bridge!"

"Security, stand ready!" Lake bellowed. "Sidearms on kill!"

The two security guards now stationed at the turbolift drew their phasers just as the recognizable whine of a transporter rose to its unmistakable pitch on the forward area of the bridge, near the main screen. A column of sparkling lights appeared and began to take form.

Lake seized the back of his command chair. "Get ready!"

Keller pushed off from McAddis and thudded down the curved steps to the main deck. He had to be down here. He was the—the first officer.

Was Lake going to order the guards to fire on whoever appeared? Keller looked at the guards, going for eye contact. Ensign Thornton shifted back and forth on his feet through the few seconds of beaming process, his phaser raised, his expression horrified. Open fire? Beside him the rookie Security Crewman Baker looked ready to throw up. Being a security guard was one thing, using phaser stun as general practice, but being told to gear up to kill somebody had them both by the gut strings.

Without turning his body or raising his arms, Keller moved one hand in a manner to get the guards' attention, easy enough since they were searching desperately for the right thing to do. Thornton saw him and drew his brows in question, then took a stiff breath as Keller gave him a very subtle back-down signal. *Hold back. Give me a few seconds.*

All this, in only the moments it took for the transporter beam to do its work and a living form to appear on the forward bridge.

The visitor was a man, fairly tall, with dark eyes and skin the color of a mountain lake. His umber-brown hair was long, woven into a simple braid that slopped over his shoulder, drawing attention to his scorched gray tunic and burned hands. The man struggled to stay on his feet by bracing himself on the forward rail. He seemed both surprised and relieved to be here.

"Shoot the bastard!" Lake belched out. "Shoot'm!"

"Captain!" Keller jolted around in front of the screen. "He's not armed!"

The guards didn't open fire. They were giving Keller the seconds he needed, but they could only hold back so long.

The stranger watched Keller briefly, not sure who was in charge, then fought to straighten up. Wisely he kept his arms down and a little out to his sides, making it quite obvious that he had no weapons, or at least nothing that looked overtly threatening. Lake clumped to the upper deck on the starboard side and came all the way around the long way, passed Keller, and stood before the ravaged newcomer.

Over Lake's shoulder, Keller watched the stranger's bruised face.

Lake swaggered a step closer. "What do you want here? Come to surprise us? Didn't think we'd be ready?"

The stranger caught the searing tenor of the captain's voice, and restrained himself masterfully. "You are Captain Roger Lake of the ship *Peleliu?*"

"How do you know? We didn't broadcast any kind of identifications."

The newcomer paused. "I can read some of your language. It says '*Peleliu*' on your hull."

"Got us there," Keller muttered, but only Makarios heard him.

The newcomer hesitated, unsure how to react. "I come with communication from Captain James Kirk of *Enterprise.*"

"Some kind of a trick," Lake accused.

Keller's legs tightened up. *Ask him who he is first.*

Dark eyes steady, alert, the stranger tried to read Lake's demeanor, but briefly met Keller's too, and this seemed to steady him somewhat.

"My name is Shucorion," he began. "I am Avedon of the Plume Savage . . . the ship you just . . ." He waved a hand in no particular direction, then paused. "Are you Captain Lake?"

"Roger Lake." Lake poked a thumb over his shoulder. "My acting first officer, Nick Keller. Why didn't you follow standard procedure for approaching a Starfleet vessel?"

Shucorion's lips dropped open as if he meant to protest, but he suddenly held back, his gaze striking Keller's over the captain's shoulder. The answer was clear in his expression—*I did follow standard procedure.*

Keller widened his own eyes just enough to get a subtle and silent message across. If Lake had done to him what he had just done to Shucorion, Keller would've been at Lake's throat by now, He expected Shucorion soon to be there. "Sir," he dared, "the signals were probably garbled in the radiation from that star. We made him veer pretty close, after all."

"Yes," Shucorion accepted. "My apologies, Captain . . . I'm new to this."

What?

This man whose ship had just been smashed to trash without provocation, who thought he had been approaching an ally and expected to be treated with civility, whose crew must be over there suffering, even dying—

Had he just apologized? Anybody else would've been on Lake already.

Or had Shucorion read enough out of Keller's undercurrent of communication to perceive the value of restraint here and now? Was that too much to suspect? To dare ask?

"There have been new developments at the planet Belle Terre," Shucorion reported. "Some kind of deep-space probe or remote units are raiding the repositories of quantum olivium and confiscating the ore. Captain Kirk has issued a planetwide alert. Kauld, people who are my enemies and yours, have noticed the dilemma and are very likely to make use of this. Captain Kirk sent me and my crew to assist you in navigating the Blind. You are not accustomed to traveling through the sensor darkness. My people have discovered ways to continue movement during these hours. I've been sent to help you navigate, that you shall arrive many days sooner."

His ship was wrecked. He didn't even mention that. He had come here with a purpose and he was sticking to it.

"Movement through the Blind is only for extreme necessity," Shucorion went on. Then, carefully, he asked, "Did you . . . have extreme necessity?"

So they'd picked up the fact that *Peleliu* was under way during the Gamma Night blackout. Shucorion watched Lake warily for an answer.

"We were being chased by a horde of attacking vessels," Lake told him.

"There were two," Shucorion said. "Kauld single-pilot patrollers. You saw them as a threat to *this* ship?"

In front of Keller, Lake's neck muscles tightened and sweat broke out on the tiny hairs. His shoulders flexed inward.

Resisting the urge to step forward, Keller abridged, "Caution is a tactical maneuver recognized by Starfleet. We just came out of a battle. We mistook you for the enemy."

"I see," Shucorion accepted, quickly digesting the message. "Captain Lake, my men . . . our ship is compromised."

Lake frowned. "What? Oh, your crew, right. How bad's your ship?"

Incredulous that Lake didn't know the degree of damage he himself had inflicted, Shucorion controlled himself valiantly. "We have massive systems failure and our engines were fused by your direct hits."

"Ah, that's too bad. Well, you'll have to dump it out here and ride with us. Keller, put all his men in the hangar deck, under armed guard. They're prisoners of war."

A ripple of shock ran around the bridge, expressing itself in a dozen tiny movements. McAddis slumped back on the edge of his console, clearly sickened that their captain could take so lightly the destruction of another man's ship at his hands. Keller's own stomach turned inside out. He fought to stay at Lake's side.

"Prisoners?" Shucorion braced slightly in amazed insult. Quietly he reminded, "We have made alliance with you. . . ."

"I don't know you," Lake repudiated. "I'm sure not about to trust you offhand. Mr. Keller, take charge and lock 'em up till we find out if their story's a fake. Take this man down to auxiliary navigation and see if he's lying about moving through Gamma Night."

"Aye, sir," Keller muttered. If only he could go back to the salad days of second matehood. How much sweeter, how much neater those had been, with Derek Hahn sturdily buffering the hard stuff. Chugging around the ship, fussing with station bills, fielding crew complaints, securing the decks, staying off the bridge except during the lovely little hours when almost everybody else was off duty . . . ah, the rambling rivers and the wide open prairee . . . some guitar twanging . . . of course, somebody else would have to play it . . .

"Anyway, I hate country music," he mumbled as he edged toward Makarios. "Anton."

Makarios flinched. "What now?"

"Hush," Keller warned, glancing back at the captain, who was suspiciously scouring the helm for readings over a nervous Hurley's shoulders. "Tell engineering to fix that wreck with a low-warp towing engine with a remote autopilot and point it toward Belle Terre. It'll show up eventually. We can use the parts for something. No point wasting it."

"Be three weeks before that thing limps in on automatic."

"Waste not, want not."

"Okay, Nick, okay. I don't care anymore."

"Oh, now, we're getting through it. Concentrate on

the ol' job there." Keller turned to Shucorion and motioned to the companionway hatch. "Come with me, please."

In silence they crossed the bridge, moving slowly, even stiffly. Keller breathed a tight sigh of relief when they climbed down and left the bridge behind, left its captain, its tension, and at the same time he sharply wished he were back up there, guarding the rest of the crew from Lake.

With some effort, Shucorion followed him down the ladder to the next deck. From here they'd be able to get a turbolift that was working. "This way," Keller invited again, and started down the corridor.

The ship was only half lit, conserving energy, still on yellow alert. Beside him, Shucorion pushed the long single braid of his brown hair over his shoulder to the middle of his back, where it hung almost to his waist, and touched a purple bruise on his face, but made no complaints.

"So you're the people called the Blood?" Keller asked.

"Yes. We are Blood."

Keller offered him a glance that might have been sympathetic. "You took the wrecking of your ship a little better than I would have."

Shucorion's expressive eyes returned the glance. "How would you have taken?"

"Boiling mad," Keller grunted.

"Mad serves no help. The wrecking is done. The suffering will make us stronger."

"How many, uh, of your men . . ." Just asking this question caused Keller's chest to constrict. He couldn't finish it.

With a comprehending expression, Shucorion looked at him. "We suffered no deaths this time, Mr. Keller. We sacrificed our ship, hoping there was some mistake occurring, that your captain was simply being cautious . . . as you said."

Humiliated, Keller shifted his feet. "He's kept us alive that way. The past few days, that's the first time he's lost any crewmen in action for over ten years. I'm sorry to do this to your crew . . . the hangar deck isn't the most comfortable place on board—"

"We will be warm and have food," Shucorion said, in something that sounded like gratitude.

Did that make any sense? Gratitude? Offered to the people who had destroyed his ship in an unprovoked and unjustified flagrant attack?

"We'll provide you with as much as we can," Keller offered, thinking about what comforts could be afforded to "prisoners" without touching off the captain's attention.

"You have provided survival, Mr. Keller," Shucorion granted. "It is always appreciated."

Embarrassed, and perplexed by the graciousness of his guest, Keller sighed. "Yeh, well, least we can do."

"This is space. Misunderstandings will—" Shucorion's words broke as he stumbled and clutched at his left thigh. He tried to recover, but fell against the wall. As he struggled, a smear of dark blood appeared on the bulkhead.

"Holy—" Keller caught the other man's arm and felt a shimmer of pain rush through Shucorion, who only winced and buried the rest. "You're wounded! Why didn't you say something?"

"What should I say?" Genuinely puzzled, Shucorion glanced up at him, then caught his breath against an obvious spasm. A short gasp got out, but otherwise he clamped his lips.

Giving him support for the bad leg, Keller tried not to sound guilty. "I'll take you to our sickbay. We'll send medics to the hangar bay for your crew. I wish you'd said something."

Shucorion drew back some. "But I should begin the work of guiding your ship to our cluster."

"No hurry on that. We just came out of Gamma Night. We've got twenty hours. Plenty of time for some rest and treatment."

"But I rested yesterday. . . ."

"No, no, you come with me. We'll see about that leg. Let me give you a hand here."

"Please—" The Blood man held back firmly now, pressing one hand to Keller's arm to stop the attempt to help him too much, and the other to the inside of his left knee. "Your captain will resist. I must earn his trust first. We must go to your auxiliary bridge and do our work. He'll know otherwise."

Keller paused. Should he admit that Shucorion had Lake pegged already? Or keep being the flak jacket? "At least let me have a medic sent up to stop the bleeding."

"If it comforts you."

"It does."

They moved on, much more slowly. "How did you perceive," Shucorion asked, "to drop the shields?"

Some light fishing going on.

"We picked up your attempt to beam over," Keller told him. "The decision was made to drop shields and allow you in. It wasn't that much of a risk, considering the ID code you sent."

Shucorion nodded thoughtfully. "And you managed to calm the situation without humiliating your captain. This was artful of you."

"Naw, that's not what happened. Does Captain Kirk have a hypothesis about who's stealing the olivium?"

"He hasn't spoken to me of any theories. I believe

he's waiting for others of Starfleet before he makes his thoughts known. I suspect Kauld."

"You think the Kauld are stealing it somehow?"

"Yes."

"Got a reason for thinking that?"

"Their motivation. With olivium, when they learn to use it, they can annihilate us, you . . . and all. Even this ship and the starship together will not be able to stand against a Kauld fleet so fortified."

Keller indulged in a canny little smile. "Oh, I wouldn't make any bets just yet."

"I make no bets," Shucorion declared. "Among my circle, I alone believed things could turn in our favor. For months I allowed myself to believe Blood could prevail, not be crushed under Kauld conquest, even after we had the dynadrive—you call it warp power. This was dangerous thinking, because I had once accepted that ultimately we would be destroyed and our energy was best spent in putting off that unavoidable time. When your Federation reached out and made me believe that people had come who wanted to live in our cluster but *didn't* want to dominate us . . . Blood had never heard of such a thing. Many of my people were afraid of this idea. Somehow the concept of Kauld conquest was easier to live with . . . but I began to reach out, just to see if the touch would burn me. I believed I was chosen to lead my people in a new direction. The Kauld turned in that direction too, and now they will possess this bright new power source, and with it they will slaughter us all. It's my fault that the Kauld have captured the olivium."

"Wait a minute—" Putting out a hand to stop their forward movement, Keller gazed at the deck and blinked at what he'd heard, went over it a couple of times, but couldn't get the meaning. Looking up, he faced the other man squarely. "I don't follow that. How is it your fault?"

The Blood captain's shoulders sagged as for a moment he let down his own shields. He let himself drop back against the bulkhead, flexed his aching shoulders, and rubbed his injured leg. His neck muscles twitched some, rippling the blue skin of his jawline and somehow calling attention to the simple gray tunic he wore. He was like a shadow come to life, waiting for something to slip behind.

"I dared to hope," he said.

Dared to hope.

What could that possibly mean? And why was it bad?

There was something about Shucorion that Keller liked, and something about him that he didn't like. But which was which?

No matter how he tried to relax, something about the day's strange happenings had set his inner sensors on overload and he couldn't shut them down.

He wanted to call Hahn and ask what to do, but that would be extreme long-distance. He'd signed on as second officer for an easy ride, with the plan of rotating back with the *Enterprise*. Suddenly he was a ship's first officer, unsure of his captain, heading into a war zone, half blind. Rats.

Damage control was under way, but the ship was a mess. Six decks had been evacuated or partly evacuated, two shut down completely, pending a well-deserved shutdown and repair cycle once they reached Belle Terre. Crew members were doubled and tripled up, rotating bunks off watch, four or five to a quarters instead of two.

He missed having a roommate. Now he and Lake were the only ones on board with private quarters. Even the guests had to share.

Even Zoa.

Problem number six hundred and one.

But who's counting?

As the shower gurgled around him, private shower in private quarters that for some reason he suddenly felt guilty about, Hahn's quarters, firstofficerland—off on another tangent, brain. Cut it out.

He closed his eyes and tried to relax his shoulder muscles. With an ill-arranged flex he discovered a pulled tendon in his right arm that somehow went all the way up and was attached to his right ear.

Ouch—all the way around to the left ear. Lake's behavior had twisted him all the way around in the wrong direction.

He turned so the hot water would strike the left side of his neck. Keep the eyes closed. He was lucky. The *Peleliu* hadn't been refitted with those newfangled sonic showers. Hahn had gone on about how great it was that ships wouldn't have to bother with tanks and heating and piping systems anymore.

Keller didn't like it. No water? Just sound waves? No splashy massage descending from On High? No steam expanding into his lungs, clouding up the stall, making his skin tingle and his hair plaster down? What good was that? No hot water sheeting down his back, taking some of the ache out of his thighs? Better enjoy it while it's still here.

There. One good reason to go out to Belle Terre. Water showers. Hold that thought.

Banish memories of first-officer troubles. Savannah's little complaint this morning, for instance.

"Nick, do something. She's a pestilence. She sits on the desk and watches me while I sleep. She says it's rude to sleep in somebody else's presence. It's like one of those paintings that follow you around with their

*eyes. Hasn't she ever shared a room before? When she
sleeps, she locks me out of my own quarters for hours.
She doesn't want me watching her. And my two Tau Ep-
silon scorpions? She ate them. She thought they were
snacks. Remember what it took to clear them through
customs? Well, do you? I know we've only got a few
days of this left, but you better change something with
this walking gargoyle before I unbraid her hair the
hard way. My scorpions were perfectly behaved."*

Mmmmm, rushing water, scalding heat, melting muscles, keep the eyes closed, breathe, breathe, breathe. In
the nose, out the mouth. He winced at the mental picture of Zoa and the Tau scorpions. Hold the mustard.

Three days, maybe, and they could be at Belle Terre.
This nightmare voyage could be over. Shucorion's navigating had kept them moving, though slowly and in
choppy jumps, through Gamma Night into the Sagittarian Star Cluster. Two accidents with minor collisions of
space matter had stalled progress, but the ship was so
banged up already that a few more dents and scratches
didn't matter at this point. Get there, get there, get there.

Once there, what about Lake? Things seemed to
have gotten better. He seemed all right. Talk of moving
him out of command had faded down to glances. Some
of the crew were ashamed they'd brought it up. The in-
tensity of those moments, though, still burned Keller
under the skin. Dr. Harrison insisted the captain's physical state turned up nothing unusual. Tim McAddis still
wanted Lake to face some kind of treatment.

At whose order? Could Keller, McAddis, and Dr.
Harrison, as the remaining senior officers, muster a
competency hearing out in the middle of nowhere? No
council of Starfleet supernumeraries to stand in judgment? James Kirk was an admiral in real life . . . but a
captain here and now.

The idea of handing over their internal problems to somebody else—that was like cheating. Keller rubbed his wet face and scratched his fingernails through his hair to wipe out the idea. Lake was his to handle.

First officer for a handful of days, and now this.

A gush of cool air hit him in the back. Fate?

"What—" His eyes shot open in the shower spray and he whirled around. The stall door stood open—all the way open, gaping into the also open doorway to the single room of his quarters. Blinking the water out of his eyes, he reached to close the stall door, but somebody was holding it open. Out of the steam a rigid form took shape.

Zoa. Her banded leather outfit had a sheen of steam on the straps, and her blue-pea eyes were completely unimpressed. The landscape of tattoos down her arms and up her shoulders and neck looked markedly darker in the steam.

Keller blurted a blank expletive. The Rassua woman blinked—which she didn't do very often—and stood still, waiting. He turned his back. Not much better.

"Can I help you?"

"You left me an message," she said bluntly. "You wish to saw me."

The water was still going, the steam not providing a very amiable shield. His hair was down in his eyes, draining. He didn't like anybody to see his hair wet.

"Ah . . . got the message, then?"

She said nothing else. Still standing there, wasn't she? Holding the stall door open?

"Em," he tried again, "pardon me, but . . ."

From over his shoulder her accented words were as staccato as the water pummeling his face and neck. "I have tolerate much."

"Have you?"

"It is impolite to turn an back on one speaking."

Order the water off? Leave it on? Was the steam much camouflage? At all?

Keller let out a miserable sigh. "Hooo-kay . . ." With a flop of his arms, he held his breath and turned to, so to speak, face her.

"Ring says you speak to me," she announced. "Speak now."

Try to act natural. Yep, this is the way we have conversations where I come from.

"As a member of the diplomatic corps," he asked, "don't you study the customs of other cultures?"

"Yes. Why?"

"Just asking."

"I knocked. You came not." She looked around, without really moving much. Her legs remained locked, one arm at her side, the other holding open the stall door. "I disturb nothing. What have I miss?"

"Not a thing."

"I know thy customs. I knock the door. You say 'come in.' I come in."

"But I didn't say 'come in.' "

"Because my knock fails."

"Ah."

"I tolerate much from you."

"From me?" Keller wondered.

"Humans."

"Oh, yeah, us."

"These." From the floor near the toilet she scooped up one of his boots and held it out to him as a demonstration of some sin or other. "You wear shooms."

Eagerly he took the boot and held it where it did some good. "We like to keep our toes covered."

Disapproval crossed her inexpressive face briefly,

then disappeared. She didn't seem to notice anything particularly ridiculous about the situation. Might as well say what he had to say.

"Well," he began, assuming what she expected, "Ring wants you to stop watching her while she sleeps. That's one thing humans consider rude."

"I must be in an quarters," she said. "I have no purpose."

"Purpose? You mean a job on the ship?"

"Yes."

Keller shrugged. "I'll give you one."

She nodded once, stiffly. Problem solved.

"And don't eat her pets."

Another nod.

She continued to stand there, unblinking. Defiance or agreement? He really couldn't tell.

Keller cleared his throat once, got a better grip on his boot, and thought about turning off the water. Steam was gone, at least.

"Anything wrong?" he asked. "Anything *else?*"

"You have no witnesses."

"Witnesses?"

"On your body. Tracing of past deeds." She scanned him up and down, and back up again. She might have been astonished, but who could tell?

"Oh, tattoos. No, I don't, we don't . . . well, most of us don't . . . some of us, anyway. Don't. Not usually."

"You have no accomplishments," she said. "We record our actions in witnesses." Holding the stall door open with one of her toenails, Zoa looked abruptly down and devoted both hands to unhooking the front of her woven leather suit, which otherwise hid enough to protect everything but her arms and shoulders.

Keller held out a hand. "Uh—I don't need to see—"

She was already moving her fingers from her right elbow up to her shoulder and down her front diagonally to the opposite hip as she stood pretty much fully exposed before him. "This testify my actions at Molifab Temple Horror, showing each day turmoil. Upon leg shows Dut Mystery in which I led an trail jump. Here, shows my action during Uprising of the Gorals. Lower is—"

"That's fine, ma'am, you have very nice past deeds." Interrupting her travelogue, Keller beat down a shiver. "But if you don't mind, I'd like to get dressed before we continue this."

She looked up, still holding her suit open. "Dress."

Sure, what's stopping you? At least he had permission.

"Computer, shower off." He eyed the towel, hanging on a hook behind Zoa. She wasn't moving out of the way.

He was just thinking about stepping on past her when the door chime out in the main room jangled. Keller opened his mouth to speak up, but Zoa was faster.

"Come in!" she called.

"No—" He winced. The door panel hissed open, letting somebody else in.

"Nick?"

"Ah. Savannah. Lovely."

Savannah Ring poked her head into the shower area, saw Keller, saw Zoa standing there with her leather unhooked, and sniffed at the fading steam. "Interrupting?"

"Nah," Keller uttered. "Want to wash your hair? Get a tattoo?"

"I like your boot." Ring leaned against the doorjamb. "Can I look at that one?"

"Little later."

"Did you two have a talk?"

"Does it matter, so close to our destination?"

"You promised. I need some sleep." She nailed Zoa with a stare. "Without an audience."

Zoa was unimpressed. Her expression remained static.

"Savannah," Keller attempted, "would you be a shipmate and toss me something to wear?"

"Oh, certainly. Let's see . . . here you go."

She tossed him his other boot.

"Thanks," Keller groaned.

"Anytime."

"Bridge to Mr. Keller."

Sure they could psychically see him standing here with his boots, he rasped, "Keller, Grand Central Spaceport, what is it, Tracy?"

"We're on final approach to Belle Terre and should be there within forty-five hours, sir. The Enterprise *is hailing on telemetry. Captain Kirk's asking for our reports."*

"I take it Roger's not on the bridge?"

"He says he doesn't want to be bothered till we make orbit. Mr. McAddis thought we better notify to somebody. Am I bothering you, sir?"

"I don't think that's possible right now." Keller found himself watching with hypnotic silliness as Zoa rehooked her outfit and Savannah sneered her opinion.

"The reports, sir?"

"Oh . . . ah, reckon they're meant to be sent, aren't they?"

"Sir, Mr. Shucorion asked me to forward Captain Kirk his log of the encounter and the loss of his ship. Should I?"

Shucorion's report about the wrecking of Kirk's emissary ship? A vessel representing a whole civilization here in the cluster? Would that be a good thing to be flapping around the waves? Keller would've preferred an in-person report, something he could have a little control over, but did he possess that authority?

Shucorion was a free agent, not part of the *Peleliu*'s jurisdiction, sent by James Kirk, who outranked everybody else out here.

He wished he knew what to do. Was there a regulation to cover it, for him to brace himself on? He hadn't reviewed the regs since getting stuck with first officer. This was his first shower since then too. Rough week.

He thought about slinking over to the coin and giving it a toss. It was still in his pants pocket. Way over there on the bunk.

The two women in his life stood watching him for his next decision.

Was this how being first officer would be? Standing without anywhere to hide, people vulturing him, judging his every choice, and betting their lives?

When had he signed up for that?

"Sir?" Tracy Chan was still waiting for his orders.

He wanted to pass it off, tell her to disturb Lake and let him be the captain. Suddenly concerned for Chan, seeing in his mind that crew manifest roll on the screen in Lake's quarters, the names of his shipmates, friends, innocent crewmen, under the skewering eye of their captain in his unknowable state of mind, Keller shrugged his naked shoulders.

"Send it. Let the chips fall."

"Aye, sir. Sorry I disturbed you."

"It's nothin'."

Chapter Nine

U.S.S. Enterprise, in orbit, planet Belle Terre
The captain's office

"I SIMPLY CAN'T imagine what could cause this much olivium to cluster and exist in such a concentrated amount in one area of space-time. And yet, here it is. When theory conflicts with reality, we must change our theories. . . ."

"Change them to what, Spock?"

"I am . . . at a loss . . ."

The Vulcan's voice tapered off to nothing. He stood with his arms tightly folded, not in the relaxed manner that was his usual style, but in a kind of protect-me stance, as if he were continually expecting to be cold and hoped to be ready.

Spock, muttering?

Jim Kirk hadn't let himself believe what he was

Diane Carey

hearing and seeing. Not until today. He'd suddenly gotten up this morning and believed everything. Just like that. Like a stone wall crumbling. Spock was his anchor, and was slipping.

"Sit down," Kirk invited. "We'll talk it through. Maybe something'll surface."

Though he resisted the idea for a moment, Spock finally indulged in his own kind of shrug and slid into one of the guest chairs, where he then sat staring at the same corner of the desk he had stared at a moment ago.

Usually they didn't spend much time in the captain's office. In fact, this was the least-used quarter of the whole starship. Only administrative duties occurred here. Kirk even preferred the austere briefing room to this place, because he felt less cornered there.

But they were waiting to have a meeting that couldn't be avoided. As he paced around behind his desk, across the tall viewports showing the constant angle of Belle Terre's equatorial zone, he wished he hadn't asked Spock to come here this morning. Disturbed and preoccupied, Spock would probably be better off working.

The dead air started to niggle at Kirk as he paced back along the windows and all the way around the desk, and around Spock, who sat in one of three guest chairs.

"The 'bots are putting olivium back into the moon, repositing it," he repeated, citing Spock's new report of only five minutes ago. He needed to hear it again, to speak the words so they would sink into his mind and he would be able to call up the image in an instant, later, when he needed it, when he had to convince himself to fight or make a decision he'd have to live with for decades. His voice sounded detached from his body,

140

as if he were listening to someone else speak. "They pass straight through the moon's body, just as they seem to do here, with buildings and ships. The moon-based harvesting process has been stopped, the facilities evacuated . . . the probes are putting the olivium back in the moon. You're certain of that."

"Yes," Spock mournfully confirmed, his eyes focused on the glossy edge of the desk. "We took every reading we could imagine to take. They are definitely confiscating harvested olivium and reintegrating it into the Quake Moon's unstable core. My concern is that, once enough mass is accumulated, the moon will once again become a detonation threat."

"This isn't over yet, Spock," Kirk assured him. He knew perfectly well this wasn't the only thing bothering Spock. What good would it do to pressure him to let his feelings be known?

Kirk felt the absence of a quip, a cut, a snide comment, and the inerrant response that always helped. For a fleeting instant he almost tossed a caustic joke himself, just to shake Spock out of his gloom.

Where was a cynical physician when they needed one? Yes, that was the missing element—McCoy. They hadn't heard from him in more than a week. The last report had been sketchy and short. Something about tracking some kind of bug or other.

Hurry it up, Bones. I need you here.

"If you're sure," he contemplated aloud, "then it means the 'bots aren't taking the olivium with them when they warp out."

"That seems to be the case." Spock's voice was hollow, troubled.

Stabbing at empty air, Kirk threw an accusative question. "Then why are they leaving at all? Just to come back later?"

Giving up on the empty stare, Spock met his eyes with a silent doubt. He had no answer, and apparently took the question as rhetorical.

Pacing like a cat, Kirk swept his gaze across the room. "Then why leave . . . Could they be going somewhere to get more fuel or energy? To be somehow repaired or recharged?"

Clinging to the captain's thin thread of logic, Spock allowed his brow to furrow in thought. "Certainly great energy is needed to do what they do. . . ."

His words petered out, like ashes cooling.

Spock was Jim Kirk's oasis of stability. To lose that oasis—it shook him deep.

A gold strike like this, once confirmed, should be nothing but sheer joy for men like Kirk and Spock, whose entire lives had been devoted to the betterment of the Federation and even those outside it. Technological advances, as Spock had long ago said, were the most fleeting. The Federation didn't hold many secrets for long. They'd hold on long enough to get an edge, and then start sharing.

And that was well. It would happen again with the olivium, in its time. That time might be another hundred years. For now, it was Kirk and Spock's duty to hold on tightly to their new possession, to get a firm grip on it and do the most with it before it could be stolen and used against the Federation. If the Federation held the technology exclusively for a while, this would be good for everyone. If someone else held it exclusively, the results could be galactic disaster.

Kirk saw all the implications in Spock's tired eyes when he looked at him today. Even Spock needed things to go just right from time to time, the sensation that luck was with them. This simple mission had turned into a monumental turning point for the Federation, and Spock felt as if he were the hingepin between the bright future and a crushing disaster.

Acute empathy pierced Kirk. Usually the shoe was on the other foot—Kirk in the clutches of his own inner struggles, with Spock bracing him from all directions. This time, things were turned around. The olivium was of supreme consequence to Spock. More than anyone, Spock grasped the imperative gravamen of possessing such a resource of advancement . . . and of losing it.

Now, the way things were going, they might actually lose it.

"We're missing something, Spock." Kirk said the words as if they were a magic formula that could summon a breakthrough.

"We're making an assumption that's throwing us off. Let's review. The 'bots are taking olivium and putting it back where it came from. What do we know about olivium?"

"Olivium," Spock said, "is a rare element that exists both in our universe and in subspace. Until now, it has existed only in laboratories and in small quantities. Theoretically, it cannot occur naturally in the quantities that we find it in here. Clearly, however, our theories are wrong, because we did find it here . . ."

"Spock, that's it!" Kirk said. He began pacing back and forth. "We're assuming our theories are wrong. What if they're right?"

"That would mean," Spock said, animation returning to his face, "that the presence of the olivium on the moon is not natural. That it was placed there by some entity or entities with a science beyond ours."

"Right," Kirk said. "Any idea on who they might be?"

Spock looked thoughtful. "When we first met Shucorion, he told us that the Blood and the Kauld had been presented with warp capacity by a technologically ad-

Diane Carey

vanced race he called 'The Formless.' The odds are that
the same race is involved here."

"I agree," Kirk said. "So what do we do now?"

"Judging from our experience with advanced
beings . . . we confront them and alter their thinking."

Kirk smiled for a moment, then got serious again. "So
how do we find them? We've been dealing with their
'bots exclusively, and that means we're one step behind
all the time. We have to start thinking more aggresively."

Still tense, even giving in to a shuddering sigh,
Spock shifted his legs and tightened his arms. "Thus
far, we've been tracking them as far as long-range sensors will allow. During Gamma Night, of course, we
have no means to continue tracking. They have been
moving off on roughly the same tangent, but of course
they may leave the solar system and change course. We
have no idea."

"Wait a minute." Kirk snapped his fingers. "If you're
tracking them? They're going somewhere, they're not
just disappearing. They're traveling."

Spock looked up, noting the change in Kirk's tone.
"Yes, apparently."

Kirk pivoted on a foot. "Then we can follow them to
their masters."

Hope sank again in Spock's eyes, after the most
fleeting of glimmers. "They break to warp nine almost
immediately, Jim. Sustained warp nine, even for the
Enterprise—"

"Yes, I know, Spock, I know." He tried to sound gentle,
not frustrated, but failed. "I hate to leave without McCoy
and Uhura . . . you haven't heard from them, have you?"

Though Spock shifted toward an answer to the pointless question, the door chime kept him from speaking.

Ah, a captain/admiral/trail-boss's work is never
done. "Come."

The door slid open. Captain Roger Lake was a stout man with sandy hair thick in the front but sparse in back, and seemed ill fit to the new design of the Starfleet uniform. Perhaps it was the day's growth of stubble and the slightly crooked belt that made him appear uneasy here, or somehow incomplete.

Less than jovially, Kirk offered, "Captain Lake, welcome aboard."

"Thanks," Lake droned. "You wanted us to check in as soon as we arrived. Okay, you got us. My first officer, Nick Keller."

"Mr. Keller."

"Acting first officer," Keller quickly corrected, and extended a handshake to Kirk. "Proud to meet you, Captain. You too, sir, really proud." He offered an appreciative moment to Spock, who simply nodded once with polite elegance.

As he rose in deference to the captain who had just entered, Spock's presence cloaked the room in sudden formality. Not in the room four seconds and already the *Peleliu*'s master was a man Kirk didn't like.

While Roger Lake barely acknowledged Spock at all, Nick Keller held eye contact with Spock a few seconds longer than necessary, a sensitive and poignant moment, almost as if they'd known each other for years. Of course, for a man Keller's age, maybe thirty, and most of the youth of Starfleet, certainly there had been a tacit intimacy between them and the tall tales of James Kirk and Mr. Spock. This—no, this was not just that. Keller wasn't just offering hero worship or hollow compliments. He really did *appreciate* Spock. How he felt about Kirk remained a mystery, but Kirk sported a sudden deep gratitude for Keller's unshielded gift to Spock, who needed it so much right now.

A pause got him a good look at this younger man.

Average in almost every way, Keller was as tall as Spock, but there the resemblance ended. Keller's eyes were astute and animated, and immediately friendly, though cloaked by the tensions of the moment. He suspected what they were in for, Kirk sensed. After all, his authorization had been on the passage clearance of *Peleliu*'s reports. Keller seemed uneasy as he stood behind his captain, yet was attenuating his unease. Good self-control. Trouble still showed in his pressed lips. Too honest to hide it all. Loyalty, and honesty too? Could be a problem mixture.

Still, Keller had bothered to offer a genuine moment of laud for Spock, a special effort that Kirk found endearing. He hadn't had to do that.

"Have a seat," Kirk suggested, though he immediately got the feeling nobody was going to be relaxed here.

Spock didn't sit down again, but came around behind Kirk's chair and retreated against the tall cool viewport. Kirk got a rush of déjà vu to those old days on the *Enterprise* when Spock stood at his shoulder in his king's-blue tunic, his charcoal hair reflecting a slick of soft light from the bridge dome. Today, framed by the planetary vista of Belle Terre and space beyond it, he appeared supremely in place, though haloed by his current bane—the Quake Moon.

"We have the reports about your voyage," Kirk began. "Without incident until eight days ago, when you confronted vessels that appeared to be Kauld. You engaged these vessels and suffered significant damage, as well as the loss of several crewmen, including your executive officer. Accurate so far?"

"For a report," Lake grunted. "Leaves out a lot. You had to be there."

"Did these ships attack you during Gamma Night? Maneuvering during the blackout?"

"Sometimes."

"Can you be more specific?"

"Gamma Night makes a mess of sensor readings. We weren't sure of all that much. Some shapes came at us, we fought them, they went away, some crew got killed. It happens."

Brick wall. Not unexpected, but Kirk wasn't reaching beyond the pale to hope for cooperation from another captain, commander of a ship as powerful as the *Peleliu*. Such power required certain obligations, and was handed out sparingly in Starfleet.

Obvious in his manner, Lake had no intention of subordinating himself to Kirk. That could be a big problem.

Hello? Had someone made a raving understatement?

"You're not an admiral on this mission, Captain Kirk," Lake stated harshly, angrier than he had any business being.

Behind Kirk, Spock's baronial voice sliced through the acrimony. "But Captain Kirk stands senior to you, sir, and the ranking Starfleet presence in the cluster."

"Senior by ten months. That won't cut much meat out here in Darkest Africa."

Oh, this man was a spinebreaker. He didn't even want to look back on his own actions, even to learn from them.

"It cuts enough," Kirk reminded. "You lost crew members, including your first officer, in a questionable encounter. That requires a *full* report, both from you and from your acting first officer. We've received neither. If Shucorion hadn't given me a report, none of this would've shown itself. Then there's the destruction of Shucorion's ship, which was broadcasting my personal authorization code of truce."

Lake's rounded shoulders stiffened. The subdued light in the office shined on his brow. "You've never lost crew members in questionable encounters? Never made decisions that seemed risky in retrospect?"

Abrupt silence clutched the office. Kirk felt the burning gaze of Keller from one side and the support of Spock from the other, but he continued to lock eyes with Lake. "You ran through Gamma Night without clear readings of what was pursuing you."

"But we were definitely being pursued," Lake said. "Our readings weren't clear. I have reason to suspect sabotage."

"Based on what?"

"That's between me and my crew."

"We had previous damage, sir," Keller stuck in. "We had to run on assumptions rather than clear readings. We *were* being chased. The captain's instincts were right."

Smart. Without moving his head, Kirk shifted his gaze to the younger man. Keller stood ready to defend his captain with evidence just vague enough to be potent.

"He was right," Kirk said, "but he almost drove you into a gas giant. Correct?"

From their reactions he guessed they hadn't expected to face their near miss a second time. The incident, he would have to admit if they pressed, was hearsay. This detail had been left out of their official reports.

It was true. That showed in both their faces, and in their stark silence. Lake's eyes grew narrow and hate-filled. At his side, Keller was covering for his captain. Lake had no interest in opening his procedures to Kirk or anyone, senior or not, and his subordinate was backing him up. Lake, of course, presented a black hole of troubles. But the real problem was in the other chair.

Keller. Very tricky. An officer teetering between his commander on one side and the monolith of the service on the other. How many of Kirk's wild decisions had been given passes at Starfleet Command? Ultimately, good had come of it. Much of that outcome was luck. His officers—friends—had stuck with him every time. Never once had Spock, McCoy, Scott, or anyone from his own ship forwarded a grievance or even uttered a criticism that went beyond their immediate circle.

If Keller wouldn't bend, wouldn't cooperate with an investigation, then prosecuting Lake for incompetence would be nearly impossible.

Prodded by Keller's devotion, Kirk found himself overwhelmed with a wish to give Lake a pass, to reserve judgment, be circumspect with another captain's turf.

On top of that, who would take over if he deposed Lake? Keller? The man had never commanded a ship. Second officer until a week ago. Not enough raw experience. Lake had over thirteen years in fighting-ship command, and ten years commanding service ships before that. Such a record couldn't be cavalierly set aside. Every captain had his own style. Perhaps Lake was just eccentric.

Kirk shook his head at his thoughts. Eccentricity couldn't explain away the reports from Shucorion, the destruction of an emissary ship with the right code signals, or the deaths of the *Peleliu*'s first officer and other crewmen who had been sacrificed to what could only be logged as skirmishes.

In any ordinary conditions, this could work. Impound *Peleliu* pending a competency hearing, find McCoy to preside over the medical aspects, and take the time needed to do this right.

But Belle Terre presented them with no ordinary conditions, ever. Kirk had no time to be conventional. He sat with his mind divided between these two problems. One ship to station here at Belle Terre, another to chase the 'bots and find out where they came from. If he shook up *Peleliu*'s command structure now, the action would effectively shut down one whole ship. Their defense would be unstable. He wouldn't be able to take *Enterprise* and leave. He wouldn't dare.

Yes, that was, by the book, what he *should* do. But did he dare? The book hadn't followed them out to Belle Terre.

The pending question demanded an answer, but neither of the *Peleliu* officers forwarded one.

Saved by the chime. The door twinkled. Somebody wanted in.

Ordinarily Kirk would've given priority to the mini-hearing, but he wanted an out.

"Come," he invited, and everybody breathed a sigh of relief.

The panel parted. Ensign Bonifay blew in. As usual his thick black hair, a little long at the neck, was brushed in a fluffy crown, with three or four wild strands craning forward into his face. Kirk always had the idea that Bonifay spent three hours every morning getting it to do that, and that he had the unruly strands named and catalogued with the Starfleet Archives. His compact body reminded Kirk of his own in younger days, though he'd never had quite the taper Bonifay was blessed with.

Bonifay was carrying a handheld cooler, which he brought straight to the desk, until he noticed the two newcomers and spun like a top.

"Keller!"

"Bonifay! That's all I need!" Keller broke out of his chair, as if on alert, and snapped to Kirk, "Sir, I'd like to apologize for anything he's done."

Bonifay shot back, "That would be perfectly normal, if you were a Libra."

"Gentlemen," Kirk snapped, barely changing it from "boys." When they both faced him, he asked, "Ensign, you have a report?"

Bonifay eyed Keller snidely as he swaggered to the desk and opened the cooler. He held up the wad of viscous goop, transparent as glasswork, though clouded by a purple coloration. Encased in its center Kirk could just make out an unevenly cut softball-sized chunk of ore, its natural glitter nulled by the gel.

"I got together with some of the other bosuns," Bonifay reported, "and we developed this plasticite compound out of a combination of inert blends we usually use as capstan shackle sealant. This node of active olivium is held stable inside the semi-solid gel. It's a little sticky, but this makes the olivium safe for handling in manageable amounts."

"To what end?" Kirk asked. He moved slightly aside as Spock came forward to take the purplish gloop from Bonifay and scrutinize it. He noticed that while Spock was interested, Lake didn't seem to be. Keller, though, put aside whatever annoyances rose at Bonifay's presence and came up close behind the ensign to get a look at the bit of Belle Terre's prize.

Bonifay's face grew tortured as if Keller had on bad cologne, but he otherwise ignored him. "We did a comparison study of the caches of olivium that are attracting the 'bots and figured the deposits are a quarter-ton and bigger. Maybe we can store it effectively in small amounts, and the 'bots wouldn't be able to—"

"Captain—" Suddenly Spock clapped his free hand to his ear and winced.

Kirk stood up and started turning to him, but never got there.

On the other side of the room, the door panel slid open—a door that should have been magnetically locked with a security encryption. As they all turned, a singsong rumble filled the room. Pulsing and whining, one of the 'bots came floating in, its three legs folded up behind so it could fit through the doorway.

"Holy—!" Shocked, Keller vaulted sideways, bumping his chair, which clattered to the floor behind him.

"Keller, freeze!" Kirk shot out a hand. "Nobody move!"

Chapter Ten

ENSIGN BONIFAY stumbled back and bumped into Lake. Lake gripped the arms of his chair and pressed forward, but had no time to move with Bonifay almost sitting on him. Keller defied Kirk's order and yanked Bonifay out of the probe's path, taking the opportunity to toss the bosun into the nearest wall in something suspiciously like exuberance.

With mechanical single-mindedness, the 'bot drifted into the room, paused as its sensors bleeped and whistled. Scanning—Kirk recognized the process immediately. The probe found what it wanted and efficiently swiveled its "front" end to Spock. From a port in the housing, it extended a telescoping metal finger out about two feet. The blunt end of the probe then broke into a talon-shaped grabber. Neatly it plucked the glassy ball with the olivium inside from Spock's hand and rotated it out of the way, then called up a recognizable nozzle from its port side.

A lather of dense foam erupted from the nozzle and

sprayed Spock's neck, chest, and the offending hand. As he stood there, splattered and bubbling, the probe backed off.

"Thk yu," the 'bot clicked.

Taking care to avoid Lake in his chair and Keller braced near the doorway, the purposeful 'bot simply backed out the way it had come, humming and bleeping in a tone that could only be described as happy.

The door closed. The bleeping faded away.

"Yikes," Keller uttered, dry-mouthed. "Clean getaway . . ."

Kirk empathized with the reaction. Reading reports was one thing. Actually seeing one of those things in action had a whole other effect.

"At least they've learned to be courteous," Bonifay mumbled out the corner of his mouth. His chalk-mark black brows crawled into an expression.

Annoyed, Kirk sighed and leered at the door panel for a moment. No point chasing the probe. They wouldn't catch it.

He turned to Spock, who stood with his now-empty hand out where it had been before, his torso dripping with decontaminant foam from neck to belt.

"You all right?" Kirk asked him.

Spock's arm squished with foam as Kirk offered a sympathetic grip, but the Vulcan could only manage a nod. Standing in a green puddle now, he didn't even lower his hand. The indignity of it all.

His glossy black hair mussed, Zane Bonifay pushed himself away from where he'd landed against the wall. "So much for our no-sensing-in-small-amounts theory."

"And they've learned to use the doorways," Kirk contributed.

Roger Lake stood up finally, bearing a caustic grin.

"So everything doesn't always go exactly right for you either, I guess, Captain?"

"Not always," Kirk admitted. "All right . . . time for plan B." Resisting the quiver of common sense running up his neck, he steeled himself and said, "Captain Lake, you have duty here at the planet. Mr. Spock and I will take the *Enterprise* and follow those probes out into space in an effort to identify and communicate with whoever's sending them. It'll be up to you and Mr. Keller to defend the planet while we try to track the source of the olivium confiscation. Can you do it?"

Lake glowered. His shoulders stiffened. "What do you take us for?"

Behind Lake, Keller visibly reined in a flinch at Lake's disrespectful tone, but Kirk said nothing about it.

However, he did have something else to say.

"I'm assigning Mr. Bonifay to *Peleliu.*"

"Me?" Bonifay gulped.

Keller grimaced. "Him?"

"Yes, him. He's familiar with the olivium storage and containment systems, as well as what's been happening on the planet with the robotic probes. Neither of you are. He'll be your planetary liaison."

"He can't even spell it," Keller revealed.

Striking a defiant posture, Bonifay trumpeted, "My people never had to read anything more complicated than a road sign. We always found our way."

"Then what are you doing here?"

Kirk came around the desk, back into the fire. No more offices, no more reports or rumors. Time for duty stations. "All right, gentlemen. We'll leave it where it is and see what happens. Dismissed."

But he got the feeling there were more problems now than when they'd come in.

Peleliu, in orbit

"Ah, the happy passenger."

"Mr. Keller," Shucorion greeted passively as he stepped by—or tried to.

Pleasantries clicked off as Keller snagged the Blood leader by one unlucky arm and boomeranged him out of his stride, pressed a hand to his chest, pinned him to the wall, and drilled him with a glare.

"Tell me your name again? Allies? Friends? Working together? Refresh my memory."

Though unintimidated by the hand pressed to his sternum, Shucorion seemed incredulous. "Some point of disagreement?"

"You told Kirk about the gas giant."

Shucorion instantly digested what this was about. "Yes, I told him."

"You weren't even on board when it happened!"

"Your engineer showed me the recordings of the event. Sensor darkness shouldn't be taken—"

"And that gives you business discussing it with Kirk?"

"Your captain's state of mind—"

"—is an internal matter and we're handling it. You've got no right talking about me or mine to Kirk or anybody."

"I see. . . . Are you actually angry?"

Keller pointed at his own hardened expression. "Does this look like joy?"

"You would not have reported the truth? For the sakes of your men? Your crew? Their reputation?"

"That's not how we do things. We don't just spew hearsay. We take proper steps, have hearings, call witnesses. These things take time."

"You have no time," Shucorion pointed out. "Swiftness of truth is important for you here. You have only two fighting ships to protect an entire star system under a siege."

"Lots of people are eccentric," Keller snarled. "Starfleet has a long-standing tradition of mavericks, eccentrics, and wildmen. You're gonna be facing one if you don't back off. Where I come from, we protect our own. I'm the one sitting on this thorn, not you. Lake got us here. Our doctor's in charge of his condition. The *Enterprise* is leaving. That makes *Peleliu* the ship in authority after tomorrow, and Lake's the ranking officer. If I hear you discussing us, it better be to say what a nice ride you had."

"Because of your captain's twisted judgments," Shucorion reminded, "my men and I have no ship. What is said in your culture of a man who destroys the ship of allies because he reacts too sharply?"

"Ah, that's it?" Keller accused. "Revenge?"

Shucorion blinked, and his expression changed to bewilderment. "Revenge? . . . Revenge . . . seems unproductive. Your captain is unbalanced. My people have never had an ally before. Now we must depend upon you and your ship, as well as those of this planet must depend upon you. I will continue—"

Keller choked off his words with a well-placed set of knuckles. "It's my problem to worry about, not yours."

Struggling only slightly, Shucorion managed a nod. "With these tidings, I would worry also."

"Don't agree with me," Keller snarled. "I hate that." He shoved off so roughly that he bruised them both. "I want you and your men off my ship and away from my crew and my captain and if you spread talk about us again I'll be on you like green on a grape. Got it?"

Intelligent eyes never wavering, Shucorion's gaze speared deep into the hidden parts of Keller's conscience and hit a sour note.

"I have it, Mr. Keller. But do you?"

"Mr. Keller."

The *Peleliu* was in orbit while a few determined crew members and one or two engineers spared by Commander Scott crawled around her, trying to effect repairs.

Keller himself had been awake thirty-five hours straight, unshaven, hungry, grumpy, trying to do both the second officer's and the first officer's jobs running interference among Lake, McAddis, the engineering staff, and almost everyone else, convincing people to give up perfection in favor of expediency. Some divisions were even arguing over who got which part or tool first. The *Enterprise* was leaving, dumping a huge responsibility in *Peleliu*'s lap. The ship had to be patched together. It had to be.

"Captain Kirk?"

There he was. In the shadows of the partially lit corridor. The ship's power had been reduced considerably, to favor certain systems that needed energy for repair work. This place was no starbase.

There, in the shadows at the turn in the corridor, in a ladder bay, stood James Kirk. At first Keller thought his imagination was playing tricks.

Kirk's face was a pattern of shadows, his clever eyes veiled, mysterious.

Intruder alert.

"Sir," Keller began, and moved toward him, wondering if something was wrong. "I'm sorry—nobody notified me you were on board."

"It's not an official visit."

"How did you—"

No point finishing the question.

James Kirk was wearing one of the new field jackets, Starfleet's answer to peacoats. Looked good in it, as if he'd always had it in the back of his mind, even before they were designed and issued. Had his hands in his pockets. Suddenly Keller was self-conscious. Kirk was leaning, with one shoulder against the bulkhead.

This was one of those holes in the road that most people had sense not to step in, but somehow the foot just kept getting sucked in the wrong direction till *wham.* Magnetic north.

Unable to resist the center of gravity, Keller found himself moving closer on thready legs, but made a last-ditch scramble for redirection. "Captain Lake's in his office, I think, sir. I'll notify him. Would you like to wait in the wardroom?"

Kirk wasn't fooled. "Can't stay. Since you're here, I'll pass along some things to you. You may want to brief your captain."

Instantly Keller understood. Since he was here?

How had Kirk come on board? Not even another captain could board a ship without permission, and couldn't tour around without escort. Not properly anyway.

But then, this was James Kirk. Not exactly Sir Propriety.

Obviously Kirk had no intention of considering Roger Lake right now. He was skirting around *Peleliu*'s assigned master and going for a completely different—and inappropriate—target.

Keller resented him for it. Officially, he couldn't resist or shoulder away Kirk's attention. He didn't have authority, and though he wished he could be rude, something stopped him. He wanted to hear what Kirk had to say. Would rank provide an excuse?

"Awright," he submitted. "I'm listening."

No "sir." No conciliations. Equal ground.

Thus, they crossed over the first line of scrimmage.

"Your name," Kirk began. "Nick, isn't it? Am I remembering right?"

Strange way to begin. Names didn't matter that much. Other things did. Where was this leading?

Keller only nodded.

"I've always been grateful for rank insignia," the captain went on casually. "Never been that good at names. Something tells me to remember yours."

Hooking his thumbs in his trouser pockets, Keller gave in to his fatigue and impatience. "Nick Jacob Keller. Thorn Bluff, New Mexico. Nearest city, Santa Fe. Help you any?"

The famous amber eyes flashed at him. "Just Nick? Not Nicholas?"

"No, not Nicholas. Captain, if there's something I should report, can we sort of pole-vault over to it? I've had a wicked week."

He made a little jumping gesture with one hand.

Kirk offered a reserved smile. "Yes. Most of the colonial expedition ships were either sacrificed to the moon-moving project or to fight off the Kauld's two attacks. We've been starved for parts, power, and the skill to use them, but between Shucorion's single-man scouts and a few picket shuttles, we've set up a fair defense perimeter on this side of the solar system. A few satellites here and there, in a cone formation that guards the solar system. You'll get a warning beacon if any ships pass into the cone. It only works if you stay close to the planet and don't get distracted."

Dazed with lack of sleep and the sudden strain of this encounter, Keller nodded. "I'll study the layout."

"Good. We've given the Kauld a bloody nose. The fact that they've been out harassing the *Peleliu* tells me they haven't decided to either go away or make nice. Until the Federation can send a diplomatic corps out here to deal with them, they're not proving to be very friendly."

Stuck in his mire of middlemanland, Keller shrugged. "Could send Zoa . . ."

"Who?"

"Sorry, nothing." Though he didn't really want to get into a conversation with this man—not now, or here—Keller couldn't stop the next sentence. "I saw the reports about your combat with Battlelord Vellyngaith on the frontier. A couple of Starfleet ships and sixty-some civilian vessels, most of the people-movers that didn't even have their own engines, going up against a whole fleet of fighters and battlebarges . . . sphering the ships was a brilliant maneuver. Defensible, without being on the defensive. A Starfleet officer on every bridge to add stability . . . I wouldn't have thought to do that. Scares me."

Kirk bobbed his brows. "Experience takes time to ferment. I wanted to give each ship self-confidence, for one thing. You have to fight using your soldiers' minds as well as their bodies and weapons."

Now Keller was even more scared. Why hadn't he known that?

"The sphering of the ships," he pushed on, "did you get that from the old British square phalanx maneuver? Rotating its front line to make for constant fire?"

"Partly. The other model was Roman tortoise formation. And a little bit of circling the wagons."

"But the British element was flexibility," Keller insisted. "The enemy couldn't get a grip on any weaknesses because the ships were constantly shifting into the geodesic. You kept opening and tightening the formation as needed. And you coordinated their weapons into barrages. Dang sphere spindled like a blowfish when it lit up. *Enterprise*'s visual logs showed eight Kauld fighters atomized in a single seizure. Made me glad I wasn't looking from outside."

The captain shrugged. What was that—modesty? Did Kirk the Great have modesty?

"It was pliant," he demurred. "Sometimes you need that. The part that nibbled at my nerves was hoping every ship would have the fortitude not to move, no matter what hit them. Have to give the civilians credit. Nobody folded."

"Any formation's only as strong as its weakest point," Keller agreed. "It was pretty foxy, that carousel you put 'em on."

Kirk's amber eyes were like a quiet yellow alert. He was almost grinning. "You know your strategics."

Not sure whether that was a compliment or a dare, Keller squeezed the coin in his pocket and shrugged. "I like military history. Just never had a chance to use it . . . or watch it being made."

Again their eyes connected in the way that proved there were underlying things being said between them.

Now Kirk let that little smile out. "Thank you."

"Welcome, sir."

"You may get your chance in the next few days," the captain said, vectoring back to his reason for being here. "We've beaten the Kauld off the planet twice. They know we'll be bringing more and more ships out here. Vellyngaith will be more cautious now. They were once superior in the cluster. Now they see themselves as doomed. That makes for desperation, and desperation is by far more threatening than anger or belligerence or greed."

Uneasy, Keller folded his arms and stretched his shoulder muscles. "I 'magine it is, sir."

Pouncing on the agreement, Kirk stepped closer to him, shortening the gap between Keller and trouble. "Don't give them an opening. Stand your ground here, in orbit. We don't need exploratory missions. You have no reason to leave the planet until *Peleliu* is back to full strength."

"We don't have to leave it," Keller said. "We just have to keep the peace."

"Peace might not be an option."

With a scowl, Keller disapproved, "What's that supposed to mean?"

"Only that peace isn't always the way." Kirk shifted his feet and pushed off the wall he'd been leaning on. "My father told me something that I've never forgotten. He got it from a Romulan friend . . . 'There's a lot of peace in a prison camp.' "

Ominous words, and he meant them. This wasn't the kind of lesson anyone expected from a wise senior. Don't expect peace? Don't believe it or accept it if it seems to come?

Keller slumped, pressing his shoulder to the bulkhead. "You're giving me a brain ache."

"Yes, McCoy usually blames that on Spock." Kirk paced a few steps and waited for two tech crewmen carrying an interfactor housing to pass the inlet of an adjoining corridor before continuing. "It's my recommendation," he went on, "that you make good use of the tools you have."

Time to do the stone-faced act, pretend to perfectly understand what a superior officer was alluding to. Actually he had no idea what Kirk was talking about.

Phasers? *Peleliu*'s banks were unstable. Patrol? With a half-wrecked ship?

Finally he gulped his pride and just asked. "What do I have?"

Kirk had been waiting for Keller to break down, or break through, as if he knew it was coming.

"You have Shucorion," he said.

"Oh . . . him."

"He's spent his life learning to anticipate the movements of the Kauld. He's survived against these people with much less powerful ships. It's something to be respected. I've already asked him to be at your disposal as an advisor."

Irritably Keller shifted his feet. "I don't think we want Shucorion around, sir. Captain Lake doesn't trust him. I don't particularly warm up to him either."

With some kind of warning Kirk's eyes brightened dangerously. "I can't order Lake to take advice. At least you know what's at your disposal. Use it. Don't let your guard down. Stay alert."

There it was again. Kirk wasn't talking about Lake. He was talking *to* Keller.

Protocol and everything else resisted. "Sir, shouldn't you be telling this to my captain?"

"Probably." The agreement was flat, unpretentious. Having made it, Kirk simply went on with his line of discussion. "Most of the known deposits of olivium have been stuffed back into the Quake Moon. Mr. Spock believes the two remaining 'bots might be the last ones. When they warp out, we'll be following one of them, both if possible. We may be back in a day, or a month, a year, or never. We're going to be following the probe at warp nine. I don't know if we can sustain. If we have to confront it out in space in ways that we didn't dare near the planet, we may end up stranded in the interstellar void. If we do, not even *Peleliu* in its best condition could rescue us. You'll have to forget about us the moment we leave here. Assume you're on your own. You'll have to take over defense of the olivium."

Keller indulged in a disapproving scowl. "Olivium? What about the people here? They can't just turn around and leave."

"No, they can't. We passed up that option." Was there sympathy in the captain's face? In his heart? It didn't show. "Do what you can for them. But the olivium, Keller . . . this discovery is nearly unmatched in the leap of technology that can be milked from it. We're not even sure how far we can go with it. What we do know is we can't let anyone else take it away, or the whole Federation could be the price, not just a colony. If hostile powers gain exclusive possession of this find, and believe me, they're thinking about it, you'll have to weigh these sixty-four thousand lives against the billions of people back home. Either we all have possession, or nobody does."

How could this corridor be sweltering and freezing at the same time?

"But we have it, don't we?" Keller asked. "These 'bot probes, they're just sticking it all back in the Quake Moon. All we have to do is dig it . . . back out . . ." He paused, hearing himself fall into a trap. "The other shoe hasn't dropped, has it?"

Kirk's airbrushed brows went up. He almost made no sound as he murmured, "No."

His innards suddenly tight, Keller couldn't move. "It could all happen again? Worse?"

This time the captain only nodded, and offered Keller time to add up the numbers.

Headache. Like sudden thunder. Keller paced away a few steps, trying to think. Disrespectful, but he didn't care. "Most of the planet suspects the Kauld are running the 'bots. I take it you don't?"

"If the Kauld had the kind of technology to do what I've seen these things do—pass through a planet without disrupting it, take a full photon hit with a chuckle and shrug—they wouldn't need quantum olivium." Taking a moment to rub his nose with a casual gesture, Kirk seemed almost human. Almost. "I've run into this kind of thing before. Mechanical probes capable of absorbing enormous energy. I never figured out just how, but I learned to deal with them in other ways. I had to. I also suspect there's a potential danger that hasn't shown itself yet. You may find yourself sitting in the path of something very dangerous going on here."

"Sir . . . what're you saying?" Keller abruptly demanded. "If there's something specific—"

"If there were something specific, I'd tell you. Starfleet can't send help or evacuation facilities in any less than six months, and we've already proven we can't fully evacuate ourselves. The Blood aren't the most secure of allies. You're alone out here. It makes for unsavory choices. I have to make one now. I have to turn my back on this colony and chase one of those probes into empty space because a geological oddity is so important to the galaxy—if it's falling into the wrong hands, if there's something bigger going on here—"

Clearly embittered, Kirk cut himself off. His shoulders were knotted under the field coat, his arms and legs tense, working. He hated the choice, yet he'd made it and was willing to stick to it.

Keller hadn't expected to see this. A captain—an admiral—possessed unthinkable power. He could do almost anything he wanted.

Or could he? Was command the beginning of freedom, or the end of it?

To hide from the future, he stuffed his hands in his pockets and slouched some. His fingers struck the *Challenger* coin given to him by Tim McAddis, who had gotten it from Zane Bonifay, who had spirited it all the way here from Earth, where it had survived two centuries, now to be in deep space, in Nick Keller's fist, hinting to him of decisions yet to be made.

"One thing I've learned the hard way," Kirk grumbled, as if to himself, "is if you wait for something to happen, it's usually a lot worse than if you go out and make it happen."

At first this sounded like pomposity to Keller. He bristled some at the imperiousness of the man before him, medals and fame and all, because the medals and fame didn't really follow Kirk out into space and didn't hold much weight. The Kauld, the Blood, the 'bots, none of them knew what James Kirk had done in his past to open up space or either save or ruin lives, the long roster of accomplishments and ancillary failures that such a man carried with him . . . yet Keller knew the history, and forced himself to remember. Before him was a man who had *moved a moon* to make happen what he wanted to happen. *Pardon me, God, but I don't like the arrangement of these planets. Mind if I shift that one slightly to the left?*

"I know what you're thinking," James Kirk bluntly declared.

Keller came sharply back to the moment. Kirk was stabbing him with those animalistic eyes. Hypnotic eyes, like grappling hooks, the kind nobody could look away from. He knew. Somehow he'd figured it out. He knew something was going on aboard *Peleliu* and that Keller had decided not to tell him. As such Kirk was putting the responsibility on Keller to make sure it didn't backfire, cost lives, whatever. *All right, you've decided, now be sure to clean up your mess. Anybody can make a mess from time to time, but accept that it's your mess and you clean it up. I'm going out to clean up mine, and I'm leaving you with yours.*

"Yes," Kirk uttered. "These sixty-four thousand lives may come second to a pile of rocks. That's the ugly side of being in charge. Command isn't choosing between a right and a wrong. After all, that's easy."

"If it's not right and wrong," Keller prodded, "what is it?"

He held his breath, cold to the gut, as Jim Kirk watched him to see if he were absorbing his words.

"Command," the captain said, "is having the spine to choose between a wrong and another wrong."

The portentous words rolled between them. Stunning—this wasn't what any manual said, or any morality play, or any legend, rule, tall tale or proverb. Right and wrong. Light and darkness. Good and evil. Those were the only ones.

Evil and evil? Choose?

Keller realized he had just been handed the culmination of a lifetime's hard choices. His expression crimped in some kind of resistance.

He bristled. "I'm not *in* command, sir."

James Kirk's eyes glinted at him now. Pride? Dare? He seemed satisfied at having done the devil's work and shredded another man's inner balance. "This is your turf, now, Mr. Keller. Protect it any way you can."

Consumed with a sensation that Kirk had somehow gotten what he wanted out of this encounter, Keller felt the weight of the whole Federation shift over to his shoulders. How did that happen? How could he shove it back?

"Mind if I beam off from here?" Kirk pushed off the wall he'd been leaning on and pulled out his communicator.

Keller stepped back. "Go ahead on."

"Thank you. Kirk to *Enterprise*. Beam me aboard."

The captain paused as the faint buzz of transport began, and he tossed one more dart with his quick eyes and his warning words.

"Don't go out at night, Nick. There are vampires in the dark."

Chapter Eleven

Mine Ship *Pandora's Box*

"HI, HONEY, I'm home. Time for another visit. I'd let you two room together, but then I'd be jealous. I'm not nice when I'm jealous, so I just avoid it."

Billy Maidenshore skimmed into Uhura's quarters with Dr. McCoy in one fist and a metal tackle box in the other, and locked the door behind him. This tactic was getting old, but it kept working. Letting her see McCoy just enough for her to know the doctor was alive kept control over her temptations to betray Maidenshore. She had no doubt he would kill McCoy, or do worse to him, if she misbehaved. Maidenshore had her pegged. She wouldn't let the doctor die.

An imposing man, physically impressive and dashing in a low-life high-horse way, Maidenshore gave Uhura a fetching grin as he dumped McCoy on the bunk and held the tackle box before Uhura. "I brought you something. Open it."

"A pair of dueling pistols?" she commented. The box wasn't heavy. She opened it and looked in. Various accoutrements of a lady's boudoir were neatly stacked and arranged in the compartments meant for electrical tools.

She looked up at him.

He swaggered in place, pleased with himself. "Makeup, perfume, talcum powder, eyeliner . . . see, even on a mining ship, there's nothing Billy can't get for you. Like it?"

"Oh, yes, I like it." She closed the lid. "You know how women are."

"Yeah, yeah, I do. Women have always done things for me." Maidenshore put in the computer cartridge he kept securely in his pocket at all other times, enabling the communications system to receive current messages. He clicked the right buttons.

"Listen to this," he invited.

"This is First Officer Spock. This is an encoded communiqué to all Enterprise *crew personnel, authorized by Captain James Kirk. All current assignments and shore leaves are hereby canceled. Return to the* Enterprise *immediately and report to your department heads for security registration. The following personnel should report directly to the bridge: Dr. McCoy. Lieutenant Commander Uhura. Commander Braxton. Lieutenant Commander Fields. Chief Lebrewski. Chief Nelson. Engineer Herne. All personnel report in by zero-six-hundred hours, Stardate 4662.1. Spock out."*

The message ended. The comm equipment bleeped in confirmation. Billy took the enabler back out of its socket and slipped it into his vest.

"Know what that means, kiddies?" he asked.

Deliberately not meeting McCoy's eyes, Uhura lolled back in her chair and struck a queenly pose.

Maidenshore seemed to like that. "No, Billy. What does it mean?"

"Means the jig is up. They're sending out a call for all their crew to come back to the starship."

"So? That happens all the time. We rotate crews regularly."

Maidenshore shook a finger at her. "Now, now, don't try to kid a kidder. There's only two reasons to recall your crew. One, you're under attack, or two, you're leaving. They're not under attack. Ergo . . . they're leaving."

"They might be," Uhura conceded. "But Captain Kirk's not that predictable."

"Jimmy? Sure, he is. He wants the two of you to report to your posts. I'm not ready to give you back, though. Don't get up hope. He's not going to hold up his whole starship to wait for you and the doctor."

McCoy rubbed his arms to ward off the chill of the barbaric conditions Maidenshore forced him to live in. Uhura knew what he was going through. Maidenshore treated McCoy poorly and herself well, probably to set them against each other in some other kind of psychological leverage.

The doctor shifted forward on the bunk. His eyes were sallow, reddened. "I don't know what you think all this is going to do for you, Billy. You can't skim enough refined olivium to make that big a difference, and the unrefined ore your men are pulling off asteroids won't yield enough to give you leverage."

"Doc, these robotoid things are doing me a huge favor by stuffing the olivium back in the rock vault. They're taking refined olivium away from the colonists and stuffing it all back into the Quake Moon. This is Miracle Maidenshore at work. Billy the Slick. I live a charmed life. Nothing can touch me. My grandmother used to tell me that. Whatever's best for Billy, that's what should happen."

Was McCoy all right? He seemed alert, though debilitated, chilly, and ill fed. Offering a kind of shrug, he managed to communicate that he was faring well enough, day by day. She suspected, though, that his value was waning. Very dangerous. Anything that lost its value to Billy Maidenshore would find its future in doubt.

Uhura tried to pay him some attention without suggesting to Maidenshore that she was less than mesmerized by his self-involvement. He certainly enjoyed hearing himself talk and anything he spilled could be used against him, somehow, somewhere, by somebody. Though she was a communications expert and famed for her speaking voice, Uhura had learned that much could be learned from keeping silent and listening.

"I decide to skim olivium off the colonists," Maidenshore was saying, "and warehouse it over there in Vellynidiot's solar system, and he comes along and begs me to let him do it. He doesn't even know what's good for him, so he does what's good for me. He spreads the word, and everybody else falls in line. I've done this before—it always works. Get the bonehead slobberdog media on your side, and you can't lose. Vellyngaith's my media this time. Last time it was the bonehead colonists. That's the trick—you just get a gaggle of clods to swallow your message, sit back and have a cigar while they do your work for you." He leaned back as if to demonstrate, nodded in agreement with himself, and muttered, "What's amazing is how rabidly they'll protect you while you suck their blood. . . ."

Chilled by the ironic truth, confidence given to such a slimeball by a lifetime of having other people let themselves be conned, Uhura found herself glad she hadn't eaten recently or she'd be forced to hold it down. "There's only so much you can do," she said, "from a ship that everybody thinks is still a mining vessel, even if you've taken over the operation."

Maidenshore shook his head and chuckled. "Haven't you been paying attention?"

"Of course not," McCoy droned. "We're losing our will to live."

Uhura warned him with a glance, then asked, "Pay attention to what?"

"To those 'bots. Think, think. When did they show up?" He paused, waiting for them to answer, but neither would play his game. "When the Quake Moon blew!"

"The probes didn't come for over a year after that, Billy," McCoy reminded. "Your evidence is—"

"They didn't come before that either. The explosion must've triggered something. Maybe it takes months to send its signal. Kirk found out they streak out of here at warp nine. Maybe they're going far. Why else would you need warp nine?"

"What signal?" Uhura asked.

"The moon. A big flare gun. It lights off, and here they come to collect the diamonds. Whatever these things are, they can swallow a full phaser hit and that means their tech's way beyond the Federation's power to stop them. The Fed can't stop them, they're coming in and collecting the olivium, and they haven't found mine. See, that's how I figure the moon was a flare. What happened here, that didn't happen in the Kauld system? No moon exploded. Nothing's showed the robots where my olivium is. Since it happened here, they won't be searching way over there. And when all the stuff here is confiscated, guess who'll be in control of all that's left. And now, to top it off, Kirk is taking the starship and blasting off. And you think I'm not charmed? This should be artwork."

"You haven't been listening to the broadcasts as closely as you think, Billy," Uhura told him. "But I have. If Captain Kirk is leaving, it's only because he knows the colony will be guarded by the *Peleliu*. Even with damage, the cruiser is strong enough to beat off a Kauld assault in conjunction with planetary defenses we've set up."

He smiled at her with a sidelong nastiness. "Come on, you're smarter than that. I've got the reports. Remember when I had you intercept the reports coming in before *Peleliu* got here? You should've read 'em. Like cheap novels! They gave me everything I need. Now I don't have to win the hard way. All I have to do is push Roger the Lake Loon over the edge. He'll take his whole ship down with him. Even Vell-in-hell ought to be able to do that much without botching it."

Shifting on the bunk, McCoy rubbed his right leg with a bloodless hand. Behind Maidenshore's back, his wide eyes communicated an unhappy message to Uhura.

Don't say anything, she willed him to understand. *Just let him posture and spout. Don't get in trouble. He already doesn't like you.*

"So Kirk's gone," Maidenshore continued, "and he's left the chicken coop in the hands of a burnt-out has-been and his overworked rookie exec in a busted-up tank. Hey! There is a God!"

Hoping at least to provide some withered example of integrity, Uhura suggested, "Is that an excuse to steal?"

The joy dropped out of Maidenshore's expression. He could don and doff sincerity like changing hats. "Stealing? I'm not stealing. I'm hoarding. There's a big difference. Stealing is silly. It's got limits. They'd figure it out, then shut down operations and have a war. I'm better than that. I'm smarter. I know to set up a situation to make them bargain with us. If you can't beat 'em, exploit 'em."

"You underestimate people in general, don't you, Billy?" McCoy observed. "It's just a habit with you."

Maidenshore wagged his satisfied-salesman expression. When he spoke, his words carried a sudden honesty. He raised his brows. "Doc . . . people in general live down to my expectations."

The disturbing truth made Uhura's insides shrink. He was right. People had played into his hands over and over, all his life, from what he had told them. An unscrupulous, unrepentant man could easily succeed if people swallowed the manure he spread, and they seemed to do that with spice. The whole colony, even the whole Federation, could find itself caught in a web under the control of a single unrepentant spider with a golden web. Justice didn't always come.

"This is the people's own choice," he went on. "You think I could succeed if they didn't fall off every cliff? This is my chance to eradicate the illusion of law enforcement in the cluster. By the time Jim Kirk gets back here, I'll own the whole Belle Terre complex. He'll be negotiating with King Billy.

"After *Peleliu*'s gone, I'll destroy all other transports, Blood ships, merchant ships, port facilities, everything, the planetary defenses, the power plants . . . if they want to deal, they'll deal with me."

Abruptly he came back to the moment, and turned to McCoy. "I have to deal with you, though, don't I?" With a swagger he came to stand over the doctor, intimidating as a vulture. "I don't think I need you anymore, Hippocrates."

Uhura bolted to her feet. "Billy—!"

He looked at her. "What? Playtime's over. I'll have to decide whether to kill you two or not. Still, I might come up with some use for you. If not, well, we don't live forever, do we?"

He turned to her, sidling nearer with his idea of warmth, as if the doctor were suddenly gone. "I could kill him now, but I'm not that bad a guy. I'll prove it to you eventually."

Repulsed, Uhura found the strength to move closer to him, measuring carefully just how much attraction he would buy from a store she knew was closed. "You've proven a lot to me already, I have to admit."

"Uhura," McCoy interrupted, "have you lost your sense of decency?"

She held out her long-fingered hand and spoke musically. "He hasn't hurt anybody yet, has he? Everybody deserves a second chance. I've known lots of powerful men, but a man who knows how to *use* power . . . I haven't found many of those . . . not in years."

The doctor sighed and glared at her with his strained ice-blue eyes. "You always did wilt at the sparkle of jewelry."

"I'm a woman, aren't I?" she agreed. Leaning back on the desk Maidenshore had provided for her, she made sure her knees were out a little and her shoulders back some. "I used to think Captain Kirk was one of those men. Then he accepted the admiralty. I lost a lot of respect for him. I only came out here to see if he had any of the old spark left."

Billy Maidenshore's eyes crinkled with satisfaction. He rolled a pinch of her hair between his thumb and forefinger. "Maybe you need a different brand of furnace. What do you say . . . is it possible?"

She tipped her head, lowered her chin, and raised her eyes to him. "It's possible, if you stretch the definition . . . but words are my life, you know. . . . Why don't you up the ante, Billy? Make me like you a little."

"Name it."

"Give McCoy heat in his quarters. A little better

food. After all, a little can go a long way between people."

A chuckle from his throat. Was he aroused, or just amused?

"Sure," he blurted. "Why not? But only because it's you."

Not giving too much, she managed part of a smile. "When I know you better, I'll introduce you to an old African ritual. Very colorful. Very intimate."

"Yeah, sure." He laughed, and moved to the doorway to cue the locking mechanism. "I like how that sounds. Why don't you two just visit for a while?" As he left, he flashed his self-ingratiated smile. "Have fun talking about me, now."

A moment later, he was gone. Yet, as always, the lingering presence of Billy Maidenshore remained a haunting reality even when he wasn't around.

Leonard McCoy gave himself the gift of a long, relieved sigh. Nothing about it, though, suggested they weren't still in trouble. He closed his eyes a moment, then opened them and looked at her. "What old African ritual?"

Uhura settled back in her creaking chair and noticed that her thighs were sore from disuse. "Cutting his heart out with his own teeth."

"Oh, that one. He's an act, isn't he?"

"He's a whole circus," she mused. "What boggles me is that anybody believes a word of his hollow promises. It makes me nervous that he tells us his plans."

"Tells *you* his plans. Remember what I said? He's trying to impress you."

"I don't know, Leonard. I think he's trying to impress himself."

"The way people give in to him, he might just have a case. Why does he leave us alone like this when he knows we'll plot against him?"

"He likes us to talk about him. Makes him feel like a man."

"Are you sure he's not bugging us somehow?"

"Believe me."

"All right, sorry . . . our problem is, he's winning and we can't stop him. Jim and Spock might be leaving, but not because they think Belle Terre'll be safe. You heard Spock's voice. He didn't sound good."

That got her attention. "You mean he sounds tired? Or ill?"

"No . . . something else. I'm not sure."

"We have to warn Captain Lake somehow." McCoy scanned the useless boards of bleeping communications equipment that Uhura couldn't make work without flagging any ten of Maidenshore's warning systems. "Oh, I know, big words—Maidenshore's anticipated every move we could possibly make. If he can inhibit this system so successfully that even you can't break through with a message—"

"You haven't been on the bridge as much as I have," she reminded. "You're not a tactician. You've been a doctor." She raised an eyebrow. "I know how the captain thinks *tactically*. This is an ideal time to use what I've learned."

"Which is?"

"First, battles are frequently decided in the first few seconds, by whoever gets in the first licks. We can make sure *Peleliu* gets it."

"How?"

"If you're being dragged through the woods by hostile natives about to attack the settlers, all you really have to do is make a noise. Right?"

"I suppose it's right. But we can't make a noise."

"Vellyngaith's going to be sneaking up on the *Peleliu* and the planet. He'll do it during Gamma Night."

"How do you know?"

"Really, Doctor."

"All right, but you still can't make a noise. He's got all the communication equipment inhibited. You told me that."

"Maidenshore expects me to do something, because I'm the signal specialist."

"I'd say that was a fair guess." The doctor stood up, grasped the pole at the end of the bunk, and used it as leverage while he stretched his legs one at a time.

Uhura watched him for a few seconds, mentally getting exercise just by watching him. "He won't expect anything from you," she said. "That's why you'll be the one acting out our plan, on my orders."

"Aye aye, Captain."

"We have to use the equipment he isn't expecting us to use, to alert *Peleliu* that there's a force approaching."

Suddenly interested, McCoy stopped moving his legs and squared her with a leer. "Like what?"

"Like ballistics. Armaments. Weapons. He doesn't expect those to have any use."

"From a mine ship? We don't have anything better than flare phasers! Oh—I heard myself say flare, didn't I?"

"Yes, you did."

"I'm a genius, aren't I?"

"Yes, you are. Doctor, you're in for a change of venue. You just became a weapons operative."

Chapter Twelve

Enterprise
Stardate 6877.1.
Speed: Warp factor nine point two four.
Course: Six one zero mark seven, zenith plus.
Leaving the Sagittarius Star Cluster.

"BACK IN SPACE, Spock. It feels good. Without all the baggage . . . no bale cubic cargo space to worry about, no passenger disputes, no arbitrations clauses, no stowage diagrams, boom capacity or obstruction dimensions, no civilians . . . just our crew, our ship . . . and space."

"Yes, Captain."

Cued by the strained voice that answered him, Jim Kirk looked to his right. Certainly concern showed in his face, but Spock didn't look back, in fact had barely paid attention as his captain mused aloud.

Good to be out in space, yes, but off kilter. Kirk tried to fool himself into feeling comfortable. He couldn't do it. Other than space and the ship, things were out of whack. Of the bridge contingent he depended upon so much, only Sulu was here with them, at his helm. McCoy was still back at Belle Terre, missing in action. So was Uhura. Both were now gaping holes in his command fabric, and a concern that he had to actively force from his mind once a quick search had failed to turn them up. Chekov had been reassigned to another ship, now as first officer. Scotty too was still back on Belle Terre, furiously working to build some kind of useful planetary fleet of utility ships from the gaggle of burned-out hulks left.

And just a few steps away was Spock, by far the hero responsible for the mind-boggling calculations and split-second maneuvers that brought the two moons together and that stopped the Kauld laser and their siliconic gel sabotage. He didn't look like a man resting upon laurels, or even particularly remembering them. Spock was here, yes, but not here too.

Holding her much-reduced family in the petal of her cupped hand, the starship that had protected them for years, extrinsic proof of their high-priced wins, streaked through space pretending there wasn't a strain on her bones at this speed. *Enterprise* gracefully turned her shoulder to the insult, proving herself once more not just a jumper but a workhorse.

Warp nine. A fiendish accomplishment, still barely possible, corrosive to the core, technology gone back to barbarism. The sheer velocity might shake them apart at any moment, without warning.

"Tell me what we're passing through, Spock," Kirk spoke up to break the mechanical bridge noises as the ship strained onward. "Be certain we're charting as we go."

Even Spock seemed to have faltered into the dangerous lull. He actually flinched and glanced at Kirk before steadying to his sensor. The colored lights played on his face from within the readout hood, and plucked at the charcoal helmet of his hair.

"This sector has twenty percent fewer stars generally than other segments of the galaxy," he reported. "However, I read many other elements of clutter. Free-roaming planets, active local attractions, large gaps in the interstellar void . . . the Sagittarius Cluster is therefore unusual. It will provide much exploration of interest for the Starfleet contingent stationed here."

Strange—though Spock could utter those hopes and anticipations, a strong hint came through that he wasn't really wishing to explore this area himself. He was unenchanted by the great unknown on the forward screen, and the tiny beacon from the 'bot they were following as it raced into the reaches. The Sagittarius Cluster was behind them now, the distance stretching out like an elastic string with every second that passed, yet the Vulcan's mind was still back there, still on the missing olivium and these robots who were taking it away, now leading them out into uncharted space at speeds to spin the mind.

Taking *some* of it away. The biggest portion was being reintegrated into the Quake Moon. Why? What interest did machines have in redepositing ejecta? There had to be a reason. Machines didn't do irrational things.

And when they were finished restocking the Quake Moon . . . then what?

Certainly not just let it explode again. Machines weren't that inefficient. Something else was going on.

Shifting in his command chair, Kirk felt out of place for the first time in years. Probably all the missing faces. Oh, the posts were manned, but that wasn't the same. He'd been spoiled by the loyalty of his primary crew, and was now crippled by their absence. Very bad.

This was one of those situations that military structure struggled to avoid—people getting too close to each other, so personally bonded that they couldn't function apart. As his fame had increased and the legend had kept their names together like Robin Hood's men, he had let himself wallow in his privilege. Most captains didn't keep the same people around them for decades, or even a few years. Fame had awarded him that. He and his merry band were an asset to Starfleet when they were together, not apart. Starfleet had never enacted its commonsense right to reassign.

He wanted to fall back on formality, but something told him that wouldn't fix the sense of urgent wrongness. He wanted to be having this conversation aloud, voice these thoughts and listen to the feedback he could count on, get peppered by McCoy and anchored by Spock, huffed at by Scott, beamed at by Chekov, scolded and worshiped at the same time by Uhura's wordless regard. But if he spoke, he would just make Spock feel worse.

Kirk suspected sabotage from within. The Vulcan disciplines made Spock far more passionate about things that really mattered to him, even more passionate than a human might be. When they embraced dispassion, they did so passionately. No other race had developed the Vulcan ways, probably because they didn't have it in them. Every race found its way to survive. Vulcans physiologically had it in them to repress emotion, but Spock wasn't physiologically pure. Just because he didn't display emotions didn't mean the emotional stress wasn't working on him from the inside out.

Being Vulcan meant his body could redirect energies to focus on particular needs, powered by the great muscle of the Vulcan mind. But Vulcans as a race hadn't been good at handling emergencies of passion or need. They had learned to control and manage their planet so there wouldn't be any crises. When one came up, they generally failed, lost, suffered.

That was why the Federation had been so good for the Vulcans. They could ask for help. They made friends with people who could change a way of thinking in an instant, and knew what to do with passion when it hit. The Vulcans hadn't done much in a hundred years or so before they met the humans. Together, the two had become the conglomerate that opened up the whole galaxy to cooperation, trade, expansion, exploration, and a rule of law. Spock was a microcosm of all that, a human-Vulcan hybrid, a little at odds with himself, somehow better than the sum of his parts.

But Kirk knew something else. He knew that, in fact, Spock's passion was unmatched. Humans would eventually reach a point where they would say, "I've done all I can." Spock would never say that to himself. He would not accept fallibility. He would continue to say, "I have not done enough." He might grasp his cause so unremittingly that he would destroy himself with his passions. Kirk was worried for him.

"Are we gaining on the 'bot?"

"Maintaining, presently. We've lost track of the second one. It pulled ahead."

"Mr. Sulu?"

At the helm, Sulu came to life. "Confirmed, sir. I've still got a fix on the one, for now."

"Engineering?"

At the console on the upper port deck, Senior Engineer Pro-Tem Johnny Herne reported, "Exceeding sixteen hundred cochranes. Crossfeed's failing on four matter reactant injectors. We're losing noticeable flux resolution and there's some failure in the coolant loops on the subspace field distortion amplifiers."

"How much?"

"Fifty millicochranes. Levels are topped off on three of the four field generators. Shield integrity is compromised, sensor focus reduced, and we're redlined on all warp systems."

Kirk's whole body seemed to sink an inch. "So everything's fine, then?"

Sulu managed a tentative smile that failed to hide his fears. "Good thing Scotty's not here."

"I'm sure he's getting psychic vibrations."

A few smiles. Not much else. Nobody wanted to blow up. Everybody knew they might.

He pushed out of his chair and circled the lower bridge, slowly, memorizing the people here. At communications, Ensign Wilma Boisjoley had been Uhura's apprentice for about a year. She could do the job. But she wasn't family. Kirk realized he was spoiled, and tried to fight it.

At engineering, Lieutenant Johnny Herne had been personally assigned by Montgomery Scott. Kirk already didn't like him much, but that didn't matter. Herne was barely a lieutenant, and had barely made the promotion. Everything he did seemed to be on an edge. His appearance was just barely inside regulations. Distractions of any sort were generally discouraged, along with blatant displays of personal attitude, but with so many aliens now joining Starfleet, demands for conformity among the humans and humanoids had taken some hits. Still, the uniform was not a bumper sticker. Military convention served a specific purpose and did its job very well. Compliance was important, sometimes critical.

Herne was human—or was he? Kirk *thought* he was. Then again, who could tell anymore?

"Captain!" Sulu called, "The thing's slowing down! It's turning, sir!"

"Match course and speed, Mr. Sulu."

"Aye, sir, matching course and speed. Warp four . . . three . . ."

Spock bent over his sensors. "Heading toward a small nebula. Sensors are reading several spatial bodies . . . large comets, asteroids, planetoids . . . no stars. Possibly some kind of gravitational force holding the bodies nearby."

"I see it." Kirk pushed out of his chair and went around the side of the helm to watch the nebula racing toward them on the forward screen. "Minimum magnification."

"Minimum mag, sir. Warp one, sir. Dropping to sublight."

The nebula, a gleaming aqua bubble, oblong with jagged spokes of gas and a red ring, shifted to a smaller size but still dominated the screen. Only sensors could see the little nut of trouble leading them in.

"Captain, the probe is circling us," Spock warned, speaking quickly.

"Turbulence, sir! Isopiestic flow's compromised!"

Sulu's call of warning provided none. Before anyone could react, the *Enterprise* lurched more violently than she would've under a full disruptor attack, and she kept lurching—upward, then farther upward, as if suddenly climbing a steep incline.

"Sir, we're losing our inertial damping," Herne warned. "SIF's breaking up. IDF failure in twenty seconds if we don't break this!"

Kirk held on to the helm. "Ride it, Sulu, do a loop if you have to!"

Like a biplane screaming into a hammerhead stall, the ship seized raw space and heaved straight upward, gravitational system screaming to keep control, keep them on their feet instead of on their heads. Had the 'bot circled and finally attacked? Had it pushed them up this way or fired something at them?

He didn't badger the crew. If they knew anything, they'd speak up.

The ship wailed so loud it hurt his ears. Suddenly the whine dropped to a horrid clatter and knock with a tympanum beat—*bom bom bom bom bom bom bom*—

"Graviton polarity's losing grip, Captain," Herne added to his previous warnings. He had the same tone Scotty usually had at times like this.

"We're inside the nebula, sir!" Spock called above the thrum.

"Shields up!"

"The grid came up automatically, sir," Sulu told him.

"That means energy," Kirk decided, choking out his words as he held tight to the helm. "We're reading something, even if we can't get a grip on—"

He hit the deck on both knees when the ship abruptly stopped climbing and twisted into a lateral spin—an amazing stress for a starship, a move she was never meant to make. If only the struts held.

Literally thrown back onto his feet and pressed into the rail behind him, Kirk felt the force change a third time when finally Sulu got control over it, or the power that had kicked the ship let go, or both.

As Kirk hung on the rail like an ape, Spock was just getting back to his feet from some other ungainly position.

"Heavy damage," the science officer reported, his complexion flushed olive. "Mostly stress points . . . the space-frame . . . reading multiple sites of collateral damage."

"Some engine compromise on the warps," Herne reported.

Kirk glanced at him and nodded. Herne seemed to know the job well enough. "Keep on top of it," he said unnecessarily, then turned to Spock. "Did it hit us?"

"Unknown." Spock straightened and looked at the main screen. "There it is."

They all turned to the forward vista just in time to see the 'bot cull out a single brown planetoid and curve toward it. Once its trajectory straightened out, the 'bot increased speed for an instant, and plowed straight into the planetoid, to be swallowed by the brown crust like a knife into frosting.

"Spock! Did you see that?"

"A force moving at that speed should have broken the planetoid into quarters!" Spock said, clearly very surprised and without the will to hide it.

"Get readings on any changes," Kirk ordered, hoping to keep him busy, "anything at all, no matter how nominal. Sulu, get us around the other side of the planetoid, minimum safe distance!"

The ship howled again with the strain they now put upon it themselves, and scored itself a path around the planetoid to the other side.

"Captain, there's no sign of the 'bot!" Sulu snapped, frustrated, even angry. "How's that possible? At twenty thousand miles per second, it should've come out almost instantly!"

"All stop. Hold position. Well, damn . . . get me some damage reports. I want to know what it did to us."

Everyone else sank back to his work, to comply with the comforting order.

The planetoid hung in front of them, turning lazily and winking its glossy mountain range in the light of a far-off star.

And over there, not so far off, Spock had gone strangely silent. In fact, he was simply sitting now, in front of his quickly changing graphics and readings, one hand on the controls but not pushing any. He seemed hypnotized.

With both hands on the rail to keep himself from poking the Vulcan in the arm, Kirk asked, "Spock? Something we should know? Something inside the planetoid?"

For a long moment, Spock said nothing, but simply shook his head, slowly.

"Captain . . ."

"Yes?"

"Captain, I believe . . . these probes may be interdimensional."

A punch in the gut. Interdimensionality opened up a very smelly can of worms.

"Based on what?" Kirk asked.

"Something I . . . missed before."

The self-deprecation in Spock's voice was touching, even a little scary. Kirk came around the rail and climbed to the upper deck and into Spock's periphery.

"It's all right," he mentioned quietly. "Go ahead. Tell me."

Spock didn't meet his eyes. "They appear to travel with no thrust."

Such a simple thing, so obvious. So completely impossible.

"What tipped you off now?" Kirk asked. Despite drilling the humiliation in a little farther, he had to know.

"When the probe struck the planetoid, there was no ejecta. No solid matter thrown out in compensation to the impact. I should've seen this sooner."

"If they're slipping between dimensions," Kirk urged on, "might be why they don't need any defense or offense, why we can't hurt them or stop them. They just ignore us. We've seen that kind of thing before. If they can phase in and out of dimension at key moments, we might as well hit a warbird with a pillow."

"Yes. And it seems, based upon this, that the probes themselves have similar properties to the quantum olivium itself."

Suddenly interested in a whole new way, Kirk leaned back on the edge of the console and pressed the heels of his hand to the bumper. "That," he congratulated, "makes a hell of a lot of sense. What properties?"

"Subtle shifts in mass. Other traits that would normally lead us to believe our instruments were faulty, were we not now wiling to accept these types of readings. I could go into detail—"

Kirk raised a quick hand. "I'll trust you. The same traits as olivium . . ." He pushed off the rail and paced aft on the upper bridge, then found himself staring at Uhura's chair with somebody else in it.

Suddenly he was thinking about McCoy too. And now, therefore, Spock again. He felt like cracked glass.

"Spock," he said, pivoting quickly, "they've been taking olivium, they have similar physical traits to olivium, they change mass and shift interdimensionally—" He cut himself off and listened to the clatter of information jockey around in his head while Spock simply watched him, frowning unhappily. "But they don't completely leave this dimension, or they wouldn't have to travel in space at all, would they?"

Spock clearly hadn't added that up, and virtually exclaimed, "Yes, of course!"

"And they didn't pick on us until the Quake Moon exploded. The olivium must've been there a long time before that, correct?"

"Yes, quite correct."

"So the explosion might have triggered some kind of—of sympathetic protocol and set them into motion. It summoned them from somewhere!"

Feeling himself zero in on a target, Kirk held out a fierce finger in Spock's face. "And they have to keep a hook or a hair or some piece in this dimension in order to stay in it."

"Although I've made no concrete correlation," Spock threw in, "I suspect this interdimensionality may be why Gamma Night has no effect on the probes."

Kirk eyed the planet, feeling like a shark stalking an eel in its hole. "Can we . . . how can we force it to reveal itself in this dimension? Can we hold it here somehow? Magnetism? Ionization? Antimatter?"

"Antimatter has some properties of interdimensionality," Spock agreed. "I have been toying with a hypothesis, although I was . . . uncomfortable about revealing it. When antimatter comes in contact with any appreciable quantity of matter under uncontrolled conditions, there is a disrupting. Perhaps we can disrupt the probe's quantum flux."

"No time like the present," Kirk encouraged. "Assuming this isn't its destination, and that it can't just disappear or it would've by now, maybe we can give it a pinch, tease the eel out of his crevice."

"Is that your decision, then, sir?" Spock took refuge from his own experience with insecurity by falling back upon protocol.

Kirk, however, wasn't ready yet to crawl back into the book. He dropped, almost jauntily, to the lower deck and slid into his chair. At last, something to *do!*

"It's always handy to keep a box of antimatter in your cupboard. Let's do it."

Spock stood up immediately and faced the port side. "Mr. Herne, we will be boring a fissure down several miles, then beaming a capsule of ionized antimatter in a plasma state into the cusp of the fissure. As it cools, which will be nearly instantaneously, it may react with the probe and interfere with its quantum flux." Having given his instruction, he looked now at Kirk. "It may work, it may destroy the probe, it may have no effect at all—"

"But everything else we've done hasn't had an effect," Kirk said. "When everything else you've tried doesn't work, you try hitting the thing with a hammer."

"This isn't that far above magic," Herne contributed.

"I'll settle for magic," Kirk said, suddenly enthusiastic. "Mr. Sulu, set phasers and fire at will."

The planetoid didn't just explode. It instantly crumbled into a hundred trillion individual pieces the size of softballs and blew outward in a fireworks shape, perfectly spherical, and perfectly demolished, almost making a *pooff* sound in their minds.

On the upper deck, Johnny Herne dropped his Señor Cool act and shouted, "Mother! Wow!"

Well, how often did you see a planet turn into a puffball right in front of you?

"There it is!" Sulu cried.

Sure enough, the 'bot's tiny form burst out of the center of the puff and split for the reaches. With a flash of propulsionless acceleration, it was suddenly gone.

"Going to warp again, sir!" Sulu scowled into his sensors. "Warp three . . . five . . . eight . . . leveling off at warp nine!" He peered over his shoulder at Kirk. "Should we turn back, sir?"

Plainly, he didn't want to. If Kirk could count on anybody *not* to turn back, that person was Sulu.

"Let's have those damage reports."

Engineer Herne made no acknowledgments, but simply reached across the gap between his station and the captain's chair and handed Kirk an engineering padd.

The bridge stood silent all around as the captain studied the information flowing from control teams dotted throughout the starship. Analyses, readings, measurements, stress limits, quick assessments, best guesses. Despite the captain's empty feeling here on the bridge, the rest of the crew seemed to be handling themselves like the clockwork they were reputed to be.

He handed the padd back to Herne. "Full ahead, Mr. Sulu. Reestablish warp factor nine."

"Aye aye, Captain." The jubilance in Sulu's voice was sharply offset by the bridge-wide understanding that they'd almost been wrecked here and now.

At the rail, Herne scanned the padd himself, unspoken opinions flashing across his face. "A burst of speed is one thing," he finally said. "Warp nine sustained, well—" He interrupted himself with a shake of his head.

Kirk ignored the unrequested comments. When he turned to face the main screen and wait out their problem, Spock was down here at his side.

"Any ideas, Spock?" Kirk asked quietly. "Can we keep up?"

"I do not believe so," Spock admitted. "However, the *Enterprise* has risen above tolerance at your call in the past."

Flattered, Kirk gazed at him. "That's quite a thing for you to say. I appreciate it."

"I never deny the facts." But Spock's expression softened noticeably.

"Mr. Sulu, return us to warp nine again. All systems comply. Shut down all the unnecessary systems taxing the warp core."

"Aye aye, sir."

"Aye, sir," Herne complained.

Spock stepped closer. "Captain, there is a possibility . . . what if these probes are intergalactic?"

"I guess we won't arrive for two thousand years."

For a moment Spock seemed unable to decide whether that was a joke or just a manifestation of Kirk's sheer will. Kirk eyed him with empathy.

"You're worried about the planet, the olivium," Kirk proposed. "I wasn't admitting to myself that my mind's back there too. But—no point worrying. After all, we've been gone for weeks. There probably won't even be a colony when we get back."

"You're concerned about Captain Lake?"

"Lake? No . . . not him. Not directly. It's Keller who worries me."

"I don't understand, sir."

"We've just left sixty-four thousand Federation citizens and the technological key to the future in the hands of a man who was rushed from second officer to first, and is suddenly the de facto captain of the only fighting ship there. He's not even a full commander yet. And that ship's a ragged mess."

Spock offered a decidedly emotional expression of solace. "You can't be two places at once, Jim."

"I know, I know . . . and I need you here with me. A man in Roger Lake's state of mind, he'll erase himself from the equation soon enough. Just how much damage he might do before that happens, Spock, I wish I knew. All my instincts tell me something's about to crack at Belle Terre."

He paused. His elbow pressed into the leather nap of the chair's arm. With that hand he rubbed his jaw and clung to his sense of physical form, willing luck and hope back through space to those who needed it most.

"When it happens," he added, "I'm afraid Nick Keller's in for the rocket ride of his life."

Peleliu
In orbit at Belle Terre

The whole ship pounded and throbbed. Or was it just his head?

And his feet. In search of a second wind, Keller ran down the corridor on deck three, the thin padded carpeting providing a dutiful bounce to each stride.

"When did it start?"

"About half an hour ago." Tim McAddis ran at his side. "I heard it start just as I went off watch. What a clatter! Sounded like somebody was peeling bulkheads!"

"You didn't call security?"

"And what? Open fire? Nothing else can stop it."

"Probably not even that."

"You better deal with it yourself."

"Stay behind me." With a cautious hand extended, Keller dropped to a quick stride as they rounded the circular corridor to the occupied quarters. Many of the bunk decks had been shut down because of damage. Only half of this deck had been cleared for use, and all crew quarters were tripled and quadrupled. Guests were doubled. Unfortunately.

He led McAddis forward. Slower now, they came around the bend in the deckscape. They passed two unremarkable quarters before spying the incredible result of what McAddis had heard.

They spotted the third door. Keller wished he were armed. But in orbit?

The blue panel of the third door actually jutted out into the corridor now, its twisted verilux layers peeled one by one into jagged spines and pressed in every direction.

"My God," McAddis gasped. "Look at the door—"

"Simmer down." Keller pressed him back and made

him stay still. The door had a gaping hole where the seal should have been. The panel had been kicked in, then pried back out until an opening appeared.

Kicked in? Bonded verilux sheets?

The quarters inside were dark, lit only by the light from the corridor. As if putting his head into a guillotine, he peeked inside.

"Savannah?"

"Come on in."

She was alive, at least, and conscious. No sound of panic or stress. Fortified, he ducked through the bent door.

Inside he found himself nose-up to Savannah Ring's belt buckle. The rest of her was hanging upside down from a pair of gravity boots attached to the ceiling brace, elbows against her sides, arms folded across her chest. Her cheeks were flushed, dark chestnut hair hanging, but she seemed otherwise alive and well.

To Keller's left, just inside her handiwork, stood Zoa. The Rassua's legs were braced, a stance oddly familiar now, her hands hidden behind her back, gold face strict. She eyed him but said nothing. She simply stood before the bulkhead, claiming her space. There was no sign of anger, no sweat, scratches or blood, nor even a sliver of the demolished door to testify against her. She protested not at all.

Both women's possessions cluttered the quarters, one bunk area with Savannah's beakers of wasps, molds, and fungi, the other bunk stacked with toothy devices that might be weapons of Zoa's preference. Keller *hoped* they were weapons.

To get down to Savannah's face, he lowered himself to one knee. "Mornin'."

"Sheriff."

"Zoa beat up the door?"

"Yes."

"Some temper. You say something about her mother?"

"I locked her out. I needed sleep."

The gravity boots hummed softly, their power system reenergizing automatically.

"She do this to you?" Keller asked.

"No." Savannah managed a shrug as she glanced at Zoa. "I sleep this way. It's good for circulation."

"Hanging like a bat?"

Her eyes shifted from Zoa to him. "What've you got against bats?"

With no way to argue, he pushed to his feet, straightened, and sighed. "Wednesday Addams grows up."

McAddis peeked in past the twisted door, but didn't interfere as Keller strode three steps over to Zoa. She didn't move, but followed him with her eyes, never blinking.

"You bend this door?" he asked.

"I bend."

"We're in orbit. You'll be debarking as soon as we clear customs and quarantine. Two days at most. Why can't you just be nice for two days?"

"She lock me out."

"Well, she shouldn't have, but this . . ." He held his hand out to the demolished panel.

Zoa's tattooed shoulders flexed very slightly, not quite a shrug. Her lined lips were silent.

"We can't have this." Keller's tone suggested he understood both sides. He didn't really. "Here's how it is with me. If you don't discipline yourself, then I'll discipline you. No explosions of temper allowed."

"Temper?" Zoa's braids swung as she snapped her dot-eyes to him. "I have no temper."

"You don't?"

"I am trained diplomat. Among my people I am

revered for being control." Her chin went up. "I am Vulcan-like."

Keller stepped back a half pace and regarded this problem as she stood before him. He didn't seem to have any effect on her.

"All right," he gruffed. "You wanted a job on board. You've got one. Unbend that door."

Leaving her there with her thoughts, if she had any, he stepped back out, trying to hide his eagerness to escape from the Hall of Dread.

McAddis was waiting with a sly look.

The crumpled door creaked a little under Keller's pressing fingers. "Ought to keep her busy for two days," he muttered.

"You're dreaming." Running his fingernails through his short blond hair, McAddis grimaced doubtfully. "Two days can be an eternity. You better find some spare quarters and separate those women."

Relieved now that he knew the port side hadn't fallen off, Keller hung a hand on McAddis's shoulder and slumped against the doorjamb. "Oh, I dunno, Tim. Something tells me those two belong together. In the same mausoleum."

"Bridge to Mr. Keller. Report immediately."

Leaving McAddis back at the bent doorway, Keller quick-paced to the nearest wall mount and hit the comm button. "Keller. You rang?"

Chan's voice was not in joke mode. *"Sir, we have yellow alert!"*

"You're kidding, in orbit?"

"Better get up here, Nick . . . please."

Yikes.

"Be right there." Keller sprang for the turbolift. "Tim, saddle up!"

* * *

Diane Carey

Nick Keller and Tim McAddis plunged out of the lift and onto the bridge, but found conditions relatively stable. At least, that was all they could see. The ship was moving, though, and it shouldn't be. On the main screen, which ordinarily would be showing a vista of space in the general direction they were heading now showed, as was usual during Gamma Night, only a clouded crackling gray mass that might be space or might be almost anything in it.

James Kirk had left them to hold the fort, and they were leaving the gates. In the command arena, Roger Lake was giving orders to Hurley and Makarios, who now glanced back at Keller, but dared do nothing more, nor even look again.

The blue-shadow form of Shucorion stood on the starboard side, watching McAddis's science boards with studious fascination and a worried expression. Whatever was going on, he didn't like it.

At Keller's side as he moved slightly to his right, Communications Officer Tracy Chan kept her voice just enough above a whisper to avoid flagging the captain's suspicious ears. "It's a distress signal from *Pandora's Box*. It came in just as Gamma Night was falling. They're on the other side of the sun. We're answering."

"During Gamma Night? We shouldn't be moving at all."

She submitted to Keller's whisper with a worried plea. "We can't even get a reading of the mining ship's position. The whole signal could be a misinterpretation."

"Or something else. Tracy, find out the last known location of the mine ship and its assignment. Tim, go, go."

McAddis stepped past him and beelined to the science station, where he set immediately to work, trying to hide a frantic edge.

To Chan, Keller murmured, "Does the colony know where we are? Did we file a flight plan?"

Her eyes full of worry, Chan simply pressed her lips tight and shook her head.

"Nick—good, you're here." Roger Lake came to life on the lower deck. "Come on down. I'll show you this. Look at the helm. We've got this Night thing whipped."

Keller dropped to the lower deck. "Sir, we shouldn't be moving at all."

Lake spread his hands. "Think I been sitting on my thumbs? I got this blackout thing figured out. I can plot the way over there without running into anything. Watch some of these tricks."

Without the slightest protocol, he butted Makarios out of the helm chair and slid in there himself. The captain at the helm? Then who would command? Would he try to do both? Under casual conditions, maybe. In a crisis—not a chance.

"Nick," Tracy Chan called quietly.

"Yes?"

"The mine ship's last known position was at the ice asteroid near the fifth planet. They were supposed to be there yesterday morning at last report. Nowhere near where we're headed."

"Understood. Hush, now." Thus armed, Keller came around and stepped down to the lower deck and spoke clearly. "Captain, the target area's not where the penitentiary ship's supposed to be. It might be a phantom call. Might not be *Pandora's Box* at all."

Could be a trap, could be a mistake, could be anything. Keller held his breath, hoping his captain hadn't crossed the desert too far to see even something so obvious.

For a moment, it seemed his words might be sinking in. Then Lake shook his head. "We'll go have a look anyway. Can't hurt and it might prove some things to some people. Jim Kirk's not the only one who can run a solar system. This is our chance to show him he's not the prettiest duck in the pond."

"What if there's something over there that hasn't been plotted? Like enemy ships?" Keller stepped closer. "Captain, somebody might be decoying us."

"Don't be paranoid. Not the Blood, the Kauld, nor anybody has a ship that can match us, even in the condition we're in."

"Captain, that isn't true. Tactics can outplay strength and you know it. We're not strong enough right now to be playing games."

"Our phaser banks are back to eighty-two percent. That means we outgun anything in this cluster. Our shields are up to eighty-five. Means we can take whatever anybody around here has to spit at us. Unless the Klingons are out here, we're all set. I've been working on this Gamma Night technique. I've been sending out mapping probes. We can do dead reckoning with the computer. Not plow into planets and asteroids. Within one system, it's not so tough."

"But ships—how can you see ships?"

"Can't. Doesn't matter. They'll stay away from us. We're the biggest kid in the yard."

Shut out, Keller stiffly climbed back to the upper deck where McAddis, tense and stiff-lipped, was waiting for him.

He couldn't quite look McAddis in the eye. Instead he turned to watch the unhelpful forward screen. "Kirk told me not to go out in the dark. He was warning me to stay home till the streets are safe. This is what he meant, Tim . . . Gamma Night."

And here they went, out into the dark, into somebody else's forest.

"I have a sudden urge to call Savannah up here," he complained. "Bet she speaks vampire."

Unable to muster a smile, McAddis could only shrug. He was scared. He deserved to be.

Were there any words of encouragement or hope a first officer should cough up at a time like this? The maneuver was risky, chivalrous only in name. If they could manage to get around the masked sun, how could they possibly track down one ship on the entire other side of the solar system? How could Lake even be sure of the integrity of the distress call?

Still, they hadn't signed onto a Starfleet ship to sit in the garage. Lake was justified in his decision, and carried the authority to render such judgments. No one had ever really made a regulation that clearly outlined the difference between hardy martial spirit and plain recklessness. Sometimes those were absolutely twins.

What was that buzz? The yellow alert notice? An underlying crackle accompanied every jangle of the constant background noise of the alert-status alarm. As he listened closer, then, he noticed that the secondary crackle wasn't quite keeping time with the alert. When it stopped for a moment, then picked up again, he started looking for it.

And found it on the deck, on the far side of the science trunks. A bosun in a spark smock and inhalant visor worked with a nozzle, a hose, and a sizable red canister plastered with warning labels. The hair— Keller knew that black ducktail anywhere.

"Bonifay! What're you doing on the bridge?"

"Sealing this crack." Zane Bonifay looked up through the visor, then pointed at an awful-looking gap between the deck carpet rim and the trunk housing. "Or would you rather fall through the deck?"

"What's this cannister?"

"Neutronium tripolymer coagulant foam. I love this stuff. Fills any gap. You just spray it in and it expands to fit. Dries instantly, hard as fused rhodinium. Don't touch!" He elbowed away Keller's venturing hand. "If it gets in your lungs, the ship'll have a new figurehead."

Keller backed off, but watched for a moment as Bonifay loaded the ominous crack with the bluish-gray foam sputtering from the nozzle he held. About the consistency of cake frosting, it had a texture like stucco as it fitted itself into the separated seam, then swelled and instantly hardened. Better living through chemicals.

"Lake's all wrapped up in this." Tim McAddis was watching the captain, there on the lower deck, eyes fixed on the main screen. "Maybe it's time to flip that coin, Nick."

"Now, don't start." But Keller pulled the commemorative from his pocket and spent a cleansing moment turning it in his fingers. "This is only for emergencies."

Zane Bonifay snapped to sudden interest, and bolted to his feet. He shoved the visor off his face and clicked the nozzle trigger off. "Hey, that's my shuttle coin!"

Keller's hand met him in the chest. "Back off, butch. The coin's mine. Tim gave it to me. Somebody I like way better than you."

"He stole it from me!"

McAddis scowled. "I *won* it. I out-slicked you for once. Fess up."

"You couldn't out-slick a five-year-old. You cheated."

"Oh, one ape saying the other one stinks."

"Keep it down," Keller warned. "Tim, how long till we get around the sun?"

"At one-tenth sublight . . . thirty-two minutes." Lowering his voice, McAddis leaned close. "Nick, you've got to influence him somehow. He'll get us killed yet."

Offering only a cautious and meagerly reassuring pat

on the arm as he turned to watch the ominous darkness on the forward screen, Keller grumbled, "I ignore, therefore I am."

In space before them, the sun Occult showed only as a gurgling gray field with a black background on the nearly blind sensors. Silently Keller cursed the faraway neutron star that bleached this whole sector with its shroud. That something so distant could affect their moment-to-moment safety suddenly irritated him. He wanted revenge. He wanted magical powers.

The bridge seemed to have too much clutter and activity for alert status. The presence of Bonifay, two other technicians, and a bosun's mate digging in the coals started to irritate Keller as he paced away from the science station toward the main screen, though careful not to block the non-view from Roger Lake's haunted eyes. As the ship felt its way clumsily across the solar system at a fraction of the speed she would indulge normally to cross such a space, he began to chafe with each movement, clatter, or utterance from the techs. This wasn't the time for repairs to be going on. Why didn't Lake shoo them off? Couldn't they see the yellow alert lights flashing? Couldn't they hear the constant beep of the warning sounds?

This ship's whole sense of discipline was falling apart. Roger Lake's carelessness had spiderwebbed throughout the whole crew. Things were happening that shouldn't. Order was compromised. Alert status didn't seem to mean much anymore.

His grumpy thoughts were confirmed when the turbolift opened and emitted Savannah Ring with a medical pouch. Behind her Zoa tramped out on her toenail sandals. Now what?

Keller stepped down to the lower deck and met them

by the helm. "What're you two doing here? I thought I left you hanging."

Savannah wagged a shoulder at Zoa. "Beats me what Hatshepsut's doing here. I'm here to give vaccinations. Part of the quarantine clearance."

"Not a good time. Why don't you go finish rushing the blood to your brain?"

"Because it's eleven hundred. 'Vaccines to be administrated one hour before each change of watch, allowing for a rest period'—out of my way, princess." She aimed her shoulder again, this time to butt Zoa back a step in order to use the helm as a table.

Zoa's eyes suddenly blew wide. Her arms flexed, shot over her head, hands clasped in a rocky knot that would've cracked Savannah's skull like a nut.

Just in time, Keller stuck out a warning arm. He never really touched the Rassua, delivering instead a clear warning. "Vulcan-like," he reminded.

With her own words to restrain her, Zoa thought twice and lowered her arms. Her anger immediately dissolved, but Keller got the feeling it hadn't strayed far.

"Savannah, off the bridge," he ordered.

She glanced at him, defiant, and continued to pull out vial after vial of hypospray. "I don't answer to you. I work for the Governor's Department of Health, remember? Haz-mat, search-and-rescue, preventative medicine—"

Pushing her back, almost into Zoa, he collected her vials and clattered them back into the pouch. "Don't come up here again during alert."

Unimpressed, she zipped up the pouch and gathered her hypos. "Okay, Sheriff. But you just delayed your planetary privileges by forty-eight additional hours."

"Off."

"Fine. I'll be in sickbay, wasting perfectly good time." She stalked aft, leaving Keller to face Zoa.

From under the rail as he sprayed sealant foam into the crack, Zane Bonifay mumbled, "Use it to brush your pet boar."

"Go retch, Bonifay."

How did they all end up here at once? Keller tipped his shoulder until he had Zoa's attention. "You too. Off the bridge."

She didn't flinch. "I have clearance. I come to watch."

True enough. The Federation Council had made an agreement with the Rassua, and Starfleet was obliged to comply.

He looked at Lake. Would the ship's master have an opinion? But the captain was completely involved with the helm and the forward screen. Attention to the muttering interactions going on around him apparently hadn't the slightest call.

Dismayed, Keller moved to the upper deck, to where McAddis nervously tended the dynoscanners. With a terse fold of his arms, Keller pressed back against the console's rolled edge and tried to stay calm. "Rassua," he grumbled. "It's got to be a bastardization of 'harass you.' "

"What do you think 'Zoa' means?"

With a little shake of his head, Keller dared a glance at the Rassua. "She's gonna cook and eat us."

McAddis cast the same glance at the lift door as it closed with Savannah inside. "Doesn't seem like Ring has much of a sense of humor either."

"She does," Keller said, "but you gotta catch it at the right moment. It's like one of those early Mars shots. You gotta wait for the window. Otherwise you crash and burn."

"Like a challenge?" The science board chirped and

worked as McAddis attended them, keeping his eyes downward now. "Here comes one."

Warned, Keller turned. He found Shucorion strolling toward him from the aft ramp, careful not to draw attention from the lower deck.

At Keller's knees, Bonifay found renewed interest in his work and pulled the visor back over his face. Beside him, the four-foot-tall tank burped and hissed. McAddis remained turned away, giving the other two men a chance at pretended privacy.

Accepting the gesture, Keller faced Shucorion squarely. "Mr. Advisor, got anything to say about this?"

Allowing their conversation to be shielded by the background ring of the constant soft whup-whup of the yellow-alert alarm—not as loud as red alert, but enough to talk under—Shucorion kept his voice low. "Most dangerous. Your crew does not yet possess the skills for this kind of attempt."

"We never had to develop them," McAddis reminded irritably, inflicting himself back into the picture. "Federation ships have constantly active sensors. We never learned to maneuver without them. We don't need to dead-reckon."

Not finished with Shucorion, Keller moved closer to the Blood visitor and pressed, "Did you suggest to our captain he could do this?"

The Blood leader seemed briefly surprised by the accusation. It took him a moment to respond. "Your captain is no fool. Clearly he attended my methods. Blood have spent generations learning to maneuver during the Blind. He did pay close attention. I never suggested—"

"Explain to me how you do it." Who cared if that sounded like an order? "Keep your voice down."

Across the lower bridge, Roger Lake's bloodshot eyes were fixed on the forward screen, while in his periphery he kept tabs on Hurley. Behind him, the confused Helmsman Makarios hovered near the command chair, without the foggiest idea of what to do. The wide main screen showed barely more than a few kilometers ahead of the ship until all of space blurred into a dark sheet. Beyond that, only the faintest glow showed where in fact the blaze of Occult should have nearly blinded them. They were circumnavigating a sun, and couldn't look at it or even read its presence.

Shucorion's voice hummed in Keller's ear like a conscience. "If you know your thrust and speed, and you know where you started, you can trust your measurements. The Blind isn't completely blinding once its signals are deciphered. Over many generations, Blood have learned to read . . . I believe you call them 'static.' As a blast engineer and Plume avedon, I've spent my life doing this. Reading space density, light shifts, the solar winds, things we can measure on the hull—for instance, temperature from nearby objects. If you know the magnitude of nearby stars, you can read the heat upon one side of your hull and judge proximity distance from them, adjusting your position with each changing degree. Also, radiation or spectral information from nebulae, clouds, and gas anomalies. Of course we must employ careful charting."

With his arms folded and one hand pressed to his lips as he listened, Keller gawked at him in admiration both unashamed and uncloaked. He pulled his hand away from his mouth after a moment. He leaned toward Shucorion and fanned his fingers to make his point completely clear.

"I'm a chimp," he proclaimed.

McAddis indulged in a nervous smile that quickly faded. "Sailors did that all the time at sea, Nick. Still do. They can see a gust of wind before it arrives. And the early submarines could move with strict, careful calculation of underwater charts."

"I just became an amoeba."

From the deck, Bonifay's voice was muffled inside his mask. "Go for blue-green algae. You're so close."

"If I want your opinion, I'll issue you one." To Shucorion, Keller quietly suggested, "Lake knows you do this kind of thing, but he might not realize you're better at it than we are."

"He does seem overly confident. Why is he not speaking to his crew? He drives the ship himself."

"That's something different. Tell me if there's specific danger here," Keller asked.

Reality showed in Shucorion's shaded eyes. "We are very close to this sun. Its radiation and heat will wash out everything else that might be read. Distance from the sun itself will be greatly distorted. Even if we succeed in going around it, you're unlikely to be able to find the ship you seek. The mission, then, is pointlessly hazardous."

From the deck, Zane Bonifay didn't turn to look at Captain Lake, but sent his message to Keller and the others. "He's trying to prove something."

Keller wanted to kick him. Still, he resisted and instead made a bet on Bonifay's intuition. "Prove what? Competence?"

"Wisdom. It's not the same. And he's not trying to prove it to us. He's proving it to himself."

Shucorion lowered his head slightly, and his voice even more. "And no one is more dangerous than a man who no longer believes in himself. I shall walk away now, slowly, thus he doesn't notice us speaking."

The incredible bald caution took the other men completely by surprise. To hear it said outright, flatly . . .

As quickly as that, like a curtain rising, Keller saw Lake for what he was—a man desperately clinging to the one thread of heroism remaining to him, in his own imagination. Lake had lost the confidence of his crew. They hadn't managed to hide it from him. He knew.

Oh, God, he knew.

"I just don't know what to do," Keller murmured. This was a bad dream, standing up here, with the captain down there, so close, yet paying them no attention at all, as if Roger Lake had retreated into single-man fighter and was making decisions only for himself and not for a crew of two hundred, and a colony of sixty-some thousand. Was it the Tavola methane kicking in? Only one out of eighty are affected . . .

How surreal it was to be standing up here, on the upper deck, talking about the captain in these low near-whispers, with him right down there. Ordinarily a captain was sensitized to every murmur going on around him on his bridge, but Lake had lost that completely. Either he no longer heard, or he just didn't care. Keller and McAddis could've kickboxed up here and the captain wouldn't have broken his mesmerization with the non-informative forward screen and the helm under his hands.

"But if I'm so wrong," Keller uttered softly, "why didn't Captain Kirk relieve him when he had the chance? You should've seen his face, Tim—he knew what was going on, but he left Lake in command. He must believe it's best for the Service and the ship, that an experienced captain is still the best bet."

"Maybe Kirk just didn't realize how erratic he's become."

"No . . . I'm the one who realized."

Fielding the idea that he wasn't getting his message across, McAddis squared off and tried again. "Listen, Hamlet, I don't know what's right. I only know he's making bad decisions fifty percent of the time. That means you, as first officer, become involved in either letting those decisions stand or challenging them. All I'm saying is, don't be afraid to do it your own way. See if it works. Don't do what somebody else told you or what the book says, or what so-and-so would do or what you learned someplace else. Look—"

With a casual turn, McAddis rearranged his stance to hook a hand on Keller's shoulder. Most of the time, that gesture was the other way around. Keller felt a little self-conscious. It was usually his hand doing the sage reassuring.

"I've served under a lot of captains," the science officer said. "I don't think one of them remembers what the heck he learned at the Academy. Most guys who go by the book are just trying to prove they've read it. We know you're new at this . . . the crew understands. Being a leader is mostly instinct. You know what they say—'Timidity isn't a plan of action.' Quit wondering what's the right thing to do, and do whatever you think might work. Flip that shuttle if you have to, but do *something*. A bad decision now is better than a good decision five minutes from now, if you're going to die in four minutes. Does that make any sense?"

Crouching on the deck again, Zane Bonifay simply gazed up at them, primarily watching Keller. He offered no opinions, but the one-man audience made Keller feel as if he were on an auction block instead of a ship's bridge. Yet somehow the advocacy of Tim McAddis and the rare silent regard of Bonifay did help him.

"Makes a lot, Tim," he awarded. "I really hate it."

With a forgiving shrug, McAddis smiled and clapped him on the back.

Keller turned the coin back and forth. "Let's see what this says."

"What's the question?" Bonifay asked.

Over there, at the helm, Roger Lake remained transfixed with maneuvering the ship. On the other side of the bridge, Shucorion watched the engineering and sensor banks, and oversaw Lake's movements every few seconds. Whether he approved or not, Keller couldn't tell.

"Don't know the question yet," he confessed, and flipped the coin.

He clapped it onto the shiny black surface of the science console. The three of them bent over the platinum dot.

Bonifay read, " 'It is decidedly so.' "

"Now your job's easy, Nick," McAddis said.

"Yes, of course it is. I think my feelings can best be demonstrated in dance."

"I'll kill you first."

"What's that!" At the nav station, sweating, Joe Hurley came to life. "Solar flare?"

Keller, McAddis, and Bonifay turned just in time to see the last gush of a reddish-orange streak running across the screen. As it faded into the cloak of Gamma Night, their suffering sensors picked up one crackle at the end of the streak. Then the screen went dark again.

"Weapon fire!" Captain Lake cried, abruptly angry and somehow thrilled at the same time.

Keller dropped to the lower deck. "Incoming?"

"No, lateral," Hurley said. "It wasn't aimed at us. There must be somebody else out there!"

Breaking everything from regulations to simple courtesy, Keller turned to Hurley and ordered, "Put the shields up right now, quick!"

At the helm, Roger Lake shot him a purely evil glare, as if Keller had betrayed him in a most horrible way, and on Lake's lips was the countermand. The shields as they came up instantly compromised the sensors under Lake's hands. He was now even more blind than he had been.

The only thing that stopped him was a sudden flashing light on his board—an alert. Sensor overload. He turned back to attend to it, and the shields stayed up.

Over Keller's shoulder, McAddis's breath took on a pant. "I can't pinpoint the source of the first shot. Definite phaser traces, though."

"Standard phasers? You're sure?"

"Absolutely."

Keller turned to Lake and very clearly said, "Then they're not Blood or Kauld, sir. They're Federation. It's got to be a warning shot."

Lake squinted at the screen. "Why would *Pandora's Box* be shooting across space?"

"It must be a warning shot, sir," he repeated. *That's why I put up the shields! Give Makarios back the helm. Do your own job.*

But neither his words nor his mental telepathy penetrated Lake's stubborn brain.

"Still no source reading," McAddis reported.

"Never mind the source," Keller suggested. "Scan where it was aimed. See anything?" On the upper row of monitors, the screen on his right was covering the area where the light had stopped running. In space, it shouldn't stop at all. He moved back to the rail, watching McAddis's struggling spectrograph. "Focus, focus, Tim—"

"I'm trying . . . There! Oh, my God!!"

A hard blast struck the ship and sent the controls screaming. Instantly, so close that the impact was almost uninterrupted, came a second hit, then a third. If the shields hadn't been up, they'd be space dust by now.

Uncomforted that his breach of protocol had saved their bacon, Keller swung around. "Kauld ships, Captain, mark three-eight! More than five of them!"

"Hell, we're almost on 'em! Security to the bridge!"

"Security? Why?" Rushing to the helm console, Keller bent into Lake's periphery. "Roger, why security?"

"Somebody set a trap for us!" The captain's face blanched. He braced his arms so hard on the helm that his elbows locked and bent in a strange direction. "I can't trust a damn soul! Which one of you set us up!"

Chapter Thirteen

THE SHIP TOOK a body blow and rocked toward her starboard shoulder. They'd been hit, blindsided. Nobody could misinterpret that.

Near the command chair, Makarios pitched all the way across the lower bridge to the port steps. The two engineers tumbled backward over the rail and landed in a tangle where Makarios had been standing a moment ago. Already on the starboard side, Zane Bonifay managed to catch the teetering cannister of sealant before it toppled and rolled into McAddis's legs. Near engineering, Shucorion had a grip on a strut to keep himself from falling. He'd been ready. He had to move aside as the turbolift opened and spewed two shocked security guards with helmets, chest shields, and two phasers each.

A few steps from where Keller clung to the rail, Zoa also pressed back on the rail, both hands gripping it, and watched the screen with passiveness that Keller decided must be a lie. He couldn't worry about her right now.

The turbulence didn't stop as it ordinarily should even in a battle. Instead they were hit again, and immediately again, as if the ship were vomiting out of control, unable to stop. Dread catapulted through the crew.

On the main screen and most of the auxiliary monitors and sensors could deliver only shadows and faint broken graphics of the enemy ships haunting the edge of the woods, appearing only in sketchy flashes from moment to moment, their brick-red hulls and lobster-clawed prows peeking like tigers in tall grass.

Because he had chosen to drive the ship instead of command it, Roger Lake forgot the most important order for such a time. Keller plunged forward and slapped his hand flat to the helm to get the captain's attention.

"Roger, let me give the order!"

"Nobody's stopping you."

"Red alert! Battle stations!"

The amber flashes of yellow alert turned to bright red and the whooping klaxon began to sound through the *Peleliu*'s corridors and arteries. Lighted panels went to scarlet. All over the ship, crewmen shifted positions, went to fighting mode, rearranged priorities. All hands on deck. Automatic mechanical systems also changed, shifting power flows to more internal routes, raising defensive grids around critical hardware, and the ship's shields popped on in full-battle readiness. Any Starfleet ship always had some nominal deflectors up to ward off space matter, but battle shields were something completely different. They siphoned tremendous power from the reserves and had to be used with discretion.

This was definitely the time. Instantly the cruiser, compromised though she was from the battles of short days ago, bristled to defend herself again.

"Threat vessels approaching on two sides and overhead, sir," Hurley squeaked, his throat in a knot. "I can't trust these readings."

Lake instantly added that up in his head and selected a course of action. "Port forward phasers, azimuth two-one, target twenty kilometers! Fire!"

Twenty kilometers. Was he right? Were they that close?

"Captain, there's damage to the drive coils," Engineer Lewiston reported, climbing back to his post. The other engineer was down on the deck, holding his knee.

"Raise the deuterium temp and flush it through," Lake said. "Then route it through to thruster power. Makarios, take your post, kid. Drive us out away from the sun, in case we lose power. Get as far out as you can. I don't want to fight the sun's gravity."

Good—he understood that he couldn't pilot and engage in strategic command at the same time. While jarring hits pummeled the ship from several directions, Lake barked orders and swung the vessel this way and that, taking shots that efficiently answered each hit, even though he couldn't see who was firing at them or with what.

Cranking on impulse drive, the tormented *Peleliu* heaved through bouts of agony. With every turn, her captain's voice cut through the alarms and bloodcurdling cracking noises and ruptured matrices quailing for attention.

"Captain, the shields are slipping!" Lewiston shouted. "I can't correct it! I can't stop it! Sixty percent . . . forty—"

"Stabilize the damn things," Lake snarled.

"Trying, sir!"

"Makarios, vector nine, hard starboard. Hurley, aim azimuth six-two-two and fire! Come about!"

That maneuver put their strongest remaining shields

in the direction of the shots. No matter his state of mind, Lake was a battle-savvy captain and he had guts. Nobody could deny that. This wasn't cowardice at work, but something completely else.

"Shields still dropping," Lewiston suffered. "Only ten percent now, sir, barely holding."

The crew did their best, but they'd lost confidence in him. Only the structure of orders and responses kept their actions flowing together, but Keller noticed they were faltering. With every order there was a critical moment of interruption before someone managed to follow it. They didn't believe in Lake anymore. They knew he'd gotten them into this. They knew the operative wisdom in this situation was to retreat, hide in the sensor darkness, confound the ambush by ducking it.

Lake wasn't retreating. In his feral savagery he was trying to fight, even with his sight masked and his arms bound behind his back. His actions demanded that the crew do the same. He'd lost his connection with wisdom, as Bonifay had suspected, and was trying to show it in a completely befouled manner.

Operational profiles—pictures of the innards of the ship, unaffected by the sensor darkness—suddenly went black. They were blind to whatever moved outside, but could no longer assess their own condition inside. Tactical and auditory feedback failed, causing alarms to go off all over the bridge, each board crying for help, assistance, power, attention, in fear for its life. The jangle was maddening.

"Torsion relief's failing in the main section!" McAddis called. "Phantoms are using some kind of solid ordnance, not just energy. We're getting hull plates pierced all over, and its taking out local systems."

Keller pulled himself to the rail under Shucorion. "What are those things hitting us?"

Shucorion held on tightly, one hand on the vestibule brace, and one on the engineering console's edge. "Javelins, propelled from launch shafts."

"Metal?"

"Yes. They're forged from ruined bridges on both our planets. A very simple type of weapon, though usually we use them only for defense, at close range, as a distracting device—"

A brain-twisting roar buried their communication. Through the side of the bridge, directly from space, bored a huge metal rod the diameter of a man's arm—a real metal rod, not just a spear of energy—leaving a hissing hole in its wake. The javelin plunged right across the bridge to the other side, where it buried its point and half its shank into the tripolymer transparent wafer, peeling it like fruit rind and exposing page edges of the embedded sensor matrix. Over that console, six of the subprocessor terminals exploded. The whole starboard side was swallowed in sparks and smoke, even open flame.

So much for Shucorion's bothering to describe the javelins.

The sheer impact drove Keller to the deck, onto his knees. Somehow he managed never to take his eyes off the horrifying presence of the javelin. Its blunt end wobbled with a metallic hum of dissipating energy.

A thump on the deck beside him almost knocked him over. Shucorion grasped Keller around the body and hoisted him to his feet. "I don't understand why Kauld would use javelins now," he called over the pounding noises and sparking. "This is a move of desperation. They clearly have advantage over us."

"All the crossfeeds are down," Tim McAddis called.

Leaving Shucorion behind, Keller forced his screaming back and shoulder muscles to propel him across to the science side. "All of them?"

"Every goddamn one of them."

"Yikes. Hold on." He turned again, this time to Lake, and spoke as forcefully as he knew how. "We need a power reallocation, Captain! I need clearance!"

"Given."

"RCS switch to manual, Tim."

"Switching. Thanks, Nick . . ."

Keller climbed to the upper deck and helped enable the switchover, he knew what McAddis meant. He'd managed to manipulate Lake just enough to get the right things done. He could shout the orders himself and by the time Lake countermanded him things might change, but the danger of that was almost immeasurable. To have two people barking commands—a perfect formula for disaster on a ship.

At his side, Bonifay made himself useful by turning the sealant foam to put out a fire where the javelin had sheared into the bridge's hidden conduits and exposed hot electrical circuitry.

"Nick!"

The turbolift had opened. A gout of smoke puffed from its maw, carrying with it the ravaged, burned, and limping Savannah Ring.

"Aw!" Keller bellowed his frustration and crossed in time to catch her as she collapsed. "What happened? Where were you?"

"Sickbay—" she wheezed. "I was—I was—just—walking out—sickbay got hit—Harrison—Harrison's dead. . . ."

The ship's only doctor. Sickbay obliterated?

"What about the others?" Keller demanded. "Nurse Mikolay? The interns?"

Savannah tried to speak, but her raw throat closed and she gagged, crumpling in his arms. Her lips moved soundlessly. Her eyes, though, were shock-clear, and told the rest.

Sickbay smashed. All the medical personnel dead.

"Decks four and five—" she gagged, "ripped almost completely out! We've got—to retreat!" The words gulped from her gullet. Her fingernails dug into his arm.

Lewiston hammered his controls, but from his expression all could see he was having no effect. "We're experiencing almost total hardware and software collapse, Captain!"

"We've got to move off!" Hurley cried from where he clung to the nav station. His chair had been reduced to a pile of splinters beside him, crushed by the javelin.

Like a magnetic field Hurley's words attracted the caustic poisoned glare of their captain. Lake's voice was guttural and burned. "Don't give orders, Hurley! I knew you were against me!"

On the upper deck, Keller pulled Savannah to her knees, hoping the position would help her breathe, but she wasn't looking for comfort. Pushing aside his attending hand, she all but struck him.

"For God's sake, Nick," she choked, "take over."

He shook his head. "I can't take over unless the captain's out of commission."

The rest of the argument took place only in Savannah Ring's eyes.

Infused by the crashing of the universe around him, he pushed to his feet and promised her with a glance that he would try to change what was happening.

He jumped over the wreckage now cluttering the steps and came around in front of the helm.

"Roger, we can't keep this up!" he shouted. "We can sink back into Gamma Night and let it protect us! They won't be able to track us if we stop firing! You're leading them to us with our own weapons fire!"

*"WARNING WARNING WARNING BRIDGE ENVI-
RONMENTAL SYSTEMS ON FULL RESERVE WARN-
ING WARNING"*

"Shut that off!" Lake snarled. He twisted his hands
into Hurley's uniform and pulled the navigator to him.
"You're trying to commit suicide, aren't you? Go out in
a blaze of glory? I won't let you do it. I'm your captain! I'll protect you from yourselves!" He threw Hurley to one side and turned on the rest of the bridge
personnel. "Everybody, hands off the controls! Hands
off! I'm taking over! Me and Nick'll do it."

"Roger," Keller bellowed, "the crew!"

"Chan, get away from communications. Get up there
and handle environmental."

Baffled, Chan stumbled up the ladder, to take a useless post. What was the captain thinking?

Lake heard the coming protest before Keller could
speak it. "Security, turn your phaser on any crewman
who refuses to give up his controls. Shoot down the
next bastard who puts his hand on a grid!"

The two security guards stepped forward out of the
lift vestibule, phasers drawn—as crazy as that order was,
they were trained to follow it. They knew, had it drilled
into them, that a million unexpected things might happen in space and the scaffold of rank orders would save
lives and fulfill missions. Do as ordered. Don't question.
There are things you might not know. The questions
happen at some other level, not yours. Keller hoped they
would hesitate, but knew better than to expect them to.

At this horrid moment a third javelin slammed
through the bridge dome from almost directly above
the helm. With a huge exaggerated *twang* it drove
downward. Makarios was instantly and obviously
killed. The javelin also raked Hurley's left thigh, but
missed killing him by millimeters. It also provided the

ironic favor of yanking Hurley out of Lake's grip and flinging him behind Keller.

Lake started forward, toward Hurley. He was still fixed on blaming somebody for this.

This time Keller stepped directly into the captain's path and with a firm hand shoved him back toward the singing shaft of the newest javelin. "Stay away from him, Roger."

Pausing, Lake held out his sweaty hands. "Nick . . . not you too. I knew they were all getting sick. I didn't think you'd catch it."

Keller locked his legs. Behind him, despite her own injuries, Savannah dragged herself down to Hurley and pressed the heel of her hand to the gash in his thigh, trying to stop the artery from bleeding him to death. Hurley's gasps of pain were as forbidding as the hissing punctures left in the ship's body by the javelins.

As Keller watched the captain's face, something changed. An appalling and gruesome alteration happened in the red-ringed eyes and perspiration-sheeted face. To watch it made Keller's stomach drop.

"Guards," Lake began, "if Mr. Keller takes one more step, stun him."

Despite the battle going on around them and the ringing blows of enemy fire, Nick Keller and Roger Lake might as well have been on a lonely moon, by themselves, as the captain uttered a new vow in his deformed idea of gallantry.

"I'll protect you too, Nick, if I have to."

Security would back him up. He was the captain. They didn't know the truth, the secret.

Whatever might have happened next, no one would know. The gods descended from above and interfered. A sonorous cracking noise busted through the tension and installed pure terror in its place.

CHALLENGER

Every face turned upward, to the cries of the bridge dome overhead.

As they watched, helpless, the bridge dome physically shuddered. A fissure appeared diagonally across the hood, first just a hair, then finger-width. Then its lips began to part into a ghastly smile. In the manner of a continent separating at a fault line, the two sides of the bridge dome began to move apart like tectonic plates. A vortex of atmosphere spiraled into the crack and raced for open space, whistling like demons.

Over their heads, the bridge dome fractured. The saucer section of the Cruiser *Peleliu* began to split down the middle like a broken cookie.

CHAPTER 14

Chapter Fourteen

UP ON THE SCI-DECK, mere inches from the dome, Tracy Chan screamed as she was lifted from her seat by the sudden suction of atmosphere fuming toward the finger-width crack in the bridge dome. Even though the gravitational compensators battled to hang on to each living body on the bridge, Chan was ninety pounds after a big meal. The crack just over her head, she soared like Peter Pan toward the overhead dome, struck the cracking sheeting with her tiny pointed shoulder, and the sheer force of the draw broke her body like ripe fruit. The dome opened its ragged lips and devoured her. She was gone—gone!

Keller bellowed in agony, fingers clawing upward. From above he felt the drag of open space, from below the draw of gravitons as the ship fought to keep hold of him. Savannah and Zane Bonifay were entangled in the rail struts and also had him by both legs.

The compensators shrieked. The ship wrestled with itself. Roger Lake held on to the command chair and stared up at the crack in complete horror. Above, the fissure grated its teeth and opened wide enough to see space, clear and black, and even a Kauld ship streaking by.

Torn data membranes and microfoamed sheeting from the destroyed panels splattered upward and raced out the fissure. In his periphery Keller caught a maddening view of Zoa's braids flapping as she too clasped the bridge rail and held on. The farther down they were, the better the ship's gravity system could hold them. New air whined into the bridge, desperately replacing the oxygen being sucked out in frosty streams. Opposite Keller, Shucorion had one arm linked through a handhold on the bulkhead, and the other around Rick Lewiston. Both their faces were distorted into grotesque masks, their hair fuming upward like flames.

Above, on the sci-deck, dangerously near the opening fissure in the dome, Tim McAddis let out a long howl—he was too close to the crack! The suction!

Keller tried to cry out, but his voice was stolen away. McAddis lost his grip on the sci-deck rail and slammed spine-first across the crack in the dome. Wider in the shoulders and bigger boned than Chan, McAddis slammed diagonally across the crack and blocked the widest part of the gap, his arms splayed out to his sides, his face twisted.

The whole bridge shook. Its two sides flexed independently from each other under Keller's feet—the deck was fracturing! In mere seconds, the compensators would lose their fight and all of them would be sucked out.

But Tim McAddis, pressed against the crack with his fingernails digging at the duranide, gave Keller precious seconds by blocking the suction. Twisting, Keller made a wild reach for the canister of sealant. His right hand failed, but his left closed around the hose. He dragged the huge tank to his chest and used its weight

Diane Carey

to stabilize himself against the two forces pulling on him from above and below. The nozzle fell into his hand, shaped like a phaser casing. He aimed it upward, fighting the swirl of air racing for space.

He looked up, but hesitated.

Pinned to the ceiling, McAddis screamed, "Do it! Do it! Doooo it!"

Seconds to live. The oxygen compensators would lose their battle any instant. The bridge would saw itself in half.

"Tim!" The nozzle in Keller's hand was actually cold. He aimed it.

McAddis screamed again. "Do it, Nick! Do it! Do it!"

Hearing his own name caused Keller's hand to close on the nozzle trigger. A narrow funnel of yeasty gray compound sprayed up at the dome structure. Each fleck swelled as it hit the ceiling, bonding until the long thin crack began to seal. Once begun, there was nothing to do but keep going, keep spraying the sealant up and down the crack, right over McAddis as he kept screaming, "Do it! Do—"

His last syllable was cut off suddenly. He sucked the chemical bond down his throat and into his lungs, where the glutinous mass swelled and hardened. Between his fingers and eyelashes, follicles and pores, the bonding agent welded McAddis to the closing crack as he gave his life to save his shipmates below. Astonished, they watched him die at Nick Keller's hands.

The suction from above wheezed and fell away. The gravity compensators gasped with relief, and turned loose of those who were left alive. When the sealant tank exhausted itself, Tim McAddis was encrusted into the silent dome overhead, the victim of a ritual smothering.

Palsied and shuddering, Keller dropped the tank and

228

staggered to the middle of the deck, turning in pathetic circles and staring upward.

"Tim!" he rasped. "Tim!"

Bits of chemical bond flecked his hands and face. He gasped upward, soulless, shuddering. His hands pressed to the sides of his head as if it might explode. "Tim! Tim!"

Roger Lake's form appeared in front of him, also turning and staring upward. "Mother of Christ," the captain uttered, his mouth moving like a gulping koi's. "Isn't that something . . ."

Lake had his back to Keller as he stared up at his entombed science officer. McAddis returned the stare, but his eyeballs were coated with curing stone.

Right in front of Keller was Lake's head, the poisoned organ that had caused all this. Emergency light flickered on the bald spot.

When Keller saw that flicker he stopped turning or calling out. As if sinking underwater, he held his breath and stared into the mirror of his mistakes, all the decisions he should've made a long time ago, and right up to today. Right up to now.

Where were his hands? He had no phaser, no blades, just empty hands.

He raised those hands. Something moved in his periphery. A movement. A solid object. A duranium cyclospanner. Zane Bonifay was holding the other end, inviting him to take it, to do something, anything.

Choose between a wrong and a wrong . . . Even a bad decision is better than no decision.

Reason left his mind, leaving only passion to rule him. He felt the balance of the wrenchlike tool is his grip. His arm drew back over his head. Power, thrust, rage all came together in the single force of his arm and shoulder. He put everything into the one strike, for he knew he could never make himself do this twice.

The spanner whistled faintly, but with purpose. The tool came down on Lake's head. Was it enough? Too much? Would the captain be killed or just angry?

Keller had no idea. He'd never hit another man before.

Before him, Lake didn't even flinch, didn't stiffen or react. His chin went up a little. That was all.

He collapsed and lay in a heap at Keller's feet.

Around them, the shocked crew stared at him, at his unconscionable act. The security guards turned their phasers on him in some kind of panic, but faltered in actually firing them. He expected to be shot. He should be.

But Zoa snatched up a piece of Hurley's smashed chair, tested the weight, didn't like it, flipped the piece over and let it fly. It pinwheeled perfectly over Keller's shoulder and struck one of the guards in the throat, slamming between his chest shield and helmet. The blunt force drove him backward and he fell.

His partner gaped at Zoa, then at Keller, and backed off. He was only eighteen.

In that instant, Keller realized the greatest error in his career, probably in his life—the reason James Kirk had come to haunt him in the corridors of *Peleliu*, and the thing Tim McAddis had tried to tell him. Keller had tried to manage a bad situation instead of leading it. Nothing could work that way on a ship.

Either be in command, or don't.

Around him, the eyes of his shipmates were sallow, injured. Yes, shocked at his behavior. The regard of Shucorion nearly crushed him. Another captain, from another culture. Zoa, representing a civilization the Federation needed to help defend itself. What was she thinking as she stood there judging these unforgivable actions? What were they all thinking?

He felt their repugnance, the intense discord he represented to them now. Estranged from people who had liked him before, he found the aloneness suddenly alluring. He couldn't do any worse in their eyes. No point caring now.

He picked up his legs, screwed them back on, and stepped over Lake, crossed the deck and grabbed Shucorion. He wheeled the alien all the way down the port steps to the helm, and pushed him into Makarios's chair.

"Drive the ship," he said. "Hard about, starboard, mark two-four."

Shucorion faltered only briefly. "About?"

"Turn us around to the right, down five degrees."

"The shots are coming from that direction."

"Never run from an animal once it's charging you. Bonifay, take damage control. Savannah, get on the science boards. Zoa, can you operate the firing systems?"

"Firing?"

"Can you *shoot?*"

Her masklike face lit up. Her heavy braids fell forward as she bent over the nav console and the weapons systems as she picked out words and symbols she recognized on the high resolution display membranes.

Suddenly calm, as if he were the one plastered and frozen, Keller scanned the master situation monitors and optical subprocessors on the engineering side. The ship was in deep trouble. Fuel constriction. Thermal overload. Thrust imbalance. Exhaust vane misalignment. It was an orchestration of disasters showing the harmonic collapse of ship's systems. What else could possibly go wrong? Amazing that they could still breathe, that they still had gravity.

"Initiators are firing out of phase," Bonifay called. "If you don't shut down, they'll rupture in less than fifty seconds."

"Valve off the deuterium flow. Prepare to shut down. Decouple the accelerators."

"Already done. We're on total emergency power supplies. Total."

Back at his ravaged station, Lewiston called, "Mr. Keller, if these readings are right, the excelinide sphere's cracked in the IRC chamber!"

"How many layers?"

"All eight."

"We're dead," Savannah wheezed.

Around them, the supercomplex integrated organism that was a Starfleet ship finally and irrevocably began to collapse. She was nearly dead. Speared, cracked, bleeding to death. Her arteries were cut. Her brains were smashed, her heart missing beats, and still the *Peleliu* forced air into the ducts, coughed coolant through her veins, to keep the gasping crew alive inside her. How was it possible? Keller could still breathe, still think, still move around. She was giving them air and gravity, the two things they needed most at the moment.

She was giving them a second chance. She didn't know what they could do with it, but she would hold on another few minutes. Time enough to think. Maybe act.

Act how? They couldn't see the enemy as anything more than hazy phantoms blowing about on the screens, and couldn't accurately tell where those phantoms were in relation to *Peleliu*. On the hull, random shots still thumped and shook, but they might as well have been hitting the carcass of a downed rhinoceros. What was left of the cruiser's shields took the brunt of impact. If those had been phasers or disruptors hitting them, the ship would've been a ball of dust by now. Only the Kauld's lack of modern technology provided a clouded window.

He began to focus his attention. Smaller and smaller thoughts, smaller targets, animal thinking. He looked into the face of the charging bull.

We're dead. We're dead. We're dead.

"No, we're not," Keller declared.

Something of a hollow assurance if he couldn't think of anything in the next couple of seconds.

James Kirk's words jerked him back to that corridor. *Use the tools you have.*

What do I have?

You have Shucorion.

Survived in the sensor darkness for years. Fought these same enemies for years—

Keller crossed the deck in a step and a half, startling Shucorion at the helm. Digging his fingers into the Blood man's shoulder, Keller demanded, "What am I forgetting?"

Though taken by surprise and pressed hard under Keller's unremitting grip, Shucorion recovered within a second or two.

"They are also blind," he said.

At first, the concept seemed too simple to be of any help.

Then it snapped into place.

"That's it!" Keller swung around. "Rick, let the field collapse. Give me overthrust, right now. Zane, go help him!"

Bonifay clumped down from the starboard side, leaped over Lake, and joined Lewiston on the port side. Around them lay the moaning, unconscious or dead bodies of their captain and shipmates. Drained of his humanity, Keller felt as if his arms and legs were separated from him. His mind went off on its own. His voice followed.

"Shut down everything but environmental, shields, and weapons. Give me photon torpedoes. Lay a pattern in a funnel shape. Zane, show Zoa how to lay a dispersal. I want automatic detonation at fifty kilometers."

Bonifay thunked to the lower deck, came around the helm, and poked the coordinates into the tactical board. Zoa nodded silently as she picked up exactly what he was doing and apparently understood. In less than five seconds she took over completely and Bonifay went back to the engineering boards to continue damage control.

The others didn't understand yet, but they would in a minute. If the Kauld were blind too, then they had to be close. Not space-distant close, but really close. Physically on top of each other—spittin' distance.

"Ready," Zoa announced.

"Fire," Keller ordered.

They heard the *phew-phew-phew* of photon torpedo launch, but saw almost nothing except a faint color change on the main screen and the two dynoscanners still working. He didn't have any way to know how many torpedoes had successfully launched. There were supposed to be seven in a funnel assault. He didn't think he heard that many.

Would the torpedoes detonate in space, or were the casings or controls damaged?

Ffffmmmmm—there it was. The *Peleliu* went up on her bow, then downward, and washed back in the photon wake. One thing worked.

"Mr. Keller," Shucorion called. "Kauld are breaking off!"

Keller rushed to his side to confirm what he saw on the helm's only working sensor outlet. "Why would they?"

"No idea."

"We couldn't have hit them all—" He divorced himself from what couldn't have happened and concentrated on the next action. "Turn us away. Move opposite to them. We'll hide in the night."

A single valiant scanner showed fuzzy streaks, constantly changing, as it tried to show the enemy ships spinning away into the cloak of Gamma Night, leaving the dying ship and her half-dead crew to float through the darkness. Leaving. For no good reason.

Why?

Overthrusting the impulse engines with minute amounts of antimatter in the IM reaction chamber had given them increased power when they needed it.

Keller counted off about two minutes of thrust, of moving into the sensor darkness.

"All stop," he ordered. "Shut down all systems but life-support. Lay silent."

They lay in near darkness, listening only to the ship's death rattle. A fritz, spark, snap of electrical arcing deep within the superstructure. Keller felt the color of emergency lights, faintly reflecting upon his bloodless cheeks, reflecting in his eyes.

The force of life drained out of him. He began the hurt of waiting.

Chapter Fifteen

Pandora's Box

"DO YOU THINK they're alive?"

"There's no way to tell."

Uhura didn't like her answer to Dr. McCoy's question. Something about the way the words fitted together, and the images they called up.

Many times in their lives, they had been on the inside of an attack, to feel the ship shudder and quake around them, the deck grow unstable and the power-loaded consoles explode.

"If we hadn't been here, no one would've known," she continued. What was that—a ray of hope? "You did a good job, getting all the way down to the array without any of the other criminals seeing you."

"They did see me. I just gave them all inoculations on the way down. They thought Billy ordered it as part of the Billy-takes-care-of-us milieu. Your timing was perfect. Not to mention your aim. Your guesses seem to be as fine-tuned as anybody else's hard data."

She smiled and stole a moment to put some of her hair back in place. "Let's hope they made good use of it."

McCoy's animated brows bobbed, not with particular confidence. "What in blazes is *Peleliu* doing on the other side of the sun in the middle of Gamma Night? Jim set up a defensive perimeter that would've warned them of Vellyngaith's approach! They couldn't pass gas in the Occult solar system without the planet smelling it, and for some reason *Peleliu* let itself be tempted out of the protective wedge!"

"Maidenshore broadcast a distress signal from this ship at Vellyngaith's position. Captain Lake fell for it."

"He must be a piece of work."

"Oh, now, that's not really fair, is it?"

"I don't even know him and I don't like him already."

The small screens on Uhura's heavily controlled console could only show them meager spectroscopy of the battle going on out there. Uhura had managed to tag the faint blurry readings of the *Peleliu* and also identify the blips of Kauld vessels from their peculiar exhaust, but only at certain distances. She could pick them up as they veered in past the mine ship to strike at the *Peleliu*, only to lose them as they veered out again. In the sensor darkness she had managed only to pick up certain elements of heat interruptions in the sun's radiation, a sun they also could barely see.

"He'll probably kill us now, you know." McCoy sat down on the little needlepointed antique bench, a new addition, a gift to Uhura from Billy. "I wish he'd get to it. Jim's gone, and there's nobody left on Belle Terre who could possibly break Billy's back. Sooner or later, it's—"

He stopped speaking abruptly as the door clacked its

magnetic lock and opened. Billy Maidenshore bumped in, his face flushed with anger.

The instant he got in the door and pinned Uhura with his electric glare, the fury in his face dropped as if he'd taken off a hat.

Amazing. Everything about him was fake.

"You lit our phaser, didn't you, hon?" he asked, swaggering the rest of the way in. "Laid into the back of one of Velly-Belly's ships. Tipped off the *Peleliu*."

Would he keep looking at her? Or would he notice McCoy sitting over there, and add up what had really happened? That McCoy was the one who could move about the ship, make it down to the defensive array, maybe arrange for a single shot before the inhibitors kicked in.

"Life's a game, Billy," Uhura said, determined to keep the attention on herself. "We're both just players."

Maidenshore approached her, then sat down on the edge of the bunk. Eerily he said nothing to the doctor, and did not even acknowledge his presence here. Instead he leaned forward with his hands on his knees and studied Uhura's face, her cocoa eyes, as if she were a piece of art in his collection.

"Pretty good," he lauded. "How'd you get out of here? You figure out my locking system?"

"Who are you kidding, Billy?" she said. "You know everything I can do is right here in this room."

"What about Hippocrates over there?"

"He's a doctor, not a gunner."

He straightened a little. "You'd be surprised what kind of people end up on a mine ship. I've got theoretical physicists, I've got ex-privateers, I've got all kinds of people here at my disposal. They all work for me now, and they had this system all sewn up. If you don't tell me where the hole is in our system here, then I won't know how to plug it. So tell me, or I'll take it out on Lenny."

She smiled. Almost. She lowered her chin a bit, and gave him her favorite melted-chocolate gaze. "Are you going to kill me if I do?"

The answer was immediate. "No, I kinda like what you did. Smart. I like smart women. In fact, you out-smarted *me*. That's not easy. Brains are way more at-tractive than anything else. Course, you got plenty of 'anything else' too, don't get me wrong. It was a good try, really good try. Doesn't matter, though. I can be back in two weeks with more Kauld ships. How long do you think it'll take them to fix that wreck?"

She reached out with one hand, flecking her fingers through his chinchilla hair, just over his ear. "My job is to stop you. You know that."

"Oh, sure." He caught her hand, held it, drew it down and looked with fascination at her fingers, and her longer nails, which had been perfect before these weeks of capture. Mesmerized, he picked the old polish off one of them. "And my job, my challenge in life, is to convince you to come with me when all this is over."

Raising a tavern eyebrow, Uhura smiled with half her mouth. "I've got a thousand tricks up my sleeve. You've still got nine hundred and ninety-nine yet to see."

There was still no sign of the anger he'd come in with, yet a lingering sense that he hadn't let it go, but only camouflaged it. Still, he smiled rather jauntily and patted her hand between his.

"This is gonna be fun," he promised.

As he stood and beamed at her, Uhura received a subliminal understanding of him. He was charming, yes, and infectious in his manners, his promises, and his lies. He did enjoy the game, the tricks and decep-tion, and he liked pushing every envelope to see just how much he could extort or bleed out of every situation. She knew that was the only reason she was still alive, and his attraction to her was the only reason McCoy was alive. Maidenshore had taken to enjoying these bizarre sessions, when he had a private conversation with her despite the presence of an endangered voyeur in the form of McCoy. There was something about being watched by the doctor that Maidenshore preferred, or he would've arranged something else.

And he always left them here alone for a while after he left. He got some kind of thrill out of knowing they were talking about him.

She also knew those filaments could snap at any moment. He could instantly lose interest. McCoy would be the first to suffer and die. Billy would make sure of that, and make sure Uhura was there to watch.

He waved merrily at her before stepping out of the small quarters. He never stayed very long, but always accomplished so much.

After the door closed, and after it had been closed several seconds, McCoy breathed a shaky sigh of relief and began to move his limbs again. "African ritual?"

"I can smell the incense." She touched her face, the rich dark skin that now had turned pasty and tired, and was glad there wasn't a mirror in here. "The time's come to stop him even if it costs our lives."

McCoy's brows popped up. "You said the olivium is just rocks."

"Yes, but now he's giving the enemy our rocks. That changes everything."

"We have a shipful of thugs. We can't outmuscle them."

"Maybe we can turn them against Maidenshore somehow . . . show them he's not the god-protector he proclaims himself to be."

The doctor shivered visibly. Fear? Probably. She didn't blame him. They'd faced death before, many times, but usually the final decision was someone else's. Odd that it should be so difficult now that it was their own decision.

"I've been thinking about his psych profile," McCoy said then, proving fear wasn't working on him quite yet. "I suspect you're the only person he has any respect for or genuine interest in as a person, probably in years. Besides himself, I mean. His pathology isn't all that unique. There have been manic egotistical people completely lacking in ethics or conscience—some even end up in high office. One of the survival techniques of this type is that he doesn't care about anyone or respect anyone, so no one else matters. Every once in a while, a need bubbles to the surface where he has to have somebody else's respect. It probably only happens once or twice in his whole life."

Uhura leaned forward and rubbed her hands to bring warmth back to the fingers. "We can use that."

Instantly McCoy digested the kind of game she was implying. "It can also be dangerous. If he thinks you're withholding your respect from him too much, he could snap in a rage."

"And kill me?"

"It's happened before. If he can't get what he wants, he may kill it. Once you're gone, he'll convince himself he never wanted your respect, or that he had it but you were keeping it from him and you deserved to die. He'll never get it, because what he wants from you is a fantasy. He's destined to be let down. Nobody will ever like him as well as he likes himself."

Uhura accepted what he had to say, and hadn't seen anything in Billy Maidenshore to contraindicate McCoy's conclusions. Maidenshore was a man much less important than he believed he was, concerned with his comfort, his legacy, his own personal aggrandizement.

"We're walking a very thin tightrope," she said. "Are you ready to step off the platform?"

Comforting places. Cemeteries, morgues, tombs. All the troubles were over by then.

In the *Peleliu*'s small hangar bay, dozens of bodies lay in pathetic order, side by side because nobody could figure out a better way. Each wore some sort of shroud. The first three dozen were draped with UFP flags. Then the quartermaster's locker had run dry. The next two rows were covered with spark tarps. After that, bunk blankets. There were plenty of those. But the crew didn't prefer to use their bed linens as shrouds unless such a mournful use became unavoidable. No one liked to sleep in his own coffin.

Savannah Ring and one of the security men picked their way through the rows of bodies, toting the remains of poor Helmsman Makarios, politely encased in a body bag. His death had, at least, been instant. Since there was no sickbay left, since there were no doctors, nurses, interns, corpsmen, or lab techs, it had become Ring's job to catalogue the dead. For that, she had to make sure they were all laid out here. After the recognizable ones would come the unrecognizable ones, and after that the grim task of matching up limbs to other body parts.

Without a word, after they deposited the latest installment, she motioned the security guy to leave. Her leg needed a rest. She reached down and adjusted the walking splint that supported her left leg from foot to knee. The leg was broken, but could function in the splint for a couple of days. Painful, though. She had to move slowly, and be careful not to turn the foot.

Once the guard was gone, she picked her way through the reposing bodies. All the faces were scrupulously covered, if they had faces. Other parts remained visible, poking from the edges of rumpled blankets, tarps, and standards. Identification would come later, then burial in space.

There lay McAddis. His body took up the space of two. Most of him, including his face, was covered by a UFP standard. The rest—both arms, one leg—splayed outward, eternally stiffened down to the last follicle and fingernail by the spray sealant, now hard as flecked granite. It would continue to cure, forever entombing McAddis in his formfitted vault. His fingers, blue-coated and spread wide, would always carry that appearance of shock and strain, every tendon showing. He only had one leg now. The other had been cut off where it stuck through the fissure in the bridge dome. There had been no other way. The edges of the hardened sealant were scorched brown from the phaser torches that had been used to cut him free.

Might not be a bad way, if you had time to plan for it.

Savannah made her way closer, paused for a moment to commune with McAddis's covered face. The thin fabric of the UFP standard came to a point over his nose. A morbid wish gripped her to pull it back and take one more look at his expression, his eyes crimped with horror and bravery, lips stretched back to scream that last awful demand.

Nick Keller couldn't take it, though.

She folded her legs and sat down. He knew she was here. He'd talk when he was ready.

He lay at McAddis's side, stretched out facedown, with his arms folded to support his head. He'd disappeared from the bridge without a word as soon as they realized the enemy couldn't find them anymore. The damage crews, what was left of them, had moved in. Keller had moved aside.

Now he was down here, under the half-lights that cast a twilight effect on the bay's quiet residents.

Two hours ago, Savannah had thought they were done finding bodies. Then more had been discovered in the twisted wreckage of decks nine and ten, and a couple in a nacelle strut where they'd been caught while trying to make mid-battle repairs.

Settling onto the deck between McAddis and the next body, she looked across the stiffened form at Keller.

His face was hidden, obscured by his folded arms, and by being turned away from her.

She pressed her spine up against the dead guy on the other side and her two feet on McAddis. The dead were always accommodating company, did what they could for you.

Though Keller didn't move, his voice scratched from over on the deck.

"Did I kill Lake?"

Savannah adjusted her injured leg. "Did you want to?"

Quiet moments passed. Almost a minute. The peaceful bay was cooler than usual, deliberately. Savannah rubbed her leg to stanch the ache.

Finally the suction of her presence pulled him over and into a mediocre sitting position. He hitched up to press his back against the accordion door of the shuttle hangar, never once raising his eyes from their unfocused relationship with the deck. His long legs tumbled out before him in no particular order. His shoulders sagged as he rested his wrists on his knees. Didn't seem very comfortable.

His hands were scratched and reddened. In his fingers he held the *Challenger* coin. He turned it and turned it.

As they sat, companionable and silent, two more

crewmen slogged in with another body. Arsini and Niedleman, carrying Melinda Clark. Sad. Clark and Arsini were a local rumor around engineering.

They put her down, met Savannah's eyes briefly, then simply left as they saw Nick Keller sitting there in his pall, enduring the nefarious confrontation. Not with Lake, Savannah guessed, but with himself.

Keller was watching the two crewmen as they picked their way back out of the bay. He noticed their condition. Dirty, ragged, ripped, weak, scorched. Pretty much the condition of the ship, except that these men could still move. He said nothing.

Nothing. The scary part was that his eyes also said nothing.

"Might as well come back to the bridge," Savannah suggested. "Zane brought some of Shucorion's crew up to clean it. They work like ants. They even polished the polyduranide sheeting. What was left of it."

Politely demonstrating her point, one of the Blood crew appeared briefly in the bay control hatchway, busily working a suction broom along the crux between the deck and the bulkhead.

Keller watched the studious Blood concentrating on the task. He wagged one of his hands in a pitiful shrug.

"Can't push the stink back into the skunk," he condensed.

Savannah laughed briefly. Something about the sound of ultimate truth gave her a tickle.

"Zane says it's all because you're a Taurus instead of a Pisces."

"He thinks a Pisces would've won?"

"No. He thinks a Pisces would've failed."

The words sank in, but still he didn't look up. He continued to peer at the deck between his knees. "Captain Kirk warned me about this. He said I'd have to choose between a wrong and a wrong."

His moccasin-brown hair still bore flecks of the sealant he had sprayed all over the dome fissure. Needed a cut. Like most country boys, he didn't like getting a haircut very often. He preferred the style he'd found useful back on his parents' ranch, just long enough on the neck to fend off a sunburn, but no longer.

No point arguing with him.

"I was all wrapped up about Roger," he went on when she didn't interrupt. "I didn't listen to the right things carefully enough. It didn't become crystal clear until people were dying around me. I had too much loyalty for my captain and too little for my crew. I didn't know about the line you cross when you become Command. Loyalty has to shift the other way."

Around them the lights went dim, wobbled a couple of times, went completely dark for an instant, then recovered. They came back on, but not quite at the level of a moment ago. Now the bay was even dimmer. Still, Keller didn't look up.

"Another power falloff," Savannah mentioned. "The generators are working overtime." She tipped her head back to enjoy the change.

Keller, though, was now looking past his knee to the covered form of Tim McAddis.

"It's doing what it knows is right," he said. "If I'd done the right thing at the right time, these people wouldn't be dead. Tim wouldn't be dead. Kirk might not have left."

"I could kick you," Savannah awarded, "if you think it'd make you feel better."

He sliced her with a caustic glare. "Beelzebitch." When she smiled, he did too, a little. He turned the coin over and over.

Savannah seized on the movement of his fingers. "You're going to wear the faces off those people if you keep doing that."

He sniffed and rubbed his nose and his bloodshot eyes. "They didn't make it, y'know."

"Who?"

"The shuttle crew."

"They didn't? You mean they scrubbed the mission?"

"Ship blew up."

"No kidding . . . on the pad?"

"Just after blastoff. Minute or two into the launch. They had a leak of some kind. They shouldn't have launched in cold weather. They made a bad call. Whole orbiter and its solid rocket booster Roman-candled."

Even Savannah grimaced in empathy at the picture they now shared.

Suddenly passive, Keller drew a long breath and sighed it out. He reached across the hangar door behind him and patted a nearby buttress. "It was the only shuttle they lost. Mighty good, when you consider they were riding a nova every time they hit that launch button. Took a lot of grit in those days. But you're only as good as your ship."

He clutched the coin in one hand, and with the other hand he rubbed the deck beside him as if he were petting an old dog.

"Did you see how long she kept fighting?"

Savannah tipped her head, wondering if she understood. "The . . . ship?"

He nodded. "She didn't give up. They had to bleed her dry. Even then we still had air. Do you know how remarkable that is? *Peleliu* never quit. A half-dozen enemy ships . . . and *they* had to do the quitting."

What could she say? Tell him the ship was finished? Describe to him what Bonifay and Lewiston had said about the collapsed grids, the missing chunks of hull, the burned driver coils, and the cracked fusion sphere? How they had described their vessel as a shell, scorched from the inside out and back again?

Or would it be better to mention that all the other command officers except Lewiston were dead or incapacitated, and that Lewiston had no command experience of any kind? Even three other department heads were dead. There were noticeably fewer lieutenants, never mind lieutenant commanders. In fact there was only one lieutenant commander. Guess who.

Keller pressed his hand to his own chest and rubbed hard. "How do you know when you're dead? I don't think my heart's beating. I just can't feel it anymore."

Savannah had already decided not to speak when one of the nearest access hatches slid open and spared her the choice.

In came Shucorion. The Blood leader had another body draped over his shoulder, wrapped in a bunk blanket, just the boots sticking out the bottom end. Laying the dead crewmen into place at the end of the row, he grunted slightly with the strain, pressed a hand to his own leg—Savannah remembered Harrison treating that wound—and turned to the two of them.

The Blood didn't seem surprised to find them here. In fact, Savannah got a subliminal telegram that he'd scooped up a body as a ticket in. She accepted delivery despite the lack of evidence.

Keller didn't look up, Savannah noted, but his expression became smoky. He fixed instead on Shucorion's gray leggings moving in and finally kneeling before him.

Shucorion ignored Savannah completely and paid strict attention to the ship's sorriest officer.

"The Blind has lifted," he informed. "Your engineer believes we can limp around the sun on docking thrusters, then send a message for assistance."

"Calling the colony for help," Keller grumbled. "We're supposed to be the help."

"We must try," Shucorion told him, speaking softly. "Kauld will return. Vellyngaith has not been defeated. When the Blind comes again, they'll return."

For the first time, Keller looked up. "Why did they break off? Do you know?"

The Blood only shook his head. His deep brown hair caught the overhead lights and turned back a rosy sheen. He shifted a little closer now that he had Keller's full attention.

"This is time to work," he said. "Your friend is shamed if you stay here with him. He doesn't want you here."

Boldly he took a grip on Keller's forearm in a manner than suggested he wouldn't let go. Savannah watched with anticipation—that grip could mean many things.

"The dead are dead, Mr. Keller," Shucorion reminded. "Rise and work."

With those words rolling between them, Keller let himself be pulled to his feet. As soon as he was on them, before even letting go of the other man's arm, he shot out a right cross that decked Shucorion in one swipe. The Blood tumbled backward, caught his heel on Tim McAddis's stone-stiff arm, dropped onto his backside, then sat there, braced by both hands and his bent legs as Keller stepped out of his self-inflicted cell and stood over him briefly before stalking out.

"Mind your own business," he pleasantly suggested.

Peleliu's captain's quarters
Two days later, in orbit at Belle Terre

"Nick! Good to see you. We squeaked out of that one somehow. I can't wait to hear all about it. Sit down. Give me a report. You want some papaya juice?"

"No, thanks, no juice."

Nick Keller hitched up onto the dresser and sat with his back to the mirror. He really didn't want to get a look at himself right now. He had nothing else now to look at but Roger Lake, confined to his bed on nominal life-support because there was no sickbay.

The captain didn't look too bad, but the head injury was serious and needed time to heal. The portable life-support crash cart next to him provided intravenous stabilizers and a brainwave monitor just in case of sudden changes.

"We're in orbit at Belle Terre," Keller reported, rather blandly. He wasn't happy about any of this, not even about getting back to the planet. That meant he had to face other things. "We came back around the sun on docking thrusters, then sent a call for assistance soon as we could. Commander Scott sent a mule engine by remote. We were towed in."

"Lot of damage?"

"Too much. Almost complete systems failure across the board. The driver coils, the sphere, the hull all over the ship—"

"How's the bridge?"

"A wreck."

"Yeah. I felt that wreck." Roger Lake sipped at his glass of juice, gazing into it as if it were a crystal ball. "Lost McAddis, I hear."

To respond in any way, after hearing Lake speak

Tim's name, somehow seized up in Keller's mind.

Lake smothered his next words in another slug of juice. "Sorry about him. Bad way to go."

Keller reached across the gulf between the dresser and the bed and pulled the cup out of Lake's hands. "How 'bout we just set this down and you talk to me."

Surprised, Lake settled back against the extra pillows. His eyes and manner were both remarkably steady.

"Sure, Nick . . . talk."

The mirror was cool on Keller's back, even through his uniform shirt. His jacket was gone, dumped somewhere. He wore only his rib-necked white shirt. The idea of wearing the uniform jacket right now just made him sick to his stomach. Even the white shirt made him feel too obvious, too easy to find.

He held the juice glass in his hands, and looked down into the orange pool.

"You're told all your life," he began, "to be loyal to those in command. They don't tell you that you get to a certain point and you cross an imaginary line where loyalty shifts in the other direction. It's what Derek was trying to tell me before he died in the lift. You start looking back to your crew instead of up to your captain."

"I don't have any worries about that, Nick," Lake claimed, raising his voice a little. "You're loyal to me. We owe each other."

Keller looked up. "I crossed the line."

"Loyalty shifted? From me to them? That pack of vipers? I don't believe it. Who got to you, Nick?"

With a huff of frustration, Keller allowed himself to moan it out. He set the cup of juice down on the desk nearby. For a moment he was no longer speaking to Lake. Lake was just overhearing.

"I always liked Starfleet discipline and loyalty. All

of a sudden I was trapped between devotion and honor, and doing what was right. For the first time in my life, they weren't the same. I'll take a lot of crap on things that aren't important. Decisions don't have to be made instantly, but once I make them, they're made. Decide to fight or to run, but once you decide, then really fight or really run. There's bad and there's worse. Pick the best thing and take the consequences. Am I going to rise to this and do my best, or am I going to duck the job I *did* agree to and shrug it onto somebody else?"

The tenor of subtle change rang like gongs for both men. Keller sensed the difference, and saw in Lake's stony face that the captain did too.

Keller didn't stand up yet, though his tone changed to something more ponderous.

"There's a security guard outside your door. You're confined to these quarters. You're going to be under some kind of restriction. I haven't figured out what yet. When Captain Kirk gets back, I'll be asking him to convene a competency hearing."

"Is this a mutiny?" Lake distilled, speaking suddenly sharply. He no longer moved, but lay perfectly still, as if encased in his blanket. "Are you trying to relieve me of my command?"

"You'd be relieved of command," Keller confirmed, "if we had a ship left to command."

Lake raised himself up on an elbow. "I'll fix the ship. You're dealing with the wrong man here. You think I'll fold just like that?"

"There's no ship to fix," Keller preempted. "She's smashed, wrecked. Her guts are blown out inside every trunk. Her arteries are fried. We just can't have any more of you, Roger. You relieved the crew of their posts in the middle of action."

"I did no such thing."

Keller stalled up short. How could he deal with someone to whom the truth was so fluid? What could he do when somebody just stood there and said, "Up's down"? He felt suddenly knocked out at the knees. How could a man look him right in the eye and believe something so vastly opposite of what had really happened? How delusional could a functioning mind become?

"You want to see the automatic log?" he condensed.

"So? Those things can be faked. Everybody knows that."

"We can't fix the ship, Roger. You can't unburn the firewood."

Lake's eyes became like a badger's. "You're relieving me of my command *and* you're trashing my ship? What then? You take over as senior Starfleet authority here? You're not qualified to take over for me."

"I'm not," Keller acceded. "But I can listen to the people around me. Their jobs will be to make me understand what I need to understand. Then I'll make the best decisions I can. I accepted this position. I have to handle it now."

His voice deep and sluggish, Lake's eyes were still sharp, his glare unforgiving. "We were one person. You, me, and Dee. You were both part of me."

Keller nodded sadly. "We were. But in the end, I was more dedicated to a captain who didn't deserve it than to a crew who did."

Sourly Lake pressed his head back against the pillow. "That's a poisoned thing for you to say to me. I'll file a breach of privilege against you."

"Wouldn't blame you a bit."

The friction between them rose like a wall. Lake clearly felt a thousand times betrayed. He rubbed his

Diane Carey

injured head, then passed his hands over his eyes. "Must be a burden, being so tenderhearted, hey?"

The erosion of a longtime friendship caught them each by the throat, but for two different reasons.

"I'll never forget this," Lake vowed. "Never."

Keller slipped off the dresser and straightened to leave. "Neither will I."

Chapter Sixteen

Planet Belle Terre

"JUST DUMP IT over there, with the other warp cores."

Zane Bonifay, once bosun, then storage steward, then bosun again, now found himself in the unenviable role of salvage foreman. As he directed other workers, Starfleet and not, over the two-mile valley before him, he felt like a bouncing ball. In space, out of space, in again, out again.

The wrecked *Peleliu* was being parted out, here in this yard, a huge clearing house for the whole planet, holding the totaled-out wrecks of about sixty-five ships, remnants of the original Belle Terre Expedition. The remains of the dozens of vessels spewed out all over this open valley, taking whatever Belle Terre's nutsy weather wanted to spit on it.

Today was an almost tolerable day. Not exactly nice, but nice days on Belle Terre were rare, even at the equator. Here, on the southern slope of the primary hemispheric mountain range, between the mountains and the desert, lay this valley. Partly protected from snowstorms by the mountain range, it was nevertheless a windswept place. Summer in this hemisphere made for an almost constant dry wind. Right now it was spring, and couldn't make up its mind between hot and cold. So, every half hour, the temperature either rose or dropped. Bonifay had taken his jacket off three times in the past hour.

Everywhere among the piles and piles of junk buzzed dozens of little sorter robots, rolling around on their six wheels or floating on their antigravs, picking their way through the hulks and delivering what they found to specified sorting grids. Some were programmed to look for certain types of metal, others synthetics, glass, fabric, circuit material, plastics, celluloids, duranides—anything else anybody could think of that might've been built into the many ships whose blown mechanics were still here.

Over the past weeks of struggle, much of the vessels' structures, furnishings, fabrics, windows, and other useful stuff had been stripped for planetary use in houses, shelters, barns, streets, or patched together into atmospheric shuttles and other vehicles for use around the planet. Most of the spacebearing mechanics was still here, much of it stressed beyond use.

Over to Bonifay's left was the beaming site, where right now six more tons of former *Peleliu* were materializing. Beside the site, twenty-odd suited workmen waited with load lifters, clamps, antigravs, and whatever they needed to separate the pieces and distribute them wherever Bonifay wanted them.

Just this morning the hulk of Shucorion's Plume had limped in, towed by a shuttle on automatic. It had arrived almost a week earlier than expected, because it didn't have the sense to shut down during Gamma

Night and had been lucky enough not to pile into an asteroid belt. Now it lay at the bottom of this ridge where Bonifay stood and supervised the dispersal of sections and parts, its wedge-like form missing a wing and part of its tail section. Obviously it was more than a spacecraft, if it needed wings and a tail. Or it used to be.

Not anymore.

A sharp hand of wind chiseled across the valley and raced up the ridge to hit him in the face as he looked down at the Plume. He winced and turned away, shielding his face with the padd he was holding.

When he looked up toward the beaming site, he saw Nick Keller walking toward him.

Keller didn't look good. His uniform jacket was missing. So was the white high-necked shirt. Instead he wore a black Fleet-issue T-shirt and trousers, but with a simple gray flight jacket such as any docking attendant might wear.

"Mornin', Badlands."

"Hey, Zane."

"You need a shave."

"S'pose so. You need a haircut." Keller turned and surveyed the sprawling acres of windblown wrecks. "You've got a new hobby, I see. What a mess."

Bonifay leaned his padd on his hip, raised his chin, and narrowed his eyes as if studying an art work. "It's only a mess to the untrained eye. To those of us who know what we're looking at, why . . . it's pure putrefied hell." He moved to the edge of the ridge, not exactly beside Keller. Together they scanned the acres of wreckage being tidily separated. "Out in that field of miserable clutter you see the thousands of dreams, aspirations, plans of thousands of people. Designers, the builders, the guys who made the blueprints, the engineers, loft techs, the guys who painted the Belle Terre

Expedition logos and the UFP standards on the hulls, the families traveling out here without looking behind . . . lot of life stories out there."

"And death stories," Keller reminded. "Aren't those the hull lights of the coroner ship over there?"

"Looks like them. Somebody took the hull and made a couple of houses out of it. Furniture and all. Same with most of the Conestogas. It's a whole settlement outside of Port Bellamy."

The wind pulled at Keller's hair, mussing up the part. "I remember seeing *Twilight Sentinel* go past *Peleliu* and the other color-guard ships during the parade as the Expedition was embarking from Starbase Sixteen. Purple hull, soft gold and white running lights . . . she was elegant. Sad, but stately."

On that thought he paused, braced against a sudden slice of wind. Together they scanned the wreckscape, but Keller was no longer paying much real attention.

Another blade of wind came down between the mountains, scraped the valley, and slapped them back a couple of steps. When it subsided, Keller was facing Bonifay instead of the valley. He stuffed his hands into his pockets. There was a little rasp in his voice.

"I know what you think of me," he submitted. "Probably not much different from what I think of me. But we've got things to do. I need help from you to get them done."

Squinting in an inhospitable streak of sunlight stabbing between the clouds, Bonifay diffidently asked, "Like what things, exactly?"

Keller spoke as if he'd been rehearsing. "It'll be six months before Starfleet can send another ship, plus the two months it takes for a message to get back there that we even need another ship. The Kauld'll be back sooner than that. All they have to do is shake off the effects of dealing with us, then come back and blow us from Monday to Christmas. We've got nothing left to stop them. But we still have a planet to protect, not to mention the olivium."

"It's stuck back in the Quake Moon."

"Still ours to protect." He sniffed at the raw dry wind, then grimaced thoughtfully. "I've got to get back out in space as soon as possible. If nothing else, I want to find out why we got a false signal from the mining ship. And who fired the shot that tipped us off to the Kauld presence. There's something going on out there, and I don't like being stuck here while it's happening."

"Planning to grow wings?" Bonifay asked. "I'm not saying it's not possible."

Keller steeled himself. "When I was a kid, I could build hoverskates with paper clips and spit." He raised his hand and pointed. "Look over there. A perfectly good warp core. Half of one, anyway . . . just past it, aren't those Starfleet nacelles?"

"From the CST *Beowulf*," Bonifay confirmed. "That was my ship."

"I know. I'm sorry."

"Me too."

Keller looked at the ground, rocked on his heels, and nodded. "Part of *Peleliu*'s engineering section's still intact, mostly the bottom half. And the saucer section's perimeter structure didn't get cracked. We've still got her bridge deck. Needs a new hat, though. . . ."

Bonifay pressed his lips, but didn't comment.

"And I heard," Keller moved on, "you've been collecting excelinide spheres for recharge, haven't you?"

Sensing where this was headed, Bonifay cocked a hip. "Sure, there are almost seventy perfectly good ships out here. Problem is, they're in fifty thousand blown-out pieces."

Once again Keller turned to the open valley and squinted into the bite of breeze. "We've still got a problem to raise up to."

"What're we raising?"

"Huh? Ourselves, I guess."

"Then it would be 'rising.' Intransitive verb."

"Oh, of course. Silly me."

"What about manpower? You might be the officer in tactical command, but there aren't enough of *Peleliu*'s personnel left physically able to crew a moon transit, never mind a fighting ship. You got no bridge personnel, no medical, you got two junior engineers left, no helmsman, navigator's laid up, and at last call the captain was recovering from a knot on the skull that matches a bruise on your thumb."

Word had already spread halfway around the colony about what happened on *Peleliu*. The captain had been acting erratically, his first officer—actually second officer hastily promoted in action—had whacked him over the head and not even made up a good story. The ship had limped back and ultimately had to be towed into orbit, and the technical diagnosis had turned into an autopsy.

Nick Keller hadn't uttered a word of protest. Not a syllable in his own defense. He hadn't made up an excuse or quoted a regulation, hadn't painted over the scratch marks or hidden behind smoke screens.

He didn't do it now, either.

"I don't have any of those," Keller admitted, "but I know where there's a heck of a bosun. If he'd have me."

With his mind already on functional realities, Bonifay glossed over the compliment. "The parts won't even work together. The tech won't be compatible from ship to ship. There aren't enough good Starfleet parts to—"

"We'll make them work together."

"How?"

"Don't know yet. What do you say?"

"You're the OTC. Why don't you just give me an order?"

"Don't feel like doing that."

"Seems to me it'd be better to wait for help."

"We don't have time," Keller said. "Besides, I don't like to wait for help. We should paddle our own canoe."

He didn't explain further, but left any details to Bonifay's intuition. After a few moments of silence, the revelation struck that Keller wasn't going to say anything else and that he understood "no" might actually be an answer. He seemed willing to take it, even seemed to think he deserved abandonment.

Keller took out the *Challenger* coin and rubbed it between his palms, thinking about McAddis.

Striking a Napoleonic pose, Bonifay raised his animated black brows and narrowed his eyes. "Go ahead," he encouraged. "Tell my future."

Self-conscious, even a little pink in the face, Keller took hold of Bonifay's hand, flipped the coin and slapped it onto Bonifay's knuckles. Together they look at it.

"That's a decision I can live with," Bonifay said. He gave back the coin, then stuck out the same hand in an offer whose best voice was silence.

Some things were better unspoken.

Deeply moved by the vote of confidence he didn't deserve, Keller clasped Bonifay's hand. A distinct fear of the immediate future set in for both of them.

"So," Bonifay bridged, "who're you gonna get to pinch-hit as a design engineer for this Frankenstein ship?"

Port Bellamy Shuttle Yard

"You want to *what?*"

"We don't have to start by winning, sir. All we have to do is show we can compete. If they know we have a ship, even if it's not the best ship, maybe we can stall them or fend them off or maybe put up a good bluff until Captain Kirk gets back or some help arrives."

"Lad, I've got barely enough here to build shuttles and planetary hovercraft and little buzzers back and forth to the moons, but a fighting ship?"

"We've got most of *Peleliu*—"

"What's left of her. She's cracked down the middle. Her skull and spine are broken. You want her to get up and walk, then dance a jig?"

Montgomery Scott carried with him almost as much legend as James Kirk and Mr. Spock, and in fact had his own legend to go on just from his innovations in deep-space engineering. He'd virtually revamped the whole engineering division at Starfleet to suit his purposes, which had thundered down for decades to youngsters like Nick Keller.

Standing under the engine of a rebuilt shuttle, Keller fidgeted with the diagnostic-and-design padd he'd brought with him and tried to bury a shudder from his shoulders to his thighs. Just talking to somebody like Commander Scott made him nervous. Something about famous people, especially when they really *deserved* to be famous.

Scott's age was lost in a strong barrel-like physique, salt-pepper hair, and a brushy mustache that framed his bright and also legendary smile, but Keller guessed at late fifties. Could be wrong. Never could guess age. The Scottish accent was thicker than Keller remembered from training tapes, but that was a while ago. Or perhaps with age Scott had settled into a colorful role and grown comfortable with the Aberdeen boatman image. Or maybe he just didn't care anymore whether anyone understood him or not.

With all that Montgomery Scott had done for the Belle Terre Colonial Expedition, from enabling them by designing the mule engines that brought them here to rebuilding a useful atmospheric fleet to traffic the planet so no one would be too isolated, he could ask almost anybody on the planet to do this grunt work for him. One colonist even claimed that the commander had fixed their ancient toaster.

Yet here he stood, welding a circuit-bearing clinker plate onto the underbelly of a patched-together surface shuttle. Looked like a twenty-seater. Keller got the idea Scott liked doing the hands-on detail work just as much as he clearly enjoyed the vista of grand-scheme engineering.

Around them, a few dozen other workers strode or floated about, working on a dozen other pathetic-looking leftovers that were being formed into craft that might serve someone here. Lifters, crawlers, and antigravs on automatic hummed and clattered all over the yard. This was one of the places making use of the garbage Bonifay's team was sorting. Other places on this side of Port Bellamy vying for parts were the mattress factory, the shelterworks, a twelve-acre horticulture hothouse, and six or seven independent metalyards.

There was almost a street outside the yard fence, a hastily carved lane fitted with rolled sheet duranium. Not exactly like home, though. Not yet.

"What about a crew?" Scott pointed bluntly. "There aren't enough Starfleet personnel left on this planet—"

"Sir," Keller sighed heavily, "I beaned my captain

over the head and took over. I'm not even sure *I'm* Starfleet anymore. Far as I can tell, my career's so shredded already, there's nothing left to lose. Starfleet'll have to make a decision on me later. Till then, I'm the OTC of a problem right here and now. If I have to cobble together a ship, I guess I can cobble together a crew too." He held up the D&D padd he was carrying. "Which reminds me, do you know what a 'connect ion' is?"

"Sounds like one of the newfangled isolinears. The old ones were more stable."

"I've got to find one."

"Who for?"

"Zoa. She's the Rassua representative we brought out with us. I've asked her to be my tactical officer, temporarily. Tactical and weapons."

"Zoa . . . ah, the lass in the neo-bondage Wellies."

"That's her."

"*Temporary* weapons officer, y'say?"

"Yes, sir. All I really want to do is make a show."

"Might as well fly a hologram, lad."

"Has to be a little tougher than that. Sir, I realize I'm asking you to do the insane and incredible and impossible, to take all this and——"

Scott waved him silent. "Third time this week."

Now that he'd done the sales part, Keller found he had to follow through. No point arguing. He paused, shrugged rather stupidly, then bluntly and stubbornly asked, "Where do we start?"

Scott wagged the welding phaser at the side of his head, not looking at Keller. "We start with your figuring out what you want."

"Oh . . . I just thought you would——"

"Not me, lad. When *Enterprise* rotates out of this cluster, I'll be going with her. There are a thousand designs for a thousand purposes. If I take over, build a ship that fits me, then I leave, it's all pointless. Figure out what you need, then build a ship to suit those needs. Do you need starship capabilities? You're dreaming if you do. Maybe a destroyer's picket talents or the composite tricks of a frigate? That's closer. You're the one who wants the ship. You got the rank, you make the choice, you get the blame. That's my advantage—nobody blames the engineer. You figure out what you want, what you need, and what'd make you like her."

"Like her?"

Scott's eyes sparkled and crinkled at the corners. His voice took on a low rumble. "Well, y'gotta like her, lad . . . or you won't fight for each other."

The concept worked on both of them, having its biggest effect on the young embattled member of the conversation.

"Y'got no slush deuterium containment facility," Scott contemplated, more or less talking to himself, "you got no straight duranium fastening rods, you'll find yourself short of tripolymer for the sensor matrices, and you can't fly in space without operational profiles and display—"

"Sir," Keller interrupted, "I generally do a lot better if I don't think about what can't be done. I'm thinking in terms of what we *do* have. We have parts of ships, we have workers from both the Federation and the Blood, and we have you. Maybe it's not much in the plus column, but—"

"You'll have to tell me how you want your bridge configured. It's got to fit your personality, your priorities, fit you like a glove."

"Oh . . . I see, yeah . . . well, I guess I'm comfortable with what I'm used to. A half-moon master situation

Diane Carey

theater, a sci-deck with optical banks up on the quarter . . . nothing too spread out—"

"Another problem," Scott threw in while he continued welding. "No spacedock at this planet yet. How you figure to build a sizable spacefaring vessel?"

Not even two steps into this dilemma and already Keller was in a puddle. As if pulling his own tooth, he made his first real tactical command decision. "Build one that can land, then."

A million micro-troubles leaped into Scott's expression, but he shrugged. "A'right. Top of the list—surface capability. Changes the hull structure, alters gravitational tolerance, thrust-to-stress ratio. What else?"

"Ah . . . a strong frame, compact . . . something that can pivot inside her own overall length, like a lazy Susan or a turning drum."

"We might be able to rig mule engines into it," Scott suggested. "She'll be muscular. Fast in short bursts, but she'll not be running any marathons."

"That's what I need," Keller quickly said. "A quarter horse, not a thoroughbred. But we'll still need warp power, of course. We've got *Beowulf*'s nacelles—"

Scott shook his head. "There you got trouble. We have very few operative warp cores, and most of them are in use as power stations around the planet."

"Can't we confiscate one?"

"Don't belong to us, lad."

"Won't the colonists be glad to give up one warp core to protect the whole planet?"

"Might. Got a better idea, though."

"Sir?"

"Use that Blood contraption that limped in the other day. The one you boys blew sky-high. She's still got her—they call it dynadrive—mostly intact."

"Shucorion's ship?" Keller paused, thinking, and

266

after a moment smiled. "I kind of like the symbolism of that."

"It'll be the devil to make 'em talk to Federation nacelles. I'll see what I can do. You come up with the rest of the list. The ability to make a decision is valuable all by itself, Keller. Second thing you've got to find is somebody else who can make a decision as well as you can."

"I don't understand, sir. . . ."

"You need a first officer. Can't do both jobs yourself. After all, chances are you'll end up dead."

Keller pushed off the hull of the shuttle and sighed. "One monster at a time, Chief. I'll be back."

As the welder buzzed in his hand, Montgomery Scott shook his head and chuckled. "I live in fear."

Chapter Seventeen

Enterprise

THE *ENTERPRISE* shot across the emptiness of space, light-year after light-year, as if borne on a single untiring wave.

"I know you're doing something, Spock. Let's talk it out."

James Kirk moved to his ship's rail and hung himself on it like a coat.

Before him, the knightly First Officer Spock, the Vulcan superpresence, the center of gravity on the bridge, sunk ever deeper into thought. It took him several seconds to bone up to answering the not-quite-question. He seemed more to be thinking aloud than actually speaking to Kirk. "This new information may supply a clue about the probe's motive power. It has no thrust, which may mean that quantum flux is how it moves."

"How does that help us, Spock?"

"We may be able to stabilize the flux, just as we used ionized plasma to disrupt it."

"How?" Kirk persisted. If he had to be on the spot, then so did everybody else.

"The unique quality of olivium," Spock explained, "is its constant random state of flux. It does not all exist in our universe at one time. Yet it must . . ."

Turning back to his readings, troubled by his own puzzlement, Spock then did something he almost never did—he disapproved of his own line of thought and stopped talking in the middle of a sentence. He was fundamentally upset, not all that down deep.

Kirk moved a little farther forward on the rail, to keep their conversation private. "So much of what we do is basic survival," he mused, gently prodding. "Fight those we must fight, drive away monsters, weather storms . . . This is different, isn't it, Spock?"

"Yes, Captain. Very different."

Go ahead. Tell me.

"This is a chance," Spock finally said, "to improve life on a galactic scale. For friends, enemies, all who live in our time and after. This will rank with the invention of sanitation, vaccine technology, warp power . . . if we lose it—"

For a man who claimed to have no imagination, he was capable of letting Kirk imagine the end of that sentence. Or perhaps he simply couldn't make himself say it.

How sad for things to have come to this for Spock, who had so looked forward to studying the enticing Occult solar system, only to discover this weird material in quantum flux, buried in the womb of moon matter, that didn't even read with conventional sensors. The moon was acting funny, constantly changing, altering the moon's gravity. The moon was too small for volcanic activity and its core registered as solid, yet it had magma and tremors and constant tectonic action. Mass was changing. Pressure was building. How?

Nobody knew, until Spock got a closer look and found a miracle. Megatons of this precious stuff, this ore, this brilliance born in the heart of a quasar. Spock had framed the value of a stable olivium source in his most high of adjectives—*inestimable*.

Obviously he thought the loss would be that also. And that preyed upon him. Pressure was building again, and his friend Jim Kirk could not help him feel better.

The least he could do was distract him some.

"Spock, let's try thinking in wild ideas, not theories. If they're high-tech, why can't we try something low-tech? Trick them somehow. Anything you can imagine about the speed of the thing, the interdimensionality, the fact that it comes halfway across the galaxy to collect rocks made out of the same kind of stuff it's made of itself . . . which way it's going, how massive it is— anything you think might be appropriate."

Bent over his boards, fine-tuning two dials at the same time while he peered into the sensor hood, Spock shook his head and sounded almost angry. "With the interdimensional flux quality, there seems no way to *make* any logical predictions."

So much for that. For Spock's imagination anyway.

Irritated that he hadn't gotten anywhere with his new angle, Kirk grumbled, "And wouldn't it be ironic if despite your trouble the universe didn't behave in a logical manner after all."

"If that were the case," Spock muttered, "then you would be right at home, Doctor."

At the helm, Sulu turned to look at them. The communications officer and Herne also both looked up.

Kirk turned slowly, brows up. Ah, what mindless mutters could reveal . . .

A good five seconds later, Spock's shoulders went down some and he straightened, still facing the boards. Another couple of seconds, and he turned to peer down at Kirk. "Pardon me . . ."

His captain's reward, to both of them, was a warm smile.

"I'll take it as a compliment," Kirk assured.

But the tiny breach of etiquette, so rare for the impeccable among us, haunted the Vulcan as he turned back to his boards.

Folding his arms, Kirk rubbed his mouth, pondering. "So that's it . . ."

The key snapped into the lock. The missing element, the conduit, the power arch. Spock had tried numerous times to throw away his humanity, and McCoy had always held it for him. No one ever needed McCoy more than Spock, or appreciated him more. Spock needed to depressurize, but that had never been Kirk's role in their relationship and he stumbled over it now. Like popping the pressure valve on the Quake Moon to make it safe, McCoy had always been here to trip the switch for Spock. Instinctively Spock must have known the relief was good for him, because he put up with McCoy and in fact counted the prime badgerer as his second closest friend. No Vulcan really had to put up with a Leonard McCoy if he didn't want to.

Now the whole weight of the Federation was on Spock's shoulders, and McCoy wasn't here to ease the pressure. As a starship captain, an exploration spearhead, a military man and an admiral, Kirk was used to the burden, though he had come to hate it.

Spock simply didn't know how to bear so much consequence by himself. McCoy wasn't here to needle him into relaxing a bit, so Spock would work harder and harder. No matter how Spock tried to be fully Vulcan, he was still part human and there were pressures working on him that would eventually crack. Humans needed some release. When he held his breath too long, a human—or anybody with a conscience—needed somebody to poke him and say, "Breathe, stupid!"

But nobody was here to do that. And when everything collapsed, Spock would blame himself and refuse comfort. There was a spirit to Spock that even he would have denied.

Reluctantly Kirk turned away from the science station when Johnny Herne dropped to the lower deck to hand over an engineering padd. "Sir, I've got the report from the damage investigation. Not bad."

Kirk scanned the padd's screen, then advanced it and scanned further. "You're got to be kidding. No significant damage?"

"Starship's tougher than I thought."

"Well, she's tough, but she's not this tough. No serious injuries either?"

"No, sir."

The unhelpful padd went back into Herne's hands. Kirk squinted at the forward screen. "Well, well. The sounds of attack, the sensations of energy, the feeling of injury, panic and fear . . . yet no significant damage."

Herne screwed up an expression. "Are you arguing? Ah—sir?"

Kirk glanced at him, but he was really interested in hearing from Spock. He turned again to the rail near the science station. "If you want to scare a tribesman away from the cave you're hiding in, you play the sounds of scary animals and things he understands as dangerous. The ship shook, all the boards lit up, we seemed to be taking prohibitive damage, but when we checked, it was a diagnostic malfunction. Therefore . . . *is* it a malfunction? Or are we listening to lions growling in the darkness?"

Spock looked down at him. "Attempting to make us select the option of turning back?"

Kirk snapped his fingers. "And what does that tell you? It says they can't completely leave, so they were trying to make us leave instead. Maybe they can't completely disappear! Maybe they have to . . . intersect with us, even just a little. Just a finger or a hair always sticking into this dimension. Like a periscope. If we've been chasing a periscope, that means there's a whole submarine attached. How else could it take full phasers?"

"Detection of phaser shifts does indicate a far more advanced civilization than ours."

"But not out of line with the type of thing we've encountered before. The Metrons, the Nomad probe, Trelane's people, the Organians—it's not unheard of."

"Not at all."

"But this one thing keeps coming back at me. If it could escape interdimensionally, why hasn't it? If it has to keep a hair or an eyeball or a periscope in this dimension, then if it leaves entirely maybe it can't come back in. And it doesn't want to leave." He leaned an elbow on the rail and rubbed his chin. "We have to find the hair and pull on it."

"That could be disastrous, Captain."

"What about a containment field? Can we use the antimatter plasma that way? A net?"

"Only if we do so within the tractor beam field, very near the ship. If we succeed and the full object manifests itself that near to us—"

"Then we're dead. But if it wanted us dead, we'd be dead already."

"If it . . . *wanted,* sir?"

"Yes, Spock, yes. It's been trying to fool us into

thinking we were in danger. They could've destroyed us anytime they wanted to. That's how I know there's an intelligence involved. Until now I thought it might be programming, but I don't think so anymore. The 'bots are being directed. I mean to force the directors out into the open."

Anticipating a change, Spock stood up. "How?"

"Mr. Herne, lower all defensive shields. That thing's threatened to kill us. Let's see if it has the stomach to follow through." He settled into his chair like a warrior into a saddle. "Mr. Sulu, overtake the 'bot. Go to warp factor ten."

Chapter Eighteen

EVER TRY surfing a tidal wave on a toothpick?

Keller felt like a clumsy magician juggling two dozen greased eggs. Every minute the toothpick was looking better. Because he had Commander Scott behind him—or at least in the life pod with him—a thousand things suddenly started to happen. Nobody questioned him anymore, uttered that immortal "Are you nuts?" that he kept asking himself, and a flurry of activity leaped up around him that kept him completely spinning. He didn't get the luxury of handling the sweeping overview. Instead, he found himself sweeping the overview and also sweeping the billion crumbs of details rushing around. Nobody had any blueprints or diagrams or schematics to follow, so Keller became the hub of a scandalous spinning ball.

Every minute somebody was pulling on the hem of his shirt wanting advice or a decision. Half the time he told them to do what they thought was best, mostly because the odds were that they knew as much about whatever-it-was as he did. He quickly discovered that his real value wasn't in any particular bank of knowledge, but in his willingness to make a decision when others weren't. Did he want flush plating or clinker plating on the dura-bonded sections? Did he want beam brackets or beam knees? Transverse bulkheads or running joiners? A bulb keel outside the ballast or an internal one? Who was going to be the administrative chain of command once the ship launched? What did he think of cannon grapples? How would the space-time driver coils work with the continuum distortion on a ship that could come into the atmosphere? Who would be his subordinate unit commanders? What did he want done with any contingency retention stock? Where did he want the bridge emergency transporter pad? Were full deflectors or full phaser power the biggest priority if he had to choose?

Most were good questions. He just didn't often have the thing that usually comes after a good question. He would listen to all sides of a problem, take all recommendations, then say, "Try that one." If he was right fifty percent of the time, then half the ship would fly.

Right now, he'd settle for half a ship. The *Challenger* coin worked overtime. Flip, flip, flip.

As for the other half of the questions, he could only hope that Savannah, Zoa, and Bonifay were running their parts of the show. Occasionally he got a question about some preference he might have regarding medical, weapons, or provisioning and support, but otherwise they were handling their new burdens on their own. After all, what did Keller know about setting up a med arena? Or a weapons bank? Or a fortune-telling booth?

Right now he was picking his way, knee deep, through a mountain of sorted parts in the salvage valley, rattling off just these kinds of decisions into his communicator as he moved while using his trusty padd for ballast.

"And don't forget to expand the bay by two meters on each side when you do the conversion. It won't do us any good if we can't get a standard shuttle inside."

On the other end, Zane Bonifay's voice sounded strained, but not impatient yet. *"Understood. What about the tractor-beam projector? You want it mounted against G deck, or higher?"*

"Just high enough to miss the elevator. We don't have time to be fancy. Just make it work right."

"We're going to have to cram the bay control room over to the far starboard side then."

"I don't care where it is."

"Then we'll cram it."

"That's well, Zane, carry on."

He snapped his communicator off, hoping for a few minutes of blessed silence, but when he turned in another direction he was startled by the approach of Shucorion climbing up the hill of junk.

"You requested to see me, Mr. Keller?"

"Oh . . . thanks for coming." Keller took the moment to rehang the padd under his arm and give his scalp a scratch. "How are your men doing since we left the ship?"

"They have work."

"Ah, good. That's good, right?"

"Always. Thank you for asking."

"Listen, I'm sorry I hit you. I was out of line."

The apology seemed to perplex the Blood leader. His handsome blue complexion flushed a bit. Was he embarrassed? He paused to think about this, then offered, "If it would help, you may hit me again."

How could someone so experienced, settled, and steady be so childlike? Were all the Blood like this?

Diane Carey

Keller knew these people could hunker down to a task like no one else, focus their attention to a singular purpose and whittle it away until their goal was met, then clean up their mess and polish the floor behind them. What in their history had made them so hard to insult?

Closing the distance between them with a few slow steps, Keller distilled, "Don't you take anything personally?"

"It's not personal," Shucorion said. "You don't know me well enough."

Interesting. In fact, downright enlightening. Keller paused and scoured him with a long look.

"You don't even take the Kauld threat personally, do you? You've had to fight with these people for uncounted generations, but you don't seem to hate them."

"Blood and Kauld have been locked in struggle since we found each other. What purpose would be served by hating them?"

"I dunno . . . it kinda helps us humans. . . . Are the Kauld like this too? Fighting because they think one or the other of you has to prevail? And there's nothing personal?"

"I imagine so. I've seldom spoken to them. Only lately, since Federation became attracted to the Cluster."

"What do you get out of winning?"

"We get to live."

"Hm." Thinking, Keller plodded away. "They use a few things we haven't bothered with since the invention of gunpowder. Spears, for one."

"Yes, the javelins." Since Shucorion didn't know where this conversation was headed, he settled down to sit on the blade of a hoverloader and took each question as it came. "Javelins are only for use in very close proximity. They can't be aimed accurately at any distance. You simply fire them and they go where they go."

278

"Our deflector shields should've stopped them. They must've fallen and we didn't even know it." He hung his hands on his hips and groaned, "No excuse for that."

"Without the Blind," Shucorion said, "ships could never approach closely enough to use them."

"Definitely a Gamma Night weapon."

"Yes."

"This is a problem. A whole new way to think about strategics. It's virtually hand-to-hand fighting, only with spaceships. We haven't had to fight that way . . . just about forever. I don't think we ever had a period of hull-knockers. You'd have to go back to pirates on the open sea to get that kind of intimate conflict. Fighting in space within twenty kilometers of each other? Whew."

Shucorion simply nodded and helped him step over a particularly snaggletoothed piece of wreckage. "Is there something I can help you search for?"

Keller held up his eternal padd, which had become permanently attached to his left arm. "Know what this is?"

"A display connection to your computers."

"Right. It's a 'personal access display device.' We can tie it in to any computer mainframe and access information we need. Some of them are unit-specific, but this is just my all-round load lugger. It's not a tricorder, it doesn't read anything, but you can pull out information when you're nowhere near a terminal. See the screen?"

"Yes."

"The diagram is a Keeling shank. I saw one on this pile last time I was here. I need a clean example, so we can have more made."

"The diagram won't do?"

"It's better if they can actually hold one. I'm about to give up, though. I just thought I saw one."

"Then we shall search." Immediately Shucorion

turned away and began scanning the lumping wreck pile for the thing in the picture.

Now that they had their back almost to each other, talking became somehow easier. "You realize, you're now their captain. You shouldn't be picking through rubbish for parts."

"Old habits die hard. There's still mostly crew in here." He thumped his chest. "And I'm not a captain. I'm what we call an OTC. Officer in tactical command. It's just the senior line officer who's still standing."

Shucorion hazarded a nod, but he didn't seem to be buying that argument.

Frustrated, Keller's mind wandered among the blur of details spinning through. "You're right about the Kauld. Vellyngaith will come back any day now. It's only because Starfleet technology was more advanced that we managed to do enough damage to beat them off. Even then, I'm still not that sure why they quit fighting after just one photon cluster strike. He must've known we'd have nothing left after that, right?"

"I have no answers. I won't guess."

Time to try again, maybe reframe the question. "You felt the detonation of the photons. What kind of effect do you think it had on them?"

Behind him, Shucorion hesitated, but Keller got the idea the hesitation was just to do a favor to the ignorant nut who was asking the question. Sure enough, after a moment the grim answer popped up. "We have no way to know."

True to his promise, he wouldn't guess.

"Any suggestions about when they might come back?" Keller attempted. "Do they have a pattern of strategy that might give me a barometer?"

"No."

"You're supposed to *help* me, you know."

Shucorion gave his version of an apologetic shrug. "I would like to."

"Watch out for that jagged brace."

His communicator beeped again, a sound he would be hearing in his sleep for the next fifty years if he didn't get a break from it soon.

He snapped the grid open.

"Keller, Grand Central."

"Crewman Riley, sir. We've got almost the whole engineering section pieced together and we're ready to start bonding them. There's just one problem."

"Just one?"

"We forgot to put in heads."

"Are you telling me that the entire engineering section, ten decks through, has no restrooms?"

"Correct, sir."

"What do you think I'm going to say about that?"

"Probably just what I said."

"Well, just flow with that river."

"Aye, sir. And, sir, the Blood workers are giving us some trouble."

Keller glanced at Shucorion. "What kind of trouble?"

"They want to paint the corridors. We tried to explain there isn't time."

"No, we definitely don't have time for home decorating. Give them something else to do. Tell them they can paint later. Carry on."

Exhausted, unshaven, dazed from sheer mental and physical stress, he stopped picking through the wreckage. Though he knew there was a real chance he'd never stand up again if he sat down, he did so on a particularly uncomfortable knot of twisted compartmental sheeting.

His arms sank to his sides. His shoulders drifted farther down, and he rested his hands on his knees. His

Diane Carey

knuckles, blurring before him, were scored and bruised, his skin raw. Those poor things looked like the hands of an old, old man. His spine screamed with the sudden relaxation, and all his back muscles seized him, squeezing a wince out of him.

"We're not in Kansas anymore, are we?"

A few tangles away, Shucorion simply asked, "I beg your pardon?"

"Just thinking of home. . . ."

"Kansas? Is this a city on your planet?"

"Hm? Oh—no, it's a state. But I'm not from there. It's just a saying we have. I'm from . . . I was raised on a ranch in another state, called New Mexico." He gazed across the windswept plane beyond the wreck field to the mouth of the valley. "We had a lot of big animals. Cattle, America bison, African elephants, cape buffalo, horses—"

"Why would you have such animals?" Shucorion asked. "I've seen pictures of these things. Very large. Most large land animals on my planet were extinct eons ago. We have few animals larger than ourselves."

"My family raises them for various reasons. Meat, tourism, leather products, or sometimes just because we like them. Earth discovered about a century ago that ranching was the only way to keep some of the species from going extinct. Instead, we did what's called 'freestyle wildlife management.' Worked, too. Just by providing the same products in a humane way, we competed the poachers out of business and increased the numbers of animals at the same time. We domesticated some of them, kept others wild or semi-wild on our property, just because we liked having them . . . lot of work. Course, I had five brothers, so we handled it. Three of my brothers are planning to take over someday when my parents retire."

282

"Why would you feed and tend the ones that have no purpose?" Shucorion asked in an endearingly naive way.

Keller shrugged, feeling suddenly wise and magnanimous. "Success allows you the freedom to just be nice sometimes. Successful businesses have always been the deepest well of charity. Scholarships, donations, sponsorships, grants—all through our history on Earth, businesses have supplied more free-flowing philanthropy than any other force, social or economic, including churches. The more productive you are, the more you're able to indulge. The more fruitful our ranch became, the more we could provide for animals that had no so-called purpose. We set up a couple of rescue habitats for abused and unwanted alien animals. People bring these bizarre creatures back from space and think they're good pets, and then the thing grows up. We also set up four scholarships in animal husbandry. One of our graduates is working out here on Belle Terre. So lots of other lives get better because ours do." He leaned back against a flow fender and nodded to himself. "Yep . . . I approve of success."

Shucorion seemed overwhelmed, but offered a humble grin. "I should like to learn more about this success method of life."

"I'll teach you."

Though Keller had paused to rest, Shucorion never did. He continued picking through the wreckage. "I would also like to experience such a ranch someday," he said.

"Maybe I'll start one on Belle Terre. Big petting zoo." Keller dropped the padd and grabbed his head with both hands. "What did I just say! That sounded like I'm planning to stay here or something. Did I say that?"

"Were you not staying?"

"I'm slated to rotate back with the *Enterprise*." He gazed out over the wind-cut valley floor. Only now, as he sat here and stared at the future, did he realize how his own personal plans had been shredded by these past days' events. "*Peleliu* was supposed to stay out here and protect the planet and the olivium . . . but there's no more *Peleliu*. There's only me and whatever I slap together. And *Enterprise* might never come back. I might actually be stuck here. . . ."

Shucorion paused in his search. "Then some day beyond, I shall see your ranch."

"Yeah, beyond." With a passive nod, Keller rubbed his face and forgot about any plans he had before this morning. "One thing you learn living on a ranch," he went on, "is never to run from a charging animal. Stand your ground. He might hit you, but if you run he'll kill you. On a ranch, there's a big difference between getting hit and getting dead." He looked up at Shucorion. "The bull's still charging. I plan to stand my ground. I agreed to this position and I have to play it out, at least until Kirk gets back. I didn't like some of the things he told me, but I have to admit he was right. You can yearn for peace and strive toward peace and work for it and aim for peace, but you can't behave peacefully while you're having a war. That's just not the right time to fill your mind with peace and try to act peaceful."

Under the crisp eccentric sky of Belle Terre, Shucorion's complexion became as deeply blue as a pure sapphire stone. His slightly less blue tunic and gray pants contributed to a particularly alien and yet somehow comforting picture as he stood on top of this salvage heap.

Keller dispensed with formalities or even basic politeness, and just said what he had to say.

"We're going to fit together a ship good enough to carry us into space and maybe fight a couple of bursts. Mr. Scott suggested we use the warp core from your ship. I'd like your permission to do that."

"Of course," Shucorion agreed. "We must not waste." He stepped closer and lowered his voice, even though there was no one to overhear them. He spoke with surprising warmth. "Your orders were to abandon my Plume. Instead you brought him in for me."

Self-conscious, Keller simply said, "It stinks to lose a ship."

"Yes, it does stick."

Keller grinned. "Stink. Smell. Bad."

This sure wasn't easy. He was having to swallow a lot more than his pride. Like his career, which didn't have any salt on it. And where was he going to get enough data-crystal membranes to hold the optical nanoprocessors?

Twenty things at a time.

"You're not Starfleet," he continued, "but I'm not sure we are anymore either. I'm just marking time till somebody comes out here to court-martial me. You're the only one in my circle who's been a command officer, who has any experience with the people we'll be fighting, and you have that navigation trick going for you. Your men are awfully hard workers. My people could use the help. They're welcome in the crew. If they don't want to stay, I'll see that they're delivered back to your planet as soon as we get all this ironed out."

He didn't mention the operative part—*if we live.*

"I find that unusually hospitable," Shucorion said. "I hope they stay."

One down. Drawing a long breath, Keller held it and went for the next level.

"And . . . I need a first officer. Somebody who can operate the Blood warps and maneuver in Gamma Night, and who knows the enemy. There's something about you that sets you apart from the other Blood. I don't know what it is, exactly, but I get the feeling you're different."

Shifting under the weight of his own past actions, Keller flinched at his proposal. It seemed awkward and out of order. He hadn't staged it very well. Shucorion had so far seen him fail to take over when he should have, then let things degenerate to a horror, whack his commanding officer over the noggin, and to top it all off, Keller had offered Shucorion a right cross in return for what was in retrospect a supportive gesture.

Oh, well, there wasn't time to redress the past. He forged on.

"I have to pick somebody my crew can follow if I die. After what you've seen on our bridge, I can't blame you if you turn me down flat. I've called the rest of my bridge crew—boy, that sounds wild to say right out like that. Anyway, Zane'll be at the site already, Zoa's coming from the lower continent where she was training with one of the privateers, and Savannah'll be arriving on the four o'clock broom . . ."

If Shucorion was flattered or put off by the prospect, none of that showed in his face. There were a lot of emotions in his eyes, but Keller couldn't decipher them.

Finally Shucorion moved off a few ungainly steps and stopped again.

"It's very hard for my people to trust," he said. "For generations we haven't been able to trust anyone. There have only been Kauld. The few others we met have looked into the Cluster and almost as quickly departed. The Formless gave us dynadrive, which turned out to be a wondrous curse. Now we have nothing but conflict. We have no rest from it as we did before, when our suns cycled away from each other. Now, we are constantly neighbors with All Kauld and must constantly fight. The space between us makes no difference anymore. Blood Many have learned that trust is usually betrayed."

He paused for a moment, then. Possibly he just didn't want to come right out and say what he thought.

Keller was about to let him off the hook when Shucorion raised his head again. "In your people, I have seen something completely new for this cluster. Someday I may understand, but for now, I confess, I remain mystified. Your people do things for the doing of them. You defend what isn't yours, but don't claim it afterward. I thought we were conquered. I find myself treated exceptionally well, spoken to with respect, even offered authority. The one who offers . . ."

Keller's stomach twisted. What had he been thinking? Why would he assume Shucorion would accept the shame of serving under a man who had bonked his own captain right in front of everybody and even after that practically got the roof pulled down on top of everybody's head?

Doing his best not to attract any attention, Keller hunked his shoulders down some and let his head hang even though he was still looking up, sort of.

Shucorion looked down at him. Somehow that was appropriate. Why didn't he just say it?

In fact he didn't say anything for quite a long time. Keller tried to keep his expression passive, but knew everything showed in his eyes, all his fears and insecurities, doubts and determinations, and the belligerence that drove it. He tried to communicate that he'd just turn around and get somebody else, but in this instant he realized he didn't really want anybody else. Shucorion carried James Kirk's stamp of approval and had given Keller just the right nudge when he'd needed it. And he was all the things Keller had said.

"You say I'm different from my own kind. You're

most perceptive, to see so much. I am different from them, though I've tried to hide it. During the last cycle, I made myself useful as a blast technician—one who scours destroyed buildings and shafts for heavy metals from meteorites after a particularly cataclysmic ore shower." He made a sweeping gesture at the pile of salvage around them. "Then I set charges and render the destroyed zone into manageable pieces that can be used to rebuild. We must rebuild almost constantly. Our planet circles a star which circles another, and when the two cycle near each other, great destruction is delivered to our planet."

"Yes," Keller supplied. "We call them 'Whistler' and 'Mother.' I'd heard they're pretty hard on you."

"On the Kauld planet also, but more to Blood Many. We are the unfortunate. We've come to call this the Blood Curse, to always be on the underside of events as we seemed to be cast. Then dynadrive came, and we thought this was good, but it turned out to be more of the Curse."

He stopped briefly as the wind lashed and nearly knocked them down. Keller put his padd up to protect his face, but Shucorion seemed hardly to notice the weather's unhappiness. Was his own planet constantly under the lash?

"I was inside a gutted shaft," he went on, "in a tall building someone had unwisely built near a fault line. It was my job to reactivate the site for mining. I was not enthusiastic that day—I had lost several family members in the ore shower, but if I failed to work, I would be disrespectful of those killed by the ore shot. I was supposed to go up in the building and start the automated machinery that would begin the sifting process. According to precaution, I was supposed to send in a mechanical unit that would take most of the day to safely rise to the top of the structure, check the integrity, then turn on the automators."

"Bet you didn't," Keller anticipated.

"No, I didn't. . . . I was hungry, exhausted, and no one was looking. I went in alone. The only safety precaution I took was to turn the emergency power off. When I did, the grid shorted out, and my arm was badly injured."

He pulled up the sleeve of his tunic, showing his right arm badly scarred by a lightning-grid of electrical burns. Keller winced in empathy. The scoring didn't look like the sort of thing that healed overnight.

"I should have taken the warning," Shucorion continued. "Instead, I went to the top and turned on the automation. The instant I did, the vibrations began to destroy the shaft. The building began to collapse in every direction around me. Down I went. Through explosions, fire, sparks, shattering glass, and crashing beams, I rode the collapsing structure all the way to the ground."

Keller clapped a hand over his mouth. "Great snakes!"

Shucorion seemed rather entertained by his own tale. "And I landed on my feet . . . utterly unharmed."

"Oh, come on, now!"

"You see, when I did the right thing, I burned my arm. When I took a risk, everything turned out miraculously fine. I began to think that perhaps this might summon a change for my people, to believe there was something about me that let me take chances and be an element of change. I even have a little cult around me, mostly those who were with me that day."

"What a story," Keller offered. "You know, people who take chances have a much better possibility of success than those who don't. We've always just taken that as a given!"

Shucorion's eyes widened. "The risks I see being taken by your people, by you—these are astonishing to me. Astonishing! What seem like mindless chances which I have taken now shrink beside the things you will do to succeed." He put his hand proudly on his chest and declared, "I thought I was a very daring fellow, before I met Humanity."

Smiling at his own revelation, Shucorion happened to look down and noticed something. He bent over, pushed his hand into the clutter of stuff at his side, and came up with a slightly scratched but otherwise laudable Keeling shank. He showed it to Keller, and came closer to present it, almost like a peace offering.

"This is the difference you see in me," he finished. "I will take a risk."

Did somebody say "peace"?

Even as Keller accepted the Keeling shank in his hand, Shucorion didn't step back. "Blood have lost countless thousands in this cycle without end. But I think if Nick Keller had been among us, we would have lost fewer."

Either the sun was melting or somebody had just sprayed ice on the back of Keller's neck. Or the wind changed.

At this remarkable compliment, gripped by both surprise and humility, Keller was on his feet before he realized his legs were working again. Despite the unevenness of the thing he was standing on, he managed to straighten and square his shoulders. He suddenly wanted to live up to the stunning award he had just been given.

"Your technology is beyond ours," Shucorion added. "I have little experience with it. I'm not qualified to be first officer in your fleet."

Keller spread his arms. "You'll fit right in. I'm not qualified to be captain."

Shucorion smiled at Keller's whitewashed humility. "In that case, we shall be a fine match."

After a whirlwind sorting expedition, the heavy lifting began immediately, with the exception of a couple of minutes to visit the head. After that, Nick Keller pretty much ditched eating or any other functional necessity for the next thirty hours. He spent all that time with either Zane or Scott, or other technicians, picking through the acres of salvaged parts, cannibalizing what he thought he might want and confounded by the fact that he wasn't sure at all what he might need.

Shucorion and his forty or so Blood soldiers showed up instantly and proved to be the most tireless laborers Keller had ever seen. They never said no, they seldom paused, they never complained, they solved their own problems, and they hardly ever rested. Such dogged determination became very quickly embarrassing. What workers!

Partly because the Blood never paused, within the first four days those parts were being welded, bonded, glued, tenoned, thermal-sealed, or fused into amalgamated ship sections. More than twice Keller had to talk Scott into thinking about function instead of form. Scott was a brilliant engineer, able to jury-rig almost anything, but it was up to Keller to think in terms of what they needed against what they had.

One of the more heartwarming moments occurred when a shuttlebus arrived with the insignia of the Colonial Governor's Office plastered all over it and two hundred colonists piled out. Summoned by Governor Pardonnet, they had come to help after all.

At that moment, building the ship became a colonial effort. Colonists trudged in from the reaches, many with good skills, and started picking at their own little areas of expertise. Nick Keller himself became the clearinghouse for final decisions. He and his coin worked overtime.

Just make a decision. Doesn't matter if it's good or bad. A bad decision now is better than a good decision five minutes from now, if you're going to die in four minutes.

Hull form was determined by salvaged parts available from the *Peleliu,* the derelict CST *Beowulf,* and other ships that had been stressed beyond their limits out here. The underhull of *Peleliu*'s saucer section, minus the pot lid, provided a basic structure. They lifted it up onto a huge scaffold, the same way old steamships were once made back on Earth, and started attaching things to it.

Scott ordered cobalt-obsidian-coated radiation-resistant hull plates from the wrecked privateer *Hunter's Moon,* to be pulled off and bolted onto a make-do top section, creating a thick "black hat" for the saucer section. Sections from the private ships *Winston Churchill* and *Mable Stevens* were used to mount the saucer onto the engineering hull, which was pieced together from four separate sections and cut to fit each other. Fan-shaped blue strakes from the loading bay of *American Rover* were used to mount the nacelles, looking more like flying buttresses than nacelle struts. Scott called them "Rover strakes," and the name stuck. The nacelles, precious cargo from *Beowulf,* were mounted below the hulls like skids on a sled.

If anything appeared to fit together, it was all cosmetic. Keller knew none of these parts or sections had been cast as single pieces. He wondered if the ship would be strong enough to leave the atmosphere at all, never mind take enemy fire, but time would have to tell. Right now all he wanted was to make an appearance, maybe surprise the Kauld into backing off for a few more weeks.

As the ship took shape, he found himself having both dreams and nightmares. Usually they had the same plot.

It would work, it might fly, and it was just ugly enough to be scary. Perfect.

On the sixteenth day, he stood below the monster scaffold and peered up at the underbelly of the engineering section. To his left were Zane Bonifay and Zoa, not standing too close to each other. To his right were Savannah Ring and Shucorion. No one said anything. The only one in a Starfleet uniform, though, was Savannah—strange, because . . . well, because Savannah was strange, but most because she was the one Starfleet had threatened to kick out if she didn't accept unsavory assignment at Belle Terre. Bonifay's uniform had been put away in favor of a more filth-tolerant work suit, and Keller still wore his favorite black Fleet T-shirt, as he had all through the dirty part of the project. Wearing the uniform tunic right now just felt wrong. He didn't deserve it.

A few feet away, one of the nacelles swept down on its flying buttress. They looked like standard Starfleet nacelles, but they hid some secrets. Expedition mule engines, for one, capable of impulse or warp speed with corresponding tug muscle, powered by the Blood warp core, in fact an alien contraption given to the Blood and Kauld by others. Scott said they were eccentric. How that would play out, no one knew. Not a thoroughbred, but a quarter horse.

Above him, way above, flew the patched saucer section, bearing signs of scorching from welders and graffiti from overanxious or cynical participants in this goofy project. Everybody wanted to have his name scratched in her. Or his mother's name. Or his opinion.

The ship was a patched-together stew, with mostly blue and gray hullplates but the odd red or green or purple one, but there was something stubbornly proud

Diane Carey

about the way she stood up in her scaffold, sticking her chin out forward and her duck-winged nacelles sprawled out underneath on their flying Rover strakes. From here they couldn't see the black hat on her saucer section, those tough cobalt-obsidian plates Scott salvaged from *Hunter's Moon* and bolted on. Somehow it was fitting that this ship should be part pirate. Keller imagined the hat would be the only pretty part of this hybrid.

As his friends stood at his sides, he felt obliged to offer a few words.

"Well, there she is," he announced. "Our one-picket wonder."

Bonifay shifted from one foot to the other. "Thank you, Commander Encouragement. Any comments from the bilious horde?"

"There will be," Savannah said, "if you call me 'bilious' again."

Zoa and Shucorion remained without opinion, or at least without voiced opinion. Keller got the idea that the reasons for their silence were myriad and probably opposite. He resisted asking. The ship was here, almost able to be launched. Whether she remained in space once they got her up there—no time for a test run. Her maiden voyage would be one of instant significance. There would be no shakedown. Either everything worked, or it didn't.

The weather had changed again. Unlike yesterday, which had been windy, dry, and cold, today it was windy, dry, and hot. Keller shrugged out of his work jacket and dropped on a nearby tarp. Suddenly he snapped his fingers. "Oh, I forgot!" He punched up the offending segment on his padd and stuck it in front of Savannah. "It's says to establish a firm 'connect ion.' What's a 'connect ion'?"

She shook her head. "Never heard of it."

He swung the padd in the other direction. "Zane, what's a 'connect ion'?"

Zane came out of his communing with the ship, which, typical of a devoted bosun, he clearly liked. "A what? Let me see that."

"Right here." Keller showed him the padd screen. "Do you know what this is?"

"'Connect' . . . oh, sure. The graphic tag skipped a space."

Keller looked again. "'Connection.' Well, for pity's sake. Have you seen my brain? It's about this big. I seem to have lost it."

"What's her name?"

At Savannah's mystic question, Keller turned again. "What? Her name . . ."

"We can't call it *Peleliu*," she said. "That wouldn't be right."

"No, no . . ." Keller looked at the ship again. "Wouldn't carry any punch out here at Belle Terre. The Blood and Kauld don't know about World War Two or the Battle of *Peleliu* or what the Marines endured there."

"At least we haven't forgotten," Bonifay mentioned.

"No, we sure haven't."

"What's its class?" he asked. "What *kind* of a ship is it? The *what what?*"

Folding his arms tightly around his chest, Keller shook his head, stumped. "I don't know . . . part cruiser . . . part cutter, part dreadnought, part lander, part scout—"

"Some light cruise, some battleship," Bonifay supplied, "and a piece or two combat support tender."

"She's a composition ship," Savannah suggested. "Composition? Miscellany?"

Diane Carey

Surveying the mottled contraption lovingly, Zane shrugged one shoulder and framed his words with animated hands. "She's a . . . an alloy. A crossbreed. A peasant. She's one of my own kind! Don't look—I may weep."

Keller looked up, up, up to the underside of the saucer section, peering straight through in his mind to the stitched together bridge.

"The U.S.S. *Mongrel?*" he said.

He won their praises in the form of dust on his boots and Savannah's hand across the back of his head.

"What's the matter with that?" he whined. "If the shoe fits—"

"Pardon me," Zane responded, "I'm gonna go over there and throw up."

Shucorion caught Keller's eye with a glint of amusement, but as usual had no creative suggestions. Zoa remained underwhelmed.

From the bosun's kit slung jauntily on his hip, Bonifay pulled a laser microtorch and held it out to Keller. "Here, Nick. Sign on."

Warmed to his toes, and scared all the way back up again, Keller took their encouragement as poorly placed confidence. He held the microtorch in both hands, turning it over and over. They were pleased, and rightfully so, with their miraculous work over the past days, but he was too aware that he may have charged them with the forging of their own coffin.

No way out of it, though.

He strode over to the nacelle, which had so valiantly, so recently and fruitlessly served another ship. He had given this nacelle either a second life or a second death.

His whole body suddenly tight, he reached up and scrawled his name nice and big in the ship's hide. *Nick Jacob Keller.*

"No rank?" Savannah asked.

He shook his head. "No rank. It's just us."

"Ahoy!"

The shout came from far overhead. They had to step back to get a look.

Far up in the scaffolding, poking out of an open access hatch in the ship's neck section like Rapunzel sticking out of her tower window, Montgomery Scott waved until they saw him.

"Mr. Keller," Scott called. "Would you like to come to your bridge for the first time, lad? She's open for business!"

Chapter Nineteen

THE INNARDS of the ship looked like something had been turned inside out and left to the elements. Actually, that was pretty much what had happened to most of this construction material. Scratches from wind and rain showed on the bulkheads and strakes and struts, beam brackets, gunwales, braces, joiners, doors, frames, and anything needed to hold them all together. Salvaged material remained at a premium on Belle Terre. The good stuff had been skimmed off almost immediately and disseminated around the planet for homes, buildings, a hospital, and the businesses needed to provide an economic base for the new Earth.

The mongrel ship, then, was made of secondhand everything, and hardly any of it was Starfleet standard. Only now did Keller realize how many of the Expedition ships had been made in far-flung spaceyards all over the Federation. Somehow Commander Scott had managed to stitch together a working bridge.

Nick Keller and his straggly team, as patched together as the ship herself, stepped onto the bridge. Some things were familiar. Others, as alien as Zoa or Shucorion. Or Zane, for that matter. Then again, Savannah wasn't exactly from this side of the spiritual divide, either.

Wonder what that makes me?

Keller stepped forward. Beneath him, there was a raised quarterdeck in a crescent shape, slightly off center, bending its centerpoint over to the starboard side. At the two ends, angled steps fanned down to the command deck, which was only one step down. To the port, then, was most of the lower deck, carpeted with burgundy low-nap, the quarterdeck with navy blue, obviously from two different ships, making the bridge look like one astral body eclipsing another.

Instead of above the turbolift, much as it had been on *Peleliu*, the sci-deck he'd requested had been mounted on the port side, and stood about five feet up with steps forward and aft of it. The space under it looked like it had some kind of panels, but Keller couldn't tell what for. This sci-deck didn't have a lattice to protect the crew from falling, but instead a short wall of alien metal with a field of quatrefoils cut into it, each big enough to put a hand through, to allow sound and light to pass through. The hand-level caprail was glossy and the color of a ripe beet, brighter than the burgundy carpet.

For an instant Keller wondered why they'd bothered to carpet when time was at such a premium. Then he remembered the noise buffer, the fire-retardant treatment, the safety factor in case anyone fell down—there were reasons other than cosmetic.

The panels below the rail were almost entirely dust brown with khaki braces, while the starboard side was black, khaki, and blue, all largely the colors of the outside of the ship. The most strikingly Starfleet element to the bridge was the rail offering a safety zone along the crescent deck. Though it too was painted burgundy instead of bright red, the rail provided a comforting tie to service ships for many generations, and the strongest thread holding Keller to this place as some kind of déjà vu. He felt, if not at home, welcome.

Burgundy, black, navy blue, gray, a bit of cream or khaki here and there . . . Keller let the colors seep into his mind until they started to feel right. This quilt-patched place was indeed an echo of the exterior of the ship. He felt as he looked around that part of him was still outside, standing at the slightly tilted nacelle, surveying the magpie hull.

The ship was looking back down at him, surveying him too. Did she like him?

Generally, Commander Scott had taken the trouble to establish a familiar work theater for him. The engineering master situation monitors and science sensors were up on the sci-deck, communications and tactical to the commander's right, and the helm in the middle. The biggest difference Keller could see was that all the work pulpits on this bridge faced the main screen. No one had to turn his or her back from the forward attractions. On the crescent quarterdeck, each station chair was nestled under a desk station that jutted out like a spoke toward the center of the bridge. The crewman manning each post would have the main control pulpit in front of him, and auxiliary panels conveniently to one side, within arm's reach.

"Somebody should've thought of this sooner," he said, pointing at the obviously sensible arrangement.

"I did," Scott said. "But you know bureaucrats." With

that, he moved away, letting Keller get the feel of his new domain without being crowded.

The helm and nav station was in two pieces rather than one console, and the two were mismatched. The pilot station was circular, like a big tube stuck in the deck with a tilted work desk, while the nav station was a kidney-bean shape, with colorful isolinear chip banks and several homing and guidance optical subprocessors for the navigator to use. All were dark now, but their little screens held some hint of promise.

In fact, all the quadritronics were dark. Some of the indicator lights were working, but no screens. Keller was relieved to see a fairly standard main screen, a little wider than he was used to and less tall, but at least there was one.

"Think she'll turn into a beautiful swan someday?" Savannah commented as she poked at the medical/hazmat/environmental tie-in boards.

A medical and life-support post on the bridge—another good idea.

"How do you feel?" Shucorion asked from just above him on the quarterdeck, running his hand critically along the rail.

Before Keller, just a few steps away, the command chair at last drew his attention. It wasn't a Starfleet chair. Silently he thanked whoever made the decision not to bring *Peleliu*'s chair here. But where had this dark green leather chair, worn to a soft sheen, with brass studs in its arms, come from? Had it always been a command chair or was this a reassignment?

"I feel," he finally answered, "like I've got a nine-hundred-thousand-ton brain tumor."

Picking at the nav station, Zane Bonifay didn't turn, but commented, "I had a brain tumor once, but it starved."

Over there, Mr. Scott chuckled freely as he powered up the revamped helm.

But now, Keller's nervous grin evaporated as he tipped his head upward, to the bridge dome. A cold dread washed through him as he looked upward, half expecting to see Tim McAddis frosted into the fabric of the ship. Instead, blessedly, there was a barbecue-black ceiling dome of cobalt-obsidian, several layers thick, standing stubbornly between them and the outside. In this light, the plates glowed with the faint hint of dark, dark blue. The cobalt.

"Sometimes the good guys wear a black hat, Tim," he murmured.

He closed his eyes a moment. A shudder of relief and other horrors shot down his spine. He thought he buried it, but when he opened his eyes, the intuitive Bonifay and the always observant Shucorion were both watching him. Beyond them, the women were interested in the bridge and their respective stations. Zoa quickly found the tactical and weapons pulpit on the starboard side. She'd been vigorously plucking various kinds of weaponry from other ships, or converting things to weapons that nobody would ever have thought of using that way. Keller had to admire the way she seized her purpose. Like him, she'd agreed to a task, and was determined to see it through. She never seemed plagued by doubts, as the rest of them certainly were. He had no idea what kind of proximity weapons she'd come up with. He could only hope they'd have the time for her to explain it all to him.

His feet cold and his hands aching with the rush of blood through his exhausted body, Keller snatched for the most sensible thing to ask for first.

"Give me the general run-down of . . . well, let's start with what we know *doesn't* work yet."

"That's easy." Bonifay raised his bosun's padd. "We

302

got no galley, no food processors, some frozens in storage, only half of the heads and showers are working, we're short on water, only three lift trolleys for the whole ship, so don't expect anybody to arrive in a split second. No internal surveillance, no automatic payload coordination, no photosynthetic processing, no particle filtration—"

"Zane! Never mind." Keller held up a staying hand. "Just put it over there. I'll look it over . . . later."

"We need your permission to move the infirmary and dispensary again."

"This is the third time! What's wrong with deck four?"

"We had a spill."

"Of what?"

"I'd rather not say."

"Then move sickbay to deck five."

"There isn't room on deck five. Deck six has no air circulation, and deck eight's not insulated yet."

"How about deck seven?"

"There's a little problem. The Blood guys misunderstood our numerical system. They skipped from six to eight."

"We have no deck seven?"

"None."

Mr. Scott was at his side now, taking his arm, pulling him away. Over his shoulder to Bonifay, Keller tossed, "Ask Ring where she wants to put it."

Bonifay scowled. "But she'll *tell* me."

Scott pulled him down to the command arena, a place Keller wasn't inclined to just go by himself. "All right, here's what it is," the elemental engineer tersely began. "You got components from a couple dozen ships under the skin here, each with its own modifications to integrate the energy and electrical synapses. There's no good way to hook this into that. We don't know what'll work and what'll cry uncle. All the lights come on for now, but we're sitting in a dock. What happens in space, under stress, in battle—I'll be taking bets."

Scott waved a hand across the mismatched systems monitors.

"What you do have is functional tripolymer embedded matrices with tactile and auditory feedback on your high-resolution displays, and you have full operational profiles of the guts of the ship—that is, of whatever's operational. I made everything as simple as I could get away with." He paused and turned to Keller with a Santa Claus expression. "Now, I don't draw in my own blood. Don't be afraid to change what you need to change. Rip it all out and start over if you find a better way. My feelings won't be hurt."

Keller wanted to explain his own ideas about function and reliability, the amalgam between crew and mechanics, but somehow that seemed unwise. In his first venture as a real commander, a new sense arose in him—the listening sense. He got a glimmer that the most foolish thing he could do now was to do all, or even much, of the talking. Becoming a shipmaster wasn't the end of a process of education, but in fact the starting point.

"Effective piloting," Scott continued, "might be almost impossible in tight quarters till you get used to the mules. The ship can go forward, back, side to side, and up and down by basic helming, but this compact design's also capable of tight turns and pivots. Might be a distinct advantage in interplanetary situations, assuming you don't pull her apart at the seams just learning to handle her. No matter what we did, there's no way to balance the hundred thousand flickers of programming still embedded in all the chips buried all over the parts we used. The only way to do that would be to let a computer do all the maneuvers, and as we know from the past that doesn't work."

"Are you saying the crew will have to coordinate their boards with each other?"

"That's right. I hope you have people who get along."

Keller stifled the urge to glance at Savannah or Zoa, but did catch a glimpse of Bonifay in his periphery before stopping himself. "What's the biggest danger?"

"Warp," Scott bluntly said. "There's no basis for computer simulation. None of these components were meant to work together. Testing it would take months and months of writing programs and computer time. You don't have that. You'll just have to experiment and try not to tear her apart. There are a million and one conflicts. The computer might throw a snit and stop working. If you push her wrong, the warp core might blow. The mules are so strong, they might tear the nacelles right off. Try not to let that happen."

Keller groaned. "Dang . . ."

"Aye, you've all got a real challenge on your hands."

An understatement's understatement. A Frankenstein ship whose parts were never meant to work together, populated by people who were never meant to work together.

Around them, more and more of the systems came on as Shucorion and the others pressed pads and buttons, flipped switches. Keller found himself abruptly aware of what was missing here, how sparse the crew really was—but did he want to take more people out into space and increase the loss numbers?

"Got an engineer picked out?" Scott asked. "I haven't seen one assigned."

"Oh, no, sir, not yet. Our last engineer died of his injuries about a week ago."

"A shame. I'll go along for your first flight."

"Commander, I can't ask you to do that. When we

come back, it might be in a million pieces blowing by on the solar wind."

Scott didn't even honor that comment with a response. He just kept on talking. "And here's my personal advice. I learned it from watching Jim Kirk, so I'll hit you with the short stick. Here it is: Get ahead of what your enemy wants. Figure out what he wants on the large scale. He doesn't just want to win a fistfight. That's for kids. There's always something bigger. Find out what that is, and you'll be ahead of him. And throw away the book right here and now, or you'll get predictable."

Keller smiled. "I already threw the book overboard, sir. I think it drowned."

"Just makin' sure. And the other thing is even more important."

"What other thing?" Keller braced himself.

"You've done well," Scott offered, his merry face beaming. "Two weeks ago there was no ship here. There's a ship now. There's something to go for. You've cobbled together a good solid chance here. Be glad of it."

The assurance, and the approval within it, had a dual effect on Keller, partly uplifting and partly dreadful. He communicated his gratitude with an expression as best he could, for he had no words that would work.

"Mr. Scott?" Bonifay cannily approached from the nav station.

Scott turned. "Hm?"

"We were wondering . . . what kind of a ship is this? We figure she's Mongrel-class . . . but . . ."

The seasoned veteran straightened and his eyes widened merrily. "Mongrel-class? I like that. But lad, she's a composite frigate."

He could've been completely snowing them and

they'd never know. A frigate, yes, was traditionally a smaller, tighter, more maneuverable vessel than a battleship or ship of the line, quick in action and mighty for its size, usually overgunned and notoriously flexible. Keller got the idea Scott liked frigates, the way he said it.

But that word "composite"—what did that mean? Was she more a frigate or less? She had mule engines, so she was part tug-and-tow boat. Her warp core was Blood, so she was part alien. She was part CST and part cutter, and about sixty percent pure mystery. Would the parts work together? Would they speak the same language, recognize each other's impulses?

"Composite frigate, Mongrel-class," he tasted.

A totally new brand of ship. A new ship for a new colony. Possibly a new war. A whole new challenge.

Scott's dark eyes twinkled. He climbed the ladder to the sci-deck and took the engineering pulpit, cued in a few undecipherable commands, then looked at Keller. "Like to give the order?"

On the lower deck, Keller's knees turned to water. The command chair loomed before him, detached from its cradle, floating free in the air over his head, getting bigger and heavier by the moment. He felt caught in the same vortex, a cyclone of responsibilities he wasn't ready for, every other whirling molecule dark and unexplained.

Cold in here . . . he rubbed his hands together. They felt chafed, dry and cracked, and strangely empty. He expected them to feel full, overloaded, weighted down, but there was something helpless about empty hands.

Dry-mouthed and shivering, afraid they could all see the not-so-internal quake, Keller tried to swallow a couple of times but failed.

Diane Carey

His chest constricted and pushed out the words.

"Power to the sphere," he ordered. "Internally metered pulse drive . . . on."

Around them the bridge began to hum with a sudden flood of energy. The sci-deck's upper grid of larger scanners popped on, only half of them with actual graphics, the other half with struggling lines and search programs as they looked for some connection or other, but the pulpit stations all came to life with lights and power.

Bonifay and Savannah let out whoops of cheer. Zoa happily pounded her board without her expression even changing. She liked being armed. Shucorion looked around the bridge with obvious satisfaction. He seemed impressed.

Hands in the air, Keller was thrilled as a teenager at a sports event.

"We've got a ship!" he cried.

And his heart began to beat again.

"Okay, first, second, and third things first. We'll need a crew manifest and we'll have to assign watch officers and establish some kind of station bill. So I need to know which stations need to be manned round the clock and which can shut down periodically. We'll have a ship check every fifteen minutes until the systems are stabilized. Let's see . . . Savannah, you'll be responsible for developing emergency procedures—"

He was cut off by an alarm going off on the communications station relay to the planetary harbormaster's mainframe. It had gone off before, but not with so many decibels, not enough to interrupt a person speaking.

Assuming malfunction, Bonifay stepped over there and picked at the data-crystal membranes, trying to turn it off.

But it wouldn't turn off. In fact, it increased.

Suddenly Bonifay stiffened. "Nick, harbormaster's getting a warning from the planetary satellite system!"

Keller spun around and caught himself on the plum-colored rail. "Oh, *please* tell me it's a malfunction."

Everyone was still and tense as Bonifay frantically filtered the signal. "No such luck. They're picking up incoming ships! A lot of them!"

Keller snapped his fingers rather rudely at Shucorion, but only because he couldn't cough up his new first officer's name right now. "Take the helm!"

Everyone else jumped to a station. So few people, so many buttons—

There was nobody on navigation, nobody to plot a clear way, watch out for spatial obstructions, handle the subspace and lateral and graviton sensor arrays, handle the accelerometers, optical gyro, inertial dampering field processors, guidance subprocessors, damage control—whoever just called this station by just one name?

Keller dropped into that seat himself. The command chair went vacant for now. Before him the kidney-shaped workstation came to life in a flood of lights and graphics as Mr. Scott fed power through to all available systems.

"Okay, this is it. Saddle up, crew. Outboard anybody who isn't signed on!"

"Done that already," Bonifay said. "We're good to go."

"Then let's rumble. Unhook the slings, pull out the tent stakes, and shove off. Main screen on."

He wasn't even sure who around the bridge was doing what job. Nobody had been given specific assignments, except Shucorion, and Scott up there seemed to be the one who was really making things happen. The ship would rise, Keller had no doubt. After that, he would be at center stage and no one, not even Montgomery Scott, could dislodge him.

At least, not without cracking him over the head from behind.

The long rectangle of screen popped on before him, showing a picture-window view of the scaffolding in front of the ship. Three workbees were frantically pulling the scaffolding down. The rest of it would just have to be knocked down.

"Vertical thrusters on," Keller charged. "Let's ride!"

Chapter Twenty

THE VERTICAL THRUSTERS lifted the dappled ship straight upward, away from the cradle of scaffolding, to the waves and swinging fists of the workers left below, the colonists who had thrown in their two bits over the past sixteen days to put this impossible dream together and get her in space. Before them the scrabbly complex of Port Bellamy grew small and shrank away, blended to white as the ship moved upward into a scowl of clouds. Heading for space. Any minute now.

Sixteen days ... had they actually succeeded in building and launching a ship in sixteen days? Or was this some kind of big illusion, just a parade balloon with nothing inside?

Maybe that would do. If the incoming ships saw that somebody, anybody, had risen to the defense of the colony, maybe the sheer determination to make a showing would serve its purpose.

At the same time, Keller couldn't imagine himself being so easily fooled. With just one ship facing him down, he'd at least have to take a few hits before he believed what he saw.

Why did he hope they'd be so easy to fool? The Kauld weren't as advanced as the Federation, but they weren't any stupider.

"Reaching the ionosphere," Shucorion reported. "I believe we can engage forward thrust now."

Ticking off a few more seconds until he saw the darkness of space instead of a haze of cloud, Keller rubbed some blood back into his lips. "Go ahead ... forward thrust, point zero five sublight."

Sssssshoooom! The frigate surged forward as if shot out of a cannon.

The automatic gravitational system didn't compensate fast enough. Keller found himself flat on his back, on the deck, with his head butted against the foot of the command chair and his legs in the air on the nav seat.

On the upper deck, Bonifay was thrown all the way back to the turbolift box. Savannah ended up under the ventilator hood. Zoa was under Mr. Scott's pulpit, and Shucorion was draped over the command chair and just now recovering.

"What the hell—!" Keller gasped as he pulled himself to a sitting position.

"Those are the mules," Scott said. He had managed to stay seated at engineering. "Sheer sudden power. The gravitons aren't compensating fast enough. You'll lose a couple of seconds before the gravity catches up to the thrust."

"Now you tell me!"

Scott threw up a hand. "Wasn't sure."

"If we go to warp speed, are we going to crash through the aft bulkheads?"

"We might."

"Let's just increase speed with some care after this."

He looked at Shucorion meaningfully as they settled back into their seats. "Go ahead and bring us up to one-quarter sublight . . . *slowly.*"

Cracking along at sublight, the frigate tolerated barrier after barrier of increase, spearing past the planets and belts that decorated the Occult system.

It really was a pretty solar system, with plenty of local attractions and color. Like Earth's solar system, it had a large scrubber planet that swept the system clean of most dangerous asteroids and debris, allowing life to exist in relative safety on Belle Terre.

Amazing—how really fast sublight speed was. After months traveling at warp speed, Keller had almost forgotten how powerful impulse engines really were. The ship barreled through the solar system in just a couple of minutes.

"Clearing the last planet," Bonifay announced, hunched over the science station. He hadn't settled back into his chair, but he was hanging on to the rolled edge of the console. "I'm getting readings of the incoming fleet. I'm reading twelve . . . thirteen vessels."

"Thirteen," Keller murmured. He tried to add up the relative power of Kauld ships compared to what he had under him, or at least what *they* might imagine he possessed. The frigate was such an unknown quantity—if only he knew what she could do, he could add up the comparison numbers and calculate the odds. For now, he could do nothing but hope to puff his feathers and look nasty.

"We'll never get there at this speed," Scott recommended. "Better to meet them in interstellar space than right on our own doorstep."

This was Scott's not-so-subtle manner of telling Keller he'd better give that one big order.

Okay. Time to give it. Real soon.

Right now. He nodded in agreement with himself, and his mouth went completely dry.

"Warp factor . . ."

When he gave the order, the ship would blow itself into a trillion microbits, sparkling all over the place and making a real nice light show. Matter and antimatter everywhere, glowing shards racing through space, and little bits of Nick stew splattered across the enemy screens, along with some of Zoa's toenails and the comb Zane always kept in his pocket for hair emergencies.

"Go to warp factor . . ."

Would the nacelles rip off? Would the core explode? Would the computer throw a snit?

Picking up the catch in Keller's voice and the pallor in his face, Shucorion leaned slightly toward him.

"Are you all right?" he asked.

The question snapped Keller out of a shudder. "It's nothing. Just a minor coronary. . . ."

"I won't take over," Scott warned from up there.

Keller hunched to his purpose. "We've heard that one before. Warp . . . factor . . . one."

Everyone held on this time. *Crack—shoooom—*a bright flash momentarily blanked out the forward screen, which then instantly settled back to a view of space, but now at hyperlight speed. Perfect! Something had finally gone right! An important something, the most important one so far.

"Very pretty," Scott commented. He looked at Shucorion. "Good antimatter core you got there, mister."

"Thank you," Shucorion quietly said. "It was a gift."

Savannah looked up. "Nick, all the lights just turned off on deck eleven!"

Keller looked over his shoulder. "You mean that's going to happen every time we go to warp?"

"Looks like, until we figure out why it happens.

There aren't any battery lights rigged in the engineering section yet. The crew on deck eleven wants a recommendation."

"Tell them to go up to deck ten and borrow a cup of electrons."

"You should also know," she continued while she had the chance, "there aren't very many safeties working on board yet. People could open a hatch and end up in space. There's no automation to stop it from happening."

"Aw, great snakes . . . what else?"

"Some of the decks aren't pressurized, and some don't have oxygen flowing yet."

He swiveled his chair in her direction. "You better get the word around for everybody to be *extremely* careful. Don't just run through a doorway or open a hatch. Work the lifts and doors manually. Check pressurization before they open anything—" Now he swung back and looked in the other direction. "Zane, I wish you'd told me about this earlier."

"What could you have done about it?"

"I—I could—get—a running start on panic, I guess, I don't know." He rubbed his icy hands again, then moved up to his bare arms under the T-shirt sleeves. "Boy, it's cold. I left my jacket outside."

"We'll find you a jacket," Bonifay promised.

"Open that starboard deck box right under the life-support station, there, ah—lad," Scott said, apparently forgetting Bonifay's name.

Bonifay crossed the bridge and pulled open one of the gray panels. Inside were stacks of tightly knitted sweaters about the same color as the burgundy carpet. Beside them were some of the same design that were navy blue, and a few the color of dried moss.

"Perfect," Bonifay said. "You look like a medium."

He pulled one of the burgundy sweaters out, shook it

free of its folds, and tossed it to Keller, who asked, "Are these Starfleet issue?"

"They are now," Scott said, "because I'm issuing them to you."

He had a point. Standing there in his blood-colored Starfleet tunic with the snappy black lining and belt and the delta-shield buckle and all, he was the supreme local symbol of that far-reaching authority that Keller so much hoped would carry weight way out here, on the spin of reputation alone.

Scott pointed at the lower carpet and added, "They match your rug. I found the red ones in a locker on the *Beowulf*, and the blues and puke-greens came in from one of the privateers. I think they're Starfleet commando surplus, but don't swear me in. Pull it on."

"Yeah, pull it on," Savannah said. "It'll match your face if you turn any redder."

Shored up by her excuse for a joke, Keller tugged the burgundy sweater over his head. It had a comfortable turtleneck that made him feel warmer immediately. Yes, this was better. Now that he wasn't so cold, he began to feel less vulnerable and was able to think more clearly. Funny how that worked.

On the nav board before him, the proximity sensors showed a display graphic of thirteen ship forms, not much more than blips, making a course adjustment and turning crisply toward the freckles on Keller's nose. They must see the frigate by now.

Go to warp two? Did he dare? Would he be pushing his luck?

Something was bumping his right shoulder. He reached up to scratch it, but found instead that Bonifay was standing beside him. When Keller looked up, Bonifay quietly said, "Let me take the nav. You shouldn't have to do this."

Immediately he felt as if he were being scolded. Defiance flared, and instantly died. He had no right to be insulted. The moment rushed back when Lake had taken the helm on *Peleliu,* making him and the whole crew very nervous. When Lake was doing the helmsman's job, then he wasn't doing the captain's job. Now Keller was making the same mistake.

Then he saw something else. The respect in Bonifay's face took him by surprise. He hadn't really stopped to think anymore about how the crew judged him for his egregious actions and failures in the past few weeks, yet the message in Bonifay's voice and in his expression were perfectly clear and enheartening.

The captain shouldn't have to do this.

Keller pressed his hand to the nav desk and stood up, then moved out of the way.

"Thanks, Zane," he said. "Thanks."

Bonifay's vote of confidence did almost as much for him as Shucorion's words on top of the salvage mountain. If he could win those two over, maybe there was hope.

On the forward screen, he saw the magnified flickers that would within minutes grow into Kauld ships.

"Shields up," he requested. "Let's have red alert."

Since Shucorion was at the helm, there was no acting first officer to repeat orders, and suddenly Keller got the feeling that might be all right on a smaller ship, with a smaller crew. Dispense with some of the racket. One watch, one officer. Might work.

"Red alert, aye," Scott responded, and engaged the system.

The ship flushed with additional power. The lights on the bridge, and all over the vessel, switched over to the scarlet that would let their eyes work without adjusting. At least, human eyes. What happened to Zoa's or Shucorion's was anybody's guess—

Then the science station started burping smoke.

"Circuit crossfeed!" Scott called. "Shut that down quick!"

"I'll do it!" Bonifay blurted. Momentarily abandoning his station to the autonav, he dashed back to the starboard quarterdeck to handle shutdown, but made the mistake of bumping Zoa's tactical pulpit just forward of the science station. Her pulpit moved firmly inward like a jackknife, giving her a squeeze she didn't appreciate.

The pulpits were hinged!

Of course—so they could be swung out of the line of traffic in case of abandon ship. Smart!

It would have seemed smarter if Zoa hadn't reacted to the inconvenience by nailing Bonifay under the ribs with her very skillful elbow. He let out a hard *oof* and crumpled, then rolled under the rail, stopped only by one of the mounting struts.

Keller rushed around the rail end, jumped to the quarterdeck and hit the safety shutdown himself. The alert immediately went silent and the science station settled down to a happy flicker again.

Then Keller knelt and kept Bonifay from falling off the ledge. "Zoa, don't hit shipmates!"

She looked down at her handiwork, unapologetic as usual despite Bonifay writhing near her toenails.

"Can that desk be locked open?" Keller asked.

"Aye, or closed," Scott said. "But the locks disengage during red alert."

"You'll have to give me a list of these things, sir."

"If we live, lad."

"Speaking of which—Zoa, arm phaser banks. We . . . do have phasers, don't we?"

"Oh, aye," Scott confirmed, "she's bristlin'."

Moaning under Keller's hands, Bonifay gasped, "I'm all right—I'm all right—she's pointy!"

"Poor kid," Keller empathized. "Can you stand up?"

"Just drag me—to my chair—where I can die on—duty."

"Come on. No hurry. Take it easy."

But there was a reason to hurry. The Kauld ships, now clearly identified by their exhaust formula and their configuration, were coming in at their full speed. As Keller deposited Bonifay back in the nav chair, he noticed that there weren't just the usual lobster-clawed Kauld battle barges, but other types of ships with them, configured completely differently. Some other kind of attack vessel he hadn't heard about?

Didn't matter. They weren't coming in to have lunch.

"Nick, do it," Savannah urged. "Hail them."

"Yeah," Bonifay said. "Give 'em hail."

"I will flay them all!" Zoa bent to her weapons boards, furiously poking the targeting computer.

On sheer reflex Keller slapped his hand to the rail beside her. When she flinched and looked up, he clearly said, "*Not* without my order. *Nothing* without a direct order. Understand?"

She didn't like it, but she understood. Keller held up a warning finger.

"Vulcan-like," he reminded again.

Zoa squared her bare shoulders and settled back in her chair. She would wait.

He turned again to the forward screen, taking a sustaining grip on the green leather arm of the command chair, even though he couldn't bring himself to sit down. "Somebody put me through to them."

Up on the sci-deck to Keller's left, Mr. Scott handled the mechanics from the engineering remote. "You're tied in."

Diane Carey

Keep it simple. He reached into his pocked and
closed his hand around the shuttle coin with its gold
rim and its spirit of hope, drawing strength from the en-
couraging face of Tim McAddis not too far back in his
mind. He mentally flipped the coin, then decided what
to say.

"This is Commander Nick Keller aboard the United
Federation of Planets Composite Frigate *Challenger.*
We're prepared to defend this solar system. Stand down
your approach immediately or we will open fire."

*And hope we don't fall into a dozen pieces in front of
God and Lucifer and everybody in the stands.*

Chapter Twenty-one

"THIS IS Vellyngaith of Kauld. We come to speak, to confer. Will you speak?"

With a ship he didn't know, Keller guessed the best plan would be a stand-still battle. He wondered if he could pull it off, maneuver the enemy into doing things his way. He tried to recall the images of classroom studies, battle plans by famous generals down through history, but his mind went blank. He wasn't Caesar or Grant or Kirk or Vercingetorix, or anybody like them.

Then again, who knows? Maybe they started out puny and miserable too. Sure. Sure, they did.

"Shucorion, bring us to a stop," he ordered. "All stations, stand ready for battle maneuvers."

Vellyngaith had asked to talk. He just didn't believe it. Even to hear that he was facing Vellyngaith himself shook him to the toes of his cowboy boots.

But now he saw something on the screen, on the lead ship. The ship's rust-colored hull was patched with an

Diane Carey

arrangement of white plates, formed in a fluid rectangle, as if it were frozen in a wave formation.

He stepped forward to Shucorion's side. "Is that a white flag broadcast on their hull? It can't be. How are they doing that?"

"We've learned your symbols," Shucorion confirmed. "It's done with what you call holograph technology on certain specially made hull plating. We developed them for visual communication in the Blind." He lowered his voice and warned, "He may not use it honestly."

The smallest of cynical grunts burst from Keller's lips. "Any suggestions?" he requested.

"Broadcast a loud guffaw," Bonifay muttered. "Maybe they'll run away."

"Shoot them," Zoa contributed.

Shucorion pressed his lips and made a little shrug with his eyes. "Ask him."

"Mr. Scott," Keller addressed, "could you patch me through again, please?"

"Aye, sir, cough button off."

Though his mouth opened and he had an idea of what to say, Keller abruptly choked on what he'd just heard. A "sir" from Montgomery Scott? When did he start deserving that? It was like being called "sir" by your dad!

He cleared his throat and tried to sound sir-like. "This is Keller. Do you know you're broadcasting a symbol of truce?"

"Yes, truce. Surrender. Treaty. Anything! I am speaking from the official barge of our Common Cabinet, our ruling assembly. All our leaders are on board. We are turning ourselves over to you. Please do not kill us!"

Scowling so hard his face hurt, Keller stood up and hung his hands on his hips. "I don't think Caesar ever faced a challenge like that. And something tells me we're not quite that scary."

Here was the frigate—what had he just named it?—coming up face-to-face with thirteen Kauld vessels of various makes and sizes racing in at them, and they were surrendering.

Forgot the question mark.

They were surrendering?

"Target phasers on the biggest ship," he said, canting his head toward Zoa.

Suddenly Shucorion grasped Keller's arm. "Wait!" He squinted at the forward screen as the Kauld ships slowed and came to a halt in front of the frigate. "Indeed that is their Common Cabinet's formal vessel. It never flies without members aboard. Never."

"Zoa, hold your fire," Keller accommodated, then asked Shucorion, "Are you absolutely sure?"

"It would violate their laws. They never violate their own laws."

"Mm . . . well, considering they could mash us like grapes—"

He glanced at Scott, whom he noticed was putting the comm broadcast on and off at just the right times.

"Vellyngaith," he called, "give me one reason why I should believe an offer of surrender instead of just opening fire on you right now, given our past relationship."

"Commander, I beg to you, general to general. Our weapons are exhausted. We have expelled them against a new enemy. We have become desperate. I wish to come aboard your ship, to prove my truth to you. Scan us. We will bring nothing. I know you can do this with what you have. Bring me there, with these people standing around me. We will prove ourselves to you."

Beam them over? Here? Who had beaten them so badly that they were "desperate"?

On the screen, thirteen very large, imposing, and well armed Kauld ships hovered. A herd of hyenas standing before a single stubborn stag. They were quite capable of ripping the stag to little leathery shreds. Why did they want to lie down before it?

Vellyngaith must know he was putting his life on the line to come over here. If he wanted to commit suicide, he could do it back home. Did he think the frigate would be somehow vulnerable if he were aboard?

No, couldn't be.

He didn't want to ask for opinions again and seem wishy-washy in front of people who needed to have confidence in his judgment. There was a certain amount of professional performance expected of him, or at least he expected it of himself. How often were captains just acting confident?

"Get out the coin," Bonifay grumbled.

Keller snapped him a look, but the clever bosun was grinning at his own comment. He hadn't meant it the way Keller was about to take it.

The little joke between them gave him a vitamin shot.

"Put red alert on standby," he said. "Maintain yellow alert and battle stations. Put the shields on manual. Mr. Scott, can you do that with the transporter? Scan them for weapons?"

As Scott worked the engineering boards, the lights on the bridge shifted from red to day-normal. Keller instantly wondered if that was a good decision. Another gamble. If the enemy was coming on board, he wanted to be able to see very clearly.

"For hardware and energy, yes." Scott's brows popped up. "Not reading any. Still a gamble, though. They've got what looks to be fifteen life-forms in a pack, ready to beam over."

That spared Keller's having to ask the not particularly ridiculous question about whether or not the frigate even had transporters.

"Okay, just let me think."

"Might not have time."

Keller held out a hand—an enormity, considering whom he was silencing. "If they're bluffing, they're gonna kill us. If they're surrendering, they'll wait a minute while I think."

The carpet fibers blurred before him as he paced in front of the command chair, turned and paced back. As he turned once again, the fibers began to sharpen, his eyes and mind to focus all at once.

He looked over to Bonifay at the nav set. "Have we got sidearms here?"

Bonifay slid out of his chair, crossed to his right and opened a panel in the wall part of the quarterdeck housing. Another smart move—the whole quarterdeck was really a huge storage locker, and every panel a hatch. He pulled open the second one from forward. Inside was a bank of hand phasers.

He looked at Keller. "No security team to use them."

"Break 'em out."

Phasers were delivered to all hands. True to the proffer, Vellyngaith was waiting, apparently patiently, and not releasing the firepower they knew he possessed.

Phaser in hand, Keller clicked the weapon to the kill setting. He would take some chances, but not all chances.

And he was strengthened, if not relieved, when Shucorion took a weapon.

The phaser felt good, secure, in his fist. He was glad to have it. There was something peculiarly stiffening about being able to defend himself, or make an ultimate decision that he had every right to make. Its presence made him calm down, settled him inside, gave him the seaworthiness to think clearly, because he knew he possessed the strongest option. Once Vellyngaith and his whoevers came aboard, then thirteen to one wouldn't matter anymore. This phaser guaranteed that.

He glanced around. Everyone was standing. To his left, Shucorion held his phaser in both hands, gripped in one, cupped in the other. On the port quarterdeck, Savannah and Scott were both standing ready.

His neck cracked as he turned to starboard. There, on the deck beside him, Zane Bonifay was pale, but also ready. Above him, Zoa had her strong legs braced, her knees bent, both arms straight out forward, and a phaser in each hand.

A whole new set of alarms went off in Keller's head. He put out a hand to get Zoa's attention. When her blue-dot eyes locked on his, he crisply instructed, "You're my last line of defense. You fire *last,* not *first.* Understand? Do you understand me?"

He held his position. She was making up her mind whether this was a compliment or something else.

Her shoulders relaxed very slightly. "I hav't."

Was her word any good? Should he tell her she was Vulcan-like again?

Welding his instruction into place with a final nod, because he only half believed her, Keller stepped back and motioned Shucorion back as well, to make room on the forward deck for the unwelcome contingent about to appear.

"All right, Mr. Scott," he began, "beam them aboard."

Only seconds later the blue-gold buzz of transporter beams brightened the bridge. Keller's chest tightened as the beams settled down into fifteen blue-skinned people. Obviously they were from the same strain as Shucorion's Blood race, but the culture was completely different. For one thing, they wore jewelry and feathers, beads and brighter colors than the Blood. In comparison with the utilitarian and thrifty Blood, these people looked instantly frivolous.

The assessment might not be fair at all, of course, but that was the first impression.

In front of the group stood a large man with long backswept silver hair that had been knotted with feathers and beads. Vellyngaith.

A warrior command of a whole new hostile culture, one of the most dangerous personalities in the Sagittarius Cluster.

Such a reputation would've been borne up rather better, had he not been holding a bundled-up baby in his arms.

If he figured Keller wouldn't shoot at a guy holding an infant—well, he was right.

And about half of these people were women. Keller hadn't expected that either. The Blood didn't fly with their women. He'd expected the same of the Kauld.

He felt suddenly silly holding a bunch of weapons on what looked just like a family reunion.

Vellyngaith met Shucorion's eyes in a moment of surprise, then simply accepted his enemy's presence on board this ship and ignored him.

"Commander Keller?" he began.

"I'm Keller."

Without another word, Vellyngaith stepped forward, shoved the burbling baby into Keller's arms, never mind the phaser or anything, then lumbered to his knees and crawled all the way down, until he was completely prostrate on the deck in front of Keller.

He took hold of Keller's ankles and pressed his face to the carpet.

One by one all the adults in the group also went to their knees, then down on the deck, until the carpet was completely obscured by a field of prone forms.

Diane Carey

"Kill me," Vellyngaith entreated, his words muffled by his arms pressed to the sides of his noble face. "Take my son. Take my wife and all these women of power. Kill the Cabinet. Arrest our generals. Imprison our soldiers. We will swear to anything! But help us . . . help us!"

328

Chapter Twenty-two

KELLER STARED DOWN.

At his feet lay a fan of mortal bodies, some sobbing freely. Whether in fear or shame, he couldn't guess.

In his arms, the little Vellyngaith cooed and waved his tiny blue fists. At least they had babies and not polliwogs. One thing in common. For him and for his crew, malevolence simply melted away.

Well, a start's a start.

A shocked silence plied the bridge. Even the bleeps and whirs of the consoles seemed to fade under the astonishment.

Keller looked to his side, hoping to get a gauge of the situation from Shucorion.

He got it. Shucorion was backed all the way up to the locker under the sci-deck, rendered completely stupefied, shocked, even horrified.

Keller wobbled briefly, but his ankles were being held in place by Vellyngaith's grip of tribute.

He managed to turn enough to shuffle the baby over

to Bonifay, who moved the little guy behind the command chair, out of the line of Zoa.

Though he almost fell over, with his legs being passionately held in place, Keller managed to lean over some and speak softly.

"Ah . . . you don't have to stay on the ground . . . but why don't you go ahead and say what you came to say."

Vellyngaith not only stayed on the deck, but spoke into the carpet, forcing Keller to listen extra carefully.

"The grantors have returned. They bring not dynadrive this time, but death. A force, a fiend, a blight— it came to the next solar system and destroyed an entire planet before our eyes. It sprayed our ships, ruining our armor. It sucks away energy as you and I take a drink. It turns now toward our planet. You have science far beyond ours. . . . Help us, we beg . . . Help us, help us . . ."

"You wrecked my ship," Keller reminded, "drove my captain to his breaking point, threatened our colony, and now you want help?"

"I beg it. Everything is destroyed. Our fleet will never recover. We are all here to sacrifice ourselves. We will sign any treaty, join you, live conquered, but let us live. Name your terms."

"You've got ships," Keller said. "Fight your own fight."

"Our science is not like yours. We've been in space but a few years. You've been for generations. Our weapons could not scratch it. We have no time to evacuate our world. You can meet this threat."

Keller pressed one hand to a hip and the other to his face. This was nutsy.

"Why don't you stand up?" he invited. "We'll handle this man to man. Get right up. All of you folks, stand right up."

Shuddering and breathing with effort, Vellyngaith got to his hands and knees. There he paused, so long that Keller reached down to pull him to his feet. The battlelord who had moments ago seemed so elegantly strong now seemed weak and aged.

With obvious effort and inner resolve, Shucorion came forward. "What is this, Battlelord?" he demanded. "What drives such as you to our ankles?"

"You were right," Vellyngaith said to him. "The galaxy is too big for squabbles. All Kauld are willing to become subjects of Federation. Anything, anything . . . anything."

"What did it do to the planet?" Mr. Scott asked. "Blow it up? Cut it up?"

Vellyngaith looked up at him, sheer terror filling his eyes. "The planet . . . is *gone!*"

His words virtually echoed.

"Vanished?" Scott demanded. "No debris? No wash?"

"Nothing!"

Certainly that was more terrifying than a giant explosion. Just—gone?

"Wait a minute," Keller interrupted. "This thing in space—it turned, you said? Was it a ship?"

"No, no ship. A blot in space. A moving poison!"

"But it changed course?"

"Yes."

"Then it's not a natural object. What was on the planet it consumed? What kind of energy?"

Vellyngaith closed his eyes. Pure shame rose in his face. "Olivium."

Exasperated, Keller huffed, " 'Zat so. And just how did olivium end up way over there, on the other side of your solar system from where we are?"

"I put it there. To hide it." Seeing where this was going and genuinely wishing to rush the project, Vellyngaith drew a breath and blurted the whole story. "I have been in collusion with a walking flaw named Maidenshore. He has been stealing olivium from the colony and giving it to me to hide on his behalf. He would then use it to—"

"Yeh, I think I've got that angle," Keller interrupted. "Skip that part."

"My thanks. He has been stealing from you, and I have been stealing from him, dividing everything he gave me and storing it not in one place, but in two. I took half of everything and buried it deep in our home planet, and the rest I buried in the planet which has been eaten by this force, this imminence that comes. This ghoul! This blight!"

Keller made a calming gesture and actually found himself patting his enemy's shaking arm. "Now, don't overreact. . . . Let's work this through. You think it's after the olivium? Because that means we've got ourselves a pattern of events going on here. Sounds the same as what's happening on Belle Terre, except on a way bigger scale."

He turned to Scott, and got a nod of confirmation for his sleuthing.

"And it eats energy," he threw in, just to see if anyone disagreed.

No one did.

"Let our people live," Vellyngaith pleaded again. "We surrender. We understand now that the galaxy is too big. We have no soldiers left who can fight. We stand ready to have done to us what we would have done to Blood Many. We will change. Execute me, all of us here—set up your own government. We will be your subjects! Shucorion, speak for us all! Tell him we are sincere!"

He was nearly in a panic. His eyes were ringed, exhausted, as he turned to his longtime opponent and made a motion that seemed he might go down on his knees again.

Shucorion watched this, and his astonishment

changed before Keller's eyes to some kind of irritation. He moved toward Vellyngaith and all the other Kauld who were watching in polite silence. He wasn't intimidated at all anymore.

"All my life," he began, "I believed we had to win by destroying all others. But these people have come here with a new way, a powerful way. They are all industrious, and they are *not* trying to break each other. They do not dominate. Understand—they have no wish, no plan to dominate you, and after this short season with them, I have no such wish either. You can live, we can live—let us rise to their level, not make them sink to ours."

"I have offered my own execution!" Vellyngaith thundered. "What more must I do!"

Disgusted, Shucorion folded his arms. "I haven't been with these people long, but I shall make a gamble with you. I gamble that this man will not kill you. Just hope he doesn't leave it to me. I am not so good in the heart yet."

Keller pressed back a flattered smile, but didn't interrupt. Shucorion paced away a few steps, troubled and now angry.

"Blood Many once believed as All Kauld," he went on, "that we had to fight or be overrun. We won not by fighting, but by refusing to fight. We have no more need to fight, because we have a mighty friend now. We're part of Federation now, and they won't allow what we've been doing to each other. We will let you live, and we expect you to do the same for us."

"What must I say to you?" Vellyngaith spread his hands beseechingly. "We will go to the ankles of Federation! All Kauld will shrink willingly, if only we can be saved!"

Passionate, Shucorion closed the distance between them in two steps. "When will you understand? They don't want subjects, Battlelord! They have no con-

Diane Carey

quered peoples among them! Everyone here is involved
for himself, for his own best interest, and this way
everyone prevails. Get this through your beads and
feathers!" He actually poked Vellyngaith in the heavy
placquet of necklaces on his chest. "There need not be
winners and losers. There can be winners and winners!"

Seemed simple. Like the punch line to a morality
play.

Maybe it wasn't so simple for the people of the
Sagittarius Cluster.

Keller remained silent, though he felt the grilling
eyes of his own shipmates behind him, and the inten-
sity of the Kauld presence. All these people were leaders of a whole planet. Here they were, on his
stitched-together bridge, begging him to save their entire world.

The burden pressed down on him. He blew it to start
with, should've taken over the other ship at the right
time, and now until Starfleet got somebody in here to
court-martial him and relieve him of command, he
owed all the colonists on Belle Terre the promised protection, he owed the Federation a safe cache of olivium,
he owed the Blood a bond of alliance, and suddenly the
Kauld rushed in and asked him to owe them too.

Mr. Scott's words flooded back to him. He'd found
out what the enemy wanted.

And he had no idea how to tell them what the truth
looked like.

334

Chapter Twenty-three

THE MOOD WAS one of amazement on the frigate's bridge. Shucorion, Vellyngaith, Keller—all were amazed at something, if not the same things.

Winners and winners.

Nick Keller felt charged to make good on that instruction.

As Vellyngaith lowered his head in salute to Shucorion's revelations, all the other Kauld also lowered their heads. They weren't ashamed, exactly, but he had humbled them with apparently new concepts.

Keller stepped between them. "How far away is this thing?" he asked Vellyngaith.

"Between our solar system and the other."

"So, between Whistler and the solar system on the far side. Is that right?"

"Yes," Shucorion confirmed, sparing Vellyngaith the trick of discovering what was whistling.

"Are you armed as powerfully as you were before?"

Vellyngaith asked. "Do you have the power of the other ship?"

Not exactly a question Keller dared answer. His head was spinning. "Don't worry, we've got plenty of firepower here. I don't suppose you can decoy it," he suggested to Vellyngaith. "Maybe pull the olivium out of your planet and move it somewhere else."

Vellyngaith's grayish-blue expression paled in embarrassment and sorrow. "Would take months."

Keller sighed. "Yeh, well, I figured if you could do it, you'd have already done it." He pulled the *Challenger* coin from his pocket, slapped it down on the helm desk and pointed accusingly at it. "Shut up, you."

Bonifay, a little nervous and a little bold, said, "Give it a toss."

"No, I don't need to. It's been sitting in my pocket, mumbling at me and biting my leg."

Vellyngaith peered down at the coin, seeming to expect it to actually speak. Perhaps it was some kind of supertech from the mysterious laboratories of Federation.

Keller knew what the coin had to say. He wanted more time to think, but he also knew he'd already made up his mind. There they were, representatives of the enemy planet, and here was Shucorion representing the whole Blood world, and over there was Zoa, here to see if she wanted to recommend to the Rassua people to join up with the UFP, and up yonder was Mr. Scott, all of Starfleet in one suit, watching him to see what he would do next. Not to mention Savannah and Zane. Why should they follow him after today? Would they have a reason?

He turned to face the rest of them. "Reckon we should go see what it is."

Vellyngaith went down on one knee before him, once again clasping Keller's ankles.

"Simmer down, please," Keller pleaded, and wriggled out of the grip. "Stand back up, will you?"

"If it's anything kin to those probes," Scott pointed out, "your phasers won't affect it. You've only got four photons, and there's doubt they'll scratch it either."

"I know, sir," Keller said. "But I can't let it go eat these people's planet. At least we can fly our brand-new jalopy in and have a look. Maybe we can figure out what how to deflect it."

Zoa nodded her braids once, sharply, and Bonifay winced at the idea. The baby wailed his single protest, then settled down to the business of fingering Bonifay's black hair.

Now that the decision had been made, Keller thought of a hundred things to do.

"Savannah, evacuate the crew personnel to the shuttlebay. Tell them to put everything on automatic or manual. I'll handle as much as I can. You load them up and go with them."

"Not me!" she protested. "I'm here now! You're not making me go back there and live with all those surface dwellers. Forget it."

She planted herself in her seat, clasped her pulpit firmly, then shot him a defiant glare. An impudent strand of her hair flopped over one eye.

Her devotion pulled a half grin from him. He looked at Zoa, but never even got the question out. The Rassua crossed her arms over her chest, each hand holding a phaser. She took a calculated step backward and stood like a carved statue guarding a pharaoh's tomb. Immovable.

He shifted his question to Zane Bonifay. "What about you, gypsy?"

Bonifay jiggled the alien baby. "It's my nomadic nature."

"You're all bats."

"But we're *your* bats."

Could the worst day of a man's life also be the best?

Strung out, he put one hand on Zane's shoulder and the other hand on the arm of the command chair to steady himself as he turned yet again and faced the port side stations. "Mr. Scott, I'd like you to take our shuttlecraft and our evacuated crewmen, and escort these people back to Belle Terre and explain things to Governor Pardonnet, please. If we fail, you'll have to gear up to fight this thing. Can't exactly move the Quake Moon away from Belle Terre. Maybe we can at least buy you some time."

"I'd rather stay with you," Scott offered, but he spoke in a tone that made clear his offer, not his order.

"I appreciate that, sir, but you're the only one who can lead these people in and not be fired upon by the planetary defense network. They just wouldn't believe anybody else, I mean, *I* wouldn't." He paused, accepting the passage of a torch from one generation to another. "Besides, I can order my own crew to go out and die with me. I can't order Captain Kirk's crew. You've done your part. It's our turn."

Scott didn't like the order, but there were a lot of things about the sentiment that he did seem to respect. He simply nodded and gave Keller one final gift.

"Aye aye, sir."

Warmed, Keller turned to Shucorion. "I can't order you either. You've got crewmen of your own to take care of. And not only that, but you have to explain to the Blood people what's going on. If we succeed, they'll have to learn how to make nice with these guys. With such a wild proclamation, they'll need somebody they can believe."

"My men will explain on my behalf," Shucorion told him. "I shall stay with you and pilot your jalopy."

The clear display of trust almost bowled Keller onto his backside just like the mule engines had. When had he earned anyone's devotion, never mind a man like Shucorion? A captain, a leader? An alien crossing over every line of contact his people had ever established?

"Thanks," he uttered. His voice rasped a little.

Shucorion smiled, as if Keller were somehow entertaining.

Turning now to Vellyngaith and the gaggle of Kauld, Keller said, "You people go with Commander Scott here. If we fail and your planet's destroyed, at least the handful of you will be alive to tell about it. Just raise that baby right, will you?"

"I will name him 'Keller'!" Vellyngaith vowed.

"No!" Erupting in an anguished laugh, Keller shook his head and pleaded, "Let's not get syrupy here! Just leave his name where it is."

"You are willing to die for our world!"

"And don't you forget it. Welcome to Humanity."

Cold now even inside the nice commando sweater, Keller paced away to put some distance between himself and the overwhelming changes of the past few minutes.

Behind him, Vellyngaith addressed Shucorion. "And you, Avedon? You will go with this man and die for All Kauld? If our planet is destroyed, this is the best thing that could happen to you. You have dreamed of it all your life."

Not denying a bit of it, Shucorion could've been rude. Instead he simply said, "Another change for us all."

Moved, Vellyngaith squared his slumped shoulders. "Then I will go with you also, and represent All Kauld." He turned to the other Kauld people and addressed one of the men. "Fremigoth, go with them and carry my final order. Listen to these humans. They are better than we are."

He shifted a step, to one of the women, and took her by both wrists.

"Raise our child human," he charged.

Must be his wife. The Kauld woman simply nodded, her eyes full of promise and adoration for him.

This was the weirdest day. . . .

But Keller was already thinking beyond all this. His fear was being overtaken by something else. How tantalizing, how infectious, to be rushing out to meet the unknown! If he could keep his breakfast down, he'd be right up there with the charioteers on that coin.

And just as a bonus, no matter what happened after this, Shucorion and Vellyngaith were standing shoulder to shoulder instead of face-to-face. How many planets, how many people were represented here on the frigate's bridge?

"Zane," Keller began, "what's the biggest supply of olivium that hasn't been crammed back into the Quake Moon?"

"Far as I know, the hold of the mining ship. *Pandora's Box.*"

"That's where we're going, then."

"Why?" Savannah asked.

For the first time, Keller slid into his command chair. The dark green leather folded around his thighs and welcomed his aching back. Not a bad chair. He raised his eyes to the forward viewscreen, to the thirteen Kauld ships floating humbly before his one cumbersome parade balloon, and past them to the dusty expanse of the Sagittarius Cluster and whatever that mysterious place held in store for them.

"Can't catch a shark without bait," he said.

Chapter Twenty-four

Pandora's Box

THE ROOM was now dimly lit by lights quickly fading. Frost rimed the edges of the console, the door, the bunk frame. The small quarters had become a strange Christmas card, etched with frozen crystals that muted every color. How pleasant it would be to wrap in a blanket.

But that wasn't the image Uhura wanted to convey when the inevitable happened. She wanted to look ready to go.

Oh, here he came. She heard the thunk and bump of heavy footsteps in the carpeted corridor of the former olivium chaser. What a strange life *Pandora's Box* had lived so far.

The door banged and bumped. Someone outside was fumbling. Very good. He was shaken up.

When Billy Maidenshore finally thundered in, he was red-faced with both cold and anger. Outside were the angry voices of other criminals, those he had conned into working with him by promising them the wind and stars. Like most people of his kind, Billy could no more deliver paradise than he could tell the truth two days in a row.

"What've you done?" he demanded.

Uhura pressed her freezing hands between her knees and asked. "About what?"

"We can't do anything! All the ship's systems are locked up! If we try to engage the drive, it'll blow up! We're losing oxygen, there's no heat, we're getting carbon-dioxide poisoning—the crew's panicking! Can't you hear them?"

"They're not a crew, Billy. They're escaped convicts. I mean to make them convicts again. Without moving them a single inch. This time, you're all in my prison instead of having me in yours."

"You better explain that, lady."

She defied him with silence this time. Whatever he wanted—answers or adoration—she would provide none.

He spun around to the bunk where McCoy lay under the finest blanket Billy had brought to Uhura. "McCoy, wake up! Wake up and die!"

"He won't wake up," Uhura said. "He's almost dead. See his sunken eyes? The cheekbones showing? No color in his lips? A few more minutes . . . and I'll be gone soon too. I just wanted to be alive long enough to tell you that you're going to die a lot more slowly than the doctor or I will. We've arranged for that."

A terrible shiver bolted through her, but she fought it, even pretended to enjoy it.

"You wanted us to talk about you," Uhura added. "So we did. We decided to put a stop to you."

Maidenshore stared at McCoy's face, the colorless complexion, the half-open but unseeing eyes. For a man who had caused so much misery, even death, he seemed stunned by the presence of it.

Uhura watched him, carefully measuring her tenor and timing. "You've forgotten, Billy. We're Starfleet officers. We're ready to die. At some point, it becomes our duty. It's my duty to make sure you don't cause any more misery or mischief or harm anyone else. It's going to get very cold out here. You may run out of air first, but I doubt it. You'll all be alive until your core temperature simply goes down so far that your hearts can't manage one more beat. Dr. McCoy explained hypothermia to me. There's nothing you can do about it. You control the *Pandora's Box,* but I've killed it."

Outside, the raging prisoners pounded on the door and called, "Billy! Get out here!"

"Shut up!" Billy shouted. "I'm working on it!"

They pounded a few more times, then fell oddly silent.

Fear. They were terrified. Why not? Hanging out here in space? All they could do was sit here and die, slowly, watching it come moment by moment.

"We've surprised you, haven't we?" she diagnosed. "That's because we discovered your secret."

"What secret?" he demanded.

She smiled. "That you won't die for anything . . . but we will."

Those words shook him to the bone. What a wonderful sight. His normally cocky eyes switched around as if to find answers on the walls, his hands clenched and unclenched, his guileless attitude fell to shreds.

"Call somebody," he ordered. "You call somebody!"

She waved her hand disinterestedly. "You've inhibited the whole system, remember?"

He fished frantically through his pockets for the code release device he'd been using on her system when he wanted messages sent. He plugged it into its socket, punched the code numbers in, fumbled the code, and had to start over. By the time he succeeded in opening up the communications system, he was thoroughly flustered and manic.

"Call somebody!" he screamed. "I'm cold!"

She gazed up at him, her own eyes sallow, her complexion patted down to a pasty tan. "What're you going to do? Kill me? What's fifteen minutes this way or that? I don't want to call anybody for you. You'll just try your shenanigans again."

Desperate, he swung to the board and began to punch out a distress call.

"Won't work," Uhura informed. "No one's going to answer another distress call from *Pandora's Box* after what happened the last time. Besides, I doubt the *Peleliu*'s in any condition to come out here and help us. Interesting, isn't it, that you arranged the ambush of the only ship capable of saving you?"

He turned to her, amazed, shaken, breathless with sheer cold and the truth she spoke. His mouth moved, but nothing came out.

"Did you think I was just a damsel in distress?" she crooned. She leaned back in her chair and put her feet up on the end of the bunk. "You're going to die in the dark, Billy."

Because of the relationship she had set up with him, he knew better than to take her words as posturing or bravado.

"Nobody kills me," he proclaimed, but he was frightened, biting his lip now, fitfully. "Nobody kills me . . . here—take it! Fix this!" He threw his hands up in the air and moved away from the console. "Whatever you did, stop it from happening. Stop it and I'll get you anything you want. I got connections, you know. Nobody kills me. Nobody kills me. . . ."

"Come here and tell me all about it." Uhura rubbed her leg on the side of his knee. "Maybe you can improve my opinion."

Apparently he picked up just the slightest perfume of second chance and grabbed for it. He moved closer, his lurid eyes fixed on her with either desire or despise. She couldn't tell which.

Didn't matter, either.

Once he was away from the bunk, he was theirs. She coiled her leg around him, slid all the way down in the chair, and yanked him off balance.

"Hey!" he wailed as his knees knocked into the edge of her chair.

McCoy appeared behind Maidenshore, who was concentrating too hard on Uhura to hear the doctor roll out of the bed. "Have a drink, Billy," he said, and pressed a hypo to Maidenshore's throat.

"Put him here." Uhura stood up and offered her chair.

McCoy steered the suddenly groggy racketeer into the chair, where he collapsed in a daze, muttering, "It's not fair . . . nobody's ever fair to me . . . what happened to simple fairness?"

Uhura looked down at him and shook her head. "He should never have left me with my makeup kit."

"Lock yourself in, just in case there's something I haven't thought of."

The doctor straightened abruptly, his teeth chattering some. "Where are you going?"

"To explain things to my prisoners. They're in a panic. I've shown them I can take them down. Now I'm going to explain it to them personally . . . what Uhura says she can do, she can do. Without Maidenshore, they'll do anything to survive, including recognize that I'm in charge of this ship and not Billy. They'll be very happy when I tell them to lock themselves into their cells and I'll take them to a nice warm penitentiary. They won't have to die with the ship failing around them, which is what they're looking at presently. After I have them convinced and confined, I'll come back and get the heat back on."

"You aren't even armed!"

"I don't need to be. I have a very big, cold knife pressing on all their throats."

"Lady," McCoy complimented, "you fight dirty."

Chapter Twenty-five

"GRAVITY!"

"Compensate! Full thrusters!"

"Thrusters are on full, sir!"

"Use the engines! Compensate! Keep compensating! Sulu, pull us back! Full power astern!"

Everyone, except Spock, was swimming in sweat. Even Spock had an unexpected sheen of amazement on his face.

Sulu fought with the protesting helm to draw the starship back, away from the enormous body that had suddenly appeared in space. Kirk was used to succeeding in his efforts, even if he had to pay a price or field a struggle—but this!

They had figured out how to attract the 'bot probe using the features of antimatter that were in similar flux to the olivium—not a good match, but close enough, apparently, to reach out and pull the tiny string that kept the probe in this universe, on this plane of existence.

Quite abruptly he found out he had pulled the string

that would unravel the whole sweater. A dangerous flicker, a wobble of space around them, and here they were, sitting next to a body, a vessel, a civilization big enough to have its own gravitational force!

Made sense. If you're going to pull something the size of a planet into your universe, you'd better expect mass and all its implications.

"Stabilizing, sir," Sulu finally gasped, exhausted and drenched in sweat.

Before them in space hung not a ship, but a mechanism or vehicle the size and mass of a very large planet. Or was it a planet in some unknown form?

A moving vessel so big that it possessed so much gravity? A planet that didn't need a sun for energy? Incredible!

The enormous body wasn't exactly round, but might once have been. Now it was more oblong, but uneven, with jagged parts and appendages that looked like huge skyscrapers, banded together at their tips with metallic filaments that flickered and glowed. Inside the filaments flowed a watery substance, some kind of energy generation or natural waterfall that changed colors every few moments. Kirk couldn't even begin to imagine what that stuff was, but he sensed the power.

And not to far from where the ship now hovered, pushing constantly against the gravitational pull of this big thing, was mounted one of the 'bots, sitting up on its table legs, fixed into a fitting that suited it perfectly.

"As you suspected, Jim," Spock said, "we were only seeing the very tip of the structure."

"Did you have any clue it would be that big?"

"None."

"What is it, Spock?"

"It reads as an amalgam of natural and constructed substances. It may have once been a planet, but was gradually fossilized into an architectural form, probably over several thousand millennia. Parts of the structure read over three hundred thousand years old. Other parts are nearly new. It is, therefore, no relic. It is in use."

"Why can I see through it every few seconds?"

"It's in flux even now."

"Doesn't sound like we can beam over and walk around," Kirk judged.

Spock closed his mouth on that idea and simply shook his head.

"Captain," Sulu said, "something I just noticed. We're within about forty light-years of the last known position of the *Rattlesnake*."

Kirk looked down at the starchart on Sulu's console. Kirk had sent the privateer, under the command of Captain Sunn, to look for possible places to relocate the Belle Terre colony in case the moon move didn't work. But Sunn hadn't come back, or reported in. After four months and a futile search for the ship, Kirk finally declared them lost.

Suddenly, a loud crack sounded in Kirk's head. Only inches from him.

"Jim!" Spock jumped down, skipping all the steps, and pulled Kirk backward, managing to keep them both on their feet.

Good thing he did too, because Kirk would've fallen forward into a suddenly available gaping opening *in the air before him.*

Not in the deck—in the air.

Around the back of it, he could still see the main screen broadcasting its picture of the archi-form in space.

With Spock's fingers digging into his arms, Kirk was relatively certain he wasn't dreaming. He was staring into a ramplike doorway, as if something had been pulled out of a dream.

"Don't shoot! Down in front! I'm comin' as fast as I can."

Far away, what seemed a mile into the illusion, came a trundling figure. As it came closer—much closer with each step than was physically possible for the distance Kirk was looking at—the form focused into a short, squarish person with broad shoulders and extremely short legs and arms.

Bearded and clenching a pipe in his teeth, the easygoing newcomer seemed human enough, but a human dwarf, no more than three and a half feet tall. He spun on strong bowed legs down an invisible ramp and out of the frameless doorway, his short arms spread in welcome.

"Holy smoke! James Kirk in the flesh! Didn't think I'd ever be rubbin' elbows with you!"

Bewildered, Kirk took the extended hand. "Who the devil are you?"

"Mitch Dogan, Captain Mitch Dogan! Me and my crew, we disappeared in a ball of flame back at that crazy moon at Belle Terre way before you guys showed up! How ya doin'?"

"Hey, you fellas look good!" Mitch Dogan said, flicking his quick eyes around at the astounded bridge crew. "I like the new uniform. Starfleet was still wearin' the grays when I left."

Kirk came forward and demanded, "How long have you been here?"

"About eight hundred years. Don't look a day over six hundred! Ha!"

Spock came to Kirk's side and looked past him at Dogan. "You were in the scout ship that disappeared during the final phase of survey at Belle Terre, correct?"

"Yeah, that's us."

"How did—"

"Yeah, how'd I end up way out here, I know, a bazillion things to ask about. The zombies pulled us out at the last second, just before our ship turned into a marshmallow. Guess they felt guilty, y'know, like you feel after you just kicked a zarr out of its hole. They asked me to come out here and talk to you, on account of I talk English so good."

Noting Sulu's terse opinion on one side, Kirk glanced at him, then back to Dogan "These beings were trying to discourage us, weren't they? Trying to get us to turn back."

"Yeah—jerks!"

"Fear of death is a potent instinct," Spock contributed. "They expected us to turn and run."

"They don't exactly understand," Dogan said. "Once time is conquered, y'know, death is too. They don't understand it no more. They'd forgot how adventurous people can get when they have a life span." He scratched his beard, then poked Kirk in the chest with the same finger. His eyes sparkled with delight. "I tried to warn 'em about you. But I ain't been around so long. They think I'm a kid. They forget how clever lifespanners can be. Just watchin' you guys come out here, you've promoted a huge discussion for hundreds of years about what's been lost in their pan-dimensional lifestyle." He leaned for a look at Spock. "See, I got some big words too, fella."

Spock congratulated him with a gentlemanly bow of his head.

"Hundreds of years?" Kirk asked.

"Well, it just happened in the past coupla hours."

"Hm?"

"In our dimension, Captain," Spock supplied. "These beings may have forgotten our driving forces, much as we have forgotten how bright and innovative Neolithic Man was to have engineered massive stone megaliths."

"Yeah, right," Dogan agreed. "You made us feel kinda fat and lazy. We gotta get out of the way of you young hawks. Gotta get crackin', maybe do some things again."

"'We'?"

"Oh—sorry. They're talkin' sort of 'with' me, get it? Sometimes it's me and sometimes it's 'we,' so if I start gettin', y'know, poetic, don't throw up, okay? It's just them pokin' their two credits in."

"These beings, Captain Dogan," Spock prodded, "are they spectral?"

"Y'mean are they ghosts? Naw. Just look like it!"

Spock lowered his voice. "We have encountered advanced beings who take on a rather sylphlike state to our perceptions. If they are noncorporeal, they may utilize corporeals to speak to other corporeals."

"Yeah," Dogan confirmed, biting his pipe.

Kirk squinted at the little man with the strong constitution. "I think I understand. Can we visit?" he asked, and gestured to the enormous archi-form in space.

Dogan looked at the main screen. "Pretty, ain't it? Nah, you don't wanna do that. You couldn't come back. They ain't figured out the go-home process."

Immediately protective of someone he considered one of his own, Kirk bristled. "Does that mean you can't come back with us?"

"Ain't so bad. Y'get used to it after the first coupla hundred years. Except, you don't happen to know the wrestling rankings, do you?"

"They exist and move through the fourth dimension," Spock concluded, "with only a few molecules in our space."

"Yeah," Dogan confirmed. "They didn't want to clutter up your space. Like you keep your furnace in the basement and just use the hot air."

"If that is the case, Captain, then these beings must exist on a multimillennial level."

"I like that!" Dogan validated. "'Multimillennial.' That's a good name for 'em! I been spendin' a coupla centuries callin' 'em 'fella' and 'you guys.'"

Spock was on a roll, not really speaking to anyone specific anymore. "This would allow the capacity to relive your experiences over and over."

"That's one of the problems," Dogan said. "They got to a point they didn't have to move around no more. Turned lazy. Quit doin' stuff for themselves. Kinda lost their muscle, y'know? Didn't build no more ships, didn't walk around, sort of cashed in their physical presence. Now they wish they could get it back. They just love watchin' you guys! They don't actually travel in space no more, except for the little suckers running around. They think your ship, mine too, are so—*so* exciting! Charging around on a block of contained power like ridin' some kind of stallion! The Blood, the Kauld, us humans and Federation guys, we inspired them. Only a few hundred years ago we was coming out of the caves and look at us now! So these guys, they want to go someplace else and start over, be a young culture again."

Kirk couldn't hold back an amazed smile. "That's very flattering."

"That these really smart, really old people want to go someplace and be us? Damn right it is. They want to go get some enthusiasm." Dogan tilted his squat body forward and warned, "And, Kirk, they mean to get out of our way."

Somehow, with all his command instincts and experiences screaming in his ears, Kirk did not like the sound of that at all.

"You want to explain that?" he required.

"Yeah . . . They're cleanin' up behind themselves. That's why they're going around suckin' back their olivium. They're about to leave the galaxy for good. Believe it or not, there are plenty of empty galaxies out there just waitin' to be explored, places where intelligence ain't got a grip yet. And after watchin' us for a coupla thousand years, the zombies—The Formless—they want to get back in the game!"

"I see no ships, no spacedocks, no mass-transportation devices," Kirk pointed out. "How are they leaving?"

"Beats me. They just think about it, and go."

"Why wouldn't they use ships to move, if they use probes to collect their olivium?"

"They don't remember how to. The probes come from an older time. They couldn't make 'em now if they wanted to. Do you know how to make fire in the jungle?"

"Actually," Spock said, "yes."

"Maybe that's a bad example. Just a minute. Let me get up here and look at you eye to eye."

Dogan wheeled about and thumped up the bridge steps to the quarterdeck, then turned and looked at Kirk with his chin just over the rail.

"We got trouble, though," he said. "Back before they figured out to use the little suckers that don't really hurt nobody, they was using bigger energy neutralizers to suck up the stuff they wanted to collect."

"What is the nature of this neutralizer, Captain Dogan?" Spock immediately asked.

"It's kind of like . . . a spot of nonexistence. A moving black hole with no gravity. It just swallowed sources of energy. A cold factor. You'd know it if you saw it. First thing that happens is your ship loses power and just quits on ya."

"What's the problem?" Kirk demanded. His fists knotted at his thighs. He didn't mean to sound angry, but didn't fight it all that much.

"They got most of 'em," Dogan bluntly said. "Then they lost one."

"*Lost* one?"

"Yeah, it altered itself or somethin.' It don't answer no more. It's being a bad machine."

"Are you telling me this thing's been out there, 'cleaning' for centuries?"

"Longer than that. Maybe ten thousand years."

"Sucking up suns? Whole populated worlds?"

"There aren't that many populated worlds that have enough energy output to attract it. On the universal scale, life's pretty rare. Whole galaxies can pass through each other without a single collision. I've seen it. What a show!"

Spock turned to Kirk. "This area of space has thirty percent fewer stars than any other known sector. Gaps of interstellar space are particularly far-reaching. There are many free-roaming planets and ice bodies. If this 'Cold Factor' has been looking for energy sources, specifically olivium, then your hypothesis about the Quake Moon's acting as a homing beacon is most inspired."

"And now it's on the way there." Determined to stay on the straight and narrow, Kirk stepped closer to Dogan and asked, "What if we confront this—neutralization device? There are forces back in the Occult system—"

"Won't work. It spreads over several dimensions. They won't be able to fight it."

Kirk got a strangely tangible picture in his mind of the wayward Cold Factor, drilling around in open space, relentlessly seeking olivium. How many solar systems had been left frozen and lifeless because of this thing? He didn't really buy the idea that such a collector/neutralizer couldn't accidentally have ruined a few billion lives, given ten thousand years.

Perhaps the Multimillenials didn't want to admit to themselves this possibility. If they had enthusiasm, as Dogan said, then they had emotion. That meant they had empathy, and guilt.

"Don't get me wrong," Dogan said, speaking very clearly, determined that they should take him seriously. "These zombies is smart, but that Cold Factor, it can still do plenty of wreckin' and schmeckin' if we don't catch it soon. That thing's gonna come in any way it can, push anything it wants out of its path, and suck back that moon stuffed with that stuff. And it don't care what it does to nobody. And right now, it's headin' right for that little solar system where you guys are settin' your new planet up. Y'know? Belle Terre? Get what I mean?"

Chapter Twenty-six

THE SHIP WAS a hydra to control. Every head wanted to go in a completely different direction. The only thing she would do without struggle was gallop straight forward. Turns, pitches, yaws, full abouts—chaos. The crew was shouting at each other over Keller's head when they finally reached *Pandora's Box*. Keller was relieved to escape and board the mining ship, only to find Lieutenant Commander Uhura in command and Dr. McCoy in charge of a subdued convict population clustered in cells or in the mess hall, under forcefield guard.

They eagerly handed over the store of refined olivium. Now it sat in its containers in the frigate's hold, pretending to be innocent.

Commander Scott now had charge of the envoy heading back to Belle Terre to be sorted out, a gaggle of ships made up of the frigate's shuttle, the mine ship, and several Kauld. The easy half of the job was done.

Dr. McCoy had wanted to come with Keller. So had Commander Uhura. Though they hadn't spoken up specifically, Keller could tell they wanted to come along, to help the whippersnappers get things right, maybe not die trying. The temptation to bring them had almost knocked Keller down.

But he could not be responsible for their sacrifice any more than he wanted to be responsible for losing a man like Montgomery Scott. When push came to shove, the three of them were more valuable to Belle Terre and Starfleet than he and his whole crew and his whole ship.

He'd sent them back there, where they would do for the future what they had done for the past.

So he drew in the reins, wrestled the cantankerous frigate about, and spurred her flanks. Now she streaked toward the Kauld solar system, on a heading that would take them beyond it to the interstellar space where an undefined danger would meet them head on.

The danger Keller could handle. The undefined part . . . he could barely concentrate on the work they were all scrambling to accomplish in the time they had. He couldn't give up the detail work. It picked at him until he ended up doing things himself that a commander should leave to the crew. After the first hour he learned to vector around Zoa, who didn't like being approached from behind. His sore rib bore that testimonial. Like a homing beacon it ached every time he came within three steps of her.

And he couldn't out-detail Bonifay. Zane was a bosun through and through, old-lady fussy down to wanting all the lockered gear to face due forward. Keller had to remind him twice that they were heading for trouble and needed to sacrifice housekeeping to other immediacies. Zane was twenty-three and had watched his former captain killed and their ship blasted to a hulk around him. How would he react this time?

What could he do against the kind of menace Vellyngaith described? What could Nick Keller kick up in the face of a power that could humble a skilled and life-long battlelord? Yes, he had some technology on his side, but his warp core was Blood, not Starfleet. Would it be as strong? Was it resilient or tempered? How far could he push it? He had a ship, but he didn't *know* the ship yet.

However, he was getting more and more intimate with the frigate as every moment passed. He now had lubricant stuck all the way up the right arm of his sweater, wire shavings embedded in his pants, and insulation in his hair. He hated stuff in his hair.

Shucorion had the ship on autopilot—after all, they were just going straight—and was on the deck with Zane, half buried in the trunks, trying to reconnect the stubborn veins that made the ship work without protest. So far they weren't having much luck.

But as they passed the Kauld solar system and drew nearer to the threat area, he had to give up picking nits and treating this like a test drive.

Once Keller was down on the quarterdeck to stay, Savannah Ring came quietly to them, her arms folded tightly. She kept her voice low, but she was looking across the bridge at Vellyngaith. The Kauld battlelord stood near the lockers on the lower deck, watching the main screen like a panther in the grass.

"How are you?" she asked.

"There's stuff in my hair."

"I think there's something wrong with that man."

"What?" Keller looked at her.

"I don't know. I think he's sick. So were at least three of the other men in the Kauld group. I can hear him breathing from here. Sounds like pneumonia or some cardiopulmonary compromise."

"But not just him?"

"They all sounded like that, and they all had the same discoloration in their eyes and lips. They're sick."

"You think it's a virus or something?"

"I'm a field operative, not a doctor."

"Sorry." Without making any bridging comments, Keller simply stepped down from the crescent and strode to Vellyngaith. He was just now learning that he no longer had to explain every choice or what was coming to everybody involved. Just go do it.

Battlelord Vellyngaith didn't look at him, but took a deep breath. He knew he would soon have to speak.

"How are you feeling, sir?" Keller asked, not disguising the significance.

Vellyngaith endured this final indignity with laudable grace. He seemed drained but accepting. "We are all ill."

"All?"

"All our soldiers. We were contaminated in an accident, an experiment at our fortress. Many have died. All the rest of our military men are ill, dying. We have no one left strong enough to fight."

"That's why you broke off the battle with the *Peleliu*, isn't it?"

"Yes. We had less than ten men in each ship. Some had no more than three. You drove us away and we had no strength to stay."

"How long has this sickness been on you?"

"Long enough to kill nearly three-quarters of our trained fighting men. The rest are all dying."

"The experiments involved antimatter? Star drive?"

"Yes."

Keller could only muster a hint of hope. "Look, like Shucorion said, there can be winners and winners. The Federation's been dealing with antimatter and star-drive radiation for a lot longer than any of you. When we get back, we'll talk to Dr. McCoy. If he doesn't know what to do, nobody will."

"My thanks for your gift of expectation." Vellyngaith offered a little bow, but he seemed resigned to his fate and trusting to change it only by dying sooner, in the coming violence.

Keller could read that anticipation in the senior warrior's face. A disturbing text.

He went back to the rail, where Savannah had been joined by a rather mussed set of Bonifay and Shucorion. Zoa, standing at her tactical board and fine-tuning the weapons, didn't look, but she was listening.

"I beat back a fleet of invalids," he mused. "Isn't that happy to know?"

"Don't get discouraged," Savannah warned. "Not at this point."

"No room left for that," he commented. "Let's saddle up and make sure we're as ready as we can be to engage this thing. Zane, how many crew have we got on board, total?"

"We only kicked off ten people to go with Mr. Scott. Four Starfleet men, because Mr. Scott wanted some security hands, and only six of the Blood guys would go. They only went because Shucorion convinced them that nobody would believe the Kauld people if there weren't some Blood to confirm the story."

"Everybody else stayed?"

"Twenty-nine, counting Shucorion's guys. Mostly people who actually worked on building the ship. We sort of got galvanized."

Enheartened, Keller was also dismayed by the heightened numbers of lives involved. Not that a few dozen this way or that way mattered much anymore, give or take the Kauld planet, Belle Terre, and anybody else in the path of the whoozit flying toward them.

Diane Carey

"What do you think our optimum crew would be?"

"I'd say . . . about sixty."

"My guess was fifty-five. We're about half manned, then."

"Would've had more," Bonifay said, "except we launched so suddenly, lot of our people got left behind. Bet they were mad."

"Bet they'll be glad later. Man the critical posts and put everything else on standby. Double up on anything you think needs extra hands. I wish I could tell them what to get ready for. I feel like I should have some predictions."

"No one expects that from you," Shucorion told him. "Tell them what you know. Then do what must be done. You must lead them, not herd them."

Keller smiled. "I like that. Thanks."

Tired, overworked, and hotheaded, Bonifay perked up and presented the chip on his shoulder to Shucorion. "Just because he asked you to exec, Nick doesn't have to run his ship your way. You're not one of us."

Though put off some, Shucorion shifted a glare of intrusion to Bonifay. "You should not address your commander so casually on his own deck, child."

"Child?"

Nick stepped between him and Shucorion. "Gentlemen," he said, consciously mimicking Kirk's tone of command. "That's enough. Bonifay, you're on report for disrespect to a superior. Shucorion, Bonifay is an officer, not a child. Now back to work."

Keller stepped out of the overflow zone, feeling like a bad actor pretending to be a Starfleet captain.

After a few moments, Keller saw Shucorion slip around to the other side of the deck, leaving Bonifay grumbling curse spells under his breath. Keller found himself missing Roger Lake.

"What's this?" Shucorion caught everyone's attention by speaking up sharply and pointing at a rectangular panel in the top of the bulkhead near the black dome. It was flashing bright amber.

The alert panel!

"Sensors must have something!" Bonifay jumped to the nav station and played the board. "Nick—"

He suddenly lost his voice. So despite his bravado, Bonifay was afraid too.

The revelation struck Keller with the force of a slap. "Put the shields up. Everything we've got. Do we know if the thing can read through deflectors?" He started toward Vellyngaith, but suddenly turned back to Bonifay. "You'd know that. You said the 'bots were raiding the storage facilities. What kind of protection did they have?"

"Not enough."

"Help me!"

"Uh—they had grade-seven shields, if we needed them."

"Were they up?"

Bonifay stared at him, thinking back. "You know, I don't think they were. . . ."

"Then keep ours up. Let's keep it from finding the olivium as long as we can. Let's get in for a good look."

Vellyngaith came to life. "If you go too near, it will drive you off."

"It fired on you?"

"Some kind of force." Obviously he couldn't be clearer.

Keller nodded and stood between the helm and nav stations, watching the forward screen. "Screen on full magnification. Confirm shields up."

"Shields are up," Zoa endorsed. "Torpedoes are ready."

As he squinted at the screen, still unable to see anything concrete out there, no ship, no form, yet knowing the phantom in the darkness had set off the alert grid.

Diane Carey

But it knew them—the ship violently heaved, then slid sideways several hundreds of meters. The crew flew against the rail or controls.

"Force, Nick!" Savannah called. "Not impact!" She was hanging on to the engineering console.

"How do you know that?" he asked.

"This screen says, 'no impact'!"

"Oh—"

"It is pushing us!" Vellyngaith shouted.

"That's what it hit you with?" Keller called back. "A blast wave? Not an actual blast?"

"It blew us into an asteroid field where we were damaged! Now it blows your ship away!"

In over his head? He was in over twenty heads.

At the nav, Bonifay twisted around. "Shouldn't we fire at it?"

"Yes," Zoa said.

On the port side, Vellyngaith's jaw hardened. He doubted success with a simple attack, but offered no alternatives.

"That's been tried," Keller declined. "Save the power."

"Photons," Zoa fumed.

Bonifay's head snapped up. "He just said no firing!"

"Shh." Keller stopped them with a gesture. "Photons . . ."

Zoa looked at him. "Yes!"

"We've tried photons against those 'bots," Bonifay insisted. "Nothing! Nothing at all! Not a scratch!"

Keller stepped to him. "You tried the torpedoes one at a time?"

Bonifay paused. "What else?"

"Zoa! Go down to the armory and bundle the torpedo casings. Put all four into one big salvo. Do you understand?"

Not only did she understand, but sheer delight

364

glowed in her emotionless blue spots. With an excited series of clumps on those platform sandals, she was gone.

Wheeeeeeezzzzzzzmmmmmm

Keller snapped up. What the hell was this?

"Losing star drive," Shucorion reported. "Slipping to sublight."

Under their very hands, every system on the bridge flickered, faded, and started to go dark!

"How could it affect us," Keller demanded. "We can't even see it yet!"

"I see it." Shucorion was staring at the forward screen.

Standing beside him, Vellyngaith had stiffened in renewed horror.

"Nick, we're losing power!" Bonifay gasped. "Half these systems just went dry!"

"Everything else is sputtering," Savannah confirmed.

Vellyngaith turned. "We must move away from it or your ship will die!"

Suddenly Keller wished he hadn't turned down Mr. Scott's offer to come along. Maybe they did need an engineer.

But there was no time left for those thoughts. If they couldn't get the engines started, they were hanging here with a belly full of bait and the shark was homing in on them.

On the screen before them, deep in the night, shone a very simple and troubling form, a wobbling water balloon of gases and mercurial liquid. It rolled through space toward them like a child's toy rolling down a hill.

It didn't look scary—until it suddenly filled the whole screen and was still coming. Directly at them. No doubt about that.

Keller knew when he'd been targeted by a charging bull. Maybe there *was* a time to turn and run.

"Full astern while we can still move!"

Shucorion nodded once, then bent to the helm and forced himself not to look at the screen.

The engines whined and coughed. The ship moved backward, but without assurance.

"We don't have the energy," Bonifay choked. "It's sapped our motive power."

"Tractor beams on. Set them on the nearest spatial body."

"Are you crazy?"

"We've got towing engines, remember? Let's use 'em."

"Oh—good idea!"

Working his white-knuckled hands furiously, Bonifay sought out the nearest solid object in space, a comet that was almost out of tractor range. "Beams on," he gasped. "I don't know if they'll hold."

"Haul away!"

With something to grab, the mule engines took a bite on the comet and sputtered back to life.

"We're moving," Shucorion reported tentatively.

"Pull away from it. Zane, reel us in as fast as you can."

Around them the ship's systems began to cough and whine, but with more eagerness, as if coming out of respiratory arrest. She was struggling to stay alive against whatever kind of damping field was being thrown by that thing.

With his fists pressed to his thighs, Keller held his breath in empathy. He peered up at the cobalt ceiling. "Come on," he whispered, "saddle up . . . come on . . ."

The tractors buzzed, sucking power from whatever was left. The lights on the bridge began to flicker.

The tactical board started bleeping furiously, demanding attention.

"Zoa! I forgot about the photon bundle!"

He spun to the command chair, but there was no access panel anywhere near the chair yet. He was obliged to jump to the quarterdeck and hit the tactical comm. "Zoa, aim and fire!"

Without acknowledgment, the forward weapons port shot a bright funnel.

Bonifay bent over the sensors. "Range, two hundred thousand kilometers . . . two-thirty . . . two-fifty . . . sixty . . ."

"Zoa, detonate!"

The screen lit up, the brightness compensators briefly failed, and the whole crew was blinded. When Keller opened his eyes, all he saw was bubbles popping. "Shucorion, keep us moving! Dang—"

He clapped a hand over his eyes. Why had he thought it would be such fun to watch four bundled torpedoes detonate at close range?

"Y'know, I *knew* that was a mistake," he grumbled. "Something inside just . . . I *knew.*"

"The thing's slowing down!" Bonifay called. "Not stopping though. The blast might've confused it."

"Confusion will not remain," Vellyngaith warned.

Keller tried to step past the command chair. "No, I don't expect—ow!"

Might've been wiser to let the eyes adjust before he tried to cross the bridge. His foot caught on something, he spilled forward and tumbled into Shucorion's chair. Shucorion, fighting to urge the ship around so she could go faster—because she could barely be handled on an astern course—only glanced at him before setting back to work. Keller caught the glance between the bursting bubbles, and somehow it sustained him. He pulled himself back to his feet.

"Are we making any headway?"

"Some," Shucorion said. "Gaining speed—"

The lights on the bridge flickered again, but this time came back on with more strength.

"Power's coming back," Bonifay reported, "but sluggish." He shook his head. "Whoa—here it comes! Nick, I've got warp power if you want it!"

"Do I ever! Release the tractor beam. Shucorion, head us away from the Kauld system, best speed."

Bonifay pounded the console in satisfaction. "I didn't think she'd recover! Are we running for Belle Terre?"

"No, no," Keller vowed. "I have not yet begun to spit and swear."

Through his clearing eyes he saw Savannah blinking at him. "We can't fight it if we can't get close enough to hurt it," she said. "What're you thinking to do?"

"Time for plan B."

"Which is—?"

"Lure it away. Zane, get down to the bay. Start pitching out cannisters of olivium with detonators on them. Blow them by remote and spray that stuff in a trail behind us. If that thing sniffs out the ore, then refined olivium ought to drive it crazy."

"I have a better idea. Let's feed it out through the impulse drive exhaust."

"Won't it overheat?"

"Might make it more potent. I can also do that without leaving the bridge."

"How could you?"

"Transporters. I'll beam the olivium out of its containers and into the mix. Won't even have to touch it."

"Maybe you *are* a wizard."

He had tried to sacrifice his ship, but she had been stunned. Now all he could do was use the olivium as a trail of breadcrumbs to attract the water balloon as far into uncharted interstellar void as he could go, as far as the ship's power and fuel could hold out, to buy time for Belle Terre and Starfleet to bring more help, or for Captain Kirk to find his way back and continue the fight.

That would be far, and it would be cold and empty. There would be no one to rescue them. No way to return.

As they streaked into the void, the ship thrumming with effort and pulsing in her own discomforts and incompatibility, the crew settled down to an uneasy silence. Soon Zoa returned from the weapons ports. Her work was done there. She took her post, and did what they were all doing—waiting it out.

"Bonifay, is it following us?" Keller quietly asked.

"At warp six," Bonifay said. "We're barely keeping up speed."

"Do whatever it takes."

Bonifay simply nodded. His dark eyes were crimped, his black hair matted with sweat.

Keller sank into his command chair, but really only got one leg all the way on before his energy sank away. He'd made the commitment that he had suspected all along would be forced upon them. The bundled photons had bought them a few seconds when they needed seconds, but no more. The thing was still chasing them.

That was what he wanted. Now he had it.

The blue autopilot light came on. He spotted it near Shucorion's elbow. A moment later, Shucorion slid out of the helm chair and approached Keller.

Casting a glance at Vellyngaith to make sure the Kauld battlelord wasn't paying them any attention, Shucorion spoke softly, keeping the words between the two of them. "Your decision is sound. If you tried to conquer it, we might be killed and never know."

Keller simply nodded, taking what little refuge could be had in knowing he came to the same conclusion.

Sympathetic, Shucorion paused a few moments, then made a new suggestion. "We should use the time we have to make repairs."

"No point," Keller told him quietly. "Repairs won't change how long the dilithium holds out. We're going to fly until we die."

Shucorion nodded. "But at least," he offered, "we will die working."

Somehow, the sentiment was actually sweet, charming. Despite its firing in a generations-old kiln of strife, Shucorion's wish carried tremendous bravery and determination. The Blood never curled up, even when they knew the end was coming. They would pick and pluck at the universe around them, leaving it a little tidier, a little neater, a little better.

Keller had no words for this. He wanted to be wise and sage, to have the right thing to say, or at least a mellow note of approval for this Blood way that had worked so well for so long. Nothing would come out.

His only offer was a mellow gesture of gratitude. He reached over and gave Shucorion a pat on the arm. Seemed inadequate.

Shucorion looked puzzled. He didn't understand what he'd done to garner that reaction. To him, work was what should be done. Breathe, eat, work.

Keller smiled at the naivete and admired it.

"Nick!" Bonifay suddenly flinched, stinging the whole bridge with his shout. "It's increased speed! It's trying to overtake us!"

Chapter Twenty-seven

Enterprise

"FROM WHAT I'VE SEEN," Kirk condensed, "these Multi-millennials shouldn't even need olivium. They don't need it, do they, Captain Dogan?"

"Nah," Mitch Dogan sputtered around his pipe. "It's a waste product. They stuck it on that moon to keep it from hurtin' anybody. Never expected nobody to need a quaking volcanic mass in an uninhabited solar system, in the middle of Gamma Night. They didn't really remember the idea of planet-hoppin' till they saw us doing it. It was long gone in their past, y'might figure. They didn't have no idea the olivium would be a gold mine for somebody. The plan is to take it all away and ditch it in the interdimensional *and* intergalactic void when they leave, where it can't be no more problem."

Spock was so moved, so caught up in the implications as to actually take Kirk by the arm. "Jim, if the

371

Quake Moon is removed from the Occult solar system, the results will be epic disaster. Not only will we lose ore of incalculable worth, but the sudden physical absence of so large a body would lay irreparable waste to Belle Terre."

"Yes, I know." As if whispering could keep these people from knowing anything at all, Kirk motioned him to back off. "Give me a moment."

Dogan, though he seemed to be enjoying a good look around the sparkling bridge, was certainly paying attention. "They know olivium's a leap for us. I mean you. Y'know what I mean. Tell you what, when I say 'you' I mean 'you,' and when I say 'we' I mean 'them.' " Dogan hooked a thumb over his shoulder at the thing on the main screen. "Get it?"

"Got it."

"They—we—know it'll change your technology a whole bunch over the next century or two or ten. They—we—gave warp capacity to the Blood and the Kauld, thinking it'd help them out of their repeating cycle of damn bloody wars. Didn't work out that way–made it worse. So they're a little antsy about doing it again."

"Wait," Kirk snapped, seizing the opportunity, the thinnest thread of a chance. "I have a proposal for your Multimillennial friends, Captain Dogan."

"Does it involve wrestling?"

"If necessary. You don't want to leave a messy galaxy. Fine. Let us sweep up. Let us keep the olivium. Then this Cold Factor neutralizer won't have to pose a danger to anyone anymore."

"That's the problem. We can't talk to it anymore. It's broke. It won't answer the recall. We can track it, but they can't go get it without a physical presence at the locale. Something about contact physics, I dunno. They don't know how exactly to go get it or talk it into coming home so they can throw a leash around it. Everybody don't know everything, y'know."

"Well," Kirk lobbied again, "let us earn it, then. You don't know how to use ships anymore . . . I have a starship. Let me locate the Neutralizer for you. You let us keep the olivium and deal with the repercussions."

"Sounds good. Okay, let me talk to 'em for a second." He closed his eyes and took a long draw on his pipe, his lower lip puffing away. "Okay, they say that the Council of Ten Thousand will take up your proposal."

Kirk's gut twisted. "Ten thousand bureaucrats? How long will that take?"

Dogan opened his eyes. "They've agreed."

Sulu pressed a hand over his eyes, overwhelmed.

Passing a weakened glance at Spock, Kirk commented, "Apparently their bureaucrats are better than ours."

"While two days may pass for us," Spock said, quite excited, "hundreds of thousands of years may have passed for them. Yet somehow they grasp our perspective of what is occurring in our own time, here today."

"Do you understand any of this?"

"In theory."

"We can't possibly think their way, can we?"

"No, sir."

"Then I won't try."

Dogan laughed. "Actually, Kirk, they conferred for over two hundred years just now, *in* the fourth dimension! Bureaucrats are still bureaucrats!"

What else was there to do? Now that he'd found his quarry, Kirk found himself caught in a swirl of events that seemed to be happening whether he wanted into the deal or not. And actually, he did.

"How do we do it?" he asked, fanning his arms a little. "Can you give us a heading?"

"Better'n that," Dogan offered. "They're gonna

mount the *Yorktown* here with all kinds of conversion equipment that'll make it temporarily fourth-dimensional. You'll get spoiled."

"This is the *Enterprise,* Captain Dogan," Sulu passively corrected, probably figuring that neither Kirk nor Spock would bother.

"Oh—sure! What was I thinkin'? Been a long time. Y'know how it is."

While he spouted, another living being—not even close to Human—came squishing down the interdimensional ramp, flipping its snorkles and leading a whole team of people who were definitely human, humanoid, a few aliens Kirk recognized and a few he didn't. They were carrying tools of some sort, and a metallic octagonal box that seemed to be no more than a box, except that it had no lid.

Impatience got to him again as his mind shot back to Belle Terre and what was about to happen there. "How long will this conversion take?"

"It's all done," Dogan said.

The team of workers was already marching back into the interdimensional doorway. All they had done, as far as Kirk could tell, was put the octagonal box on the helm, touch parts of the bridge with some of their tools, then turn around and leave.

"Thanks, Roib!" Dogan called up the passageway. "Thanks, fellas! Good job! You're gettin' fast!"

Dogan waved merrily and came back down to the command arena, apparently meaning to follow his friends back into the interdimensional vortex. "You need anythin' else? Wanna come and have breakfast for a decade or two before you go?"

Tempting as that was, Kirk already had plenty to digest. "If it's all the same to you, I'd rather get going."

"Yeah, I get it." Dogan wobbled back to the doorway

and put one foot on the glossy ramp. "Now, when you find the thing, we'll take over. But look, don't get too close too fast, or it'll freeze your fanny! I sure hope you're in time to keep the Factor from chompin' down that pretty planet. Lotsa luck. Nice t'meet you, damn sure. Don't get up—I'll close the door behind me."

Chapter Twenty-eight

KELLER FLEW out of his chair. "Increase our speed."

Shucorion returned quickly to the helm, but had nothing hopeful to offer. "Speed remains at six, Commander."

"Bonifay, choke some more out of it! Zoa, can you give us an aft view on this screen?"

He hoped she could figure it out, so Bonifay wouldn't have to take his attention away from the engines.

She did, though it took several seconds.

On the forward screen, the water balloon filled nearly half the screen.

"Speed, Zane," Keller begged.

"Maybe warp seven," Bonifay gasped. "Maybe."

Keller's chest seemed to cave in as he stood there gripping the unoccupied nav chair. "Not far enough . . . we've got to get farther!"

"The thing's at warp eight." Bonifay's announcement chilled them all.

There was no warp eight in this ship, not yet, not with a Blood warp core and muscular but cumbersome towing engines and a crew who didn't know the mismatched systems well enough.

The balloon was coming to get its olivium. Any second now the ship would die of power drain and the thing would be on them.

He looked around. Zoa was on her feet, searching the weapons board for a possibility. She found none.

On the sci-deck Savannah gripped the engineering pulpit, but she had no experience to do anything with it. Shucorion did his best to pilot the ship, but there was only one course, one speed. He too could only stare at the oncoming threat.

Vellyngaith stood on the port side of the command deck, one hand on the rail, his eyes closed, and his chin raised.

The balloon filled the whole screen in seconds.

"Hell with this." Keller kicked the nav chair, climbed to the engineering console and shoved Savannah brutishly out of his way and began hammering the controls.

"What are you doing!" Savannah cried.

"Flying a big bomb, that's what. I've got a warp core. Matter and antimatter are only this far from blowing up half the time anyway. It wants energy? I'll give it a gut full."

An instant later, Bonifay squirreled to the sci-deck at Keller's side. "Rig to overload?"

Keller could only nod and strike the right buttons. The warning system popped on. The ship took herself to red alert—something he had completely forgotten to do, yet another symptom of his inexperience. She knew she was about to blow up.

They'd thrown the ship together so fast that she had no safeties, no reason to abort their orders, and she didn't need any authorization to rip herself into a billion glowing shards. She would go happily, and very bright. She was brand new, and somehow she was already a good old warhorse, running herself into the ground at her master's whim.

"Thirty seconds to—to detonation," he gagged. Even though he had committed himself, this was hard to do.

"Ready," Bonifay whispered. He cleared his throat and spoke a little louder. "I'm ready. Guess you can spit and swear now."

Somehow a smile popped up on Keller's sweat-glazed cheeks. He couldn't look up. He didn't want to see Bonifay's expressive eyes.

"It's on us, Nick."

Savannah's words from behind him were surprisingly soft.

He didn't turn. "I'll push the button, Zane. Get your hand away."

"I wouldn't do that if I were you, Commander Keller."

The strange defiance made him look up. Who had said that?

Something pulled at his half-numb brain. He straightened, and looked around.

"Captain Kirk!"

James Kirk had welcomed himself aboard the frigate. On the starboard side of the command deck, right at the foot of the fan-shaped steps to the tactical station, the captain stood in an unframed doorway through which Keller and his crew clearly saw the last thing they might've imagined—the bridge of the *Enterprise*.

Behind Captain Kirk, Mr. Sulu stood near the starship's helm. The two men looked supremely authoritative in their crisp red jackets and white collars.

Stunned like a fish, Keller thumped down to the lower

arena. Was this a trick? A dream? Dead already? Where was the tunnel with the light? Granny? Is that you?

On the forward screen, the picture of the bloated water balloon was gone. The screen was now placid, showing a vision of sparkling space, but everything in it seemed distorted, as though looking through a prism.

Zoa clumped forward. Keller motioned her back, but moved forward himself.

"Captain?" he tested.

Kirk offered him a snide grin. "Welcome aboard? I suppose I should say the same." He pointed at the engineering board. "You'd better turn off the destruct mode, Mr. Bonifay. And Mr. Shucorion, I think your commander would like to go to all stop now. He's getting nowhere fast."

Keller nodded, hoping they both saw his confirmation, but he still couldn't make himself turn away from the remarkable sight. Through the rimless doorway, the bridge of the *Enterprise* seemed a beautiful and ethereal place compared with the ill-fitted, rough, worn-edged frigate bridge.

James Kirk held out a beckoning hand. "Come with me, please, Nick."

Keller swallowed his astonishment and asked, "Where?"

"To deck three. I have something to show you."

"Spacefaring ability is one of the talents the Multimillennials lost in their extreme advancement. Ten thousand years ago, when they decided to leave, they built a collector/neutralizer that we call the Cold Factor. Later they found they couldn't control those very well, so they converted to the smaller 'bot probes. But this one last Cold Factor was out roaming around, looking for their waste product."

"Olivium, I bet."

"Yes."

"We were trying to lure it away from the Cluster. Guess we failed."

"No, you didn't have the chance to fail. We overtook you. I'd say your odds were fair of succeeding. At least in drawing it away for several months, maybe years."

"Not enough."

"No. Not enough. Eventually it would've come back and left Belle Terre and possibly the whole solar system cold and barren. They converted the *Enterprise* to a fourth-dimensional vessel in order to come back here. We've actually been six weeks at high warp to get back."

"You've barely been gone that long!"

"It's hard to explain."

Forcing himself back to the immediate problem, not at all sure it was solved, Keller asked, "Now what? How can we stop it now?"

"Come this way."

On deck two, James Kirk led him through the *Enterprise*'s sparkling corridors, the spongy carpet giving a lift to their steps, to a curved ladder that led to the lower deck. Kirk stepped jauntily onto the ladder, glanced up to make sure Keller followed, then disappeared.

Numb and trembling, Keller almost fell twice. "Where are we going?"

"I told you. Deck three."

But when they got there, deck three was gone. In its place was an entire solar system.

Stars, sun, planets—and they were standing on a platform of completely open space.

Keller's arms flared and he staggered back, but Kirk caught him and pulled him forward again.

"You'll get your spacelegs in a minute," the captain said. "Don't worry."

"You're enjoying this!" Keller accused.

"You will too."

"Captain!" A third voice broke, with a slight echo.

There stood Mr. Spock, two planets down.

Keller choked down a rock. "Pay no attention to that man behind the curtain. . . ."

"This way, gentlemen," the Vulcan directed.

Kirk pulled Keller along. Keller was breathing in gasps, but he managed to stumble along on the big empty. When they got to Mr. Spock, he motioned beyond the second planet.

"There's your problem," Kirk announced.

Floating in some kind of containment field, as big as any of the planets, was the water balloon. It still rolled and bumped around inside its cage, looking for a way out, but it couldn't break free.

Keller shuddered. "Oh, m'God . . ."

"It's all right," Kirk told him passively. "They've got it tethered now. They'll be taking it home. And we get to keep the olivium."

Spock strode over to them, as if he skated solar systems every day. "Good afternoon, Commander Keller. Where is the *Peleliu?*"

"Oh—" Keller blinked. "That's not a real good story, sir."

At his side, Kirk pivoted to face him. "Try us."

Epilogue

U.F.P. Frigate *Challenger*

NICK KELLER sat in his command chair, relaxed for the first time in weeks. They weren't going anywhere. In fact, the ship was once again propped in her scaffold on the planet Belle Terre, getting work done on her that should've been done before she ever left the solar system. She deserved it.

And he was having some work done on himself as well. His sweater lay across his knees, and the sleeve of his black T-shirt was rolled up on his left arm as he flinched and winced his way through the current adventure.

Beside him, Zoa hammered tiny needles into his arm, embedding colored dye in the shape of the frigate.

"Understand you," she said, concentrating, "this be not right place for thy first witness."

"Never mind—just never mind," he drawled. "The arm is *fine*."

Zane Bonifay stomped past them then, without a greeting, carrying some tools in each hand, and crossed directly to the nav station, where he dumped his tools and started working with a small drill. Keller craned some to see what he was doing, but Zoa kneed him in the thigh and he decided holding still was better.

"What're you doing, Zane?"

"Installing a precautionary unit."

"A what?"

"Stand by."

"Nick." Savannah Ring came onto the bridge from the lift. "Captain Kirk wants to see you down on the surface."

"When?"

"Right now. He's down there."

Keller sighed. "I can guess what this is about. Zoa, better wrap it up. You can do the other nacelle later."

Without a word she backed away and turned off her dye injector.

Twisting to look at his own arm, Keller smiled at the inspiring picture of the funny frigate, looking much better in artistic rendition than in real life. "Thanks," he said. "This is foxy."

Zoa stonily said, "You will have many witnesses. I will inflict them."

"Bet that's right," Bonifay grumbled. His drill whizzed, then finally stopped.

Keller stood up and flexed his stiff legs, then stepped down to Bonifay. "What're you up to, trouble?"

"I told you." Bonifay stepped aside. "Precaution."

Mounted now on the kidney-shaped nav console, up where it was out of the way, stood the Shuttle *Challenger* half-dollar. It was framed in a specially fashioned lollipop-shaped stand with the stick embedded in the console, allowing the coin to show both its sides.

Self-conscious and touched, Keller chuckled. "Now, what is this supposed to be on the bridge of a fighting ship?"

"A talisman," Bonifay said.

"Figurehead," Savannah corrected.

On the sci-deck, Montgomery Scott unfolded himself out of a trunk and contributed, "Hood ornament." When Keller could only offer a flattered smile and a nod, Scott added, "Better get crackin', lad. Captain Kirk doesn't like to be kept waiting."

"After a while, you won't even notice it," Bonifay said, and spun away, proud of himself.

Keller moved forward to commune briefly with the mounted coin. His new "witness" stung some as he reached out and thumbed the raised image of the space shuttle.

"Thanks, Tim."

On the planet's surface, the cluttered shuttleyard bore its biggest burden with sturdy grace. The enormous frigate was far bigger than anything else being worked on.

When Keller got down there, he saw the Federation's favorite headliner standing near the port nacelle, peering up, up, up to the underside of the saucer section with its mismatched hull plates. Way up there, workers in hoversuits were affixing letters and call numbers onto the skin of the ship.

U.F.P.F. *Challenger*. OV91951-L.

After a deep breath to sustain him, Keller strode over there.

The rakish Jim Kirk didn't even look at him. "You call this a ship?" he asked.

Keller broke into a laugh. "Snob . . ."

"Who came up with the phony serial number?"

"I did. It's the serial number off the Shuttle *Challenger* combined with its last mission number."

"An excellent choice."

"You wanted to speak to me, sir?"

Might as well get the worst over with.

"Yes," Kirk said. "Very commendable work you've done here. Not having a ship or crew is pretty big odds. Patching one together out of what's lying around, that's above and beyond the call. You remained at your post and held the stability of your jurisdiction against insurmountable odds."

Embarrassed, Keller hooked his thumbs into his pockets and scuffed at the ground with the toe of his cowboy boot. "Oh . . . we just did what we had to, sir."

"But your choice of crew is questionable. A woman with talons on her feet, for instance."

"Ah—Zoa."

"And another one suggested I take a rest period of hanging upside down . . . like a bat."

"Ah," Keller resigned. "Then you've met the whole coven."

Kirk nodded and watched a second crew as they affixed an enormous UFP standard onto the mismatched khaki-colored neck of the frigate. "Your idea?"

"Hm? Oh, yes, sir. I don't want anybody making any mistakes about who we are. At least, as long as I'm here."

"You'll be here a while. There's no one else to effect law enforcement once the *Enterprise* leaves. I'll be executing a field order. You'll be promoted to post captain until Starfleet makes a decision regarding your extenuating circumstances."

A big rock landed in Keller's stomach and sat there, laughing at him. "Sir, I'm perfectly content to be OTC. You might not want that promotion . . . reflecting on you."

Temperately, Kirk blinked his eyes and rubbed them, then stopped watching the work up above. He paced around to Keller's other side.

"I've taken a look at your report," he said. "Tavola methane. Very serious mistake."

Keller stiffened, then owned up. "Wasn't a mistake, sir. It was a calculated bad decision. It was only my first error. I don't know if it was the worst one."

"You know the regulations regarding Tavola exposure."

"Yes, sir. Starfleet personnel are on their honor to report exposure. You can't run a scanner over somebody and prove he was exposed. It causes changes, but you can't prove that it has. That's why it's a court-martial offense not to report exposure. Loyalty or not, you report it. Changes normally show up within three months, but with Roger they didn't. Not until he was under stress . . . halfway to Belle Terre."

"What does Captain Lake have to say about all this?"

"He doesn't think he's changed at all. He thinks I'm just grabbing his command. He's under surveillance and analysis at the hospital across town."

"Hurts," Kirk sympathized, "when your idol thinks you've betrayed him."

Weakened now that everything was out in the open, Keller felt as if he were physically sagging. "I broke one of the most important regulations around, sir. I don't want to complicate things by trying to powder over it or have it dirty up your record too. I'll take whatever decision Command brings down, without contest."

Diane Carey

With a little shrug, Kirk clasped his hands behind his back. "Regulations also say you don't risk the ship for one person, but occasionally you do. Usually they're right, but not always. You make your hard choice, and accept that you might be court-martialed, but it's worth that price. You made the choice. It didn't turn out right. Sometimes that's the only difference between glory and the grave."

They were silent for a few moments, together watching the final touches on the new coded call letters and numbers for local communications buoys. *D.I.T 405.*

"Who's code is that? Yours?"

"Yes, sir," Keller said. "Delta India Tango."

"I'll remember," Kirk promised. "I'll follow your wishes and file a report with the admiralty. It'll be a black mark on your record. Fortunately, as long as you're on duty at Belle Terre, nobody'll be reading the record. The value to the Service now is that you stay, not that you go. You still have a while to catch up to me and my black marks." Kirk's sharkish eyes flashed at him. "Dare you to try."

Keller smiled uneasily. "Any advice?"

"None. You'll figure it out. *Peleliu* had a two-year mission here. You're taking it over. If it's good, you'd be surprised what the admiralty can forget to read. Besides, chances are you won't survive two years out here."

"Oh, bless you, sir . . . At least the Kauld have lined up with us now. The Cluster might settle down and be a pleasant place to live after all."

Kirk smirked at him without pity. "Trust me—it's big out there. We've got plenty yet to discover. You'll have your hands full."

"Again, bless you."

With a star in his eye, the captain jauntily finished, "I

388

could throw you in irons, but what a waste of iron. Fair weather, Nick . . . I'm afraid you're the sheriff in these parts now. Protect your turf."

Without waiting for an answer, he stepped back and snapped out his communicator.

"Kirk to *Enterprise*. Beam me up."

Epilogue Two

Enterprise, the next morning

"I DON'T LIKE MYSTERIES. When I left, Billy Maidenshore was a syndicalistic, charismatic prancer without a conscience. When I come back, he's absolutely subdued. He almost seems ashamed of himself. What happened over there?"

"Oh, nothing significant, Captain. He thought he was one ape in a million because he was devilish and savvy and had no conscience. Once I understood him, handling him was a minor matter."

James Kirk pressed his thigh to the communications console and peered suspiciously at Uhura, who sat in her familiar position with her lovely legs crossed, flicking a stylus through the crown of hair over one ear.

"Minor?" he repeated. "Billy almost wrested economic control of the olivium supply. Now he's sitting in triple security, and he's not even arguing. His spirit's gone." Leaning forward a little, arms crossed, Kirk queried, "What've you done with it?"

Uhura's exotic Nubian features took on a queenly presence. "Why, Captain," she said, "it's in my top left dresser drawer."

She swiveled a shoulder to him, enjoying her victory. Who ever said a woman couldn't keep a secret?

He was about to pursue the interrogation when the turbolift door opened with what sounded like a sigh of relief, and Spock's voice broke the peace on the bridge.

"You're being emotional, Doctor. Any advancement throughout history, from fire to warp drive, on balance, despite problems, has been a change to the good."

"The problem with you, Spock, is you've never sat on a front porch and watched the kids play and the corn grow."

Kirk turned to see McCoy and Spock, literally arm to arm, arguing in the vestibule.

"Review the delay in personal mobility had Thomas Edison never encouraged Henry Ford to pursue developing the automobile. The entire progress of the most productive single century in mankind's history may have been set back by decades."

"The bloody twentieth?"

"Yes, including the bloody vaccines, the bloody sanitation, the bloody personal computer—"

"It used to be a problem when your family moved into the next county," McCoy protested. "Then we start leaping whole sectors, and now we have something that'll help us go even farther away, even faster. How is this good?"

"Doctor, had you been in charge, humankind would still be conducting business from the counter of Maw and Paw's corner feed store."

"You never look at the other side, do you? There's

something to be said for *slow* advancement. That's how wisdom comes. How often have men taken one of these great leaps and almost ended up at the bottom of the canyon?"

"Had Copernicus embraced your attitude, doctor, we would indeed be having this conversation with the corn stalks in the holler."

"There! You see? Rapid advancement doesn't necessarily bring wisdom. Nobody grows corn in a holler!"

"Perhaps," Spock skewered, "we shall use the olivium to develop advanced programming and eventually replace doctors. At least a programmable physician will keep his mind on business."

"Oh!" McCoy pivoted to Kirk and Uhura. "Can you just see that? You're lying there and some machine with a head painted on it is hovering over you deciding whether to remove your brain or clean under your fingernails! Maybe it'll hold your hand at the same time!"

Sharing a brief glance with Sulu, who was smiling at the helm, Spock folded his arms casually. "Doctor, I sense no threat in such a probability."

"Of course not, Mr. Spock," McCoy parried. "We could replace you with a machine this afternoon and nobody would notice. You already have an asbestos personality."

The Vulcan nodded and swaggered in place. "A mechanical doctor would have at least one distinct advantage . . . an 'off' switch."

"Gentlemen, good morning." Kirk pushed off the comm console and stopped their conversation with his approach.

"A very good morning, Captain."

"Hi, Jim."

"I see you two have both recovered from our respec-

Diane Carey

tive adventures," Kirk commented. "What's your prognosis for the Kauld soldiers' disease, Bones?"

"We don't know, yet, Jim. They made a mess during their antimatter experiments. It could be radiation, but it's been complicated by their physiology."

"Can they be saved?"

"Some of them are beyond help. Vellyngaith himself may be too far gone, but we've set up a clinic at the medical center on Belle Terre. I've handed over the research problem to Dr. M'Benga. He's worked on more aliens than anyone else down there. Who knows? If they can cure the Kauld, maybe they'll make Sagittarius Cluster history because the Kauld will be forever grateful. No more conflicts here."

"Again, Doctor," Spock commented, "your shortsightedness reveals itself. History is full of convenient friendships. We shall see if the Kauld remain friends once they no longer need our help."

McCoy confronted him again. "You don't have any faith in simple goodwill!"

" 'Faith,' sir, is what a weak mind clings to when it possesses no evidence."

"Pagan."

"Thank you. Captain, should I transfer the report to Starfleet about Captain Lake?"

Kirk perked up, realizing he was once again involved. "No, Mr. Spock. I'll deliver the report in person when we get back. I want to add a few comments."

"In six months?"

"Is there a rush?"

Spock's dark eyes shined. Back to his incombustible self, he didn't mind showing his pleasure in Kirk's decision. With great meaning and even sentiment, he sanctioned, "No, sir. No rush at all."

"Very well. All hands, take your posts and prepare to leave orbit."

He stepped down and slid into his command chair, charged with the adventure of going home, back through the dark empty tracts of space between here and the Federation, reaches full of mysterious and uncharted tributaries. Even the trail home promised sparkling chances. His starship, his familiar crew— Uhura at her post, Sulu's hands on the helm, Scotty at engineering where he belonged, Spock at his right and McCoy at his left.

"Ready to leave orbit, Captain," Spock reported, sounding almost jaunty.

"Thank you, Mr. Spock. Doctor, is the crew settled and ready to depart?"

"They are, Captain," McCoy merrily confirmed.

Kirk smiled. He looked at the main screen, with its picture of the planet Belle Terre, a struggling but hopeful place, patched by tiny agricultural centers and growing factories, a frontier gold-rush town, determined to make good for itself and everybody back home.

"Mission accomplished," he said. "The colony is secure. The Blood and Kauld are speaking to each other. It's time to pass the torch. Mr. Sulu, move us into the spacelane."

"Aye aye, sir. Point zero two impulse speed."

The starship slowly broke from orbit, her swan-shape gleaming proudly in the sunlight as she soared into the first established departure lane in this new solar system.

Kirk smiled again at the half-built spacedock flickering like a Christmas tree hanging over the planet. In the boxdock, just now being pulled up to the umbilical mooring, floated the half-breed ship Nick Keller had conjured from scraps.

A composite frigate, Scott had called it.

Diane Carey

And a repository, Kirk thought, for composite aspirations. He wouldn't know for months upon months whether that ship and her young master could keep a grip on the tiger he had by the tail.

But for today, for Kirk and his own crew, the future was somewhere else. With Spock and McCoy on either side of him and Belle Terre pulling itself up by the bootstraps in front of him, James Kirk felt supremely complete.

"Mission accomplished, gentlemen," he said. "A very long mission. My compliments to the crew."

"We'll pass them along, Jim," McCoy accepted.

"Thank you, Doctor. Mr. Sulu, bear us off. All running lights, signals and pennants render honors to starboard . . . the United Federation Frigate *Challenger*. May she hold the fort, crack the frontier, and live to tell the tale."

Look for STAR TREK fiction from Pocket Books

Star Trek®: The Original Series

Enterprise: The First Adventure • Vonda N. McIntyre
Final Frontier • Diane Carey
Strangers from the Sky • Margaret Wander Bonanno
Spock's World • Diane Duane
The Lost Years • J.M. Dillard
Probe • Margaret Wander Bonanno
Prime Directive • Judith and Garfield Reeves-Stevens
Best Destiny • Diane Carey
Shadows on the Sun • Michael Jan Friedman
Sarek • A.C. Crispin
Federation • Judith and Garfield Reeves-Stevens
Vulcan's Forge • Josepha Sherman & Susan Shwartz
Mission to Horatius • Mack Reynolds
Vulcan's Heart • Josepha Sherman & Susan Shwartz
Novelizations
Star Trek: The Motion Picture • Gene Roddenberry
Star Trek II: The Wrath of Khan • Vonda N. McIntyre
Star Trek III: The Search for Spock • Vonda N. McIntyre
Star Trek IV: The Voyage Home • Vonda N. McIntyre
Star Trek V: The Final Frontier • J.M. Dillard
Star Trek VI: The Undiscovered Country • J.M. Dillard
Star Trek Generations • J.M. Dillard
Starfleet Academy • Diane Carey
Star Trek books by William Shatner with Judith and Garfield
Reeves-Stevens
The Ashes of Eden
The Return
Avenger
Star Trek: Odyssey (contains *The Ashes of Eden*, *The Return*, and
    Avenger)
Spectre
Dark Victory
Preserver

#1 • *Star Trek: The Motion Picture* • Gene Roddenberry
#2 • *The Entropy Effect* • Vonda N. McIntyre
#3 • *The Klingon Gambit* • Robert E. Vardeman
#4 • *The Covenant of the Crown* • Howard Weinstein
#5 • *The Prometheus Design* • Sondra Marshak & Myrna Culbreath

#6 • *The Abode of Life* • Lee Correy

#7 • *Star Trek II: The Wrath of Khan* • Vonda N. McIntyre

#8 • *Black Fire* • Sonni Cooper

#9 • *Triangle* • Sondra Marshak & Myrna Culbreath

#10 • *Web of the Romulans* • M.S. Murdock

#11 • *Yesterday's Son* • A.C. Crispin

#12 • *Mutiny on the Enterprise* • Robert E. Vardeman

#13 • *The Wounded Sky* • Diane Duane

#14 • *The Trellisane Confrontation* • David Dvorkin

#15 • *Corona* • Greg Bear

#16 • *The Final Reflection* • John M. Ford

#17 • *Star Trek III: The Search for Spock* • Vonda N. McIntyre

#18 • *My Enemy, My Ally* • Diane Duane

#19 • *The Tears of the Singers* • Melinda Snodgrass

#20 • *The Vulcan Academy Murders* • Jean Lorrah

#21 • *Uhura's Song* • Janet Kagan

#22 • *Shadow Land* • Laurence Yep

#23 • *Ishmael* • Barbara Hambly

#24 • *Killing Time* • Della Van Hise

#25 • *Dwellers in the Crucible* • Margaret Wander Bonanno

#26 • *Pawns and Symbols* • Majiliss Larson

#27 • *Mindshadow* • J.M. Dillard

#28 • *Crisis on Centaurus* • Brad Ferguson

#29 • *Dreadnought!* • Diane Carey

#30 • *Demons* • J.M. Dillard

#31 • *Battlestations!* • Diane Carey

#32 • *Chain of Attack* • Gene DeWeese

#33 • *Deep Domain* • Howard Weinstein

#34 • *Dreams of the Raven* • Carmen Carter

#35 • *The Romulan Way* • Diane Duane & Peter Morwood

#36 • *How Much for Just the Planet?* • John M. Ford

#37 • *Bloodthirst* • J.M. Dillard

#38 • *The IDIC Epidemic* • Jean Lorrah

#39 • *Time for Yesterday* • A.C. Crispin

#40 • *Timetrap* • David Dvorkin

#41 • *The Three-Minute Universe* • Barbara Paul

#42 • *Memory Prime* • Judith and Garfield Reeves-Stevens

#43 • *The Final Nexus* • Gene DeWeese

#44 • *Vulcan's Glory* • D.C. Fontana

#45 • *Double, Double* • Michael Jan Friedman

#46 • *The Cry of the Onlies* • Judy Klass

#47 • *The Kobayashi Maru* • Julia Ecklar

#48 • *Rules of Engagement* • Peter Morwood

#49 • *The Pandora Principle* • Carolyn Clowes
#50 • *Doctor's Orders* • Diane Duane
#51 • *Unseen Enemy* • V.E. Mitchell
#52 • *Home Is the Hunter* • Dana Kramer Rolls
#53 • *Ghost-Walker* • Barbara Hambly
#54 • *A Flag Full of Stars* • Brad Ferguson
#55 • *Renegade* • Gene DeWeese
#56 • *Legacy* • Michael Jan Friedman
#57 • *The Rift* • Peter David
#58 • *Face of Fire* • Michael Jan Friedman
#59 • *The Disinherited* • Peter David
#60 • *Ice Trap* • L.A. Graf
#61 • *Sanctuary* • John Vornholt
#62 • *Death Count* • L.A. Graf
#63 • *Shell Game* • Melissa Crandall
#64 • *The Starship Trap* • Mel Gilden
#65 • *Windows on a Lost World* • V.E. Mitchell
#66 • *From the Depths* • Victor Milan
#67 • *The Great Starship Race* • Diane Carey
#68 • *Firestorm* • L.A. Graf
#69 • *The Patrian Transgression* • Simon Hawke
#70 • *Traitor Winds* • L.A. Graf
#71 • *Crossroad* • Barbara Hambly
#72 • *The Better Man* • Howard Weinstein
#73 • *Recovery* • J.M. Dillard
#74 • *The Fearful Summons* • Denny Martin Flynn
#75 • *First Frontier* • Diane Carey & Dr. James I. Kirkland
#76 • *The Captain's Daughter* • Peter David
#77 • *Twilight's End* • Jerry Oltion
#78 • *The Rings of Tautee* • Dean Wesley Smith & Kristine Kathryn Rusch
#79 • *Invasion!* #1: *First Strike* • Diane Carey
#80 • *The Joy Machine* • James Gunn
#81 • *Mudd in Your Eye* • Jerry Oltion
#82 • *Mind Meld* • John Vornholt
#83 • *Heart of the Sun* • Pamela Sargent & George Zebrowski
#84 • *Assignment: Eternity* • Greg Cox
#85-87 • *My Brother's Keeper* • Michael Jan Friedman
    #85 • *Republic*
    #86 • *Constitution*
    #87 • *Enterprise*
#88 • *Across the Universe* • Pamela Sargent & George Zebrowski
#89-94 • *New Earth*

#89 • *Wagon Train to the Stars* • Diane Carey
#90 • *Belle Terre* • Dean Wesley Smith with Diane Carey
#91 • *Rough Trails* • L.A. Graf
#92 • *The Flaming Arrow* • Kathy and Jerry Oltion
#93 • *Thin Air* • Kristine Kathryn Rusch & Dean Wesley Smith
#94 • *Challenger* • Diane Carey

Star Trek: The Next Generation®

Metamorphosis • Jean Lorrah
Vendetta • Peter David
Reunion • Michael Jan Friedman
Imzadi • Peter David
The Devil's Heart • Carmen Carter
Dark Mirror • Diane Duane
Q-Squared • Peter David
Crossover • Michael Jan Friedman
Kahless • Michael Jan Friedman
Ship of the Line • Diane Carey
The Best and the Brightest • Susan Wright
Planet X • Michael Jan Friedman
Imzadi II: Triangle • Peter David
I, Q • Peter David & John de Lancie
The Valiant • Michael Jan Friedman
Novelizations
Encounter at Farpoint • David Gerrold
Unification • Jeri Taylor
Relics • Michael Jan Friedman
Descent • Diane Carey
All Good Things... • Michael Jan Friedman
Star Trek: Klingon • Dean Wesley Smith & Kristine Kathryn Rusch
Star Trek Generations • J.M. Dillard
Star Trek: First Contact • J.M. Dillard
Star Trek: Insurrection • J.M. Dillard

#1 • *Ghost Ship* • Diane Carey
#2 • *The Peacekeepers* • Gene DeWeese
#3 • *The Children of Hamlin* • Carmen Carter
#4 • *Survivors* • Jean Lorrah
#5 • *Strike Zone* • Peter David
#6 • *Power Hungry* • Howard Weinstein
#7 • *Masks* • John Vornholt
#8 • *The Captain's Honor* • David and Daniel Dvorkin

#9 • *A Call to Darkness* • Michael Jan Friedman
#10 • *A Rock and a Hard Place* • Peter David
#11 • *Gulliver's Fugitives* • Keith Sharee
#12 • *Doomsday World* • David, Carter, Friedman & Greenberger
#13 • *The Eyes of the Beholders* • A.C. Crispin
#14 • *Exiles* • Howard Weinstein
#15 • *Fortune's Light* • Michael Jan Friedman
#16 • *Contamination* • John Vornholt
#17 • *Boogeymen* • Mel Gilden
#18 • *Q-in-Law* • Peter David
#19 • *Perchance to Dream* • Howard Weinstein
#20 • *Spartacus* • T.L. Mancour
#21 • *Chains of Command* • W.A. McCoy & E.L. Flood
#22 • *Imbalance* • V.E. Mitchell
#23 • *War Drums* • John Vornholt
#24 • *Nightshade* • Laurell K. Hamilton
#25 • *Grounded* • David Bischoff
#26 • *The Romulan Prize* • Simon Hawke
#27 • *Guises of the Mind* • Rebecca Neason
#28 • *Here There Be Dragons* • John Peel
#29 • *Sins of Commission* • Susan Wright
#30 • *Debtor's Planet* • W.R. Thompson
#31 • *Foreign Foes* • Dave Galanter & Greg Brodeur
#32 • *Requiem* • Michael Jan Friedman & Kevin Ryan
#33 • *Balance of Power* • Dafydd ab Hugh
#34 • *Blaze of Glory* • Simon Hawke
#35 • *The Romulan Stratagem* • Robert Greenberger
#36 • *Into the Nebula* • Gene DeWeese
#37 • *The Last Stand* • Brad Ferguson
#38 • *Dragon's Honor* • Kij Johnson & Greg Cox
#39 • *Rogue Saucer* • John Vornholt
#40 • *Possession* • J.M. Dillard & Kathleen O'Malley
#41 • *Invasion!* #2: *The Soldiers of Fear* • Dean Wesley Smith & Kristine Kathryn Rusch
#42 • *Infiltrator* • W.R. Thompson
#43 • *A Fury Scorned* • Pamela Sargent & George Zebrowski
#44 • *The Death of Princes* • John Peel
#45 • *Intellivore* • Diane Duane
#46 • *To Storm Heaven* • Esther Friesner
#47-49 • *The Q Continuum* • Greg Cox
   #47 • *Q-Space*
   #48 • *Q-Zone*
   #49 • *Q-Strike*

#50 • *Dyson Sphere* • Charles Pellegrino & George Zebrowski
#51-56 • *Double Helix*
    #51 • *Infection* • John Gregory Betancourt
    #52 • *Vectors* • Dean Wesley Smith & Kristine Kathryn Rusch
    #53 • *Red Sector* • Diane Carey
    #54 • *Quarantine* • John Vornholt
    #55 • *Double or Nothing* • Peter David
    #56 • *The First Virtue* • Michael Jan Friedman & Christie Golden
#57 • *The Forgotten War* • William Fortschen
#58-59 • *Gemworld* • John Vornholt
    #58 • *Gemworld #1*
    #59 • *Gemworld #2*

Star Trek: Deep Space Nine®

    Warped • K.W. Jeter
    Legends of the Ferengi • Ira Steven Behr & Robert Hewitt Wolfe
    The Lives of Dax • Marco Palmieri, ed.
Millennium • Judith and Garfield Reeves-Stevens
    #1 • *The Fall of Terok Nor*
    #2 • *The War of the Prophets*
    #3 • *Inferno*
Novelizations
    Emissary • J.M. Dillard
    The Search • Diane Carey
    The Way of the Warrior • Diane Carey
    Star Trek: Klingon • Dean Wesley Smith & Kristine Kathryn Rusch
    Trials and Tribble-ations • Diane Carey
    Far Beyond the Stars • Steve Barnes
    What You Leave Behind • Diane Carey

#1 • *Emissary* • J.M. Dillard
#2 • *The Siege* • Peter David
#3 • *Bloodletter* • K.W. Jeter
#4 • *The Big Game* • Sandy Schofield
#5 • *Fallen Heroes* • Dafydd ab Hugh
#6 • *Betrayal* • Lois Tilton
#7 • *Warchild* • Esther Friesner
#8 • *Antimatter* • John Vornholt
#9 • *Proud Helios* • Melissa Scott
#10 • *Valhalla* • Nathan Archer
#11 • *Devil in the Sky* • Greg Cox & John Gregory Betancourt

#12 • *The Laertian Gamble* • Robert Sheckley
#13 • *Station Rage* • Diane Carey
#14 • *The Long Night* • Dean Wesley Smith & Kristine Kathryn Rusch
#15 • *Objective: Bajor* • John Peel
#16 • *Invasion!* #3: *Time's Enemy* • L.A. Graf
#17 • *The Heart of the Warrior* • John Gregory Betancourt
#18 • *Saratoga* • Michael Jan Friedman
#19 • *The Tempest* • Susan Wright
#20 • *Wrath of the Prophets* • David, Friedman & Greenberger
#21 • *Trial by Error* • Mark Garland
#22 • *Vengeance* • Dafydd ab Hugh
#23 • *The 34th Rule* • Armin Shimerman & David R. George III
#24-26 • *Rebels* • Dafydd ab Hugh
   #24 • *The Conquered*
   #25 • *The Courageous*
   #26 • *The Liberated*
#27 • *A Stitch in Time* • Andrew J. Robinson

Star Trek: Voyager®

   Mosaic • Jeri Taylor
   Pathways • Jeri Taylor
   Captain Proton! • Dean Wesley Smith
Novelizations
   Caretaker • L.A. Graf
   Flashback • Diane Carey
   Day of Honor • Michael Jan Friedman
   Equinox • Diane Carey

#1 • *Caretaker* • L.A. Graf
#2 • *The Escape* • Dean Wesley Smith & Kristine Kathryn Rusch
#3 • *Ragnarok* • Nathan Archer
#4 • *Violations* • Susan Wright
#5 • *Incident at Arbuk* • John Gregory Betancourt
#6 • *The Murdered Sun* • Christie Golden
#7 • *Ghost of a Chance* • Mark A. Garland & Charles G. McGraw
#8 • *Cybersong* • S.N. Lewitt
#9 • *Invasion!* #4: *Final Fury* • Dafydd ab Hugh
#10 • *Bless the Beasts* • Karen Haber
#11 • *The Garden* • Melissa Scott
#12 • *Chrysalis* • David Niall Wilson
#13 • *The Black Shore* • Greg Cox
#14 • *Marooned* • Christie Golden

#15 • *Echoes* • Dean Wesley Smith, Kristine Kathryn Rusch &
   Nina Kiriki Hoffman
#16 • *Seven of Nine* • Christie Golden
#17 • *Death of a Neutron Star* • Eric Kotani
#18 • *Battle Lines* • Dave Galanter & Greg Brodeur

Star Trek®: New Frontier

New Frontier #1-4 Collector's Edition • Peter David
   #1 • *House of Cards* • Peter David
   #2 • *Into the Void* • Peter David
   #3 • *The Two-Front War* • Peter David
   #4 • *End Game* • Peter David
#5 • *Martyr* • Peter David
#6 • *Fire on High* • Peter David
The Captain's Table #5 • *Once Burned* • Peter David
Double Helix #5 • *Double or Nothing* • Peter David
#7 • *The Quiet Place* • Peter David
#8 • *Dark Allies* • Peter David

Star Trek®: Invasion!

#1 • *First Strike* • Diane Carey
#2 • *The Soldiers of Fear* • Dean Wesley Smith & Kristine Kathryn Rusch
#3 • *Time's Enemy* • L.A. Graf
#4 • *Final Fury* • Dafydd ab Hugh
Invasion! Omnibus • various

Star Trek®: Day of Honor

#1 • *Ancient Blood* • Diane Carey
#2 • *Armageddon Sky* • L.A. Graf
#3 • *Her Klingon Soul* • Michael Jan Friedman
#4 • *Treaty's Law* • Dean Wesley Smith & Kristine Kathryn Rusch
The Television Episode • Michael Jan Friedman
Day of Honor Omnibus • various

Star Trek®: The Captain's Table

#1 • *War Dragons* • L.A. Graf
#2 • *Dujonian's Hoard* • Michael Jan Friedman
#3 • *The Mist* • Dean Wesley Smith & Kristine Kathryn Rusch
#4 • *Fire Ship* • Diane Carey
#5 • *Once Burned* • Peter David
#6 • *Where Sea Meets Sky* • Jerry Oltion
The Captain's Table Omnibus • various

Star Trek®: The Dominion War

#1 • *Behind Enemy Lines* • John Vornholt
#2 • *Call to Arms...* • Diane Carey
#3 • *Tunnel Through the Stars* • John Vornholt
#4 • *...Sacrifice of Angels* • Diane Carey

Star Trek®: The Badlands

#1 • Susan Wright
#2 • Susan Wright

Star Trek® Books available in Trade Paperback

Omnibus Editions
    Invasion! Omnibus • various
    Day of Honor Omnibus • various
    The Captain's Table Omnibus • various
    Star Trek: Odyssey • William Shatner with Judith and Garfield
        Reeves-Stevens
Other Books
    Legends of the Ferengi • Ira Steven Behr & Robert Hewitt Wolfe
    Strange New Worlds, vols. I and II • Dean Wesley Smith, ed.
    Adventures in Time and Space • Mary Taylor
    Captain Proton! • Dean Wesley Smith
    The Lives of Dax • Marco Palmieri, ed.
    The Klingon Hamlet • Wil'yam Shex'pir
    New Worlds, New Civilizations • Michael Jan Friedman
    Enterprise Logs • Carol Greenburg, ed.

STAR TREK
THE EXPERIENCE
LAS VEGAS HILTON

Be a part of the most exciting deep space adventure in the galaxy as you beam aboard the U.S.S. Enterprise. Explore the evolution of Star Trek® from television to movies in the "History of the Future Museum," the planet's largest collection of authentic Star Trek memorabilia. Then, visit distant galaxies on the "Voyage Through Space." This 22-minute action packed adventure will capture your senses with the latest in motion simulator technology. After your mission, shop in the Deep Space Nine Promenade and enjoy 24th Century cuisine in Quark's Bar & Restaurant.